Dear Reader,

This is a spoiler alert: No one is murdered in this book!

Only Son was my second novel, written in 1996, before I started writing thrillers. While the body count is zero, I think you'll still find plenty of suspense, surprises, and excitement in *Only Son*. If you've read some of my thrillers, you'll be in familiar territory here. The story is set in the Pacific Northwest. There's a single mother, searching for her missing son. There's also a devoted single dad with a dark secret. And then there's Sam Jorgenson, the first in a long line of complex teenage characters to appear in my novels—he's still one of my favorites.

Since this novel is over twenty years old, you'll have to go back to a time before smart phones, global warming awareness, the Internet, Facebook, Twitter, X-Boxes, DNA testing, security lines in airports, Fox News, and the Kardashians.

So please adjust your reading accordingly.

Many readers—good friends and family members among them—have told me that *Only Son* is still their favorite of my books. I've always had a soft spot for this novel. I wrote it when I was still a railroad inspector. But thanks to the sales from this book, I became a full-time author. It was also the first of sixteen books (so far) that I've written with my editor, John Scognamiglio, at Kensington Publishing.

I'm thrilled Kensington has brought *Only Son* back into print after two decades. I hope it's a hit with you.

Thanks so much for picking it up!

Kevin O'Brien

BOOKS BY KEVIN O'BRIEN

ONLY SON

THE NEXT TO DIE

MAKE THEM CRY

WATCH THEM DIE

LEFT FOR DEAD

THE LAST VICTIM

KILLING SPREE

ONE LAST SCREAM

FINAL BREATH

VICIOUS

DISTURBED

TERRIFIED

UNSPEAKABLE

TELL ME YOU'RE SORRY

NO ONE NEEDS TO KNOW

YOU'LL MISS ME WHEN I'M GONE

HIDE YOUR FEAR

Published by Kensington Publishing Corporation

KEVIN O'BRIEN

ONLY SON

PINNACLE BOOKS
Kensington Publishing Corp.
www.kensingtonbooks.com

PINNACLE BOOKS are published by

Kensington Publishing Corp.
119 West 40th Street
New York, NY 10018

All Kensington titles, imprints, and distributed lines are available at special quantity discounts for bulk purchases for sales promotions, premiums, fund-raising, educational, or institutional use. Special book excerpts or customized printings can also be created to fit specific needs. For details, write or phone the office of the Kensington sales manager: Kensington Publishing Corp., 119 West 40th Street, New York, NY 10018, attn: Sales Department; phone 1-800-221-2647.

This book is a work of fiction. Names, characters, businesses, organizations, places, events, and incidents either are the product of the author's imagination or are used fictitiously. Any resemblance to actual persons, living or dead, events, or locales is entirely coincidental.

ISBN-13: 978-0-7860-3986-9
ISBN-10: 0-7860-3986-8

First Pinnacle paperback printing: March 2017

10 9 8 7 6 5 4 3 2 1

Printed in the United States of America

First electronic edition: March 2017

ISBN-13: 978-0-7860-3987-6
ISBN-10: 0-7860-3987-6

This book is for Adele, Mary Lou, Cathy Bill, and Joan—with love, from the guy who is very lucky to be their kid brother.

ACKNOWLEDGMENTS

Many people helped me with this book, and I didn't have to sleep with any of them. My thanks and love goes to Mary Alice Kier and Anna Cottle, my agents, literary guardian angels, and dear friends, who never lost their vision for this book.

I'm also grateful to John Scognamiglio, my editor at Kensington Publishing, and a terrific guy.

To my friend, Stephanie Ogle, of Cinema Books in Seattle, for introducing me to Mary Alice and Anna; to family and friends, especially those who read early drafts of this book and came back with "atta boys" or suggestions for improvement: Joan O'Brien, Mary Lou Kinsella, George and Sheila Kelly Stydahar, Dan Monda, Kate Kinsella, Shannon Russell, John Bentz, and my dad, The Honorable William O'Brien.

Near last but not least, I couldn't have written this book without my "Writers Group" authors and buddies: Bonny Becker, David Buckner, and my dear, dear pal, Cate Goethals.

Finally, thanks to Adele Bevan O'Brien (1915–1992) for being such a wonderful mom.

PROLOGUE

Sam didn't know there was a cop car behind him until he saw the flashing red strobe in his rearview mirror. All at once, he couldn't breathe, and his heart pounded furiously. He switched on his indicator, then pulled over to the side of the road.

Until tonight, he hadn't driven much farther than the mall and back. But he'd just put close to three hundred miles on his mother's Toyota; five hours from Seattle to Eugene. He'd been secretly planning this trip for a month. What had made him think he could get through it without an accident or a cop stopping him? Now his mom would find out that he'd come here, and it would kill her.

The patrol car pulled up behind him. Sam squinted at the headlights in his rearview mirror. He watched the cop get out of the car, but could only see his silhouette: a baseball player's stocky-muscular build. As the cop approached the Toyota, he switched on his flashlight, then Sam couldn't see him anymore.

"Can I see your license and proof of insurance?"

the officer said, very authoritative. His face was still swallowed up in the shadows.

"Yes, sir." Sam fumbled with the seat belt and reached back for his wallet. "I've never been stopped by the police before. I—I'm a little nervous." He still couldn't breathe right. He noticed the cop direct the flashlight to his gym bag on the seat beside him. WEST SEATTLE HIGH SCHOOL was emblazoned across it. He pried the license out of his wallet, then handed it to the cop. "This is my mother's car," he explained. "I'm sorry, but I don't know where she keeps the proof of insurance."

"Ink on this driver's license is barely dry," the cop said. "You're sixteen?"

"Yes." Sam tried to smile into the blinding flashlight.

"Pretty far away from home, aren't you? Does your mother know where you are?"

"Yessir," he lied.

"What exactly are you doing down here?"

Sam was afraid he'd ask that. He made up a story about visiting his cousin, who was going to show him the University of Oregon campus. "I might go to school here," he said.

The cop finally turned off the flashlight. "The reason I stopped you, Sam, was that you were weaving slightly and seemed to have difficulty staying in your lane."

"I'm sorry. I'm kind of lost. I've been trying to read the street signs."

He really was lost. He might have asked his dad for directions. But Sam wasn't even supposed to talk to his father, much less visit him.

"Um, are you going to give me a ticket?" Sam asked.

"Just a warning," the policeman replied, handing back the license. "Watch where you're going."

"I will, thanks. Um, can you tell me where Polk Street is?"

It was where his dad lived, a big secret. He wasn't supposed to know.

"Polk Street?" the cop said. "Yeah, you're only five minutes away. What's your cousin's address?"

The cop was right. It didn't take Sam long to find Polk Street. But he didn't like what he saw. He drove past lot after lot of neglected lawns, and run-down houses and apartment buildings. God, please, don't let my dad live here, he thought. He kept waiting for the neighborhood to get nicer. Then again, his father must have gotten out of jail less than a year ago. He probably couldn't afford to live someplace nice.

Sam wondered if prison had made him mean. Would he look like someone who had "done time"? Maybe he was a wino, or a drug addict, or he'd gotten a bunch of really creepy tattoos while he was in jail. Sam didn't want to think about his dad in there. He didn't want to think of him as a baby snatcher either. But that was what Sam's real father called him: that bastard, that pervert, that baby snatcher.

Sheila, his stepmother, was the one who had let it slip that he was in Eugene. She'd had a few too many beers at a barbecue during one of his bogus "family weekends" in Portland last month. Sam remembered feeling trapped as he sat across from her and his real father at the picnic table. Both of them had on "I'M WITH STUPID ➜" T-shirts. They were oblivious to *their two younger sons, fifty feet away, throwing rocks at each other. Sam's bratty half sister, Brandy, the preteen queen, had wandered off with some of her delinquent friends.*

"Well, I for one don't feel safe," Sheila said, puffing on her Virginia Slim. "I mean, Eugene isn't so far. Okay, so he's not allowed in the same state as Sam. But we live in Oregon, and Sam stays with us at least once a month. So how come they let this crazy live in Eugene?"

"Drop it, will ya, hon?" her husband said in a low voice.

"You're the one who started talking about how laws are made to protect the criminal. I was just agreeing—"

"I started the talk, and I'm finishing it," he said firmly.

Sheila looked ready to give him an argument, but just then, the nine-year-old, Todd, bounced a rock off his younger brother's forehead. There were screams and tears, some blood, too. Sheila puffed on her cigarette and inspected the cut on the younger boy's forehead. She handed him a napkin to soak up the blood.

Little Todd stared at the ground while his father yelled at him: "Hey, shit-for-brains, what the hell is wrong with you?"

"I'm sorry!" *Todd cried miserably.* "I'm really, really sorry. It was an accident!"

Sam's heart went out to the kid. But his father, clutching a beer and shaking his head at the boy, wasn't moved by the tears. "Hey," *he called to Sam.* "What should I do with this brat, huh? Maybe smack a rock on his head, see how he likes it . . ."

"I'll take him for a walk, Dad," *Sam said, grabbing*

Todd's hand. He frowned at the boy's father, their fa-ther. He had to remind himself that the creep now on his way to the cooler for another beer had sired him, and that the "crazy" in Eugene was indeed a criminal.

When the heinous weekend ended, he returned home and sneaked a peek at his mother's daily plan-ner. Under the "J" section, he found a Polk Street ad-dress in Eugene, Oregon; but there was no name written above it.

He passed a 7-Eleven that must have been a divid-ing line between Polk Street's high- and low-rent areas, because suddenly the neighborhood became cleaner. Lawns were tidy, flower boxes decorated win-dows, and stately houses stood next to apartment build-ings that had what people called Old World charm. Sam wondered if he'd passed his father's address a while back—before the 7-Eleven.

Then he saw the building, about a block ahead. He couldn't see the number, but he knew. It was a three-story, tan brick building with an awning over the front door, probably built during the thirties. He'd grown up in an apartment building very much like this one. In fact, the similarity was eerie.

He parked across the street from the place and saw the numbers over the door. It was the right address. He didn't like it that his father had found a new home so similar to the one they had shared years ago. It was as if his dad wanted to repeat the past or something. The phrase "repeat offender," came to mind, and Sam tried to block it out. His dad would never repeat what he'd done sixteen years ago. Never.

PART ONE
THE BABY SNATCHER

CHAPTER ONE

June 7, 1977—Portland, Oregon

The overweight, copper-haired nurse waddled into the waiting room. "Mr. McMurray?" she asked.

Paul McMurray tossed aside the copy of *Sports Illustrated* and hopped off the light green vinyl couch. He was twenty-seven years old, with straight flaxen hair and a tan. His athletic good looks were just starting to slide, and his Trailblazers T-shirt didn't quite camouflage a slight beer belly.

In fact, he hadn't been in the waiting room very long before he'd left and returned, smuggling in a six-pack of Budweiser and some cigars. He'd slyly pulled a beer from the grocery bag and offered it to another expectant father, who had shown up just a few minutes after him. The guy said, "No, thanks," and that was it. Didn't say another word the whole time—and they'd been in the waiting room for over two hours.

But now the man was standing up along with Paul McMurray. The nurse looked confused for a moment, her eyes darting back and forth between the two of them. "Mr. McMurray?"

"Yeah," Paul said anxiously. "I'm McMurray. That's me."

The nurse broke into a smile. "Congratulations. You're the father of a healthy, eight-pound-two-ounce baby boy."

"ALL RIGHT!" he yelled, shoving a fist in the air.

"You can see him in the newborn room in just a few minutes. And the mother's doing fine. She's resting, but you can see her in a little while."

Paul McMurray had another beer, then went to the window outside the newborn room. He waited, his nose fogging the glass. In his hand he clutched the cigars. He gave one to the man standing beside him, the other expectant dad. He was a tall, well-built man with light brown hair. He looked like the country club type, handsome and well dressed. He had on a green sport shirt with some designer logo on the breast pocket.

"Congratulate me," Paul grinned. "I'm a daddy. Got myself a little boy. How about that, huh?"

The stranger gave him a limp smile. "Congratulations," he murmured, tucking the cigar in the breast pocket of his sport shirt. "Thanks for the smoke." He turned back toward the window, a sad look on his face.

"This is my first kid," Paul said. "My name's Paul McMurray."

"Jack Spalding," the man said, shaking his hand. But he still didn't smile. He glanced back at the infants.

Paul wondered if the guy's trip to the hospital had started much earlier today. He looked so goddamn gloomy. Maybe there were complications with the birth. Maybe his kid had already been born—perhaps born dead or deformed. "Is—ah—your baby in there?" he asked.

But before the man answered, Paul saw the nurse on the other side of the glass, holding something in a white blanket. She came up to the window. Paul pointed to himself and mouthed his last name. She nodded. He blinked at the purple, no-eyed thing—the face all squashed and its head lumpy. And it was so dark.

He mouthed his name for the nurse again, and she nodded emphatically. She showed him the baby's hands so he could count the fingers. The nurse was talking to the baby, pointing at Paul. He could read her lips: "There's your *daddy*," she said.

Paul let out a surprised laugh. "That's my boy!" he cried. "That's my little Eddie. Hi, slugger."

The nurse gently rested the infant in a bassinet, then pinned a tag at the foot of the little bed: *"McMurray."*

Paul glanced at the man, who also seemed mesmerized by little Eddie. "That's my little boy," he said.

"He's beautiful," the man whispered. There were tears in his eyes.

"Um, which one is yours?"

The man pointed to an infant three cribs over from Eddie.

"A boy?" Paul asked.

He nodded.

"Uh, he's a handsome little tyke, too," Paul said, trying to be polite.

"Not as handsome as yours," the man said.

Paul McMurray gazed at his son and smiled. But then it struck him as pretty damn strange. What a weird thing for a new father to say about his own little boy:

"Not as handsome as yours." Was the guy's kid really that ugly? He glanced over at the other baby. He wasn't deformed or hideous-looking. The tag on his crib read: *Copeland.*

Paul McMurray scratched his head. "Hey, what did you say your name was?"

He turned, but the man wasn't there anymore.

At a stoplight on his way home, Carl Jorgenson was about to toss the cigar out the car window. But then he changed his mind and tucked it back inside the pocket of his sport shirt.

"Nights in White Satin" came over the car radio. He cranked up the volume. "Suicide Music," Carl called it. This song and Brook Benton's "A Rainy Night in Georgia" were his favorite I'm-depressed-and-want-to-wallow-in-it tunes. The music certainly fit his mood now. He almost wished it would rain. The night was too beautiful, with a gentle, early summer breeze and the clear, starlit sky. He never felt so lonely in all his life.

When the light turned green, Carl suddenly realized he was headed in the wrong direction. "You don't live there anymore, stupid," he whispered to himself. He made a U-turn. His new apartment was on Weidler, another part of town. He wasn't crazy about the place. But it beat the Best Western, where he'd stayed for two nights after walking out on Eve. Two nights of limbo. He'd longed for a sense of permanency, and wanted his things out of the house. He also wanted Eve to know he wasn't coming back. So he signed a lease on the first apartment he'd seen.

Carl parked in front of the building, a homely four-story brick structure built in the Eisenhower era. Maybe he'd taken the apartment because he felt sorry for the landlady. Old Mrs. Gunther didn't look long for this world. She had short, curly hair, and cat-eye, rhinestone-studded glasses. While she'd shown Carl the apartment, she'd clutched to her bosom a mangy old poodle she had introduced as Sparkle. Sparkle had a crooked jaw and yellowish grey hair the same shade as her owner's. In fact, the two could have passed as sisters—if you put rhinestone-studded glasses on the dog.

"It's a warm, friendly building," Mrs. Gunther had explained, stroking Sparkle's head. "You'll like it here . . ."

But Carl found the other tenants a cold assortment of forgettable faces. He didn't recognize the man now following him up the walk to the front door. Carl guessed he was around his own age, thirty-nine—maybe older. The dark-haired man wore tennis clothes, and ate an ice-cream cone. A few paces behind him straggled a little boy, also working on an ice-cream cone. Carl glanced back at them, thinking the father ought to walk beside his son so he could keep an eye on him and make sure he was safe.

Carl unlocked the door, then held it open for them. Without a look at him, the man strolled by and called back to his little boy, "Come on, quit dawdling."

Carl felt like the invisible doorman. "You're welcome a helluva lot," he said, loud enough to be heard.

But the man ignored him. He grabbed his son's hand and moved toward the elevator.

Carl let the door swing shut. "Hey, don't thank me, buddy," he growled. "I love holding doors open for ingrates like you . . ."

The man stepped inside the elevator, let go of his son's hand, then turned around and flipped him the bird. "Fuck you very much," he said. The elevator doors shut.

"Oh, nice!" Carl yelled after him in vain. "And in front of your kid, no less. You got a lot of class!" He stomped toward the elevator and jabbed at the button. *Creeps like that shouldn't even be allowed to have children,* he thought; *damn, it was so unfair . . .*

As the elevator took him up to the fourth floor, Carl wanted to hit something—someone. He'd come very close to belting Eve that night, the week before, when she'd told him what she'd done. It had taken every drop of restraint to keep from knocking her across the living room. But he'd left her unharmed; both of them angry, in tears. Now, he was glad he'd held back. A blow to the side of that pretty raven-haired head would have smacked some of the guilt out of Eve, and she deserved to feel one hundred percent terrible for her actions.

Carl stepped inside his new living room, dark and cluttered with half-unpacked boxes. The hide-a-bed sofa he'd ordered from Meier & Frank had arrived. It was still shrouded with plastic. Mrs. Gunther and Sparkle must have let the delivery people in. At least he wouldn't have to use the sleeping bag tonight.

Switching on the kitchenette overhead, he dug a frozen pizza and a beer out of the refrigerator. The telephone rang. He stared at it a moment, fancying that it might ring off the daisy-patterned kitchenette wall. Maybe Eve, calling to make amends? He hated himself for hoping it was. Finally, he shoved the pizza in the oven and went to the phone. "Hello?"

"Carl?"

It was his lawyer. "Hi, Jerry," he said, opening the beer. "How are you?"

"I've been trying to get you all day. Where have you been?"

Carl sipped his beer. "The old neighborhood pool, the movies, here, there. What's up, Jerry?"

"Eve called me this morning, asking for your new phone number. She wants to talk with you—"

"Well, I don't want to talk with her. Another thing, Jerry, please tell her to stop calling me at work."

"Carl, she thinks the two of you ought to see a marriage counselor and try to work things out."

"There's nothing to work out," Carl sighed, setting his beer on the yellow Formica counter. "All the counseling money can buy won't change things. Now, have you filed the petition for divorce or whatever it is you do to get the ball rolling?"

"Not yet, Carl. I thought maybe—"

"Jerry, please, get off the pot and do it."

"I just want you to be practical about this. Now—"

"She can have the house, the second car, everything she can get her bloodstained hands on. I don't care."

"Carl, you're not acting rationally . . ."

"For God's sakes, how do you expect me to act?" he said. "That was my baby, goddamn it! I wanted that child more than anything."

"I know that," Jerry said. "And I understand—"

"Then you understand why I can't have anything to do with her right now. So—please, please file that petition. Okay?" Carl didn't want to give him time for any more arguments, and he quickly said: "Listen, I have a pizza burning up in the oven here, so I've got to go. Just file the sucker. Thanks for calling, Jerry. G'night." He hung up. Friend or no friend, if Jerry didn't file on Monday, he'd find a new lawyer.

Screw dinner. Carl switched off the oven. He needed a shower. He hadn't taken one after swimming his laps that afternoon, and hated the idea of dried community pool water covering his body. He'd been in such a hurry, throwing on his clothes over the damp swim trunks and running to his car to follow that young couple home.

Two weeks before, elated that at last he would become a father, Carl had first spotted them at the neighborhood pool. The guy looked like an ex-jock, a bit out of shape. The wife was cute with brown hair and dimples, but no stunner like Eve, whose *haute couture* looks always turned heads. He wouldn't have given the girl a second glance if not for the beautifully swollen belly that stretched the fibers of her lavender swimsuit. *That's Eve in just a few months,* he'd thought, a satisfied grin on his suntanned face. How radiant the girl had seemed, carrying new life inside her.

Seeing them again today, he'd felt as if they had something that used to be his. He noticed them after finishing his laps, and he moved his blanket over to the grass, near where they sat in lawn chairs. The guy had brought the newspaper and a cooler with him. He opened a beer and stuck the can in one of those Styrofoam receptacles to keep it cold. The girl was wearing her lavender swimsuit again, and she looked overdue for the delivery room by several days. "Promise me, honey," the girl said as she rubbed suntan lotion on her husband's shoulders. "Don't let me get one of those ugly postnatal haircuts like my sister got. She looked so frumpy in her pictures with the baby."

The husband was deep into the sports section.

Some kids were screaming "Marco Polo!" in the shallow end of the pool, and Carl couldn't hear the young couple for a minute.

"—might as well be talking to myself half the time," the girl was complaining. She applied lotion to her legs, barely able to reach them past her inflated midriff.

Carl watched as a skinny, wet kid in baggy trunks raced past the husband, a little too close. Apparently, the kid had shed some water on his sports page. The husband looked very annoyed, and grumbled something to his wife.

"Oh, relax!" Carl heard her say. She tipped her head back.

Carl saw something that the guy hadn't noticed yet. Down by his feet, his precious beer had spilled over on its side. If the skinny, wet kid had done it, Carl hoped the boy was long gone. One of the worst beatings Carl had ever gotten in his life was from knocking over his father's beer; and he imagined that this guy was a lot like his old man.

"MARCO POLO! MARCO POLO! MARCO POLO!"

In between shrieks, Carl heard the husband say, "Somebody should get them to shut the fuck up."

Oh, bub, you'll be great for those 2:00 a.m. feedings, Carl thought, sitting at the edge of his towel.

The wife muttered something to the guy, and he laughed. He reached down for his beer. Carl waited for him to make the discovery. But just then, the skinny kid ran by once more, giggling and flailing his arms.

Again, he must have doused the guy with a little water.
The husband threw down his paper and almost leapt up
from the lawn chair to chase him, but then he sat back
down.

Carl watched the boy gleefully threading around
people, chairs, and towels.

When he looked back at the couple, the father-to-be
had discovered the spilt beer. He was cursing, but the
Marco Polo game had gotten loud again, and Carl
couldn't hear exactly what he was saying.

Her head still tipped back, the wife dismissed his
anger with a wave of her hand. But the guy took off his
sunglasses, and seemingly out for blood, he sat forward in the lawn chair and scouted the area for that
poor dumb little kid. He didn't see the boy coming up
from behind him—not until it was too late. He made a
grab for his skinny arm, but the boy unwittingly escaped.

The wife must have nodded off, because she didn't
seem to notice. Carl wanted to get to the kid and tell
him to keep away from that man in the lawn chair, but
he lost sight of him in the crowd. The boy was about
eight years old, simply having fun at the neighborhood
pool. How was he to know that he'd made somebody
so furious at him?

Carl heard his by-now-familiar giggle. So did the
husband. He set down a new can of beer he'd just
opened and watched the kid play by the foot shower.
The boy started running again, weaving around towels
and sunbathers, toward the man and his sleeping pregnant wife.

The children were screaming again: "MARCO POLO!
MARCO POLO!"

Helplessly, Carl watched as the kid sprinted along the grass. The father-to-be inched forward in his chair, and he stuck his foot out.

"Oh, Jesus," Carl whispered.

The kid tripped, and that skinny little body hit the ground hard. He let out a sharp cry. No one saw who had tripped him. The husband quickly grabbed his newspaper just as the wife sat up to see what all the crying was about. There was a tiny smirk on the guy's face.

Creeps like that shouldn't even be allowed to have children.

The kid was crying and at the same time, trying to catch his breath. Somebody helped him to his feet. The boy glanced back toward the couple, apparently looking for what had made him stumble. There was a grass stain all up and down his leg. He wiped away his tears and limped toward the pool house.

Carl wanted to confront the man, maybe even beat the crap out of him for picking on that pathetic skinny kid in the baggy trunks. Instead, he didn't move—and said nothing. He followed the young couple as they left the pool that afternoon. They had a bumper sticker on the back of their VW: a leering cartoon billy goat, and the slogan, HONK IF YOU'RE HORNY! Probably the husband's idea. They seemed like a couple of greasers. He imagined a pair of fuzzy dice dangling from their rearview mirror as well.

Carl parked in front of their town house and sat in his car for two hours. He was in no hurry to return to his empty apartment. Later, the couple came out again and got into the VW. Carl followed them to a movie theater. He went inside, sitting two rows behind them.

The guy had a way of eating popcorn that was really annoying. From the bucket he'd scoop out a handful, shake it like loose change, then shove the entire fistful into his mouth, crunching loudly. Only God knew how the wife put up with him.

The movie was pretty good, and Carl started getting interested in it; but then, the young couple suddenly got up. They whispered back and forth until someone in the row behind them asked them to be quiet. *"Can't you see my wife's in labor?"* the creep of a husband snarled.

Carl kept a safe distance behind them in his car. His heart beat faster and faster as he watched them pull into the hospital's emergency entrance. He had to go inside and see.

Of course, three hours later, when he finally set eyes on the baby boy that could have been his, Carl was miserable.

He didn't want to talk to the father. Then the guy asked him his name, and Carl lied. He lied, too, about having a son of his own in that roomful of infants. Why should this McMurray guy think he had something over him? But he did. He possessed something Carl had wanted for a long, long time.

The warm spray from the showerhead felt wonderful, as if it were washing away his troubles and heartaches. Some people he knew drank to ward off depression, but Carl took showers—long, leisurely showers. He was sitting down, his head tipped back against the tiled wall. He'd put the plug in the drain, and the shower made a poor man's whirlpool in the rapidly filling tub.

For the first time that day, Carl smiled. He rubbed a bar of Irish Spring over his broad, hairy chest, then down the rippled stomach. He soaped up his flaccid penis with hygienic apathy. It hadn't seen any action in almost two weeks—not even from his own hand. He'd sort of lost interest in sex, because it only reminded him of Eve.

"You have a wonderful physique," Eve had told him after the first time they'd made love.

The memory of her nude body—so taut and tan— was still painfully fresh in his mind. Just seeing her naked had never ceased to fascinate and arouse him. He enjoyed giving her massages as a postlude to sex. The feel of her body always made him hard again. There was one spot, at the small of her back, where he loved to rest his head. He'd stare at the upward curve of her buttocks and lazily caress the soft flesh. She said she liked his foot rubs the most, and he saved them for last, often nibbling and sucking on her toes.

He'd met her on a blind date. A teacher friend at the grade school where Carl taught physical education had set it up. Friends at work were constantly trying to fix him up. They seemed more anxious to see him in a re-lationship than he ever was. Some of the dates were abysmal; and some were abysmal—but with sex. But most of these attempted matchups just left him feeling awkward and sad. The women had a certain despera-tion to them. They'd laugh hysterically at his mediocre jokes, quiver at his casual touch, and worst of all, they'd want to know all about him. Carl had always been well liked, but no one ever really knew him; and he wanted it that way. There were certain things about himself that he didn't want people to know. When these women expressed interest in seeing him again, Carl ran in the other direction.

But Eve was different. She was more beautiful than any of the others, more confident, with a dry sense of humor. But there was also a haughtiness to her that proved challenging. He actually had to chase after her. When they made love, Carl wanted to stay with her for the rest of the night—maybe even remain in bed with her forever, holding her in his arms, whispering, kissing. He was thirty-five years old, and for the first time, Carl felt really *intimate* with another human being.

Eve had also come along at a time when Carl felt ready to settle down and start a family. This was the woman he wanted to have children with. Even her name meant mother.

But Eve was in no hurry to get married or fulfill the origin of her name. She was very wrapped up in her work as a tennis instructor, and played in minor pro tournaments. Sometimes, she criticized Carl for his lack of career drive. There were better jobs with higher salaries than he made as a grade school P.E. coach. It was a waste of his college degree. After eight years with the job, wasn't he ready for something more challenging?

Not really. He loved acting as a father figure to all those kids, guiding the young athletes and building up confidence in the weak, underdeveloped ones. His only complaint about the coaching job was that the kids weren't his own.

But for Eve, he reluctantly hung up his coach's whistle, then worked like hell to climb into a management position at an insurance corporation. The job was a yawn, but his reward came when Eve finally agreed to marry him.

Then came the blow: "Maybe in a few years down the line," she said. "I'm twenty-nine. There's no need to rush into starting a family. I want you all to myself for a while."

It seemed the real reason she didn't want a child was because she always had some tennis tournament coming up.

At least *one* of them liked their work. Carl began to resent her for driving him into the insurance game. He'd done it for her. Why couldn't she make a career sacrifice for him—and a temporary one at that? Sure, she didn't have to worry about the clock ticking away, but he'd be forty in a year, and he wanted to start a family *now*. He loathed the sight of that slim, fashionable box which contained her birth control pills—the only thing standing between him and his dream of fatherhood.

One spring morning, Eve bolted out of bed before the alarm went off. Carl followed her to the bathroom, and found her hovered over the toilet, throwing up. She thought it was a bad stomach fiu. But Carl had an idea what it really was—divine intervention. He didn't want to think that she was just ill. All day long, she was tired, and the following morning, she threw up again. Carl hid his enthusiasm in the face of her misery. Eve would be all right, he told himself. As soon as she realized it was their child growing inside her, she'd accept it, embrace it.

"Oh, Christ, of all the shitty things to happen!" she cried over the phone. Carl was at work. "I just got back from the doctor's, and guess what? I'm pregnant, he says."

"Well, that's wonderful, honey!" Now he could bring home the rattle he'd bought three days ago.

"It's awful! How the hell could this happen? I've been taking the pill religiously for the last four years. I should sue our pharmacist . . ."

"Oh, you read in the papers all the time about women getting pregnant while on the pill. It's nobody's fault. Maybe it was just meant to be, honey. In fact, I'm really thrilled about it."

Over the next two weeks, Carl gave her pep talks. There would be other tournaments to play after the baby was born. She wasn't the type to let herself get out of shape. Hell, she'd bounce right back. Maybe they should enroll in one of those natural childbirth classes. He'd help her along through the whole experience. Carl bought baby things and made plans to convert the spare bedroom into a nursery. He began watching pregnant women on the street, and they fascinated him. Bringing home books on childbirth and child development, he pored over them eagerly. But Eve refused to crack open a cover.

"Can't you get it through your thick skull that I don't want to have this baby?" she screamed.

"You wouldn't say that if you knew how much it means to me, honey. I swear, I'll be with you all the way through this—"

"Yeah, well, you don't have to *have* it." She paused. "And I don't have to have it either."

"Don't talk like that, Eve. I won't listen. I mean it."

He chalked up her tantrums to the hormonal changes and nausea. Carl tried to be patient, and he pampered her.

One night he came home from work to find Eve sitting up in bed, half-awake. Her face was pale, and the long, black hair limply hung down past her shoulders. No, she didn't want him to fix her some dinner. She just needed to be left alone. Carl kissed her forehead and as he crept out of the bedroom, he heard her: "I feel so sick and miserable, I just want to die . . ."

God, what I'm putting her through, he thought; *the poor, brave thing.* There had to be some way of making it easier for her. The next day, at the office, Carl asked the advice of every coworker who was a parent.

He returned to the house that night with a list of temporary remedies and recommendations. But he didn't need them. Eve looked incredibly healthy when she met him at the door. Dressed in jeans and a white knit top, she even seemed a bit more tan, and her hair was freshly washed. "God, honey, you look great," he said. "You must be feeling better."

"I do feel better, Carl. I—"

"In that case, wait a minute." He ran back out to the car, pulled the cumbersome box from the trunk, then carried it inside. "I brought this yesterday," he said, catching his breath. He ripped open the box. "But since you were so sick, I figured you weren't in the mood to see it then." Getting down on his knees, he took out the parts, encased in plastic bags.

"What is it?" she asked listlessly.

"A bassinet. I'm going to assemble it tonight . . ."

Eve just stared at the box and bit her lip. Carl began to tear at the plastic. *"Don't,"* she said.

He looked up at her. "Why not?"

"Because you won't get your money back when you have to return it," she murmured.

He laughed. "What does that mean?"

"I didn't want to tell you last night, because I was still recuperating, but I *miscarried* yesterday."

"What?" The little headboard slipped out of his grasp. He gazed at her. "You're joking . . ."

Eve's hands wrapped around her forearms as if she were suddenly cold. "No, that's not right," she whispered steadily. "The truth is, yesterday, I went in for an abortion."

Carl only shook his head.

"I never wanted to have that baby," she said. "I tried to tell you over and over again. The timing was all wrong. I wish you'd listened to me, Carl . . ."

She kept on talking. Carl's hand trembled as he rubbed his forehead. He reached for another plastic bag and ripped it open. "I want to put this together tonight," he said loudly. "It'll take a while to assemble. I'll need my screwdriver . . ."

"—It doesn't mean we won't have children sometime later, but this one—"

"You know what I'll do tomorrow? At the place I got this, I saw a neat, little mobile with wooden giraffes, tigers, and monkeys. I'm gonna buy that tomorrow and fix it on the crib . . ."

"I know how much you wanted this baby, Carl. I just wish you knew how much I didn't want it."

His hands shook terribly. He tried not to listen to her voice, so steady and controlled. Suddenly, he hurled the little wooden headboard across the living room. It smashed into a lamp and clattered to the floor. *"God-damn you!"* he cried. He wanted to kill her, and the more he fought that impulse, the sicker he felt, so sick and miserable, he just wanted to die.

* * *

Naked, he wandered around the darkened living room, peeking into boxes until he found the one holding his socks, shirts, and underwear. Then Carl pulled on a clean pair of undershorts.

He stopped to stare at all the boxes. The place was a mess. He'd been living there three days; everything should have been unpacked and put away by now. Usually, he liked things very tidy, organized, in their proper place. Eve used to say he lived his life like that, in rituals and routines. He had to have his morning run, his Post Raisin Bran breakfast, and his two cups of coffee every day before work. Coming home, he needed his forty-five minutes alone to look at the mail, enjoy his beer, then take his second shower of the day. Eve claimed these routines were the result of being an only child and living alone so long in adulthood. She said he made his "rituals" a companion to him. Eve was a real pain in the ass when she analyzed him like that.

Carl started unpacking one of the boxes, but only got halfway through it before he went to work on another. Soon, the living room was even more of a mess. Clothes, books, records, towels, and kitchen supplies lay in piles around the boxes—none of which had been completely emptied. He found the box containing parts to the bassinet, and he began to assemble it.

Two hours later, Carl was asleep on the new sofa. He hadn't bothered to open it up and test the bed, because he couldn't find where he'd packed the linens. A thawed-out pizza still sat in the cold oven, and nothing he'd unpacked had been put away. But the bassinet—sturdy and complete—stood in the corner of the living room. It was the only thing Carl had finished that night.

* * *

He felt a little lost on his morning run. The new neighborhood meant charting a new route, and he wasn't sure he was getting enough miles in. He explored unfamiliar streets for something picturesque, shady, or level; but it just wasn't the same as his old route. Carl felt his lungs reach that last-mile burning point, and decided to head back to the apartment.

He wondered if Eve was trying to phone him right now. *Fat chance.* That business about wanting his number from Jerry was a crock. All she had to do was call directory assistance. The calls to his office were a joke, too, just a pretense that she was *trying* to get in touch with him. She always made the calls during his lunch hour, for God's sakes. If she really wanted to talk with him, she knew where and when to call.

He wasn't about to phone her, although he'd been tempted so many times in the last six days. He missed her terribly and still loved her. But he couldn't forget what she'd done. There was no way of bringing back the baby she'd destroyed. He wanted to tell her that.

But the bitch probably wouldn't call, so thinking about it was a waste of mental energy.

As Carl rounded the corner to his apartment building, he noticed a small crowd gathered on the street. He heard an old woman's anguished cries. Everyone was staring down at something on the pavement, but Carl couldn't see what it was.

"Oh, gross me out!" a teenage girl was saying.

Her friend giggled. "That old lady is crazy . . ."

It was Mrs. Gunther, his landlady. With her pointed glasses off, she looked even more ancient and feeble. Tears streamed down from her puffy eyes. She wrung her hands and stood over the mangled, bloody thing on the pavement. Mrs. Gunther kept crying the dog's name over and over again. Carl saw some of the people in the crowd snickering at her. "God, she's acting like it's her kid or something." One of the teenagers laughed.

Carl bumped against her, hoping he'd smeared some of his sweat on the girl. "Excuse me, you little dipshit," he mumbled.

"Hey, I heard that, asshole," she called after him.

Carl went to Mrs. Gunther. Putting a hand on her shoulder, he led the old woman inside.

The next day, he played hooky from work. He spent the morning at the Humane Society's animal shelter. "I want to buy a dog," he told the man at the pound. The place smelled like hell, and the caged dogs were howling and barking. "I'm looking for a white or grey poodle," he said over the noise. "Preferably house-broken and—well, this sounds crazy, but if you've got a poodle like that with a crooked lower jaw, it would be terrific."

The mangy mutt, which cost fifteen dollars, could have passed as Sparkle's twin. He spent another seven dollars on a leash and collar. Carl felt like a jerk walking the rodentlike thing up the walkway to his apartment building. He tied the leash to the knob on Mrs. Gunther's door, then fixed a note to the dog's collar. *"Will you take care of me?"* it said. *"Yours Hopefully, Sparkle II."*

Carl pressed the doorbell, then ran up the corridor. He ducked around the corner and peeked back down the hallway.

Mrs. Gunther opened her door, yanking the leash so the poodle yelped and tumbled to the ground. The old woman let out a horrified gasp. Her frail, bony hand came up to her mouth. "Oh, no," she cried. "Lord, no . . ."

Carl felt his well-meant plan backfiring. He'd been so sure this dog could replace the one she had lost.

The poodle bounced back up and sniffed at Mrs. Gunther's feet. She just stared down at it, shaking her head. "Oh, who would do this?" she cried.

Carl watched her stoop down to read the note. He got ready to step forward and beg her forgiveness. But after a moment, he heard her laugh. "Oh, of course. I'll take care of you!" she said, wiping the tears from her eyes. Mrs. Gunther gathered the poodle in her arms and carried it inside her apartment.

Carl retreated upstairs to his own place. Maybe he should have gotten a dog for himself at that pound. Even some obnoxious barking would have been better than the lonely silence greeting him now. After sharing his life with someone for four years, he wasn't sure he could live alone again. He wanted something—someone—that would ask of him: *"Will you take care of me?"*

He flopped down on the new couch. His shirt from the day before yesterday was strewn across the armrest, and he dug the cigar out of the pocket. He studied it. *Congratulate me. I'm a daddy.*

A package under his arm, Carl returned from his lunch break. He had his own office, but not much privacy. Half a wall and a glass partition separated him from his best friend at the office, Greg Remick. Carl set the package on his desk.

Greg waved at him from the office next door. Greg

was forty-two, lean, with straight, black hair and thick, Coke-bottle-bottom glasses. He came in and sat on the edge of Carl's desk. "I've got one for you," he said. "'Wild Thing.'"

"The Troggs," Carl said, sticking the package in his bottom drawer.

"What'd you buy?"

"Just some underwear," Carl replied. "How about 'Five O'Clock World'?"

"The Association?"

Carl made a noise like a buzzer. "Oh, we're sorry. That song was by The Vogues. But we have a lovely parting gift for you. This slim, elegant ballpoint pen from the people at Paper Mate." He set the pen in his friend's hand.

Greg laughed weakly. By the time he'd stuck the pen in his shirt pocket and loosened his tie, his smile was gone. "Listen, Carl," he said. "This might not be any of my business, but—well, Eve called while you were at lunch. She asked me if I had your phone number. I didn't even know you two had split up . . ."

Carl looked down at his desk blotter and nodded. "Yeah, well, it happened last week. Just one of those things, as they say." He glanced up at his friend. "Did you talk to her long?"

"No." Greg shrugged. "Kind of threw me for a loop. I mean, I thought you two were really happy, with the baby on the way and everything. This seems so sudden. You moved out?"

Carl smiled tightly and nodded.

"Listen, you want to go for a drink after work?" Greg asked, leaning toward him.

He shook his head. "Really, thanks anyway, Greg. But I still have stuff to unpack and I've got to get my new place in order—"

"Just as soon not talk about it, huh?"

"No, that's not it," Carl said. In fact, Greg was probably his closest friend, which suddenly struck him as very odd, because he never really *confided* in Greg much. Up until the week before, he'd considered Eve his best friend. It had been difficult the last few days. So many times, he'd wanted to call up his best friend and tell her about the awful thing his wife had done. He had only his lawyer and Greg as confidants now, and he really didn't feel like talking about it with Greg. "Um, maybe later in the week we can get together, okay?" he said.

"Sure." His friend nodded. "Whenever you're up for it." Greg climbed off the desk, but he hesitated at the door and looked back at him. "One thing though, if you don't mind my asking. What about—the baby?"

"I'm taking him," Carl said. "Eve didn't want the baby."

Greg let out it little laugh. "That's unusual. She's going to have it, and you'll be—"

Carl nodded. "It's all settled. I'm taking him."

"Him, huh? What makes you so sure it'll be a boy?"

"I just know." Carl smiled.

His friend gave him a puzzled look. Then the telephone rang next door, and Greg hurried back to his office to answer it.

Carl turned in his swivel chair. He slid open the bottom drawer to his desk and took out the package. Setting it on his lap so no one could see, he carefully pulled out his lunch hour purchase and admired it once again. It was a little mobile, with wooden giraffes, tigers, and monkeys.

That night, after work, Carl once again started driving toward the old neighborhood. He could have turned back, but didn't. Instead, he drove to the town house, and parked across the street. No one came outside or arrived during the two hours he just sat in his car and watched. But he remained there, until the last light went off inside the McMurrays' house.

CHAPTER TWO

Mrs. Gunther and the poodle met him in the lobby of his building. "Oh, Carl, there's something I need to ask you," she said, clutching the dog to her sagging bosom. "We had a bugsprayer here yesterday, and while we were in your apartment, I couldn't help noticing all the baby things . . ."

Carl stood by the elevator, a blank smile stretched across his face. He wore his swim trunks and a sport shirt; a damp beach towel was thrown over his shoulder. It was a glorious, hot July Saturday. He'd been so certain he would see them at the pool today, but they hadn't come. He'd even checked the kiddie pool. He'd returned home still damp from his laps and very disappointed. His landlady had caught him totally off guard.

From behind the rhinestone, pointed glasses, Mrs. Gunther squinted at him. "I wasn't sure what to think with the crib, and the changing table, and what-have-you."

He nodded. "Oh, yes, well, I—should have told you when I signed the rental agreement last month. But I—wasn't sure then." He dropped his voice to a whisper.

"See, my wife died giving birth to our son. And the baby was very premature. They didn't think he'd live either, but now it looks like he'll pull through." Carl wondered if she was buying any of this. "They say I might be able to bring him home soon. Anyway, I'm buying some stuff for him. I'm sorry I didn't tell you earlier. It won't be a problem, will it?"

"Oh, of course not," she murmured, stroking the dog's head. "I'll just change the number of occupants to two on the rental agreement. Don't you worry. You poor man . . ."

"Thank you, Mrs. Gunther." He pressed the elevator button. "I see you have a new dog."

"Yes!" She grabbed the poodle's paw and waved it at him. "Twinkle, say hello to Mr. Jorgenson."

"Twinkle, huh?" He wondered what happened to Sparkle II.

"I found her on my doorstep the day after Sparkle died." With a tiny pout, she shook her head, "I never thought I could replace Sparkle, but Twinkle here is the sweetest pooch." She pressed her cheek against the dog's head.

He smiled. "You really love that new poodle, don't you?"

"Oh, yes. She's my baby . . ."

In his living room, Carl surveyed the purchases he'd made in the last three weeks. In a way, he was relieved Mrs. Gunther had seen the bassinet and everything else. Now, he didn't have to worry about their being discovered. He could take some of the baby's clothes and toys out of their boxes now.

Grabbing a beer, Carl sat on the floor, and went through the packages. He smiled at the little tennis shoes, the tiny pajamas with a Superman emblem on the chest, and the toy tiger. Then he pulled out a Felix the Cat clock from another box. He found a nail on the wall, hung up the clock, and plugged it in. He laughed. The dial was on Felix's belly, and his eyes and tail moved back and forth, keeping time. He'd gotten a kick out of it in the store. But now he imagined the clock in his little boy's room after dark, those big, cartoon eyes darting from side to side, the whiskered grin—almost sinister. *Jesus, it would scare the hell out of the kid.*

He'd have to take the god-awful thing back. How quickly adults forgot that certain "cute" decorative items for a kid's room were nightmare material for the kid.

He remembered a clown portrait that hung in his room when he was a little boy. It was a Bozo-type clown, with a bald, white head with red tufts of hair at the temples like horns; the huge, painted smile, and laughing eyes that seemed to look back at him. Sometimes in the night, that clown picture looked so evil and scary. Carl would turn his head away, yet still feel those eyes studying him.

Throughout his childhood, he was plagued by bad dreams. He had no brothers or sisters; and the Jorgenson house was large and formidable. There were rooms that Carl was afraid to enter alone. He was convinced that a monster lurked in that house.

And he was right.

*   *   *

"When's Amy going to bring the baby by so we can see him, Mrs. Sheehan?" the checkout girl asked.

Carl stood in the next line at the Safeway. After four weeks of watching the slim, sixtyish blond lady come and go from the town house, he'd assumed she was the McMurray guy's mother. She looked nothing like the girl. The elegant way she dressed and carried herself, she seemed to have a lot more class than either of them. He was more willing to acknowledge her as the baby's grandmother than he was to accept that young, white trash couple as the parents.

Those nights of sitting in his car, parked across the street from the town house had become a routine—something he looked forward to after work, before going to his empty apartment. Back in high school, he'd made the same kind of lovesick surveillance on Mary Woodrich's house. Nothing had ever happened with that secret crush. Sometimes, he thought this business in front of the McMurrays' house was just as pointless. Still, he wanted to find out everything he could about them, the child especially. But from where he watched, he only caught an occasional glimpse of someone in the window. He'd yet to get a good look at the baby. If they took the boy outside, it must have been during the day, while he was at work. Like the checkout girl, he too wondered: *When can I see him?*

"Maybe we'll bring Eddie by on our way to the airport," Mrs. Sheehan was saying. She gave the girl a playful pout. "I have a 2:40 flight tomorrow afternoon. I'm going to be one lonesome grandma. Little Ed is so sweet and lovable, I just want to take him back to Chicago with me."

* * *

"Thank you for calling Northwest Orient. This is April. Can I help you?"

Leaning over the kitchen counter with the receiver to his ear, Carl doodled on a notepad. He'd written down the names of twelve major airlines, and already crossed out four. "Hello," he said. "I'd like to make a reservation on your flight to Chicago that leaves Portland at 2:40 tomorrow afternoon."

"One minute, please."

He waited. The four other airlines he'd just tried had no such flight.

"Yes, there are still seats available on our flight 57 to Chicago O'Hare. How many will be traveling?"

Bingo. He'd only wanted to find out the airline, so he could see them at the boarding gate, but Carl heard himself answer: "One. Just me. Um, my mother-in-law's on that flight, and I'm wondering if I could sit next to her. The name's Sheehan . . ."

At two o'clock the next afternoon, Carl stood at the boarding gate for Northwest Flight 57. He'd been assigned a middle seat—ordinarily the least desirable place to be stuck for three and a half hours; but he'd be sitting next to the grandmother. This whole trip had him deliberately seeking the in-flight situations he usually tried to avoid. This trip, he hoped to sit next to a chatty grandmother. He wanted to see photographs of her grandchild. He wanted her to talk all about the baby.

Carl glanced down the terminal's long corridor, then checked his wristwatch. He'd left work early, saying he had a dentist appointment; and he still wore his light blue seersucker suit. He liked looking neat and presentable for plane rides. He never understood how some people allowed themselves to appear as if they'd just finished cleaning the garage before jumping into the car and driving to the airport.

The father of the baby boy looked exactly like that. He wore a dirty T-shirt and cutoff jeans. Carl cringed a little at the sight of him, holding the baby in his sweaty, dirt-stained arms. Beside him, the grandmother was a sharp contrast in an airy, yellow, "Sunday-go-to-church" dress; immaculate, every blond hair in place. The girl seemed like a compromise between the two, sporting a white shirt and khaki shorts. But she looked a bit haggard and bloated. Her brown hair was pulled back in a limp ponytail. Carl couldn't quite see the baby's face.

He put on his sunglasses as they approached the gate area. It had been almost a month since seeing Paul McMurray at the hospital; still, he thought he might be recognized.

"Hey, would ya take him for a minute, hon?" McMurray said. He unloaded the baby into his wife's arms. Then he pulled a thin paper bag from under the front of his T-shirt. "Lauraine, I got you a going-away present."

"Oh, Paul, how thoughtful," she said. "You shouldn't have."

Carl saw what McMurray pulled out of the paper bag. It was a bumper sticker that said, "FOXY GRANDMA."

The blond lady's smile seemed to lock on her face. "Well, my, isn't that *sweet*?" She almost sounded sincere. She kissed his cheek, then examined the sign again, a trace of mystification in her eyes. "Um, I— think I'll frame it . . ."

"You don't frame it, Lauraine." He laughed. "It's for the back of your car. Even glows in the dark."

The girl giggled and said how cute it was, but Carl detected a desperation in her enthusiasm—as if she'd support her husband to the point of embarrassment.

They turned and started to move away. Carl could no longer hear them, but he finally got a look at the baby's face. The beautiful little golden-haired boy seemed to peer back at him from behind the girl's shoulder. His tiny hand stretched out. *He's reaching toward me,* Carl thought; *he wants me to take him.*

"Would you like my nuts?"

She looked up from her book, the bumper sticker inserted in the back pages. "Beg your pardon?"

Carl showed her the packet of peanuts. "Would you like these? I'm not going to eat them."

Setting the book in her lap, she took the foil packet. "Well, thank you."

He smiled. "Do you live in Chicago?"

She nodded. "I was in Portland visiting my daughter and son-in-law and my new grandchild."

"I bet you took a ton of pictures of him while you were there," Carl said, hoping to see some photos.

"I was just about to tell you it was a boy." Mrs. Sheehan gave him a puzzled smile. "How did you know?"

"Didn't you just say you were visiting your grandson?" he asked. But she'd said *"grandchild."* He wanted to kick himself for slipping like that.

She shrugged and nibbled on a peanut. "I must have . . ."

"Did you take any pictures?" Carl realized how pushy he sounded, and quickly explained: "My folks could have filled a whole album with the pictures they took of my little boy. During a one-week visit, they must have gone through ten rolls of film."

"You're married?" She glanced at his left hand.

He'd taken off his wedding ring three weeks ago, when Jerry had filed the divorce petition and Eve's calls to the office had stopped. "Um, I'm a widower," he said.

"How awful," she said. Then Mrs. Sheehan blushed and shook her head. "I'm sorry. What I mean is that you seem so young . . ."

"Oh, I'm thirty-nine."

"Really? I thought you were my son-in-law's age. He's twenty-seven. In fact, you look very much like him."

Carl didn't appreciate the comparison as much as he did her estimation of his age. "Do I?" he said. "I'd like to see what he looks like. Do you have a picture of him?"

"Not with me, but I do have one of my grandson," she said, reaching under the seat in front for her purse. "His name is Edward. He's four weeks old. Isn't he handsome?" She handed him a cardboard folder frame from Sears Photography Studio.

Carl gazed at the photograph. The baby clutched a toy stuffed elephant. He wore a light blue pajamalike outfit with a little choo-choo train embroidered over the left breast. He sat propped up against a blanket backdrop. His eyes were bright and big, and he had an open mouth, toothless smile. The baby's sparse, dark blond hair was exactly the same shade as Carl's. He could have been the father. "He's beautiful," Carl murmured.

"Maybe I'm biased," Mrs. Sheehan said. "But he has the sweetest disposition. Oh, and what a smile. He's a real cutie." She reached for the photograph.

Carl hated surrendering it. "He doesn't cry much?" he asked.

"Well, less than most babies, and I speak from experience. But Amy—that's my daughter—she's had a few sleepless nights with him. That's to be expected at this stage."

"It's easier after a couple of months, isn't it?" Carl asked. He heard the naïveté in his voice and tried to cover himself. "I mean, it was with my own little boy . . ."

"Well, at least when they start sleeping through the night, it's easier," she agreed.

"My son had colic," Carl said. He'd read about it in one of the baby books he'd bought for Eve. "And he was allergic to dairy products. We had a tough time with him for a while. Your grandson doesn't have any problems like that, does he?"

"No, thank goodness. It'll be hard enough on my daughter. See, she has to go back to work in a couple of weeks—part-time."

"What does your daughter do?" Carl asked.

"She's a cashier at the Safeway in her neighborhood. I think she'd rather have another kind of job, but she never finished college, so her choices are limited."

"Why didn't she finish school?" Carl asked. "Grades?"

"Oh, no, her grades were good." Mrs. Sheehan sighed. "No, see, Amy and my son-in-law met in college. They eloped during her sophomore year. My late husband—

well, he wasn't too happy about it. We'd been paying for her college, but he felt they were on their own after that. So Amy had to quit school.

"Last year, I gave her some money to go back for her degree, but then she found out she was pregnant, and they used the money as a down payment for their house. It's a sweet little town house. I think they'll be happy there."

"Pardon me for saying so, but you don't sound very sure."

Mrs. Sheehan gave him a wry, sidelong glance. "You're pardoned, and quite correct." She lowered her seat back and sighed. "Juggling a job, a house, a husband, and a baby . . . I don't know. Amy feels terrible leaving the baby with this daycare center, like she's abandoning him or something. She's my youngest. I suppose that's why I worry about her more than I do my other two children. I still think of her as my baby." Mrs. Sheehan smiled tiredly. "It never really gets easy, does it? Do you just have the one? The little boy?"

Carl nodded. "Yes, he's three years old."

"What's his name?"

"Sam." That had been the name he'd wanted for Eve and his baby. He'd been so sure it would be a boy. "It's tough being away from him on these business trips," Carl thought to add. "Um, what kind of work does your son-in-law do?"

"He's a salesman for Hallmark."

"A salesman," Carl echoed. That had been his father's profession. He was retired now, still living in Santa Rosa, in the same house in which Carl had grown up.

"Yes, they both work," Mrs. Sheehan was saying. She glanced briefly out the plane window. "I think it was much easier back when I was a young mother. Nowadays, these working moms have it the worst. Their mothers were always there for them, and they feel badly that they can't do the same for their own children. I know my Amy feels that way."

"Isn't your son-in-law helping out?" Carl asked.

"Well, it's not that Paul isn't trying. I mean, there's the rub. He can diaper or feed the baby a couple of times a week and *rightly* feel he's doing more than his father ever did, but it still isn't enough."

"Well, my wife never had to worry about that with me," Carl said. "I wanted to spend as much time with my baby as I possibly could, even with my full-time job . . ."

She smiled. "I'd say you were an exception. I don't know if it's due to the economy or women's liberation or what. I just know I don't envy my daughter's position right now."

"Personally, I'm in favor of *men's* liberation," Carl said. "That's all you hear about now, women saying they want to 'choose for themselves.' When have men had that luxury? Married or not, they've always had to get a job. When a war comes along, we get drafted. Talk about never having a choice! And if a man wants to have a child . . ." He laughed bitterly. "Nowadays, an unmarried woman can have a baby without becoming a social outcast. It's even fashionable in some circles. She doesn't have to 'commit' to the child's father. But a man who wants a baby needs some woman to cooperate—not just for one night, but for nine months, and usually a helluva lot longer than that."

Mrs. Sheehan started to laugh.

"I'm serious," Carl said. "When parents split up, who gets the kid? Nine times out of ten, it's her."

"That's because nine times out of ten, the father doesn't want the child—"

"Some fathers, yeah. But not this one. That's another thing, a woman doesn't want her baby, hell, she can take care of that before it's even born. She doesn't need the father's consent to go off and have an—operation . . ."

Mrs. Sheehan stared at him.

Carl suddenly realized how crazy he was sounding; the fervency in his own voice was almost embarrassing. He chuckled uneasily. "Sometimes, I take the—the idea of single parenthood too seriously," he said.

Mrs. Sheehan smiled tightly. "You certainly sound like someone who"—she paused—"who wanted very much to be a father. I'm sure you're a good one to your own little boy."

Glancing away, Carl nodded. "I hope to be," he said.

When they landed at O'Hare, he helped Mrs. Sheehan with her bag from the overhead compartment. They shook hands and said good-bye in the terminal. Carl watched her walk away, then he went to the ticket line for the next flight to Portland.

For the trip back, two hours later, Carl sat beside another old lady. She was peppy and talkative, with breath that smelled like an old people's home. Carl got a whiff of it when she asked him what he thought the weather would be like in Portland.

"Oh, a lot milder than Chicago, I imagine," he replied.

She wore a kelly green pantsuit, with a button on the collar of her polyester jacket: ASK ME ABOUT MY GRANDCHILD.

Carl didn't ask. Shortly before takeoff, he closed his eyes and feigned sleep. But he didn't doze. The kid behind him kept kicking his seat back; and the grandmother loudly chatted with a young woman in the aisle seat; now and then she'd lean over him to look out the window, and she'd comment to the girl.

He kept thinking about the coincidence: his father and Paul McMurray, both salesmen. Although Carl's father would have outweighed McMurray by about fifty pounds, the two men looked like the same type: crudely handsome, swaggering ex-jocks. Carl guessed that both men had something else in common, maybe a sadistic streak. After all, he'd seen McMurray in action, the cruel way he'd tripped that poor little kid at the pool. Of course, as a child, Carl had routinely endured a lot worse.

He'd been five years old when Walter Jorgenson quit his sales job to enlist in the army. Despite Mr. Jorgenson's absence, an abundance of money kept coming in—from where it had always come, Grandfather Jorgenson's estate. Carl's father was gone three years, and during that time, Carl's bad dreams gradually faded away—along with the bruises on his little body.

Carl's father returned with his honorable discharge and a chestful of ribbons and medals. He had them mounted on red velvet in a mahogany display case that adorned the living room mantel. With his money and war record, Walter Jorgenson became a big man in

Santa Rosa. Instead of going back to his old job, he got involved in a lot of civic causes, contributing money and spearheading campaigns for buildings, parks, and monuments.

At home, however, he hardly looked like a "pillar of the community," sitting in his favorite chair in the living room, smoking Camels, and slowly getting tanked on scotch and waters.

A few weeks after his father's homecoming, Carl got to tag along with him on his Saturday afternoon poker game. It was held in the bar of a bowling alley a few miles from their house. Carl's mother was sick; otherwise, he figured, the old man never would have taken him. For three hours, Carl bowled alone, ate a hot dog, and played pinball. Every now and then, he checked with his father to see if he wanted to go home yet. The last time Carl checked, his father's poker game had disbanded, and he was sitting in a booth with a red-haired woman who had a beauty mark on her cheek. His father still wasn't ready to go yet. But five minutes later, he was tapping Carl's shoulder over by the gumball machine. He had a surprise for him, he said. Then he led him out to the parking lot, where the bicycles were parked. He pointed to a shiny, blue Schwinn. "Look what I won for you in my poker game."

Carl studied it with awe, running a hand over the leather seat. He rang the St. Christopher bell on the handlebars. From the handgrips dangled plastic red, white, and blue streamers. "Is it really mine?" he asked.

His father nodded. "Think you can ride it home from here?"

"Boy, I sure can! Thank you, sir," and he shook his father's hand.

"I have to go to another poker game. Won't be home till late. Enjoy the bike, son."

Of course he'd enjoy it. His old bike was a rusty, pint-size two wheeler. This was a big boy's bike, and he was in love with it. For two days, he rode his "blue bomber" everywhere. Then one afternoon he came out of the five and dime and caught another kid trying to steal it. The boy was older—maybe ten—but skinny. "Hey, whaddaya think you're doing with my bike?" Carl said, stomping toward him. He made a fist.

The other boy looked past Carl's shoulder. "Hey, Dad!"

Carl spun around. A balding, fat man came out of the store. Carl couldn't figure out what was happening. He glanced back at the boy pulling his blue bomber from the bicycle stand. "Hey, take your grubby mitts off my bike!" he said, grabbing the seat.

Suddenly, the man's hand came down on his shoulder. "Now, hold on a minute, young man," he said. "We reported this bicycle stolen three days ago . . ."

"Not this bike," Carl said, still clutching onto the leather seat. "My dad gave this to me. He won it in a poker game."

The fat man squeezed Carl's arm even tighter. "Listen you, I'm not going to stand here and argue." He nodded up the street. "There's the police station. We'll walk the bicycle over there and discuss this with them. It's a police matter anyway."

On their way to the police station, Carl clung to the seat while the other kid gripped the handlebars, both of them in a silent tug-of-war for ownership. He glanced back at the kid's father, who frowned at him. They were treating him like a criminal, and he hadn't even *done* anything.

"Jorgenson?" the policeman said, after Carl told him his name. The cop was big, with an acne-scarred face. He didn't seem very old, just stern and scary-looking. He stood behind a tall desk that hit Carl at neck level. The station was starkly lit, but seemed gloomy nevertheless. "Your father isn't *Walter* Jorgenson, is he?" the policeman asked.

Carl nodded nervously. "Yessir."

The boy's father touched Carl's back. "You're *Walter Jorgenson's* son?" he asked.

He nodded again. His dad was very well respected in town. He'd clear all this up. They'd listen to him.

The policeman smiled. "Um, why don't you have a seat, Carl? I'll be right back." He retreated to an office down the hallway.

Carl sat on a long, wooden bench against the wall. The kid and his father situated themselves on the other end—far away. After what seemed like an eternity, the policeman came back. "Your father's on his way here, Carl," he said. "Just sit tight."

Carl nodded. He couldn't figure out why his dad didn't just tell the cop over the phone that the bike was his. But Carl kept silent. He stared at the clock on the wall, behind the desk; then at the cigarette stubs in the dirty ashtray stand by his side, and at the fat man's underthighs hanging over the bench. He spied a water fountain down the hall. His mouth felt dry, but he was too scared to ask for permission to get a drink.

Finally, his father came through the swinging doors. "I'm Walter Jorgenson," he told the policeman.

Carl got to his feet, but he remained silent in his father's presence.

"Mr. Jorgenson," the policeman said. "We're terribly sorry to inconvenience you—"

"No apologies necessary. We'll straighten this out in no time." He turned and smiled at the fat man, who stood up. "We haven't met. Walter Jorgenson." He shook the man's plump hand. "I hear your son got his bike stolen, and you think my Carl here is the culprit."

"Well, Mr. Jorgenson, I—"

"Oh, call me Walter."

The man nodded timidly. "Well, the bicycle your son has, it—it's exactly like the one that was stolen, right down to the St. Christopher bell on the handlebars."

"And you think my boy did it?"

The fat man looked very uncomfortable. "It appears to be my son's bicycle. But your son claims that you gave him the bike."

Suddenly, his father seemed agitated. "Well, if that's what my son says," he replied hotly, "then on top of being a thief, he's also a liar. And believe me, he'll be punished."

Carl couldn't believe what his father was saying. "But Dad, what do you mean? You—you *gave* it to me!"

"I'm going to give it to you, all right." He grabbed Carl's arm, then looked at the policeman. "I'd like a word in private with him."

Carl fought back the tears. He didn't understand how this could be happening. His father's grip nearly cut off the circulation in his arm. The other boy smirked at him.

"I think we have an empty office," the policeman offered.

"The men's room is good enough," his father said.

Carl was terrified. "Dad, why don't you tell them they made a mistake?" he whispered. "Please, Dad . . ."

Silent, his father dragged him into the men's room, past the urinals and stalls. He checked each one to make sure it was empty. Finally, he shoved Carl into the last stall, stepped in after him and locked the door. Carl cried uncontrollably now. He knew his precious blue bomber was lost to him, and he'd have to endure a beating from his father. Maybe even jail, too.

"Quit that slobbering!" He grabbed Carl's hair. "I'll give you something to cry about." He smacked him across the face with the back of his hand. "Want another?"

Carl stifled his sobs. Biting down hard on his lip, he stared up at his father with trepidation. His whole head hurt, and he thought he might get sick. The old man let go of his scalp, and several hairs fell out of his hand. "Tell me how you're going to apologize to them," he whispered.

"Apologize? But I didn't—"

His father grabbed his head again before Carl got another word out. He forced him to his knees on the dirty, tiled floor. Carl bumped his cheek against the toilet bowl. Before he knew what was happening, his father pushed his head into the water. It entered his nose and he swallowed some when he opened his mouth to breathe. The big hand held him down, pressing his face against the porcelain. The toilet water got into his ears. He no longer heard what his father was saying—not until the old man dragged him up for air.

"—peep out of you. Understand?"

He was coughing and gagging. "I didn't hear you," he gasped. "I'm sorry—"

"That's right. You're sorry for stealing the bike, aren't you? Aren't you?"

"I'm very, very sorry, sir," Carl told the fat man five minutes later. His hair was still wet, and his face felt swollen from the slap he'd gotten. He stood by the officer's desk, eyes downcast. His father had a tight grip on his arm. Carl had never hated anyone so much in all his life. "It was wrong of me to take the bicycle," he mumbled to the man. "And I shouldn't have lied about it. I hope you won't press charges . . ."

While he carefully repeated all the lines his father had fed him in the lavatory, the old man kept interrupting, joking with the cop and the other boy's father about the "licking this little criminal's got coming to him."

The charges were dropped. His father shook hands with everybody, then led him to the car. "For your sake, young man, I won't mention this to your mother," he said. "And neither will you."

As they drove away, Carl looked back at the other father and son. The boy was hopping on the bicycle, laughing and ringing the bell. His father stood beside him. He was laughing, too.

When they got home, Carl ran up to the bathroom and looked into the medicine chest mirror. He ran a hand through his damp hair and studied the side of his face—already turning an ugly grey color. Why, he wondered, didn't the cop or the fat man say anything about it? They must have noticed.

Of course, his mother had reacted the same way as always. She'd met him at the door, her eyes widening at the sight of his battered face. Yet she, too, said nothing.

From that day on, Carl became suspicious whenever his father gave him something. He'd never show the gifts to any of his friends, he kept them secret, hidden, and unused. He was forever afraid that the things he loved would be taken away from him.

"The captain has turned on the No Smoking sign for our approach to Portland. Please extinguish all smoking materials at this time and return your seat backs to their upright positions."

Carl opened his eyes. The chatty grandmother was smiling at him. "Have a good nap?" she asked.

"Yes, thank you," he lied.

"You from Portland?"

He nodded, then glanced out the window. It suddenly dawned on him. If he wanted that child, he'd have to move to a new city. There were too many people who knew him in Portland. He'd have to go live somewhere else with his new son. Then there would be no questions, no explanations, no fear of having yet another precious thing taken away from him.

CHAPTER THREE

The *Sergeant Pepper* album jacket—opened up and covered with a sheet of Reynold's Wrap—made a good reflector. Amy set it on the lawn chair and kicked off her sandals. She was in the side yard, by the kitchen door—so she could hear the phone in case it rang. She wanted a few quiet, selfish moments to relax.

Unfortunately, Eddie wasn't cooperating. He was cranky and wouldn't fall asleep. She rocked the carriage. "C'mon, guy-guy. Mommy needs rest. Give me a break." But he kept crying, so Amy picked him up. "This is the last time," she sighed. "Then it's off to dreamland, okay?"

Pushing aside the reflector, she eased back into the lawn chair and cradled him to her shoulder. He wore diapers and a T-shirt with Sesame Street's Bert and Ernie on it. His skin felt cool and soft. He quieted down a little. "That's right, go to sleep, guy-guy. Mommy needs rays. She looks like an albino."

Working four days a week at the Safeway and looking after Ed the rest of the time had taken its toll on her appearance. It had been four months, and she still hadn't gotten down to her normal weight before the baby. Miss Thunder Thighs 1977. She could barely squeeze into her old uniform.

But she didn't really care about her appearance when it came to impressing people with her gorgeous child. They'd taken scores of pictures of Eddie, and whenever she was in one with him, she looked awful. Still, if it was a good photo of her little guy-guy, Amy stuck it in the family album anyway.

She was head over heels. She'd do anything, go anywhere, lie, steal, and cheat for him. She thought about him all the time, even in her sleep. Most of her life, she'd wanted someone who would love her; and now she had someone *she loved.* Did Paul have any idea? Did he suspect that the real love of her life was this miracle child?

No, he probably didn't have a clue. Just as he'd never had an inkling that she'd been ready to leave him a year ago. That was when she realized that the marriage was a mistake. Sure, it had been sweet and romantic at first, playing the struggling college bride, having friends over to their modestly furnished newlyweds' nest. Amy knew they were envious. Plus Paul was so cute and sexy. But then he lost his job at the sports equipment store. For several months, Amy was the only one bringing home a paycheck—from the Safeway. She watched her friends graduate from college; she listened to their stories about budding careers, boyfriends, and vacations their parents were paying for. And here she was, in her ugly orange polyester uniform, chained to her cash register and a jobless husband.

Paul wasn't beating the pavement too hard for work

either. He wasn't so cute and sexy anymore, spending most of his time with his beer-drinking buddies. He had a lot of time on his hands, too. They were living like white trash, and Amy hated it. She'd come from an upper-middle-class Catholic family in the North Shore suburbs of Chicago. She wanted to go back— alone, for good. Her father was dead, but Mom still had the house. Amy imagined living in her old room again, perhaps day-hopping at Northwestern, and applying for a nice Catholic annulment. Secretly, she started to make plans for her second chance.

Then she got pregnant. Everything changed. It put a fire under Paul. He got a sales job with Hallmark Greeting Cards in Portland. She was able to transfer to another Safeway there. Amy considered his sudden burst of ambition a positive sign.

At that time, she'd told herself not to expect miracles. It didn't matter that Paul was no superhusband, just so long as he would be a good father.

Her sweet guy-guy deserved a terrific daddy.

He didn't deserve a father who bathed and changed him so infrequently that he always had to ask where the diapers were. Paul would step around a glob of baby puke on the floor without ever thinking to clean it up. He seemed to treat Eddie like a toy he'd grown tired of. Amy resented him for that most of all. He no longer shared with her the wonder of this terrific baby. The dumb lughead didn't seem to give a shit.

Amy patted little Eddie on the back. He'd finally fallen asleep. Gently, she set him in the carriage. He stirred for a moment, then sighed and went back to sleep. Amy turned the carriage around so he wouldn't get burned. The sun was strong for late September.

She sank back in the lawn chair and picked up the homemade reflector. The warm sun baked her face and she felt herself drifting off—almost floating in a sea of semiconsciousness.

The telephone rang. "Shit!" Dropping the reflector, Amy jumped up and ran inside the kitchen. She grabbed the receiver on the third ring, then listened outside for a moment. No cranky cries; Eddie hadn't woken up. "Hello?" she said.

"Hi, hon."

She rubbed her eyes. "Oh, hi. What's up?"

"Well, you know what tonight is?" he asked.

Amy edged toward the sink, as far as the phone cord stretched. From the window, she could see only the top of Ed's carriage. The side yard was unfenced and awfully close to the street. She didn't like leaving him out there. "It's just a plain old Monday, Monday, can't trust that day. Why? What's going on?"

"It's 'Monday Night Football,' the season premiere!"

"Oh," she said, turning from the window. "Well, you're gonna have to watch it in black-and-white, because I've got dibs on the color set. *West Side Story* is on tonight."

"Sorry, hon. But I've already invited Don, Allen, and Rich over for dinner and the game."

"You *what*?"

"Oh, c'mon, don't have a hissy fit on me. It's no big deal. You know you'd fall asleep during the movie anyway."

"God, that's just like you to be so selfish—"

"What the hell is that supposed to mean?"

"It means I've already got plans for tonight," she answered. "Besides, we're having leftovers, and there won't be enough for five." She opened the refrigerator. "And we're out of beer."

"I'll pick up some steaks and beer on the way home. I'll barbecue. For cryin' out loud, you won't have to lift a finger."

"Oh, bullshit! The place is a pigsty."

"Well, like that's *my* fault?"

"I seem to recall you live here, too." She heard something outside, the carriage squeaking. "Just a second," she said into the phone. Amy went to the window again, and once more, she saw just the top of the baby carriage. She couldn't hear Ed.

"All I'm asking is that you straighten up the living room a little," Paul was saying. "Christ, you'd think I wanted you to donate a kidney."

Amy turned and stomped toward the breakfast table. "Dammit, Paul, I was really looking forward to this movie . . ."

"Okay, fine, fine. You want me to call Don, Allen, and Rich, and tell them you don't want them over, fine. Great."

She looked toward the screen door. At times like this, Ed's silence caused more worries than his crying. "Oh, all right," she sighed. "Bring them over, have a blast. I haven't got time to argue with you now. Just do me a favor and get some Midol while you're at the market. Better get some Tater Tots, too."

"No problem," he replied. "Oh, and hey, hon, clean up the bathroom a little. Okay?"

In response, Amy slammed the receiver on its cradle, then glared at the dirty dishes piled up on the counter. Defeatedly, she wandered over to the sink and turned on the water. She reached for a plate. "God,

Eddie!" she whispered. What an awful mother she was, leaving him out there. How could she forget her own child? She ran outside, her heart pounding. There hadn't been a peep out of him. She half expected to find him gone.

But he was there, asleep in the carriage, his little hands cupped beneath the double chin.

"Dammit, Amy," she scolded herself aloud. She'd never do that again. God only knew how long she'd left him out there.

Four and a half minutes. She'd left the baby alone that long, and he'd just sat in the car, too scared to make a move. Hell, in the past nine weeks, he'd used up almost all his sick days from work so he could watch the house and possibly get an opportunity like the one he'd just blown. *Stupid, stupid . . .*

Pulling away from the curb, Carl gripped the steering wheel tightly. Maybe it wasn't meant to be. He just didn't have the nerve to pull it off. He didn't have the money either.

He'd found an apartment up in Seattle, and on weekends he was furnishing the place that would be his son's new home. His money had wings; paying rent on two apartments put an extra bite into his wallet. He was down to his last thousand in the bank.

All the baby things were still at the place on Weidler. He liked having them around, but he couldn't afford to indulge himself much longer. Everything had to be ready in the new apartment if he took the baby. What he'd do for money when he got to Seattle was another question.

Shit, don't think about that now, Carl told himself. *You need a nap. Hardly got any sleep last night. Everything seems worse when you haven't had enough sleep. Just a few winks and you'll feel better. . . .*

But back in his apartment, stripped down to his undershorts and sprawled across the living room sofa with a blanket over him, Carl couldn't fall asleep. Typical. And he was dead tired, too. Even as a kid, he'd been plagued with insomnia.

Back then, he was never sure when closing his eyes to sleep if he'd make it to morning without a beating.

The attacks during the night were the worst. Carl was never quite sure what he'd said or done during the day that set his father off. Maybe he'd eaten the last of the Toll House cookies that night; or yesterday, forgotten to take out the garbage; or last week, been late for dinner. Then again, the old man didn't always need an excuse to start in on him. Sometimes, all it took was a bad day or too much scotch. He'd wake up Carl with a slap or a blow to the stomach. Often during the night attacks, the old man would grab Carl's pillow and press it over his face to muffle the screams. Carl would feel the knee come down hard on his stomach, the breath squeezed out of him until he'd think he was going to die. The pressure of the pillow crushing his face sometimes caused a nosebleed.

At first, Mrs. Jorgenson tried to dismiss the attacks as "bad dreams." Her stock explanation for the blood-stained pillowcase and sheets was: "Well, you must have hit yourself in your sleep again, honey." Still, she nursed the bruises and cuts. Carl often noticed a puffy discoloration by his mother's lip or eye that makeup didn't quite camouflage, and he knew the old man was beating up on her, too. But she never let on, not even when Carl asked her. She was adamant that he keep his own suffering a secret as well: "You mustn't let anyone know about this. It would ruin us." She made it a point to casually mention to all the other mothers that eleven-year-old Carl was "accident-prone."

Despite such gloomy credentials, many of his friends' parents welcomed him into their homes—for supper or to spend the night. He'd learned early on not to confide in anyone; yet for survival, he sought out and won several friends. He was safe in their homes—away from his father.

He couldn't predict what the old man would do. Days, even weeks could go by, and his father wouldn't touch him, then suddenly, he'd just explode. The assaults always managed to catch Carl unprepared and vulnerable. Carl decided to build himself up—like that skinny weasel in the Charles Atlas ads on the back of his comic books. Then he'd be strong enough to defend himself. Carl exercised, and checked out books from the library on bodybuilding. His efforts boosted his athletic status at school. He held the record for chin-ups in his seventh grade class, but he was still no match for his father.

On the frame to his closet doorway, Carl had penciled a line at six feet, two inches—his father's height. He marked off his growth every week. When he entered high school, he stood just three inches short of his father's line, and he became the freshman team's first-string quarterback.

Carl was often mentioned in the town newspaper's sports pages; once there was even a whole article written about him, predicting a great future for him on the varsity team. Walter Jorgenson wasn't mentioned in the story. As one of the town's "leading citizens," he'd become accustomed to seeing his name in the newspaper. But he'd gotten another sales job and stopped devoting so much time to civic projects. He hated the new mayor. And he seemed to hate Carl, too, because now he was the only Jorgenson who got written up by the local press.

"So how's the football star tonight? Drop any more passes?"

Suppertime at the Jorgenson household was always a semiformal occasion: candlelight, tablecloth, and polite conversation amid the clanking of silverware. Carl was not expected to talk. It was unusual for his father to address him at the dinner table—unless something was about to happen. And Carl felt it coming. "I'm the quarterback, Dad," he answered quietly. "I'm the one who does the passing."

"Must have a classload of fairies if they made *you* quarterback," the old man grumbled.

"We've won eight out of nine games so far this season," Carl pointed out.

"Is the roast beef all right, honey?" Carl's mother asked, looking at her husband. She fidgeted with her pearl necklace.

He wasn't eating. With his fork, he idly pushed the food around his plate, "Huh, thinks he's a big man just because he got his name in the newspaper a couple of times." He tossed his head in Carl's direction. "Football hero. He's not worth a damn around here. Sits around on his ass all day."

Carl took a deep breath. "Mom," he murmured. "Can I please be excused?"

"Excuse you?" his father said. "Why? For being so worthless? For being a lazy, good-for-nothing—"

"Shut up," Carl growled. His whole body tingled as he talked back to his father for the first time.

"What did you just say to me?" The old man reached over to grab him by the hair.

Carl knocked his hand away. "Cut it out!"

His father got up. "Why, you little shit—"

"No, Walter, don't," Carl's mother was saying.

Carl jumped up and backed away. With a clenched fist, his father swung at him, but Carl dodged it. He was getting too fast for the old man; didn't have all that extra weight to slow him down. Cursing, his father got redder in the face with each failed swing until he managed to connect, cuffing Carl on the side of the head.

Carl had gotten tagged worse during football scrimmages; it dazed him for only a second. Then his father grabbed him by the hair. Carl could no longer hold back. Years of silent submission and powerlessness suddenly ended. He punched the old man back, a hard blow to his soft gut. He didn't stop there. Without thinking, he hit him across the mouth with his fist.

His father stumbled back into the table. Food, plates, and silverware toppled to the floor. He fell to his knees and held a hand over his mouth. As if in shock, he gazed at the blood on his fingertips.

Carl stood there, paralyzed with fear. He could barely hear his mother, pleading for them to stop. He'd never seen his father look so angry.

"I'll show you," the old man whispered. He grabbed a steak knife off the floor and got to his feet. "C'mon, football hero."

"No, Walter . . . God, please . . ."

Carl backed away until he bumped into the break-front.

Cutting at the air, his father came closer and closer. He jabbed the knife toward Carl's face, but Carl lurched to one side. The old man took another swing with the blade. Carl put his hand up, and blood suddenly sprayed onto his father's white shirt. He'd sliced a deep line across Carl's palm.

He came at Carl with the knife again.

"Fucking asshole!" Carl kicked the old man in the balls. The knife flew out of his father's hand. Carl didn't even realize what he'd done until he blinked and saw his father curled up on the floor, writhing in pain, his hands cupped between his legs. He made a strange, choking sound as he gasped for air. Carl knew what it was like to have the breath knocked out of him.

He grabbed a napkin and wrapped it around his bleeding hand. The cut would need stitching. It stung, worse than any burn. He looked down at his mother, now kneeling over the old man. "Mom?" Carl said. "Mom, can you drive me to the hospital?" The napkin was already soaked through, dripping blood. "Mom, please . . ."

But she just shook her head helplessly, not moving from her place by the old man.

Carl left them there together, and ran down the block to his friend Timmy Monda's house. He told them that his folks were gone for the night and he'd cut himself fixing dinner. Timmy and Mr. Monda drove him to the hospital. Carl gave the same story to the doctor who put six stitches into his hand.

"It'll be sore for a couple of days," the doctor told

him. Then he squinted at Carl and touched his bruised cheek. "Say, you've got quite a shiner there. How did that happen?"

"Oh, well, after I—I cut my hand, I ran into a cabinet. Pretty stupid, huh?"

"Put some ice on that cheek when you get home," the doctor said.

Carl nodded and looked away. Just once, he wished someone wouldn't believe his lies.

"You're Walter Jorgenson's boy, aren't you?"

"That's right," he murmured.

"Give him my regards. He's a fine man . . . fine man."

Carl spent the night at the Mondas' house. He phoned his mother, and she said his father was packing for a business trip. It would be safe to come home the next morning.

Never again would his father get the best of him. Carl put a swift end to every attack. He didn't allow the old man to catch him vulnerable or unprepared. He bought a hinged padlock and screwed it to the inside of his bedroom door. He hid the lock and key inside an old pair of gym shoes at the back of his closet, and pulled them out before going to sleep. No more sneak attacks. Often, he'd wake up at night to the sound of his father beating against the secured door, the muted curses as he vainly tried to force it open.

The knocking wouldn't stop. Then the doorbell. Carl opened his eyes. He squinted at the shades drawn against the living room windows, and he threw the blanket aside. Climbing off the couch, he glanced at his wristwatch: 4:40. Must have fallen asleep after all.

The doorbell rang again. "Just a minute!" he called,

almost tripping as he stepped into his pants. He grabbed his shirt—draped over the railing of the baby's crib—put it on and fumbled at a couple of buttons in the front. Staggering to the door, he checked the peephole.

It was Eve.

What the hell does she want? he wondered. It had been over three months since he'd even spoken to her. All communications were now handled through their attorneys.

Damn. Their first meeting after the divorce: she should find him looking terrific, healthy, and happy. Not like this: tired, disheveled, his ugly apartment barely furnished—*and full of baby things.*

She was looking directly at the peephole. "Carl, I know you're there. Are you going to open the door or what?"

He opened it only a crack. Then he stepped outside, set the catch and quickly shut the door behind him. "Hi," he said, running a hand through his hair. "How've you been, Eve?"

"Fine." Her eyes avoided his. "I guess you're not going to ask me in . . ."

"The place is kind of a mess right now. Otherwise I would."

"I tried you at work. They said you called in sick today."

"I'm feeling better now," he said. Carl smiled at her. She looked beautiful, that relaxed, "natural" beauty which took her twenty minutes in front of the makeup mirror to achieve. Carl hated himself for still feeling drawn to it. She wore the lavender blouse he'd given her last Christmas, his favorite on her. Had she come to try for a reconciliation? He wondered if it were possible. "You look very nice, Eve," he managed to say.

She glanced down at his bare feet, then at the undone buttons on his shirt. "I seem to have caught you at a bad time." She looked beyond him at the door. A tiny frown came to her face. "You have company, don't you?"

He swallowed. All the baby things, he couldn't let her come in and see them. "Yes," he said. "Sorry."

She took a deep breath. "Well, then I'll get right to the point, Carl. I almost gave them your number here, but I thought, well . . ." She shrugged. "I felt you shouldn't hear it over the phone from some stranger. I got a call from this man in Santa Rosa, and he said he'd been trying to locate you for two days. It seems your father had a severe stroke. He—he passed away on Saturday, Carl. I'm sorry."

Carl stared at her for a moment. "You're kidding . . ."

"The funeral is day after tomorrow," she murmured.

He wondered why he didn't feel anything. There was no sorrow, not even relief. It merely struck him as ironic, since he'd been thinking so much about the old man recently. "Well, thank you for telling me, Eve," he heard himself say. "It was very thoughtful of you to come here . . . very considerate . . ."

Was that the only reason she'd come? Had she made herself so alluring just to give him this news, or was there more? He kept telling himself that his father was dead, but he'd never loved him. Yet he still felt something for Eve. And she stood in front of him now, touching his arm. Against all his resolves, he hoped she'd missed him too, and been as lonely as he.

"Are you going to be all right?" she was asking. "I have a feeling this isn't sinking in yet."

"Oh, I'm fine," he said. "It's sweet of you to be so concerned." He smiled shyly. "Listen, Eve, I'm alone here. There's no company. I just said that because, well, this place is kind of a rathole, and I didn't want you pitying me—like I was living in squalor without you . . ."

"I wouldn't think that, Carl," she said.

"Listen, maybe if you're not busy tomorrow night. we could have dinner together." As he spoke, Carl felt he shouldn't be so honest and impulsive. It was like opening a wound. "Just dinner," he mumbled.

"You're expected in Santa Rosa tomorrow for a memorial service," she replied. "They'll be calling you tonight about the arrangements. In any event, I don't think dinner together is a good idea, not at this time. But I'm flattered."

Could she have sounded more impersonal? he wondered. *But I'm flattered,* that was a polite "get-lost" line to some schmuck trying to pick her up in a bar. Hell, he was still her husband. Maybe if she'd said it with a smile instead of that glacial expression, it might not have been so humiliating. What was he thinking anyway? He didn't really want to be with her again. It would spoil all his plans for the baby. How could he be so stupid? "I see what you mean," he said finally.

She studied him in a pained and wondering way— as if staring at some juvenile delinquent in jail. "It doesn't faze you at all, does it?" she asked quietly. "I know you and your father had problems, Carl. Maybe if you'd told me just a little more about that, I'd understand. But he's dead. And you don't seem a bit sorry. Isn't there an ounce of forgiveness in you?"

"Not for him," he said. "But for you, Eve, yes. Only you don't want my forgiveness, do you?"

Her eyes narrowed at him. "Carl, I don't think I did anything wrong. It's my body, my decision. I'm sorry you got hurt, and I'm sorry you don't understand. But I don't need you to forgive me for what I did . . ."

The little speech seemed more carefully thought out than when she'd given it before, and he imagined Eve rehearsing it in the car on her way to his place. In all the time he'd known her, in all the fights they'd had, not once had she admitted to being wrong. She'd never said to him, "I'm sorry." Instead, it was: "I'm sorry you misunderstood," or "I'm sorry you're upset about it,"—always qualifying the apology so it came back to him, as if he were too thickheaded to accept something hurtful she'd said or done. He often wondered why she couldn't ever tell him she was just plain sorry.

"I haven't done anything wrong," she said with finality, her head held high, tilted to one side.

He just nodded. "Well, Eve, I guess that's where we'll never see eye to eye." He reached for the doorknob. "Listen, it was very nice of you to come here in person to tell me the news about my father. I appreciate it. Thanks." He nodded again and smiled. "Take care." Then he ducked inside and closed the door.

Carl felt proud of himself for keeping his cool, acting so civil and friendly when she'd probably expected an argument. It was almost like a victory for him—but a small, sad one. He had no connection to anyone at all anymore, not her, not the father he'd hated. He was alone in the ugly, nearly barren apartment now. And the baby's crib was still empty.

Natalie Wood danced alone on a rooftop. *West Side Story* lost a lot of its impact on the twelve-inch black-and-white screen. The portable TV sat on the breakfast table, while Amy slouched in the chair, trying to ignore all the noise from the living room. Nearly every tender moment in the movie was spoiled by loud cheers or groans, or Paul coming in for more beer.

He was right, damn him. If she were on the living room sofa watching this, she'd have fallen asleep before Tony and Maria even met. She hated the heaviness dragging down her eyelids.

A chorus of hoots and applause from the living room made her sit up. Someone must have scored a touchdown. Did they have to be so damn loud? They'd wake up the baby . . .

Then, as the noise died down, sure enough, she heard Eddie crying—his sleepy cry. If she went in to him now, he'd never go back to sleep. And she had work in the morning. Didn't Paul realize that? Didn't he care at all? She might as well have been a single parent. Sometimes, that didn't seem like a bad idea.

Amy turned down the volume on the movie and listened. Eddie got a little quieter. *That's it, honey, go back to sleep . . .* She closed her eyes and felt herself drifting off in the lull.

"OH, SHIT! THE BALL WAS RIGHT IN HIS HANDS!" someone boomed.

This was followed by the sound of stomping on the

floor, loud moans, and hisses. Then Eddie—screaming.

Amy snapped off the TV, got to her feet, and marched into the living room. *All of you, get the hell out of here right now!* she wanted to yell. But she put on her best cordial smile, although four sets of eyes were glued to the set. "Paul," she said steadily. "Can I see you for a second?"

"Can't it wait until next commercial?"

She kept the smile stretched across her face. "Now, sweetheart, okay?" Amy swiveled around and walked into their bedroom. Ed was still crying, but his voice was weak and sleepy.

Paul came into the bedroom. "Hey, hon," he whispered. "Can't you do something to quiet him down? We're trying to watch a game in there."

"Anyway, that's when I hit him," Amy told her mother on the phone. It was ten-thirty her mother's time; Amy knew she'd woken her, but thought she'd go crazy if she didn't talk to someone.

"Well, *where* did you hit him?"

"Just on the shoulder," she sighed. Amy was sitting in the dark, on the bed.

"What did he do then?"

"He said 'ouch' and laughed." Actually, he'd said: "What the fuck is the matter with you?" Then she'd torn into him about the racket he and his friends were making. They were quieter now, and she didn't want to pass through that living room with them still there. Eddie hadn't let out a peep in the last ten minutes. "Anyway,

Mom, everything's okay now." Amy got up and pulled the phone to the window. "Listen, one of the reasons I called," she said. "Would it be okay—just as soon as I get some time off from work—if we came for a visit?"

"Of course, dear. I'd love it. There's plenty of room—"

"I think it would be just the guy-guy and me, Mom," she said, leaning against the drapes. "Paul—I don't think he could get the time away from work. See, I'd like to stay a couple of weeks, maybe even a month—if that's okay with you."

There was a silence on the other end of the line for a moment. "Well, um, that's fine, dear," her mother said. "Stay as long as you want. . . ."

CHAPTER FOUR

Carl's face hurt from maintaining a stoic smile. And making small talk with all the strangers outside the church was wearing him out. "Yes, he was a great man," Carl would lie, pumping one hand after another. "My father mentioned you in his letters. Thank you for coming."

The old man had written about once a month: dull updates and invitations to come visit. The letters had been addressed to a Portland post office box which Carl had rented. Several of them had alluded to *"the Oriental gal who works for me,"* a widow named Han Serum, his father's live-in "housekeeper."

Carl never met her. Yet she was the only one he could pick out among the strangers. When he spotted the petite Asian woman climbing the church steps, Carl broke away from an old city councilman and called to her: "Mrs. Serum?"

At the top of the steps, she turned to stare at him.

He'd extended his hand. "Mrs. Serum? I'm Carl . . ."

She shot him such a cold look that Carl pulled his

hand back. "I do not want to talk with you," she said evenly. "I'm surprised you even bothered to come."

"What? Wait a minute—"

But Mrs. Serum ducked inside the church.

A senile former mayor gave the eulogy: *"Walter Jorgenson was a loving husband, devoted father . . ."*

Carl sat in the front pew, stifling a yawn. He glanced over at Mrs. Serum, alone in the pew across the aisle from him. She was around fifty. With her gaunt, vulturine features and the grey streaks in her sixties-throwback beehive hairdo, Mrs. Serum didn't seem to fit the "mistress" mold. But she'd been living with his father for years. Carl studied her face for bruises, but there were none. She caught him staring. Carl smiled timidly and faced forward.

He wondered what the hell his old man had told this lady to make her so bitter and mean toward him. God only knew what kind of lies the old bastard fed her.

Carl felt on the outside of everything. So many familiar sights, yet he no longer had any connection to his "hometown." Last night, he'd driven his rental car past the house, knowing he would have to step inside eventually. But the red brick estate held too many memories. After seventeen years, he couldn't enter that house again just yet. He'd spent the night at a Travelodge.

The only thing he cared about was in Portland. He hated missing his nightly vigil outside the McMurrays' town house, and feared something might happen to the baby in his absence. He'd have to take him as soon as he got back. This funeral—this charade heralding his father's kindness—had Carl desperately wanting to disprove the theory that abused children grew up to become abusive parents. He wasn't like his old man. He'd be a wonderful dad to that boy. At his own funeral, his son wouldn't have to put on an act for strangers. His tears would be genuine.

Carl wished he could cry. He wanted to feel something besides fatigue and alienation. But for so many years, fear was the only emotion his father had induced in him. The old man had died for him long ago—on that night over dinner, when Carl had first struck him back. But there had been someone else in the house who couldn't stand up to the old man.

As Carl grew stronger, his mother seemed to deteriorate. The bruises she used to conceal with makeup were poorly camouflaged in the last years of her life. She was only forty-two, but could have been mistaken for Carl's grandmother. Carl day-hopped at a local college so he could be close to her.

One afternoon, he returned home from classes and found her facedown on the floor in the front hallway. She lay at the foot of the stairs, her periwinkle blue tea dress wrinkled up near the top of her sprawled legs. A dark puddle of blood framed her head and mingled in her blond hair. She wasn't moving at all.

On the way to the hospital, Carl rode in the back of the ambulance with her. The medic had rolled an ugly bandage around his mother's head, and a spot of blood bloomed on the gauze over her left eye. Carl held her limp hand. The medic had said he wasn't sure she'd regain consciousness. He'd asked how it happened. Carl said nothing, but he knew.

The old man must have come home for lunch, then started in on her. How could he have just left her there?

It was criminal—attempted murder, or manslaughter. If she died, they'd put his father in jail. *I won't have to stay here and look after her anymore,* Carl thought. *I'll finally be free of him—if she dies.*

He pushed the thought out of his mind before he dared wish for it. Carl squeezed his mother's hand.

Three hours later, she was sitting up in the hospital bed. The room was dark, because she said the light hurt her eyes. The clumsy bandage around her head had been replaced by a smaller patch. They'd said she'd suffered a slight concussion and she would have to spend the night at the hospital. This seemed to worry her; but Carl, seated in a hard wood chair by her bed, was more concerned about how it had happened.

"Quit protecting him, Mom," he whispered. "He did this to you, didn't he?"

"Carl, I was alone in the house all morning," she said, still very groggy. "I fell down the stairs all by myself. It's silly—I know. But I'm telling you the truth."

The stories were always the same: *I tripped over the coffee table—so clumsy,* or *I slipped on the kitchen floor.* She'd be so bruised or weakened by these "accidents" that Carl never had the heart to browbeat her into admitting what had really happened. But he knew. After all, throughout most of his childhood, he was the one who was supposedly accident-prone. One word from her, and Carl would have taken his father apart. But she protected the old man, and never gave Carl that chance.

"I won't fall asleep tonight," his mother was saying. "I know I won't, not in this hospital bed, with nurses running up and down the corridor. I won't sleep a wink. . . ."

"They'll give you a pill, Mom," Carl sighed. "Don't worry."

"The pills won't work. Listen, honey, you—you're coming back to see me tonight, aren't you?"

He nodded. "Sure, Mom."

"There's a bottle in the back of the kitchen cupboard, where I keep the spices. Could you bring me that bottle, honey?"

"What's in it?"

"Oh, just a little bit of gin. I think if I had a drop or two at bedtime, it would relax me, help me sleep . . ."

"You want me to bring you some gin?" Carl asked numbly.

"That's the last thing you need."

Carl looked over at his father, silhouetted by the light coming through the doorway. He'd called his father's office three hours before, and now the old man finally had come. He lumbered into the hospital room and dropped his hat on the foot of her bed. "Three quarters of your liver's destroyed and you want him to smuggle you a bottle of gin. Christ Almighty, woman, what am I supposed to do with you? Doctor just about told me the blood from that cut on your forehead was ninety proof . . ."

She bit her lip and slowly—almost painfully—turned her head away from him.

"Mom, were you drinking?" Carl said. "Is that why you fell down the stairs?"

She closed her eyes. "Would you both please go? I don't feel well. Come back later . . . but for now, I need to rest."

They drove back from the hospital in silence. His father stared at the road ahead, and the headlights of passing cars cast shadows across his stern face. Carl sat on the passenger side, close to the car door. He wondered why he hadn't seen it before. Most of the townspeople considered Teresa Jorgenson a teetotaler. But then, she'd always been an expert at camouflage. He knew his father beat her, but now, he'd never be sure how many times she'd been telling the truth about her "accidents," and when she'd been covering up for the old man.

"How long has she been drinking?" he asked quietly.

"Long enough that it's made her sick. I give her a year."

"Until she's well again?"

"Till she's dead." His father glanced at him for a second. "Get used to the idea."

Eventually, he did. His mother began to spend more time in the hospital than at home. Visiting her after classes became part of his routine. Sometimes, they just watched TV together; but all too often, she was delirious from pain or her medications.

"You're leaving him after I die, aren't you?" she asked him, one rare afternoon when she'd been lucid.

"You're not going to die for a long time, Mom."

"I've made my will," his mother said. "You'll be twenty-one this November, won't you?"

"Yeah, Mom. But I—"

"You'll get everything. With my furs and jewels and the savings, it comes to about twenty thousand dollars. That's what the lawyers said. It'll be enough for you to go away and finish up school. I should have sent you away a long time ago. He wanted to put you in one of those military schools. I should have agreed to it, but I wanted you here—selfish. I didn't think about what you had to go through living at home—with him."

"Let's not talk. Okay, Mom? Let me turn on the TV . . ."

Her bony hand wrapped around his. "Forgive me, Carl . . ."

"What for? You didn't do anything, Mom."

"That's right," she murmured. "I didn't do anything. From the very beginning, I knew. When you were just a baby, and you'd cry at night, sometimes he'd wake up first. Then I'd check on you after, and I'd find—" She shook her head and tugged at the bed covers. "I'd find he'd stuck a rag or a washcloth in your mouth to stop the crying. God knows how many times you could have choked to death when he did that. And I kept quiet about it. All these years, *I didn't do anything.*" She started to cry. "I'm sorry, Carl. I should have been a better mother to you. . . ."

"Well, I survived," Carl mumbled. He handed her a Kleenex. "Here. Don't talk anymore, okay? Don't talk, Mom."

She died three weeks later. His father didn't shed any tears—not until the funeral mass. He suddenly started blubbering in front of the congregation. Carl couldn't tell if the tears were genuine or for show. He stood beside his father, but the old man never took hold of his arm for comfort. Nor did Carl reach out to him.

Perhaps the townspeople in St. Matthew's Church now expected the same show of emotion from him that they'd witnessed from his father eighteen years before. Then again, Mrs. Serum and several others probably figured he'd returned only for his father's money.

Well, he'd need it. Yesterday, he'd asked the funeral home for an estimate: $4,880.00. He couldn't swing that—even if he cashed a bond he'd been saving for "baby money." He'd be broke.

But with the inheritance, he could give his son a good home, something better than the one that Mc-Murray couple gave him. The sale of his father's house alone would see him through a few years of unemployment and full-time parenthood.

But he hadn't come all this way just for money. No one would understand the real reason. All his life, he'd kept his father's abuse a secret, not so much to save the family's reputation, but to carry on the pretense that his father loved him. He didn't want anyone thinking that he was unworthy of a father's love. He needed to play out the charade to its finish now, and a few tears— however forced—might help. He wished he could cry.

"That's what I remember most about Walter," the former mayor was saying from the pulpit. "His generosity. He always gave so much of his time and money to this community. He left behind a bountiful contribution to the city of Santa Rosa . . ."

A tiny alarm went off in Carl's head. After listening to all the lies, he heard something which seemed horribly true—and so much like the old man. All of his money was going to the city, not his son.

"Just two weeks ago," the ex-mayor went on, "Walter discussed with me his plans to leave a large part of his estate to our city, his beloved hometown . . ."

Carl felt as if he were being yanked out of a childhood slumber again, a terrible, wakening blow to the side of his head. How could he be so stupid? Of course, it all made sense now. One final act of hatred, made public: cut the estranged son out of the will and stick him with the funeral cost.

There went his "baby money." He couldn't afford to quit his job and move to Seattle now. All hopes and plans for his son, shattered. He shifted restlessly in the pew. He just wanted to run out of the church and disappear someplace where no one could find him. He glanced around, wondering if they saw the panic and pain on his face. He caught Mrs. Serum staring at him.

She smiled.

Mrs. Serum sat beside Carl in the other green chair at the law office of Bracken and McCourt. Carl had said hello when she'd come in. She'd nodded curtly.

"Why didn't you want to talk to me yesterday?" he'd asked quietly.

But just then, Mr. McCourt cleared his throat. A heavyset man in his late fifties, he had glasses and a full head of white hair. He shuffled through some papers on his large maple desk and announced it was time to read the will. The housekeeper got to keep the house and all the furnishings with the exception of those items Mrs. Jorgenson had bequeathed to Carl back in 1960.

Carl slumped lower in the chair. That was all he'd get—junk already belonging to him. Was that why he'd come to this reading? Or did the old man have a hateful good-bye for him too?

Fifteen thousand dollars in stocks and bonds also

went to his father's housekeeper. Another ten thousand went to the city of Santa Rosa to help erect the monument to its World War II veterans.

Carl straightened in his chair when Mr. McCourt looked at him from over the rim of his bifocals. *" 'And to my son, Carl,' "* he read, *" 'I leave the remainder of my estate: approximately fifty-five thousand dollars in savings, insurance, and stocks.' "*

Carl waited to hear more—some explanation. But the rest was mere legal jargon. He couldn't believe the old man had been so generous to him, and he wondered if perhaps this wasn't just another one of his father's gifts he couldn't keep. Yet it was legitimate, and the lawyer was now explaining that after taxes and the funeral costs, he'd get about forty thousand dollars. It was enough for him to start a new life with his son in Seattle.

He sat in a stupor until it was over. Then Mrs. Serum got up, shook the lawyer's hand, and without a glance at Carl, she went out the door. He caught up with her outside the building, just as she was about to climb into her car. "Mrs. Serum?"

She opened the car door, then hesitated and gave him an icy, imperious look.

Carl felt foolish under her cold, silent stare. "Um, I just wanted to say, if there's anything I can do for you, you can—"

"I can what?" she said. "Write to you care of that post office box?" She shook her head at him. "I was with your father twelve years. And in all that time, you never visited him. He waited and hoped. I never knew a son could be so indifferent toward his own father. My God, you would not even give him your phone number or home address. Well, you got what you came here for, Mr. Jorgenson. You are fifty-five thousand dollars richer."

"Now, wait a minute." He touched her arm, and the Asian woman reeled back. Carl held up his hand as if to show that he wouldn't dare touch her again. "It's true," he said. "I wanted to keep a distance from him. I had my reasons—"

"You do not deserve all the love he had for you."

"What?" Carl let out a bitter laugh. "If he loved me, he had a peculiar way of showing it. You've no idea what he did to me when I was a kid."

"And you do not know what it was like for him the last twelve years," she said. "You were all he ever talked about. He wanted so much to see you again. If there were bad feelings, maybe he wanted to resolve them."

"My father didn't love me, Mrs. Serum." It hurt to admit that truth to someone. "Please, don't make me out a lousy son, just because he might have had a few regrets in his old age. He never loved me."

"You would not say that if you knew how happy he was whenever he received one of your *infrequent* letters. It broke my heart the way he carried on over a son who wanted no part of him. You do not seem to understand. You were all he had."

"He had you. . . ."

"I worked for him. You were his son."

Carl shook his head. *You were all he had.* For the last few months, Carl knew what it was like to have no one—except a boy that wasn't quite his. He'd invested all his love and hope in that elusive son; perhaps his father had done the same.

"He didn't love you?" Mrs. Serum whispered. "Why, you were his whole world."

"I'm sorry," Carl heard himself say as tears filled his eyes. "If that's true, it's such a shame. And it's not going to happen to my little boy. He won't have to wait until after I'm dead to know how much I love him."

"You have a child?" she murmured.

Carl hesitated. He never wanted to be like his father. He wouldn't go on loving a son that was not really his. "Yes," he said. "My boy is five months old. I miss him a lot right now. The couple looking after him, I don't have much confidence in them. I'll feel better once I take him home." Carl smiled at Mrs. Serum. "He's all I have."

CHAPTER FIVE

Halloween afternoon, Amy loaded Ed into his car seat and drove to town. She had a flight to Chicago the next morning—and a load of last-minute errands now: the bank, the cleaners, then the Safeway for—among other things—trick-or-treat candy and a supply of Swanson's for Paul during her absence.

The last couple of days, everything seemed to be going so well that she'd practically considered canceling the trip. Paul was suddenly very helpful with Ed; and the night before, he'd made love to her. It had been wonderful. He'd managed to make her feel like a desirable college girl again. He seemed to rediscover her body in the hungry, urgent way he'd worked his hands and mouth over it. For the first time in weeks, they'd fallen asleep together, naked in each other's arms.

If all this attention to her and Eddie was a last-ditch effort to keep them from leaving, she didn't mind. As sweet as he was, it didn't change her plans. Better to go knowing she'd miss Paul. Better for her mother to see her pining for her husband than harassed, tired, and bitter.

Eddie was in a happy mood. Amy liked showing him off to the girls at the market. She'd dressed him in his cutest outfit: yellow OshKosh overalls, yellow-striped shirt, and a baby blue cardigan. A tiny pair of Adidas covered his feet, which dangled and kicked over the car seat. He laughed and sang, keeping time with the Supremes on the radio. "It's Rockin' Baby Eddie!" Amy announced. "He digs the Motown beat. Rock on, guy-guy . . ."

She found a parking spot right around the corner from the bank's new outdoor cash machine. "You're going to see Grandma tomorrow," she said, searching through her purse until she found her bank card. "Haven't seen her in four whole months . . ."

Eddie was still babbling and kicking in rhythm, although she'd turned off the engine—and the radio. She tried to unfasten him from the car seat. "Cutie, keep still for Mommy. Jam session's over . . ." He kept wiggling and she couldn't get the strap loose. "Oh, Amy, forget it," she mumbled. It wasn't worth the time and aggravation for a quick trip around the corner. It would take twice as long to get him out of the car seat.

Amy stuck the bank card in her teeth, shoved her purse under the seat, and climbed out of the car. She locked her door and shut it. If there was a line for the cash machine, she'd come back and get Ed. He'd start to cry once he realized she was gone.

She folded up the $150 in fives and twenties, then grabbed her receipt and bank card. It had only taken a minute. Amy trotted around the corner. Eddie would be crying, and she'd have to turn on the car radio to quiet him.

She walked toward the car. From the distance, it looked empty. A sickly pang hit her in the stomach, and suddenly she couldn't breathe. She imagined the worst thing that could possibly happen, then immediately blocked it out. *No, it's just the sun on the windshield,* she told herself. That was why she couldn't see him. He was in there. It had only been a minute . . .

She'd never leave him alone after this. She'd learned her lesson. She didn't want to feel this kind of panic ever again. Oh, why couldn't she see him? Eddie had to be in there. . . .

Amy rushed around to his side of the car and tugged the door open. The unfastened seat belt slid down, its metal buckle dangling toward her feet. She gazed into the empty car. Even the infant seat was gone. *Please, God, this isn't happening . . .*

Amy swiveled around. She looked up and down the street. Whoever took him, they couldn't be far.

"Eddie!" she screamed, and she ran toward the corner. Amy stopped, frantically looking around at a streetful of strangers. She glanced back at the empty car, his door still open.

Someone must have taken him into the bank. That was it. Somebody got concerned when they saw him alone in the car. . . .

She rushed to the front entrance and opened the glass door, hoping—half-expecting—to hear Eddie crying. But there were only muted voices. Blindly, she wandered through the bank. At first, she just whispered his name, then she began screaming it. Someone grabbed her arm, the security guard. Amy struggled to get free. She started toward the side door to check the parking lot. She imagined someone right now loading Eddie and his infant seat into a car, ready to drive off with him forever. For some reason, she imagined it was a woman who had taken him.

"Let go of me!" she cried. "Somebody took my little boy . . ."

Later, they told her that she'd knocked the guard down and run out to the parking lot. She'd gone from car to car, pounding on the windows and peering inside each one until the police had come. Then she'd fainted. Amy had no memory of it.

She suddenly found herself back inside the bank, in a chair by some desk, surrounded by policemen and bank employees. They were all staring at her. Some of them wore strange costumes, and she felt as if she were awakening from a nightmare that wasn't quite over yet. Then she remembered it was Halloween. And Eddie was gone. She wanted to run outside and search for him. But someone held her down.

It was Paul. She almost didn't recognize him among all the strangers. They must have called him, although she didn't recall giving them his number. Still, he was there. But he brought her no comfort. He seemed as bewildered as the rest, just another stranger who couldn't comprehend what she'd let happen.

The baby cried and cried. Carl imagined the shrieking could be heard for blocks. He navigated through the slow city traffic. His hands shook despite a taut

grip on the steering wheel. Every two minutes, a stoplight held him up, and he'd glance down at the baby in
the car seat—on the floor of the passenger side. Carl
prayed it wouldn't tip over. He still couldn't believe he
finally had him. It had been so easy. Too easy.

Carl kept checking his rearview mirror for police
cars. More than anything, he wanted to have the baby
in their new home. Then he'd feel safe. But Seattle was
three hours away.

What had he left behind in the apartment? Not
much. If there was anything, he had a whole month to
go back and get it.

At the traffic light just before the expressway on-
ramp, he hoisted up the baby and buckled in the infant
seat. All the while, the kid kept screaming. The light
changed and Carl drove on.

LEAVING OREGON, said the sign on the bridge.
Somehow, it made Carl feel better—they'd made it
across the state line. He kept waiting for the baby to
fall asleep. But the kid wouldn't stop crying. His feet
kicked at the car seat—as if protesting what was hap
pening to him. Carl reached over and patted his head.
The baby seemed to recoil and shrieked louder.

Carl saw another sign, posted along Interstate 5:
SEATTLE—123 MILES. It was still too far. He sped
down the left lane, not certain he could take another
two hours of this. Maybe there was something on the
news already, a bulletin. Carl switched on the radio.
But he could barely hear it over the incessant screams.
He fiddled with the selector buttons and glanced at the
rearview mirror. *Jesus, a police car.*

He'd already passed it, parked along the highway's

shoulder. Instinctively, he tapped the brake. He could only think that they'd already gotten a description of him, the car, the baby . . .

He checked the rearview mirror again. *Please, stay there, don't move.* But the squad car pulled onto the highway.

The baby's cries seemed to get worse. There was no way to quiet him down—or hide him.

The cop car veered into the left lane and sped up behind him. The red strobe went on. "Oh, shit," Carl whispered.

He felt his stomach turn. For a crazy moment, he pressed harder on the accelerator. But then he signaled and steered to the side of the highway. He clung to a tiny grain of hope that the cop had pulled him over for speeding. The patrol car parked behind him. Carl turned off the engine, then gazed at the baby. With a shaky hand, he reached over and gently rocked his infant seat. He hadn't even gotten him home yet, hadn't even held him in his arms.

The tapping started on the window.

Carl turned and saw the pudgy, blond-haired cop— a little older than him, maybe forty. He hadn't drawn a gun, but he looked as if he were about to read him his rights.

Carl rolled down the window. He couldn't look the cop in the eyes, so he focused on his badge instead. If his nervousness didn't give him away, the infant's angry cries would.

"In quite a hurry," the policeman remarked.

Carl said nothing.

"Can I see your license, please?"

His hands still trembling, Carl pulled out his wallet, then gave him the driver's license. Across from him on the passenger side, the baby screamed and tugged at the infant seat's cushioned bar like a prisoner wanting to be freed.

The cop studied Carl's license. "I clocked you going at sixty-four, Mr. Jorgenson."

He doesn't know, Carl thought.

"Were you aware that you were going so fast?" the cop asked, having to shout over the baby's crying.

"I'm sorry," Carl said. He tried to laugh. "Um, somebody needs a nap. Guess I was in a hurry to get him home and in bed."

The policeman frowned a little. "This your correct address?" he asked, squinting at the license again.

"Yes—"

"Well, if you're headed home, you're going the wrong way. Says here you live in—"

"Yes, I'm sorry," Carl said. "Actually, I—I just moved to Portland—I mean, Seattle. We just moved to Seattle a week ago."

The cop's eyes narrowed at him—then at the baby, but it was only for a moment. He walked around to the front of the car and checked the plate. The baby's shrill cries continued. Carl waited. A drop of sweat slithered down from his underarm.

Finally, the patrolman returned to Carl's window. "I'm letting you off with a warning this time, Mr. Jorgenson," he said. "Take it easy the rest of the way to Seattle, then you and your little boy will stand a better chance of making it there. All right?" He gave him back the license.

Carl took it. He nodded a few more times than necessary. "I will. Thank you, Officer." He turned the key in the ignition.

But the cop still stared at him, unmoving. With a brief nod at the baby, he cracked a smile. "Powerful set of lungs. How old is he?"

Carl hesitated. "Five months. Why do you ask that?"

"I've got a two-year-old at home myself. What's his name?"

Again, Carl didn't answer right away. He looked at the baby for a moment. "Um, Sam," he said. "Sam Jorgenson."

"Well, Sam," the policeman said. "Tell your daddy to obey the speed limit." Then, with a grin, he waved him on.

Carl rolled up the window, put his license away, and slowly started back onto the highway. He checked his rearview mirror. The cop was getting inside the squad car—perhaps to an APB over his radio about a Portland kidnapping. Certainly, by now the McMurray girl had given the police a description of her missing child, and what he was wearing. The cop would remember.

Carl picked up speed. He wondered if he should get rid of his car after today. Thank God the new place in Seattle had an underground garage. He could keep the car down there for the next few days until he figured out what to do. The police wouldn't be looking for it there. But they'd be looking for him.

He wished the baby would be quiet for just a minute. His head was pounding. "Oh, please, shut up," he said hotly. This red-faced, screaming urchin wasn't anything like the happy baby in the portrait Mrs. Sheehan had shown him on the plane.

If only he could drive back to Portland, bring the kid into a police station, and claim he'd found him in an abandoned car someplace. With a little luck, they might have believed the story. But it was too late now. That cop had seen him.

The damn crying wouldn't stop. *"Oh, for chrissakes, can't you be quiet?"* he hissed. *"Shut up!"*

One hand on the wheel, Carl frantically dug into his pocket. He pulled out a handkerchief. The car rocked and swerved as he reached over and got ready to stuff the handkerchief in the baby's mouth. Then Carl remembered what his mother had once told him: *"I'd find he'd stuck a rag or something in your mouth to stop the crying . . ."*

Carl threw the handkerchief to the car floor. "I'm sorry," he murmured, rubbing the baby's leg. He turned and gazed at the road ahead, then started crying with his son. "I'm sorry. Hush, now, Sammy, please. I'll never hurt you. I'm not my father. I'll take good care of you. . . ."

When Carl lifted him out of his car seat, the baby let out a howl. His cries took on a staccato rhythm as Carl hurried up the back stairwell with him to the second floor. Carl could hardly breathe without gagging, because the kid had loaded up his diaper shortly after they'd pulled off the interstate at Seattle. Staggering inside his apartment, Carl set the smelly, wiggling, screaming thing on the carpeted floor.

He heard the baby crying as he ran into the nursery and tore open a box of Pampers. All the neighbors could hear the screams, too, no doubt.

The nursery was completely furnished, loaded with Pampers, clothes, and toys. The rest of the apartment wasn't far behind, except he hadn't gotten a phone yet. It was a spacious two-bedroom with a fireplace and bay windows. He'd even figured out where to put the Christmas tree already.

But he didn't know what to do with this crying, stinking kid. Carl spread a bath towel on the living room floor. "All right, Sammy, okay," he whispered pulling him by his feet onto the towel. He ripped apart the snaps on the insides of the overall legs. The baby kicked and squirmed. "Please, keep—keep still," Carl pleaded, choking at the smell.

The baby kept screaming—that inhuman squeal—and Carl worked quickly, cleaning him off, then fastening a new Pamper around him. It seemed so haphazard and temporary. He'd studied diapering in a baby book, but wasn't sure he put it on right. He had a feeling he wasn't doing *anything* right.

"Stay," Carl said. He left him—still crying—on the living room floor. He threw the soiled diaper in the garbage under the kitchen sink. Then he switched on the stove to heat some milk. He'd bought it during his last trip to Seattle four days ago.

He hurried back to the living room to check on the baby. *"Oh, Jesus . . ."* He ran over and yanked the remote control out of his tiny hand. It was slimy. The baby had been gnawing at it, and he screamed in protest. Carl clicked on the TV, and pressed the volume button until the noise matched the baby's shrieks. "The Flintstones" came up over the tube. "Hey, gonna watch TV! Okay?" he said in a strained, cheerful voice. Then he retreated back to the kitchen.

Carl tested the milk he'd been heating in a sauce-pan: lukewarm, good enough. He spilled some on the counter as he filled one of the new plastic bottles he'd bought.

Back in the living room, Carl scooped up the boy and carried him to the couch. The baby wiggled and cried. It was as if he didn't want any part of him. "Okay, okay, now," Carl whispered, showing him the bottle. "Calm down." He sat back and stuck the nipple in the infant's mouth.

Silence.

It lasted a couple of seconds. The baby started to cry again—louder and more angry than before. Carl shook him. "C'mon, I thought you were hungry . . ." He tick-led his lips with the nipple, but the kid turned his head away and kept screaming. The milk couldn't have been that hot, the bottle was hardly warm. Carl felt his diaper. "You're not wet. What's the matter with you? Hush now . . . come on . . . please . . ." His hand trembled as he poked and poked at the child's mouth with the nipple. He rocked him in his lap. "Take it! C'mon, take it, drink it. What's wrong with you? Please, stop crying, goddamn it!"

Carl was ready to start crying himself. He quickly set the baby down on the cushion, then he took a deep breath. Didn't help much. What did the kid want? Was he sick? God, if the baby was sick, what would he do? He couldn't call a doctor. He couldn't call anyone.

Maybe the baby was used to being breast-fed. Carl examined the nipple, turned the bottle upside down, and shook it. Nothing came out. "What the hell?" he murmured. He twisted off the top and found a disk inside the nipple portion. "Shit, no wonder." He pried out the disk, then screwed the top back on.

The baby screamed and tried to pull away when Carl reached for him again. "C'mon, c'mon," Carl pleaded. He poked the nipple in the baby's mouth once more. He waited, counting the seconds of silence and praying it would last this time. The baby's wet cheeks moved. The large, tear-filled eyes blinked. *He was swallowing.*

Carl let out a weak laugh. "Hallelujah."

The baby still wiggled and kicked a little, but the angry, red color had left his face. His little fingers spread out from the dimpled fists, and he grabbed hold of Carl's shirt.

Carl smiled at him. The loud volume of the TV spoiled the moment and he wished he could get up and turn it off.

The cat was throwing Fred Flintstone out of the house and Fred pounded on the front door as the credits rolled over the screen. Then a newscaster came on, sitting beside a typewriter, his tie loosened. *"Among our stories on KING-5 News,"* he said. *"Authorities suspect that four-alarm fire in Tukwila was arson; in part three of our series on abducted children, Dan Alder is in Portland examining the disappearance of a baby boy today; the Seahawks take it on the chin, and some safety tips for your young trick-or-treaters. All this and more, next on KING-5 News."*

The baby started to cry. The nipple had slipped out of his mouth. Trembling, Carl stuck it in his mouth again, and the baby took it eagerly.

The headline story was about a fire at some water-bed store. Carl's gaze turned toward the window, to the apartment building across the street. He noticed the flickering light of a TV set in one of the windows. How many others were watching this broadcast right now?

"In Portland tonight, the search continues for five-month-old Eddie McMurray . . ." A fuzzy snapshot of the baby appeared in a box behind the newscaster's shoulder. *"The infant was abducted from his mother's car this afternoon. In a special series on missing children, KING-5 reporter, Dan Alder, has the story from Portland . . ."*

A windbreaker over his shirt and tie, the thirtyish, mustached man spoke into a handheld mike. He stood in front of the bank's cash machine. *"At one-fifteen this afternoon, Amy McMurray made a transaction at this cash machine at the Hollywood Branch of the First Interstate Bank. She'd left her five-month-old son, Edward, in the car, parked around the corner, just three hundred feet away."* There was a shot of the Volkswagen, parked by the curb—its door open. *"Mrs. McMurray thought she'd locked the door. The transaction took only a minute, but when she returned to her car, little Edward McMurray was gone . . ."*

The picture switched to the McMurray girl and her husband. They sat on a beige couch, a blank, white wall behind them. Carl wasn't sure if they were in their house or not. She still wore the same brown sweater she'd had on at the bank. But she looked as if that had been days ago. Her face was ravaged. *"I just want my little boy back—safe,"* she said in a strained, tearful voice. *"We're praying and waiting . . ."* She clutched her husband's hand, then looked directly at the screen. Carl felt as if those red-rimmed eyes were staring at him, and he wanted to shrink away. *"Whoever took my boy, you—you have to know . . ."* She started to break down. *"He's teething now. I've got his teething ring. He's not sick. He—please, don't hurt him."* She brought a hand up to her face. *"Please . . ."*

The baby suddenly struggled. He knocked the bottle away and screamed. Carl realized it was the sound of his mother's voice. He wanted her.

"What in God's name have I done?" Carl murmured. He clutched the crying infant to his chest. But once again, the child seemed to want no part of him.

CHAPTER SIX

Amy was used to the darkness in the nursery. By nightfall, Eddie was always asleep in there. Even when he'd wake up, Amy never turned on the light. She'd grown accustomed to changing diapers, feeding him his bottle, and singing lullabies in the darkness of this room. She didn't turn on a light now; it would have been like violating something. Bad luck.

She stared down into the empty crib. The room still had his smell. Then again, why shouldn't it? Eddie had only been gone eight hours. It seemed like days to her. Their doctor had been by, and he'd given her Valium or something. Whatever it was, the medication made her tired and numb. If the roof were to cave in right now, she'd just stand there watching it come down on her.

She could hear her mother in the kitchen, talking on the telephone to a neighbor. The police had put a tap on the phone, though they'd seemed skeptical about anyone calling to demand a ransom. For that, Amy would have been grateful, because it meant they stood some chance of getting her little guy-guy back. There had been dozens of calls: friends, reporters, the police, some cranks. Paul and her mother had taken them all.

The doorbell kept ringing, too: trick-or-treaters. Amy couldn't bear seeing the children in their costumes. Her mother answered the door, giving out quarters and explaining with strained cheerfulness that she'd forgotten to buy candy.

Three baked hams and two casseroles sat in the refrigerator—from concerned friends who had stopped by. There were others who stopped by, but they were strangers who never rang the bell. They crept up to the windows to peek inside. Paul always chased them away. Still, he could do nothing about the dozens of cars that slowed down and stopped for a moment in front of their town house. "Goddamn snoops," Paul would growl, his voice hoarse from crying. But Amy kept hoping that the driver of each idling car was the one who would bring Eddie back to her.

She stared down at the crib and heard Paul walk into the darkened room. In all this time, he'd hardly said anything to her. He'd held her hand while the TV reporters had interviewed them. He'd spoken to the police and then told her of their lack of any leads, but he never whispered a word about his own grief and confusion. He'd embraced her mother when she'd arrived by airport taxi, but Amy hadn't felt his arms around her all day.

She glanced back at him for a second, and thought she saw tears in his eyes. Then she looked at the crib again. Amy waited for him to hug her, or maybe just squeeze her shoulder. But he didn't touch her. "Paul?" she murmured. She felt him staring at her back.

After a moment, she heard him crying, and he whispered. "Why did you leave him alone like that?"

Amy just shook her head, and Paul left the room.

Brushing his teeth, Carl wandered back into his bedroom. He'd moved the crib in there. After weeks of coveting this child, he wasn't about to shut him off in a room alone for the night. As he got ready for bed, Carl kept checking on the baby to make sure he was still there. Everything seemed so tentative—even the sound of his breathing. What if it suddenly stopped? Too many precious things had been taken away from him in the past; he was terrified of losing this child.

Returning to the bathroom. Carl rinsed out his mouth and washed his face. He hurried back to the living room to catch the eleven o'clock news. They were reporting world and national events—Carter supporting a U.N. embargo on South Africa, something about the Concorde. Carl gathered up all the toys that had failed to amuse his new son. He threw the yellow overalls, the shirt, and blue cardigan into the fireplace, then set a match to them. It was a cute little outfit and the clothes looked brand new, but he had to get rid of them. *Destroy the evidence.* A description of these garments was probably on every police file in the Pacific Northwest. He held a match to the baby clothes until his fingers burned. Still, the clothing didn't ignite. He tried again, then finally checked the labels: flame-retardant fiber. He'd bought the baby over three hundred dollars' worth of clothes, and had never checked to see if they were nonflammable. The McMurrays had thought of something he hadn't.

Defeatedly, he gathered up the evidence of both his crime and his negligence, then stuffed the clothes into a paper sack. Maybe lighter fluid would do the trick. He'd try later.

"Portland police still have no leads in the disappearance of five-month-old Edward McMurray, abducted from his mother's car."

Carl turned up the volume on the TV.

"KING-5 News Reporter Dan Alder spoke to the child's parents, Paul and Amy McMurray . . ."

Once again, they showed the tape of the girl. Carl was about to switch off the TV, but—almost masochistically—he forced himself to watch. His heart broke for her. He wished he hadn't spoken to Mrs. Sheehan on the plane, because now he remembered everything she'd said about her girl—especially the part about how hard she tried to be a good mother to the baby.

"He's teething now . . . I have his teething ring . . . please, don't hurt him . . ."

Carl shut off the set. He'd have to buy a teething ring in the morning. And if he wanted any sleep tonight, he'd have to call Amy McMurray. She needed to be reassured that the baby was in good hands.

Don't be ridiculous, Carl, he told himself. *Not only is it stupid and risky, but you don't even have a goddamn phone.*

There was a phone booth down the street.

And leave the baby alone here?

Carl went to the bedroom to check on him again. Still asleep, still breathing. He could leave him alone for a couple of minutes. And in that time, he'd alleviate some of that poor girl's suffering, tell her the baby was safe and healthy. . . .

That won't help her at all, stupid. She wants him back. You'd just be stringing her along. She's better off thinking he's dead. . . .

It seemed so cruel. Yet wouldn't it be just as heartless to let her know the baby was all right, then tell her she'd never get him back? So he wouldn't tell her that part. Maybe just hearing that the baby was okay was all she wanted to hear right now, and that was all he'd tell her.

Carl checked his pockets for change. He'd need a lot for long-distance to Portland. He'd have to talk to an operator, too. And there was bound to be a tap on the McMurrays' phone. He wondered how long it took for the police to trace a call.

For the next ten minutes, he paced around the living room. Then he finally came to a decision.

"If you're not going to bed, dear, let me fix you a ham sandwich—with plenty of mustard, the way you used to like it . . ."

"I'm not hungry, Mom," Amy murmured. She sat at the kitchen table, rubbing her forehead.

But Mrs. Sheehan was pulling one of the baked hams out of the refrigerator. "You haven't eaten all day. Maybe if you had something in your stomach, you'd feel tired enough to go to bed."

Amy could hear the television set in the living room. Paul was in there. The eleven o'clock news was ending. It was strange to hear her own voice on TV, and not care. *"Police have no leads,"* the anchorman had said, and Amy stopped listening. Now "The Tonight Show" was on. She heard the theme song.

She couldn't go to Paul, knowing how much he must hate her. She didn't blame him a bit.

The telephone rang. "I'll get it, Paul," her mother called. She grabbed the receiver. "Hello?"

Amy had tried to give up hoping each call would be the one to end this wait. But each time the phone rang, she couldn't help herself. And there was always the terrible letdown after the call turned out to be from a reporter or a crank. Biting her lip, she stared over at the empty high chair.

"Hello?" Mrs. Sheehan said again.

"Is this Mrs. McMurray? Amy McMurray?" It was a man's voice.

"No, this is her mother. Who's calling?"

"She doesn't know me. I'm the one who took the little boy. I'd like to talk to her."

Mrs. Sheehan looked down at her daughter for a second. Amy glanced up at her listlessly. "I'll let you talk to *Mister* McMurray," she said into the phone.

"No. I'll only speak to the mother. Now, please, put her on. I'll have to hang up soon. I know this call's being traced. I might not call back."

"She's asleep," Mrs. Sheehan said. "I—I'll have to go wake her. Can you hold on?"

"Just hurry," he said.

Mrs. Sheehan put the phone down, then ran into the living room. Amy sat at the table, bewildered. She heard her mother whispering to Paul: "I have someone on the line who says he's got Ed. But he'll only talk to Amy . . ."

"Put her on," Paul said. "I'll get the other extension."

Amy reached for the phone, but her mother grabbed it out of her hands. She covered the mouthpiece. "Wait for Paul to pick it up in the bedroom," she whispered. "It might be just another crank, honey . . ." She listened to the receiver for a click. "I'm hanging up now," she said into the phone. Then she pressed down the cradle for a second and handed the receiver to Amy.

"Hello?" she said. Her heart was racing.

"Is this Amy McMurray?" the man asked.

"Yes . . ."

"I saw you on the news tonight. I'm the one who took your baby."

"Is he all right?" she asked, her voice cracking.

There was silence.

"Please, tell me if he's okay . . ."

"I have your little boy here right now . . ."

"Then he's all right?"

The man on the other end made a strange snickering sound. "I cut off his head. Shall I send it to you?"

The receiver dropped out of Amy's hand and she collapsed to the kitchen floor.

An hour later, she woke up startled—the phone again. Amy found herself on top of the bed, still dressed, but covered with her robe. That was her mother's work. Back in her high school days, she'd often woken from an afternoon nap to find her mother had crept in and laid a robe or blanket over her.

She heard Paul talking on the kitchen extension now. Then he must have hung up. He was mumbling something to her mother.

Amy squinted at the clock on the nightstand: 12:45 a.m. Her mother tiptoed into the room. "You awake, honey?"

"Who was it on the phone?" she asked.

Mrs. Sheehan sat down on the bed. "The police."

"He's dead, isn't he?"

"Oh, no, no." She smoothed back her daughter's hair. "They just wanted to tell us, that call earlier, they traced it. They've got the man in custody. It was just a crank, honey, a very sick man. He didn't have Eddie. Try to go back to sleep now. I'll be here, darling. Just go to sleep. . . ."

Amy closed her eyes.

Mrs. Sheehan moved to the easy chair at her daughter's bedside. She didn't tell her what the police had also said. A woman had phoned headquarters saying she'd been outside the bank that afternoon. She'd seen a man with a baby, getting inside a car, and it had looked very suspicious to her. The police were following it up now.

There was no use in building up Amy's hopes right now. The lead might not pan out. This news was the kind of thing that might get her through the day tomorrow, but it would have kept Amy awake tonight. And her daughter needed sleep.

Mrs. Sheehan decided to stay with Amy until Paul came to bed. She waited an hour, then got up and padded out to the living room. He was asleep, face-down on the sofa. A nearly drained glass of scotch sat on the coffee table nearby.

She went to the linen closet and pulled out a wool blanket. Mrs. Sheehan gently laid it over Paul. He stirred. "Who is it?" he asked, squinting up at her.

"I thought you might be cold," she whispered.

"Oh." He rolled back over. "Thanks, Lauraine."

"Amy's asleep in the bedroom. Maybe you should join her?"

"It's okay," he mumbled, waving her away. "I'm fine here."

Mrs. Sheehan wandered back into the bedroom and sat down beside her daughter. She cried before falling asleep in the chair.

"It's good news," Paul said. "I really think so. I feel it. I wouldn't be surprised if they found this guy today, and—and we get Eddie back by tonight."

They sat at the breakfast table. Amy's mother set two cups of coffee in front of them. "Thanks, Mom," Amy said, looking up only for a moment. With her thumbnail, she scratched at some dried baby food on Eddie's high chair tray. Working up a smile, she nodded at Paul as he spoke.

"The lady gave the cops a complete description of him—and his car. She even remembers part of the license plate number. They got it in the afternoon editions of every newspaper in the Pacific Northwest. The guy won't get far . . ."

Amy nodded some more, but she refused to think it could happen that easily. Why set herself up for more disappointment? Paul was wrong to invest all his hope in this one lead. Then again, maybe he was just placating her; part of his "crisis duty," along with handling the police and reporters. Meanwhile, her mom had taken it upon herself to cook and clean. Between the two of them, they left her with nothing to do but worry—and replay in her mind that awful moment outside the bank, when stupid carelessness had cost her the most precious thing in her life.

Amy sipped her coffee. "We can't expect the police to do everything," she said. She couldn't quite look at her mother or Paul, so she stared down into her coffee cup. "Don't you think we ought to be *doing* something? At least, let's hire a private detective, someone whose business is finding missing persons."

Paul let out an exasperated sigh and glanced at Amy's mother. She met his gaze for only a second, then turned away, busying herself over a pan of scrambled eggs on the stove. "Let's just let the police handle it," he said, his voice strained. "They know what they're doing, Amy. I feel good about this lead, I really do."

"We can't just sit here. We ought to distribute Eddie's pictures all over town, Xerox it or something. Maybe even buy some airtime on TV and radio stations—"

"We can't!" Paul hissed. He hit the tabletop with his fist. "We can't afford it, goddamn it! We don't have the money. Understand?"

Amy turned to her mother. "Mom?"

She shrugged. "I have a little left over from when I sold the house—"

"No!" Paul broke in. "We're not borrowing from your mother again. Thank you, Lauraine, but no."

"What about your parents?" Amy said hotly.

"Look, they're barely getting by on my dad's measly pension. We've taken enough money from them, Amy. We can't borrow from the bank either. I don't even know how we're gonna make the damn mortgage payment next month."

"You're worried about money? Paul, our son is missing."

He pulled away from the table and stood up. "Don't you think I feel bad? Think I'm not frustrated?"

"So you're just going to sit back and let the police handle it?" she asked. "That's the man I married. Let everyone else do the work—"

"What the hell are you saying?"

"It's all Amy's responsibility!" she snapped. "I always had to look after the baby. I never got any help from you. It was all left up to me!"

"Well, it looks like I left it up to the wrong person."

Amy let out a wounded cry, as if he'd slapped her.

Paul quickly shook his head. "Forget it," he mumbled. "I didn't mean that. Forget the whole thing." He stomped outside, slamming the back door behind him.

He was raking leaves in the side yard when Mrs. Sheehan came out twenty minutes later. "I thought you might need this," she said, handing him his jacket.

"Thanks, " he said, putting it on.

She folded her arms. "Amy's asleep on the living room sofa. Whatever the doctor gave her yesterday must still be in her system. Paul, about the money. With my savings and what I have from selling the house, there's about thirty thousand dollars. It's yours if you think it'll help get Eddie back."

"Thanks anyway, Lauraine."

"Well, it's there." Mrs. Sheehan's voice dropped to a whisper. "Be patient with her, okay?"

He nodded, then started raking leaves again. "Maybe you ought to go inside in case the phone rings. She's not making any sense this morning. She shouldn't be talking to anyone."

But Mrs. Sheehan didn't move. "Don't blame her, Paul."

He kept working and didn't look at her. He didn't see the tears in her eyes.

"That girl in there is *my* baby. And she's suffering, Paul. I know you are, too. So am I. But she's got it the worst. She feels this whole thing is her fault."

He went on raking.

"Paul, this could have happened to anyone. It could have happened to you. Imagine how you'd feel if it had. You can't expect Amy to let herself off the hook when she feels you blame her for what happened to Ed. There's nothing I can do to help her anymore. It's up to you."

Paul continued his work on the leaves. "You know, I think the cops are really going to come up with something from this eyewitness," he said, not looking up. "Maybe you should go inside and call them. Thanks for bringing the jacket."

Sighing, Mrs. Sheehan wiped her eyes and wandered back to the kitchen door. As she entered the house, she heard her daughter crying again.

His lungs burned. Carl's usual six-mile run became a frantic, four-block, uphill sprint to the convenience store. He was giving himself ten minutes to get back home. Even that seemed too long to leave the baby alone in the apartment.

Sam had woken up—screaming—at 6:10 a.m. With only three hours' sleep, Carl was suddenly busy changing, feeding, and entertaining him—so busy that he didn't get to take his morning pee until after ten. He hadn't eaten, shaved, or even made his bed. He fed

Sam a disgusting dish called Strained Vegetables for lunch, then put him down for his afternoon nap. Sam finally fell asleep around one-thirty. And that was when Carl put on his winter sweats, double-locked the front door, and left his son alone for the first time.

Carl never ran so fast. He must have been a mere faceless blur to everyone he passed; and that was just how he wanted it—no one recognizing him. He needed a teething ring. But more important, he needed to see a newspaper. A lot could have happened between last night's newscast and this afternoon's edition. For all he knew, the newspaper's front page could be carrying a police composite sketch—maybe even a photo—of him. *"HAVE YOU SEEN THIS MAN?"* the caption would say. He needed to know what the police had so far.

Staggering into the 7-Eleven, he felt everyone's eyes on him. He hurried down the aisle to the Pampers and baby things. He was in luck, they had teething rings. Grabbing one, he headed toward the front of the store.

Swell, a line. Just three people, but he couldn't afford to wait. After his sprint through the cold, it seemed like a hundred degrees in the store. He felt woozy. Wiping the cold sweat off his forehead, he saw the newspapers by the front window. Carl grabbed a *Seattle Times* and went to the end of the line.

The teenage boy in front of him glanced over his shoulder. Carl looked away. Maybe the kid recognized him. The five-dollar bill grew damp in Carl's sweaty hand. He peeked at the front page of the newspaper. At least his picture wasn't splashed beneath the headline.

But he could be on page two or three. He folded up the newspaper and began tapping it against his leg.

What if the baby woke up? He crawled around pretty well, maybe he could crawl out of the crib. Carl imagined running home to find an ambulance in front of the building—a rescue squad, fire trucks. *Good God, what if there's a fire?*

One customer left. Then an old woman unloaded an armful of groceries on the counter. The tall bonehead of a clerk rang up the merchandise like it was his first day at the register—turning over each item to find the price, then punching it in with one finger.

Carl just wanted to get the hell out of there and run home. He glanced up at the clock behind the counter: 2:10. He'd left Sam alone fifteen minutes ago.

The old woman just stood there while the spastic clerk rang up her goods. She hadn't even reached inside her purse yet. *"For Christ's sakes, lady,"* he wanted to yell, *"get your goddamn money ready!"*

"Do you have those tiny little packets of Kleenex?" she asked. A checkout line shopper. He was ready to strangle her. The cashier moseyed away from his register and wandered up the aisle. Carl glanced up at the clock and tapped the newspaper against his leg again. Finally, the clerk found the tissues and ambled back to the register.

"Do you have them in any other colors besides white?"

Carl hurried to the front of the line, tossed the damp five-dollar bill on the counter, and called: "A teething ring and a newspaper. Keep the change!" Then he ran out of the store.

Carl's hands were covered with newspaper ink and he smeared it on the white-painted woodwork as he unlocked the door to his apartment. He staggered inside.

Silence.

He hurried into his bedroom and checked the crib. The baby was still there, still asleep, breathing. He even stirred a little. Carl backed out to the hallway and sagged against the wall. He held the crumpled newspaper to his chest.

With a shaky hand, he opened the *Seattle Times*. Sam's teething ring and the newspaper's back sections all fell to the floor as Carl moved toward the living room. He rifled through the front section until he saw the baby's picture on the bottom of page eleven. The McMurray girl held him in her lap; they were both smiling. *"BEFORE THE NIGHTMARE: Paul McMurray took this photo of his wife, Amy, and their son, Edward, two weeks ago,"* the caption read.

Carl stopped at the window and read the headline: *INFANT BOY ABDUCTED IN PORTLAND*. Then he saw the subhead. "Oh no," he murmured.

"Police Question Eyewitness to Kidnapping; Encouraged by Leads."

How could anyone have seen him? He'd been so careful. Carl read the article, searching for something to explain this new development, and he found it in the bottom two paragraphs:

Portland Police Sergeant, Hollis Trumbell, said that they "had little to go on" until fate Thursday night. After viewing an account of the abduction on the 11 o'clock news, Mrs. Evelyn Royce, 56, telephoned the police. She remembered having seen a man with a baby outside the First Interstate Bank around 1:30 PM Thursday. "I thought it looked peculiar," Mrs. Royce said. "But it wasn't until I watched the story on TV that I figured I should tell the police."

Carl read the next line, and he flopped down on the sofa. "Oh, God . . ." He let out a weak laugh.

Mrs. Royce described the suspect as a tall, slender black man in his late twenties, wearing a tan jacket. She said the child was "fair-skinned and blond, with a blue sweater." She saw the man carry the child into a red Datsun, and was even able to recall for police part of the license plate number . . .

Earl Armstrong was thirty-three years old. He'd been at a pharmacy across the street from the First Interstate Bank twenty minutes before Amy had been there. He'd parked his red Datsun in the bank's pay lot. With him had been his daughter, eleven-month-old Shauna, who indeed was fair-skinned and blond, like her mother. The "eyewitness," Mrs. Royce, confirmed that Armstrong was the man she'd seen.

Amy felt Paul was betraying her when he told her this. The next morning, *The Oregonian* carried the story—on page seventeen of the front section, just a couple of paragraphs and a statement from the justifiably outraged Mr. Armstrong. The local TV news didn't even bother to report it.

A week after Halloween, the police told them they were taking the tap off their telephone.

Paul reluctantly borrowed five thousand dollars from Mrs. Sheehan and hired a private detective. The detective spoke to everyone who had been in and around the bank at the tiine of Ed's disappearance. The police had gotten to most of them first. After six days—at one hundred dollars a day—the detective told Paul and Amy he couldn't take any more of their money.

It seemed as if their lives were supposed to return to normal again. But that was the last thing Amy wanted. Maybe the police and that detective had given up, but she wasn't about to quit. She wanted to stir things up again, keep it alive.

"City Desk, Art Garcia speaking."

He was with *The Oregonian.* He'd interviewed them on Halloween night, and left behind his business card. Amy barely remembered talking to him—or what he'd looked like. But she tried for a tone of familiarity now. "Mr. Garcia? Hi, this is Amy McMurray. IIow arc you?"

"Fine, just fine, thanks . . ." There were a few seconds of silence from the other end of the line.

"You interviewed me two weeks ago," she said. "My baby boy was kidnapped . . ."

"Yes, of course. I'm sorry. How are you, Mrs. McMurray?"

"Well, not so hot," she said, tugging at the phone cord. "See, we haven't had any—tangible leads yet. The police have just about thrown in the towel. I'm beginning to think everyone's forgotten about my little boy, and I know he's out there."

"Yes . . ."

She was trying to keep some control in her voice. "Anyway, I'd really like to talk with you again, Mr. Garcia. Maybe you could run another story on—what happened."

"What happened two weeks ago?" he asked.

"Yes. I thought you could do—what do you call it?—a follow-up story?"

"What exactly did you want to discuss? I mean, if there haven't been any new developments . . ."

"Maybe we could get people *interested* again." Amy felt so stupid and pushy. She'd figured this guy would have jumped at the chance to interview her again; and here she was, groping to recapture the interest he'd shown in her two weeks before, trying to sell her tragedy to him. "I miss my son," she said, her voice cracking. "Can't you see how important it is that people know he's still out there? We've got to keep looking for him."

"I wish I could help, Mrs. McMurray, really—"

"My husband and I, we're not going back to work until our son is found. Anytime you want to set up an interview . . ."

"Mrs. McMurray? I'm sorry. I have another call coming in. I hate to cut you off. Um, if there are any new developments, please, give me a call, and I'll do what I can for you. Okay?"

She was silent.

"Mrs. McMurray?"

Amy hung up.

She'd hardly stepped outside the house in the last two weeks. Paul didn't want people recognizing her from the TV and newspaper stories, then upsetting her with stares or tactless questions. Amy's mother had been taking care of all the shopping.

But Amy stood in the checkout line at the Safeway now, unloading a cart full of groceries. Her coworkers wanted to know how she was holding up, and when she'd return to work. She was vague in her replies. At one time, these women had been her closest friends in Portland. But once Eddie had come along, she hadn't had much time for girlfriends. They were like strangers now.

Amy paused at the exit door and glanced at the bulletin board, where Paul had posted a Xeroxed photo of Eddie: *"MISSING,"* the caption read. *"EDWARD ANTHONY McMURRAY. Abducted: 10/31/77; 5 months old; curly blond hair, blue eyes; 20 inches high, 19 lbs. If you have seen this child, please contact the management of this store. Thank you."* Paul had posted copies all over town.

From her boss, Amy had gotten a list of Safeways in the Pacific Northwest, and she'd sent copies of the bulletin to sixty-two Safeway stores, from Bellingham, Washington, down to Eureka, California. She'd gotten addresses of seventy pediatricians in the region from her doctor, and sent Eddie's bulletin to offices in Eugene, Portland, Seattle, Spokane, and other major cities. Maybe someone—someplace—was looking at Eddie right now and remembering one of those bulletins she'd sent out.

She stared at the bulletin board, and her optimistic heart sank. Someone had covered up half of Eddie's face with an advertisement for a church raffle. Amy set down her bags and tore the raffle poster from the board, then threw it in the trash. Thumbtack punctures marred the picture of Eddie, and there was nothing she could do about it.

Where was the goddamn silver lining to all this? She didn't feel any wiser from this tragedy, she didn't feel closer to God; she wasn't a better person for it. No, she was left with just this big hole in her heart and life the way it had been before her guy-guy came along and made it bright.

Paul was on the phone when she plodded into the kitchen with her bags. She dumped them on the counter, pulled off her coat, and began to unload the groceries. "Where's Mom?" she asked.

He cupped a hand over the mouthpiece. "Living room. Can't you see I'm talking here, hon?"

"Sorry." Amy pulled a six-pack of Coors from a bag.

"No, don't worry," Paul was saying into the phone. "I'll be in the office tomorrow all day. It'll get done. No problem . . ."

Amy stopped what she was doing. She held a jar from the bag and stared at Paul until he hung up the phone. "Did I hear you right?" she whispered. "How can you go back to work when we still haven't found Eddie?"

Paul rubbed his forehead. "Because, honey, it's my busiest season, and I've missed the last two weeks. Want me to lose my job on top of everything else?" His mouth twisted into a frown. "Amy, what the hell is that in your hand?"

She held a jar of Gerber's Custard, Eddie's favorite. "We can't afford to throw money away like that,"

Paul whispered. "There's already enough baby food here to—"

"You don't think we'll get him back, do you?"

"Don't start—"

"You've given up! That's why you're going back to work."

"How's my sitting around here all day going to bring him back sooner? What good is it accomplishing? If we get him back—"

"What do you mean 'if'?"

He took hold of her arms. "All right, all right. Say we do get him back, I'll still need a job—some means of supporting him. So don't make me out the bad guy in this. I'm going back to work tomorrow, and that's it."

She pried herself away from him. Paul started unloading the rest of the groceries, frowning each time he pulled out another jar of baby food. "You ought to think about going back to work yourself," he said. "Do you good, take your mind off things . . ."

"But I don't want to take my mind off things, and neither should you." Besides, she could never go back to her old job. Once they found Eddie, she'd have to stay with him—all the time. "Did you hear me, Paul?"

"Amy, if you want to pick a fight, do it when your mother isn't within earshot. Then I'll take you on. Okay?"

Amy turned away and wandered into the living room, where her mother sat on the sofa, working a newspaper crossword puzzle. She sank down on the other end of the couch.

"Saint and Gabor," her mother said, studying the newspaper. "Four letters. Second one's a 'V.'"

Amy stared at her. Every time she and Paul had a fight, her mother would suddenly act interested in something—TV, the dishes, cooking dinner, a crossword puzzle—anything but the confrontation in front of her.

"Never mind. I have it. *Evas.*" She filled in the squares.

"I'm sorry, Mom." Amy sighed. "You could hear Paul and me, couldn't you?"

Her mother shrugged. "I was working my puzzle . . ."

"But you heard us just the same."

Her mother put the newspaper down. "Darling, I think I should be heading back soon. I'm just in the way here."

"No, you're not. C'mon, that's silly." She grabbed a sofa pillow and hugged it to her chest. "Don't even talk about leaving. The house seems empty enough as it is. I need you here, you know that. I haven't got anyone else."

Her mother frowned. "What about your husband?"

"He's quit, Mom. He's going back to work."

"That's not quitting. He has responsibilities, Amy."

"You sound just like Paul," she grumbled.

"Well, maybe you should listen to him, pay more attention to him. He's suffering, too. At a time like this, you should be—" Mrs. Sheehan shook her head. "I promised myself I wasn't going to meddle. That's why I should leave. I'm in the way here."

"No, you're not. . . ."

"Amy, I see you two hurting each other, and it's hard not to say anything. You ought to cry on your husband's shoulder, not mine. You only go to Paul when you're angry and frustrated. I haven't seen you turn to him for comfort once."

Amy rubbed her eyes. "He doesn't want anything to do with me, Mom. And I don't really blame him. If I were a better mother, this wouldn't have happened."

"Then I guess I wasn't a good mother either," Mrs. Sheehan said. "It could have happened to me a hundred times over, all the times I'd leave one of you kids in the car for a minute—or in the shopping cart seat, because I needed something down another aisle in the market. When you were a toddler, I'd park you in the toy section so I could shop in another part of the store. You've heard me tell that story about losing you in Marshall Field's when you were four. . . ."

Amy managed a smile. "Only about a hundred times. But you found me a half hour later, and I was all right."

"Yes, I was lucky. That's the only difference between what happened in Marshall Field's twenty years back and what happened two weeks ago with Ed. Luck. You can't go on blaming yourself, honey. And shutting the door on Paul, because you feel he blames you, isn't going to help either. It just happened. And it could have happened to anyone—even the best of mothers."

Amy stared at a picture of Eddie across the room and thought of how she didn't have much chance to be a good mother to him

"I'm going to get him back, Mom," she said. "No matter what Paul says, no matter what happens, I'm not giving up on him. I'm going to get Eddie back."

CHAPTER SEVEN

"Please, don't be sick," Carl whispered. He hovered over Sam in the crib. The baby cried, not his shrill screams from hunger or crankiness. No, these cries were weak, heartbreaking. He had sweat so much that his golden hair was in damp, dark ringlets. Yet he shivered, too. Carl tucked a blanket around him and tried to get him interested in a rattle, but Sam didn't even look at it. He just cried and clutched his "blanky," a small, yellow cotton blanket that rarely left his hand nowadays. It was filthy and smelled, because Sam often sucked his fingers through it. Even his blanky didn't seem to comfort him now.

For the last three days and nights, Carl had tried to convince himself that the baby wasn't really sick. He kept hoping it was just Sam teething—or at the very worst, a flu bug that would pass. Still, Carl worried. What if he had pneumonia or something? He'd had the baby only three weeks. He couldn't risk taking him to a doctor yet, not so soon after all the newspaper stories. Hospitals and baby doctors probably kept files of recently reported missing children. They'd recognize the baby. They'd take Sam away from him, and he'd end up in jail.

"Go to sleep now, Sammy," he said, with tears in his eyes. "Please, just sleep and get well. You'll be okay. . . ."

But the baby was sick and he knew it. Sam needed a doctor's attention—not his new father's useless prayers.

There was no one Carl could turn to for advice. All he had was a stupid book called *Know Your Baby,* and that didn't explain Sam's sudden listlessness, why he couldn't keep his food down, why he sweat so much and slept so little. Carl looked up every symptom in the baby book, and he read the same thing each time: *". . . If this persists, consult the child's physician."*

But he didn't know *anybody* in town. Even if he risked taking Sam to a doctor, there would be countless questions he couldn't begin to answer—about the baby's regular pediatrician, the vaccinations he'd received, his medical history . . .

Carl had been too afraid to even take the baby out of the apartment. And he hadn't ventured outside much either—except for the frantic sprints to the store for food or Pampers while Sam slept. He still felt like a fugitive. And it still seemed as if the baby wasn't his yet—like those suspicious "gifts" his father used to give him; Carl had always been too afraid to take them outside, show his friends, or get too attached to them.

He wondered now if the baby might die on him.

Sam choked on his cries, and he shook violently beneath the blanket. "Hush now, Sammy," Carl pleaded. "Sammy? Sam?"

The baby didn't even focus on him. Carl reached down and felt his forehead. *Christ, he's burning up.*

Carl rushed into the bathroom and ran a washcloth under the cold water. When he got back to the crib, Sam was throwing up. Carl quickly turned him over on his stomach so he wouldn't choke on the vomit. He caught some in his hand as the baby retched again. It was all down the front of his Big Bird T-shirt and on his yellow blanky. Finally Sam stopped. Carl tried to clean him up with the damp washcloth. He just lay there, shaking in the soiled blankets of his crib.

Carl realized he could no longer keep this baby a secret.

The landlady answered the door wearing a flowery housecoat and pink curlers in her silver hair. She was a stout woman in her late sixties with the face of a veteran Walgreens waitress.

"Hi, Mrs. Kern," Carl said, He nervously rocked Sam in his arms. The baby was naked, but swaddled in a clean sheet. "I'm Carl Jorgenson—y'know, in 208? I hate to bother you, but my son is very sick. He's got a fever. I'm new in town and don't have a doctor yet. Could you—"

"Come right in, honey," she said. "I got the number of my granddaughter's pediatrician by the phone. I keep it here, because I baby-sit so much. How old is he?"

"Six months." Carl followed her into the kitchen. The dimly lit apartment smelled of stale peanut butter and was cluttered with a child's toys. The chirping from a caged pair of canaries competed with Sam's weak cries.

"Has he been upchucking?" Mrs. Kern asked as she riffled through a notebook by the telephone.

"Yes," Carl said, past the tightness in his throat. "I didn't know what to do. . . ."

"Dr. Durkee's office isn't far from here—"

"I haven't got a phone yet. Could I use yours?"

"Sure thing, honey. You just give him to me."

Mrs. Kern had written down directions to the doctor's office—only twelve blocks away. She'd also gone back to the apartment with them, deaf to Carl's polite objections that it wasn't necessary. "Getting a baby ready to go out is like making a double bed," she'd said. "It's easier with two people doing it." She'd helped get Sam dressed, and even carried him down to the car. Sam had seemed to find comfort in her chubby arms; and she'd immediately taken to him, too. "You be sure to tell me how this little angel is doing when you get back from Dr. Durkee's," she'd said, after Carl had buckled Sam into the McMurrays' car seat. "Tell me first thing when you get back. Never mind about the garage doors. I'll get them."

But Carl was unsure if he'd ever return from the doctor's office—if he'd even make it there at all. He hadn't driven this car since that day he'd taken the boy. The police could have a description of it, and the Oregon plates were a dead giveaway.

Sam was quiet now. He babbled softly and clung to his blanky, which recked of vomit. The smell filled the car. While the convulsions had stopped, Sam still didn't look well. Tiny red spots seemed to emerge on his face and hands. At the first stop sign, Carl reached over and felt the tiny bumps—maybe chicken pox or the measles. They were even in Sam's scalp.

Carl stepped harder on the accelerator; at the same time, he dreaded reaching their destination. He tried to convince himself that no one there would recognize Sam from that blurry photo in the newspaper two weeks ago.

He found the address—a two-story, redbrick building across the street from Swedish Hospital. Approaching the glass doors with Sam in his arms, he wondered if this was the last time he would hold him.

The waiting room was modern, with soft, indirect lighting and an array of hanging plants. Muzak played at a discreet volume. A brunette in her late twenties sat on a long, green sectional, paging through a copy of *Highlights* from one of the chrome-and-glass end tables. Her toddler daughter fussed with a Fisher-Price toy in the little play area. The woman stared at Carl as he walked in with Sam. Instinctively, he turned away and clutched the baby closer to his chest, then he hurried up to the receptionist's window. "I'm Carl Jorgenson," he muttered to the nurse. "I called for Dr. Durkee."

"Oh, yes. This must be Sam. We're ready for you."

A moment later, the nurse was leading them into a small examining room. She pulled a pen out of her frizzy brown hair and consulted a form on a clipboard she carried. "You said on the phone he was throwing up and had a fever . . ."

"Yes. He's been a bit under the weather for about three days now," Carl answered, rocking him gently. "But it wasn't until this afternoon it got really bad.

And driving here, I noticed these spots. See? They weren't there when I called you."

Her eyes narrowed as she studied the baby's dotted face and felt his forehead. "Has he had a R/M shot?"

Carl hesitated. He shifted Sam into his other arm.

"Oh, I'm sorry, Mr. Jorgenson," she said. "You can put him on the table and take off everything except his diapers. Okay?"

Carl started to peel off Sam's little jacket. The baby was crying again, but with more strength in his voice. He didn't seem so clammy and hot anymore. Still, the awful rash had spread all over his face, neck, and hands.

"I need Sam's full name, please," the nurse said, leaning over the table, pen to clipboard.

"Sam Jorgenson." Carl spelled it.

"No middle name?"

"Uh—no," he answered, struggling with Sam's overalls.

"Date of birth?"

"Um, six-ten-seventy-seven."

"Oh, June tenth? That's my birthday, too."

Actually, Sam's was the seventh of June. But that newspaper account of the kidnapping had carried the baby's birth date. Why make it any easier for them to see a connection?

He'd been prepared to lie about everything. All those years of covering up for the old man had made him an expert liar. But Carl answered truthfully when she asked for his name, his address, then his phone number. "I haven't got a phone yet," he said. "I'm new in town. Just moved up from Santa Rosa."

"Your employer?"

He busied himself pulling off Sam's socks. "Um, I don't have one. My father passed away recently and left me enough money to—to look after Sam full-time. I'm a single parent. My wife died in a car accident last month—down in Santa Rosa." *You're telling her too much,* he thought. *Wait until she asks.*

The nurse was silent for a moment as she looked at her clipboard. "I'll need your wife's full name, please."

"Anne Marie Brewster Jorgenson." He'd just seen a "That Girl" rerun while feeding Sam that morning. In the show, Anne Marie had considered changing her name to Marie Brewster. Carl spelled it out for the nurse as he pulled the T-shirt over Sam's head. The pimplelike rash covered his stomach and legs.

The girl drew a thermometer from the silver canister on the counter, shook it, then slipped the tube under Sam's armpit. "Could you hold that there for me?" She picked up her clipboard again. "Are you insured, Mr. Jorgenson?"

"I'm—switching companies. I'll get back to you on it. I'm prepared to pay for everything myself."

"The baby's regular physician?"

"He's—in Santa Rosa," Carl answered, holding Sam still.

"We'll need his name and address so we can have Sam's records transferred up here—that is, if you want Dr. Durkee to be Sam's pediatrician."

"I don't have the address on me. I—think I have Sam's medical records at home. I asked for them when we moved. I put them in a drawer or a box someplace. I'll try to remember the records for his next appointment."

She looked up, a tiny frown on her face. "Yes, well,

we'll need them." The nurse pulled the thermometer from under Sam's arm, then studied it. "Ninety-nine point two," she announced, writing on her clipboard. "Dr. Durkee will be right with you, Mr. Jorgenson. You and Sam make yourselves comfortable." She gave him a slightly strained smile. Carl wasn't sure she believed a word he'd said. She left the examining room and closed the door behind her.

Climbing onto the table, Carl set the baby in his lap. "At least you're not dying, Sammy," he whispered. He felt the tiny red bumps on Sam's stomach. But the spots covering his face and scalp seemed to be fading already. He could almost gauge Sam's speedy recovery by his increasing restlessness. The baby wiggled and kicked in his lap. Carl tried to keep him still as he watched the second hand sweep around the clock on the wall. They'd been waiting ten minutes.

Carl began to worry. Once again, he wondered if pediatricians kept records of recently missing children. He heard the nurse whisper to someone on the other side of the closed door: ". . . *from Santa Rosa, he said, but he didn't . . .*"

Sam let out a bored cry, and Carl gently rocked him. "Sammy, please," he hissed.

". . . *something wrong. I really think so,*" he heard the nurse say in a hushed voice. But Sam kept crying, and Carl could hear nothing else. He watched three more minutes go by on the clock.

At first, the distant wail of the siren seemed like nothing more than an echo of Sam's crying. But then it became louder. Carl looked toward the single window in the examining room. The venetian blinds shut out any view of what was going on outside. He hugged

Sam tighter. He could no longer hear the nurse—only the siren drawing closer and closer. *They've called the police,* he thought, staring at the door. It was too late to make a run for it. They had his name, his address . . .

Suddenly, the door opened. "Mr. Jorgenson?" It was a tall man in his mid-forties, with glasses and unkempt, curly salt-and-pepper hair. He wore a navy blue crew neck sweater beneath the white coat. "I'm Bill Durkee."

Carl was still listening to the siren. He just stared back at the doctor, who stepped inside and closed the door. "You're one of Hester Kern's tenants, I understand," he said, pulling a stethoscope out of the cabinet drawer.

"Yes, I just moved here from Santa Rosa," he managed to say. The noise of the siren suddenly stopped— just when it seemed right outside the building. He thought he heard the nurse whispering to someone.

"Does she baby-sit for Sam, too?"

"Who?"

"Mrs. Kern," the doctor said. "She looks after her granddaughter five days a week, I figured—"

There was a knock on the door. Dr. Durkee turned to open it. Carl sat frozen, clutching Sammy to his chest. The nurse stuck her head in. "Mr. Jorgenson?" she said. "I think you left your headlights on."

He quickly shook his head. "No, I didn't."

"Is that your silver Chevy in the lot?" she pressed.

He nodded.

"Well, the lights are on."

It was a trap. They wanted him to leave the baby, so the cops—waiting outside—could pounce on him. They were being very clever about it.

The doctor smiled at him. "It's okay, go ahead. You don't want a dead battery." He reached for the baby.

Carl wanted to pull away, but reluctantly, he let the doctor take Sam. Moving to the door, he turned and took one long, last look at his son.

The nurse followed him to the hallway, closing the examining room door after her. Carl thought he heard the lock click—and Sam crying. "That's the way out, Mr. Jorgenson," the nurse said, pointing to another door.

Slowly, he started through the waiting room. No police. No sign of the brunette and her daughter. Carl stared at the parking lot beyond the glass doors. There were no squad cars or police. And his headlights were on. He stepped outside, and looked around the lot: no one. He noticed the ambulance parked by the hospital across the street, and realized it hadn't been a police siren after all. But he still didn't feel safe. He hurried to his car, climbed inside, and turned off the lights. Then he swiped Sam's smelly blanket off the car seat and ran back inside the clinic.

"Thanks," he said to the nurse, out of breath. "Can I go back in there with him? He probably wants his security blanket."

She smiled. "Of course. He probably wants *you* is more like it. You should have heard the shrieks when you left him alone with Dr. Durkee."

Sammy reached out for him the moment Carl stepped into the examining room. The doctor had already put his T-shirt back on him. "He has a touch of roseola," he said. "But he's past the worst of it. The rash ought to completely disappear by tomorrow. Give me a buzz if it persists or the fever returns."

Carl gathered Sam in his arms. The baby grabbed his blanky and started sucking on it. "That's all?" Carl asked.

"I'd like to see him again in two months and bring those medical records over as soon as you can. That's all. No problems outside of the roseola." He started humming a Beatles tune while he jotted something on the nurse's clipboard.

Carl buttoned up Sam's shirt. "Um, is it okay to take him outside, to the store, things like that?"

"Sure. Just keep him warm." The doctor resumed his humming.

"Then he's really going to be all right?" Carl asked.

Dr. Durkee laughed. "He's fine. Don't worry, Mr. Jorgenson."

"Sorry." Carl shrugged. "It's just that I'm new at this single parent business. My—late wife, she was so good with him. I didn't have a worry." He slipped Sam's little arms into his jacket. It was such a relief to talk to another adult—even if the truth had to be mixed with lies. After three weeks of enslaved solitude, just to be *around* another grown-up was like a reprieve. "I keep thinking I'm doing everything wrong," Carl confessed.

"Looks like you're managing fine," the doctor replied. "Roseola is pretty common in babies Sam's age. Don't worry." He finished writing on his medical form, then stopped to gaze at Carl and Sam. "You'd never guess he was your son," he said.

The words hung in the air like an accusation. Carl was dumbstruck for a moment. "Well, he—takes after his mother—"

"I was joking," the doctor laughed. "He looks just like you, Carl. A regular chip off the old block." He slapped him on the back. "See you in two months. 'Bye, Sam." Then he started for the door, humming again—as if nothing were the matter at all.

Driving home from Dr. Durkee's office, Carl wondered why the nurse hadn't noticed the Oregon plates when she'd seen the headlights. He imagined her talking to the doctor now: *"But he said he was from Santa Rosa, California. That doesn't make sense. He must have been lying . . ."*

"Shit, Carl," he whispered to himself. "Don't be so paranoid." The nurse hadn't mentioned the license plates. People didn't notice those things. They didn't remember stories in the newspaper that were two weeks old either. He had nothing to worry about, the doctor had said so.

Carl smiled. Now Sam had a pediatrician: Dr. Durkee, the Humming M.D. And Carl had made his first friend in Seattle too—at least, his first acquaintance.

He made another friend that day. Mrs. Kern stopped by the apartment while he was feeding Sam. Carl told her Dr. Durkee's diagnosis.

"Oh, roseola," she said. "I should have guessed. Two of my own had that. The rash will go away, honey. Don't you worry. Now, I know what a chore feeding time can be. But before I skedaddle, let me tell you, if ever you need to go out, feel free to leave that little angel with yours truly. I mean it now."

Carl realized that this stout woman with the flowery housecoat and the canaries in her apartment knew about babies. He had a seasoned, willing baby-sitter right in his building, someone who would give him a break once in a while. No more frantic sprints to the 7-Eleven. He could actually shop for things now. He could pick up Washington plates for his car and stop worrying. He'd be free to go out and get a telephone now. He could *call* an insurance company, a diaper service, even order pizza when he was too tired to cook. His fugitive days were over. He wanted to kiss this woman. "God bless you, Mrs. Kern," he said. "God bless you . . ."

Carl couldn't fall asleep and he'd have to get up for Sam in about five hours. Still; he lay in bed, restless and depressed. He told himself everything would be all right from now on. He'd come out of hiding today. Sam was off the critical list. He'd found a doctor and a baby-sitter for Sam, his first two friends in Seattle. In time, he would make more friends.

But he couldn't risk getting close to anyone—ever. For the rest of his life, he'd be looking over his shoulder, always lying to people about his past and his son, He'd always have to lie to Sam as well.

What kind of father was he anyway? For the last three days, his baby boy had been sick. Yet he'd waited until this afternoon to find a doctor. He'd been too worried about getting arrested. He'd let Sam suffer for three days. It was negligence. Certainly the McMurrays would have gotten him to a doctor sooner. And he'd taken their baby believing he would make a better parent than either of them.

Now Carl couldn't sleep, because he wasn't sure what kind of father he'd be to that little boy sleeping in the next room.

As Sam climbed out of the car, the cool night air hit him, and a pang of homesickness swelled in his gut. He stared at his father's apartment building, so much like their home together years ago. Sam walked up to the front door and checked the names by the buzzers. There it was: Jorgenson—309.

Sam hadn't seen him in four years—not since before the trial. He'd wanted to testify on his father's behalf, but they sent him to stay with his grandmother in Chicago during the trial and sentencing. They'd made it so he couldn't be a help to him.

Suddenly, all the pain and wondering during the last four years came back to him now. Did his father even want to see him? His letters, forwarded through some lawyer, had stopped coming. Sam still received cards from him on his birthday and Christmas. But the notes inside had become more impersonal with each passing year. Maybe his dad was trying to pull away from him, figuring it was the right thing to do, under the circumstances.

A thin black man in spandex bicycling garb brushed

past him, unlocked the door, then stepped inside. Sam slipped in after him.

At that moment, someone came down the front steps, toting a couple of garbage bags. Sam's heart stopped.

His father looked older. The hair was almost completely grey now, and his face seemed a little droopy; more lines, darker around the eyes. He'd always appeared younger than his age; but now he looked like a guy in his fifties. He wore khakis and a white shirt. He smiled and nodded at the bicyclist without really looking at him, then rounded the corner. Sam heard a door open, then the clatter of a dumpster lid.

The black man moved to the mailboxes and opened one up.

Sam waited for his father to reappear—that guy who had passed through the lobby a moment ago was almost a stranger. Still, there was a gentleness to him that Sam recognized. He'd been afraid that prison would make his father mean, but he didn't look all that different. Sam had no idea what it had been like for him. In his letters, his dad had never talked about jail, no mention of a cellmate, or work programs, or how many months he had left. His dad just wrote about him, and how proud he was; and occasionally, he'd share a memory with him.

All the lawyers, and everyone involved thought it best that he not know where the jail was, or how long his dad had to stay there. They hushed it up pretty well, too. Press coverage had died down by the time of the trial. When Sam had returned from Chicago, he'd scanned through week-old newspapers in the library, but couldn't find anything on the trial or the sentencing. He'd asked his mom, but all she told him was that *he was someplace in California, minimum security, and they could still write to each other through the lawyer. They must have figured this was how they'd keep him from making direct contact with his dad. Well, it had worked pretty well up until now.*

The back door opened and closed once more. Sam watched him pass through the lobby again and start up the stairs. His father didn't even glance at him. Wounded, Sam had to remind himself that he'd changed, too. He'd grown at least ten inches, and filled out. Besides, his dad certainly wasn't expecting him. Maybe he and the black guy looked like buddies or something.

He started up the stairs after his father. It no longer mattered that his dad looked old, or that he'd stopped writing to him. He just wanted to see his father's tired-looking face light up with recognition and love.

Sam watched him walk to the far end of the hallway. And the old guy began to whistle "Sweet Baby James," one of his favorite songs. At that moment, the stranger became his father. Tears brimmed in Sam's eyes as he listened to his dad butcher the melancholy tune. He was never very good at whistling. Sam almost called to him, but his father stepped into the apartment and closed the door.

PART TWO
THE SURROGATE FATHER

CHAPTER EIGHT

"He pointed right to it and said, 'Look at the baby giraffe, Daddy.' I mean, he said it almost like an adult—clear as that."

"Hot damn," Frank Tuttle said, dropping his fork with mock surprise. "Call Ripley's, Carl!"

Frank was thirty-three, with black, curly, receding hair, a mustache, and about twenty excess pounds. He occupied the cubicle neighboring Carl in the accounting department at Allstate.

At first, Carl's inheritance had seemed like a bottomless pool of security, but it had diminished to a few thousand dollars in a fleeting sixteen months. So, begrudgingly, Carl had started looking for work. He'd landed a job in Allstate's management trainee program. All of the guys in his section were younger than he, all married with kids. But they acted like a bunch of horny frat boys—with their after-work beer chugalugs, and the way they hit on the waitresses during group lunches at the Red Robin Burger Emporium near the office. Carl rarely went along on these excursions; this was only his second lunch with Frank.

"Okay, so I'm a bore on the subject," he said, grinning tiredly. "How old were your kids when they started talking in complete sentences?"

"Same age as yours, Carl—two years. Frank Jr. and Janey were walking by then, too."

Carl frowned. "Do you think Sam's—backward? I mean, he'll stand up if there's something to hold on to, but he won't even try walking—no matter what I do. I'm starting to worry about him."

"I'm starting to worry about *you*," Frank said.

"How do you mean?"

Frank looked up at the pretty, blond waitress, who stood by their table, a coffeepot in her hand. "More?" she asked.

He nodded, almost leering at her. She refilled his cup, but smiled at Carl. She had pale, cream-colored skin, and breasts that seemed too ripe on such a nubile body. "A warm-up, Carl?"

"Sure, thank you." He tried not to gawk at the display of cleavage beneath her scooped-neck white blouse as she leaned forward to replenish his coffee cup. Then she sauntered away.

The leering smile fell off Frank's face. "That's how," he whispered. "Shit, buddy. Connie is the best-looking waitress in the place. Everyone in the office is hot for her. I've been eating lunch here twice a week for over a year now, and the girl probably couldn't pick me out of a lineup. You've been in here only once—what? two weeks ago?—and she remembers your name . . ."

"So?"

"So you're telling me about how you took your kid to the zoo this weekend. Meanwhile Connie's bumping her hip against your shoulder while she takes your order. Man, she's warm for your form. Why don't you do something about it?"

"Gee, think I ought to try to bang her behind the salad bar, Frank?" Carl sipped his coffee and noticed Connie smiling at him from across the restaurant. The girl made him nervous.

The last time he'd been with a woman was Eve— over two years ago. No girlfriends, no dates, no one-night stands, nothing, Carl got by with an ever-increasing collection of *Playboy* and *Penthouse* magazines, which he hid under his bed. He spent Saturday nights alone with Sam asleep in the next room and the Channel 13 Eight O'Clock Movie on TV. There were only three commercial interruptions. He'd order pizza, and usually fell asleep before the movie ended. Last week he'd shared his dinner and dreams with Audrey Hepburn. It was Lee Remick the week before that. These were the only women in his life.

Now this blond waitress over by the kitchen door was smiling at him.

"Connie's giving you the eye," Frank whispered. "She wants it, man."

"For chrissakes, Frank, she's just a kid . . ."

"She's twenty-eight. Bernie in Claims found out from one of the other waitresses. Unmarried, unattached, unyielding in her lust for your bod. So are you going to make your move or what?"

"Frank, she's just being friendly. I'm too old for her . . ."

"What are you giving me with this 'too old' bit? Jesus, you look younger than half the guys at the office." Frank leaned forward, and his voice dropped to a hush-hush confidential whisper. "Y'know, Carl, we're really disappointed in you. We're all married, getting spare tires around the middle. Then you come swaggering in—good-looking and single. We thought you'd be the office stud. We counted on living vicariously through you and your sexploits. We even had a pool going. Half of us bet you were nailing Pam in Personnel during lunch hour. The other half were sure it was Morton's secretary, Barbara. . . ."

Chuckling, Carl shook his head.

"What a shame it ain't so," Frank said, pushing his coffee cup away. "You've been telling the truth about your lunch hours, haven't you? You really have been brown-bagging it and eating with your kid at the daycare center."

Carl tried to laugh. "You make it sound like a crime."

"It's a *waste*—guy with your looks and all."

Carl often said the same thing to himself. Vain as it seemed, he'd study his reflection in the bathroom mirror and wonder how long he could hold on to his deceptively youthful handsomeness. He didn't have many years left before women like Connie would take no notice of him.

"Don't you ever get lonely, Carl?" he heard Frank ask, his tone suddenly serious.

"Of course I do," he replied edgily. "But I have an obligation to my boy. You just don't understand what it's like to be a single parent, Frank."

"Maybe you're right," he said, glancing at the check. He pulled out his wallet. "This is on me, Carl, if you'll take a little bit of advice." He slapped a ten-dollar bill on the table. "Kids grow up, buddy. If I were a single parent like you, I'd be looking for someone so I wouldn't be single anymore."

Frank went to the men's room. Carl was waiting by the restaurant door, when Connie brushed up against him. She slipped a matchbook into his hand. "My phone number's inside," she whispered. "Call me some-time, okay?" She smiled, then turned around and hur-ried to a tableful of people.

Returning to the office with Connie's phone number in his pocket, Carl turned into his cubicle then stopped dead.

Eve sat at his desk. She wore a light trench coat, and her black hair had been trimmed and curled at shoulder length. She held a framed photo of Sam from Carl's desk and she was studying it. Then Eve looked up at him. "Hi. The girl said you'd be back soon, so I waited."

"What are you doing here?" he whispered.

"Like I said, waiting for you." She laughed. "That's not a very warm greeting after two years, Carl."

"I'm sorry," he heard himself say.

She put the picture frame down, crossed her beauti-ful legs, then swayed from side to side on the swivel chair. "Maybe I shouldn't have surprised you like this. In fact, I was in for a surprise myself. When I told the girl out there who I was, she said she thought Mrs. Jor-genson was dead. I was about to check my pulse when you came in." Eve glanced at the photo again. "Who's the little boy anyway?"

"Eve, I can't talk to you here," he said, under his breath.

She let out a wry laugh. "I wouldn't doubt it, since you must have told *everyone* here that I'm pushing up daisies."

She looked so very smug, rocking from side to side in the desk chair. Carl frowned at her. "Eve, the *second* Mrs. Jorgenson died in a car accident shortly after our son was born. That's him in the picture. His name's Sam."

The smirk fell from her face and she stopped playing with the chair. "Oh, Carl . . . I'm . . . I'm sorry . . ."

"It's okay. If you want to talk, we can go somewhere else."

"Of course," she whispered, then got to her feet. "I'm sorry, Carl. You should have told me—and not let me go on like that. Somehow, I just never figured you'd remarry so soon."

"Let's go outside. I still have fifteen minutes of my lunch hour left." He led her toward the elevators, ignoring the curious stares from his coworkers. Carl congratulated himself for the "second Mrs. Jorgenson" story. He could use it on the people at the office: *"Yeah, the brunette dish was my first wife. I don't know why she still calls herself Mrs. Jorgenson. It's been years since we've even spoken . . ."*

They were alone in the elevator. Eve gave him a strained smile. She was even prettier than he remembered. The new hairstyle flattered her. But Carl didn't feel any attraction left. "You look good, Eve," he remarked.

"Thanks, Carl. You too." She looked up at the lit numbers above the door.

Carl took her to a delicatessen, where they sat by the window and ordered coffee. It was one of those brightly lit places with plastic tables and chairs like patio furniture. The lunch crowd was starting to dwindle.

Carl asked how she'd tracked him down. Eve explained that she'd gotten his Seattle address from his father's attorney. Then she'd met Mrs. Kern, who had Carl's work address. "She thought 'Mrs. Jorgenson' was dead, too," Eve said, frowning. "I figured you must really hate me if you were telling people that. Now I feel rather silly." She leaned back in her chair. "You certainly didn't waste any time after we split up, did you?"

Carl stirred his coffee. "Why did you want to see me, Eve?"

"I'm attending this tennis tournament in town, and figured I'd look you up." She shrugged. "My therapist recommended it. She thought I should try to resolve the bitterness between us."

"What bitterness? It's ancient history, Eve. My life's going well. I'm happy."

She gave him a sad smile. "Yes, you finally got the son you always wanted."

He nodded.

She glanced out the window for a moment. "You know, that whole abortion thing wasn't easy for me, Carl. You never seemed to understand that."

"Well, c'mon, Eve," he sighed. "At the time, you acted like all you'd done was go in for a haircut or something—like I had no say in the matter. 'My Body, My Choice,' you said."

She leaned forward. "Listen, back when I first got pregnant, you were the one who wouldn't let me have any 'say in the matter,' Carl. I tried to get through to you, but you didn't take my feelings into account at all."

"All right, fine." He tried to smile. "Let's not argue,

Eve. It's history. I've put it behind me. Time wounds all heels."

She frowned. "What's that supposed to mean?"

"It's a joke," he said tiredly. "It's been a long time, and a lot has happened for me. I'm happy with my life now. I wish you the same, I really do."

Eve drank some coffee. "I'm seeing somebody," she said. "An architect."

"That's nice," Carl said.

She smiled awkwardly at him. "So—when did you remarry? It must have been pretty soon after the divorce. . . ."

"That's right." He glanced at his watch, then pulled out some money for the check. "I should get back to work now, Eve. Thanks for stopping by to see me." He got ready to stand up.

"Well, are you free for dinner tonight?" she asked. "We haven't had much of a chance to—"

"Oh, I'm afraid not. Thanks anyway, Eve."

"Then that's it?" she asked.

"Then what's it?"

"I thought we might be friends, Carl."

"What for?" he said. Then he smiled gently. "I'm sorry. What I mean is, you live in Portland, and you're seeing an architect. I live in Seattle and have a son. Why be friends? So we can send each other Christmas cards once a year? Where else could a friendship between us go?"

Eve raised her eyebrows. "And you said you weren't bitter."

"I'm not, honest. I just don't see any point in trying to keep in touch and be friends." He didn't want her pulling any more surprise visits, or asking about his son, or his "dead wife." He wanted Eve to go back to Portland, marry this architect, and forget about him. "Listen, Eve," he said. "I want you to be happy. There are no hard feelings."

"No, as a matter of fact, you don't feel anything at all, do you, Carl?" she whispered. "It's just like that time I told you that your father died. You didn't feel anything then either."

Carl glanced around the delicatessen. They'd been talking in strained whispers, and people were starting to stare. He'd seen couples quietly arguing in restaurants, making everyone around them uncomfortable; and he hated being half of that kind of couple now. It didn't seem to bother Eve.

She let out a sad, embarrassed laugh. "I didn't expect it to turn out like this," she said. "I certainly hadn't counted on you remarrying. Funny thing is, you've hardly mentioned your dead wife. . . ."

Carl automatically shook his head. He tried to think of some details that might lend credence to his fabrication. But he was stumped—and afraid Eve knew it was a lie.

"I shouldn't be surprised you don't talk about her— or that her picture isn't on your desk beside the one of your little boy. You have a way of sweeping your painful past under the rug, Carl. Not just the pain, but the whole works. I imagine our six years together are buried under that rug—along with your father and the mother of your child. The trouble with that is, Carl, it'll catch up with you eventually. You'll have to pay a price for not facing your past. It'll come back to haunt you."

Carl gave her a strained smile. Eve was two-thirds

right; he hadn't thought about her much—nor about his father. But not a week went by without him remembering—and wondering about—someone he'd never even met. Every time Sam did something charming, every time he was sick, and every time he seemed to take another step toward growing up, Carl would think about Amy McMurray. And he'd want her to know just what Sam had done.

"Maybe you're right, Eve," he said, to stop her from analyzing him any further. He stood up. "Thanks for stopping by. Take care, okay?"

Before she got another word out, Carl leaned over and gave her a quick kiss on the cheek. He felt nothing. Even the old, familiar, bittersweet scent of her perfume didn't move him. Carl hurried out of the deli, never looking back.

"Well, we've been married—what, honey, about five years, right?" She glanced over at Paul, who sat beside her in the other tan sofa seat.

Staring down at the carpet, he nodded.

"Um, Paul's a sales rep for Hallmark, and I work in Housewares for Frederick and Nelson at the Lloyd Center. I got the job a month ago. Before that, I worked at a Safeway." Amy twisted her wedding ring around her finger. "Paul and I met in college. We got married my senior year. I never finished school, but Paul did. He's a couple of years older than me. He's twenty-eight and I'm twenty-six. This October, we'll be married five years."

"You already told her that," Paul mumbled. He propped a foot on his knee and began to wiggle it.

At fifty bucks an hour, she could hardly afford to repeat herself. Amy smiled at the tan, starved-thin, middle-aged woman. Her shiny black hair was pulled back in a bun, and she wore gobs of Mexican jewelry around her neck and wrists. From her chair on the other side of Paul, Dr. Amberg coolly smiled back and nodded for Amy to continue.

"We had—one child," Amy said. "A little boy, Edward. But he was abducted when he was five months old. It happened a year and a half ago. I wanted to have another child right away, but . . ." She shrugged and glanced at Paul.

He wouldn't look at her. He glanced around the office, frowning a little at the Navaho artwork and contemporary furnishings. He'd been dead set against this whole thing: *"I don't have any problems. If you want to go see this lady shrink, go by yourself."* It had taken Amy three weeks of pleading and browbeating for him to consent to one trial visit.

"Have you consulted a therapist before?" Dr. Amberg asked. Her voice was soft and so passive that she sounded like she was on Librium.

"No," Amy answered. "I wanted us to see a counselor after we lost Eddie, but Paul said—well, we both agreed that we couldn't afford it. Anyway, we're a bit better off now, moneywise that is. Right, honey?" Amy reached over and took hold of his hand.

He nodded and threw the doctor a strained smile.

"You look a little pale," Amy told him. "Are you okay, honey? Did you take your pill today?"

He sighed. "Don't worry. I took it. I'm fine."

She turned to the doctor. "Paul's an epileptic, but

you'd never guess it—thanks to this medication he's on. He's got—"

"She doesn't have to hear my medical history," he cut in.

Amy tried to smile. "Of course not."

"Why do you feel you need counseling?" the doctor asked.

Amy looked at Paul. He offered nothing. Amy shrugged. "Well, I'd like things to be better between us."

"Better in what way?"

"Well, we don't talk much anymore." She realized how lame that sounded and rolled her eyes. She glanced at Paul again; no help. "The truth is, Dr. Amberg, Paul and I haven't made love in over a year. I mean, I'm not saying it's entirely his fault. But whenever I try to talk about it, we end up fighting. That's one reason I thought—we thought we should come see you."

Paul coughed and pulled his hand away from hers to cover his mouth. He tugged at the knot of his necktie as if it were pinching him.

"Paul, we haven't heard from you," Dr. Amberg said in her dreary voice. "Does talking about this make you uncomfortable?"

"Hell, yes, I'm uncomfortable," he said, laughing curtly. "I just met you ten minutes ago, Doctor, and I'm supposed to spill my guts about our sex life? I'm sorry. I feel like I'm on trial here, sitting between the two of you. We haven't made love in over a year, so something's wrong with *me,* right?"

"Honey, I said it wasn't your fault entirely," Amy interjected. "I'm to blame, too."

"In what way are you to blame, Amy?" the doctor asked.

She drew a blank for a moment. "I don't know," she said, fidgeting with her wedding band again. "For a while there, after the baby was stolen from us, I—I wasn't ready to go back to what you might call a 'normal married life.' And, naturally, Paul was pulling away, too."

"What do you mean, 'naturally' he was pulling away?"

"It was my fault we lost Eddie," she said. Amy had rehearsed this speech many times, and had it whittled down to the emotionless facts. "See, I had him in the car, and I left him there alone for a minute. When I got back, he was gone. I'm to blame for the whole thing."

"Do you blame Amy for what happened, Paul?"

He glanced at Amy. "Have I ever said I blamed you for it?"

"Not in so many words. But you've just about proved it to me, honey. I know what you're thinking. . . ."

"How? You just said we don't talk anymore. So how can you know what I'm thinking? Are you a mind reader? *We don't talk anymore.*' Where do you get that anyway? We talk all the time."

"You talk," Amy snapped. "You bend my ear about work, and then when I try to tell you about my day—" She turned to the doctor. "Last week, after listening to him go on and on about his boss, I start to tell him something that happened in the store, and he reaches over and turns on the TV."

"You know what she was telling me?" Paul said.

"She's telling me about this little boy she saw in the store, and how much he looks like Ed. After a rotten day at work, I'm supposed to come home and subject myself to that? I didn't want to hear about it. I'm sorry."

"Why, Paul?" Dr. Amberg asked. "Was it painful for you?"

He rubbed his forehead. "Well, it didn't exactly lift my spirits, Doc."

"Would you object if Amy told us about it now?"

He shrugged and looked up at the ceiling.

"Amy?" the doctor said.

"It was nothing unusual," Amy muttered. "There's always a steady stream of mothers with babies coming through the store. But I've never really gotten used to it—since Ed's been gone. I compare every baby to Ed. Sometimes, I'll see a child with his mother, and I'll wonder if he's Eddie's age, or if he's actually Eddie himself. I know it sounds crazy . . ."

"Go on," Dr. Amberg said.

"My girlfriends at work—I've made a lot of good friends through work, except for my boss, who's awful. Anyway, none of them know about Ed. I'll listen to stories about their kids, and they'll usually finish by saying something like, 'You'll know what it's like when you have one of your own.'"

"Why haven't you told your friends at work about your son?"

"I don't know. I'm ashamed, I guess." Amy took a deep breath. "Anyway, the baby I saw that day seemed only a couple of months older than Eddie was when we lost him." A dreamy, tearful smile came to Amy's face. "His mother was wheeling him around in his stroller. He had the same kind of hair as Eddie—light brown and curly. Even wore a little pair of Adidas, just like Eddie's. I remember he looked at me and smiled. . . ."

Paul slumped lower in the chair and tugged at his suit jacket. Amy glanced at him. "That's about as far as I got in telling Paul. That's when he turned on the TV."

"What more did you want to tell him?" the doctor asked.

"I was going to tell him how much seeing that baby made me want another child," Amy said. Then she shook her head as if she were wishing in vain. Ed's room was just the same as it had been before that Halloween almost two years ago, as if they were awaiting his return—or for a second child that would never come. The nursery was like a shrine—a grave she frequently visited. Sometimes, she'd see Paul go in there, too, late at night, when he didn't think she'd notice.

"I can't let go," Amy said shakily. "Every baby, every little boy I see reminds me of him. At work, I'll hear a song on the Muzak system and remember how I used to sing it to Ed. God, I can't go to the market and pass a box of Pampers on the shelf without practically falling apart." She wiped a tear from her eye and tried to laugh. "I told myself before coming here that I wasn't going to cry. I purposely didn't bring any Kleenex."

Silent, Paul handed her a handkerchief.

"Thanks, honey." She blew her nose and sighed. "I don't know. It's like neither one of us will let ourselves be happy."

"Do you think that's true, Paul?"

He frowned at Dr. Amberg. "I think she doesn't want us to be happy." He glanced toward Amy. "A day doesn't go by without you bringing him up. And it hurts. You won't let me forget."

"That's because I know Eddie's still out there some-where," she replied, squeezing the handkerchief in her fist. "And I'm not giving up on him. I don't care how long I have to wait or how much it hurts. I'm not giv-ing up on my baby."

A half hour later, they walked to the car in silence. Paul slid behind the wheel, and Amy climbed into the passenger side. He sat there, his head turned away from her as he gazed out the window. Amy rubbed her forehead. "Thanks for going through with this for me, Paul," she murmured. "I know you hated every min-ute. I know you hated *her,* too."

He was silent.

"Paul, I have to ask you something," Amy said. She stared at the dashboard. "You never really answered her when she asked if you blamed me for what hap-pened to Ed. Do you blame me, Paul?"

More silence.

"Paul?"

"I'm sorry," she heard him whisper.

"You still haven't forgiven me, have you?" Her eyes filled with tears.

Paul turned the key in the ignition, then pulled onto the street. "Forgive and forget," he said. "They go to-gether, Amy. Maybe if you let me forget, I'd forgive you for losing him. It's been eighteen months. I'd like to put it all behind us. Why can't you do that, too?"

Because he's the only thing keeping us together, she wanted to say. Didn't he know that? She'd been on the verge of leaving Paul when she'd gotten pregnant. Eddie had saved their marriage—or at least the baby had given her a reason to stay on with Paul. Even with him gone, she still clung to his memory—his possible return. Now Paul was asking her to give up on Eddie. He might as well have asked for a divorce. Her love for their absent child was all she had left of their lives together.

Carl set Sam's blanky on the grass. It was a warm Saturday morning at Volunteer Park—just six blocks from their apartment. On his more masochistic days, Carl would try to force a little culture on Sam and push him in his stroller through the park's art museum or the conservatory; but Sam favored the diversions offered outside: the playground, amateur ball games, people throwing Frisbees, joggers doing laps around the large reservoir, and all the other toddlers and their parents. Most of the children around Sam's age were walking—even running—already.

Two years old, and Sam was still moving around on all fours. Carl imagined him a couple of years down the line, crawling to kindergarten, dragging his lunch box the whole way.

This was for his own good.

Sam cried and pointed to his cherished blanky, discarded on the grass. Carl lifted him out of the stroller. "Try walking to it, Sammy," he said, careful not to sound overly demanding. "I know you can do it." He lowered Sam to the grass.

"No!" Sam kicked as if he were afraid the ground might swallow up his feet. He clung on to Carl's hands. He looked like an angry cherub, his hair shimmering in the sunlight, the wet lower lip in an outraged pout.

Once Sam's little Adidas hit the ground, Carl announced: "Okay, I'm letting go now. Walk to the blanky. Here goes . . ."

He pulled back. Sam squatted down and softly fell on his diapered butt, then he started to crawl toward the blanket.

Carl scooped Sam up and set him on his feet again before he reached the bait. Sam shrieked in protest. He had a way of hitting those high notes that drove Carl crazy. "Oh, now, don't be a pill," Carl hissed. "Give it a try at least . . ."

Sam was shirtless, and he wore a pair of pale blue overall shorts. His chubby arms were slick with sweat, and the way he wiggled and screamed, it was difficult to hold him. As Carl set him on his feet again, he saw a thin young woman in a peasant dress, staring narrowly at him from behind a pair of granny glasses. She stood several feet away. Carl may as well have been a child molester the way she scowled.

"Walk for Daddy," he said gently, not happy they had an audience. He forced himself to laugh as Sam sank to his butt again and crawled to the blanket. "Okay, partner, we'll try again some other time," he said loudly—for the girl to hear. He kissed Sam on the forehead and put him in the stroller. The prized blanky in his grasp, Sam finally stopped screaming.

The nosy girl kept staring at him, her lip curled slightly. Carl turned his back to her and pushed Sam in his stroller. Was he really being too rough with Sam? Was it cruel to deprive him of his blanky? Was that girl just a nosy twerp? *Yes!* How dare she look at him as if he were mistreating his child? What the hell did she know about raising kids? He was a good father—

and resented the snoopy girl for making him question that.

He knew real child abuse. In a way, it made fatherhood even tougher. How could he measure discipline against what he'd experienced growing up? So many times, saying "that's a no-no" or giving Sam a light slap on the hand didn't seem to work. For a kid who could only crawl, he sure got into a hell of a lot. He was going through the terrible twos. There were times when Carl thought he might lose it and smack him. But he never got angry enough at Sam to go past that line. Hell, he could hardly even bring himself to spank Sammy—even when the boy *needed* it. Even if the youngster wound up a little spoiled, so be it. His son would never have to suffer the wrath of an angry, frustrated old man.

He collapsed the stroller, then hoisted it and Sam up the stairs to the apartment.

"I'm hungry," Sam said, twiddling his ear.

"I'll fix you a peanut butter sandwich, partner," Carl said. "You know, you're getting too big to be carried around like this all the time."

"Sannich," Sam said, and he sucked on his blanky.

Between Sam's attachment to that smelly, dilapidated old blanket and his unwillingness to walk, Carl was deeply concerned about him. Dr. Durkee the Humming M.D. surmised that the child of a single, working parent might develop a fixation for a security blanket in lieu of the parent's presence. He added that Sam could be a little slow in his motor skills, and said he'd run some tests if Sam wasn't walking within a couple of months. He told Carl not to worry. But even

Ms. Petesch at the day-care center had expressed some concern, since Sam was the only one there in his age-group still on all fours.

Carl set Sam on the living room floor, then watched him crawl toward a Fisher-Price toy. Frowning, Carl headed into the kitchen. He made Sam's peanut butter and jelly sandwich, then went back into the living room to check on him.

Sam was standing—on his own. His back was to Carl, who froze in the kitchen doorway. He held his breath and watched his son take a few steps toward the TV. Sam didn't know he was being watched. Carl counted each teetering step with amazement and pride: one, two, three, four . . .

Tears swelled in Carl's eyes. Five, six, seven, eight . . .

Sam plopped down on his little bottom after nine steps. Then he reached for the channel dial on the TV set.

"Sammy!" Carl cried, elated. *"You walked*—all by yourself!" Carl scooped him up in his arms. He kissed his son, then lifted him up over his head. "That's a good boy!"

Ten minutes later, Sam sat in his high chair, eating and painting the lower part of his face with peanut butter and jelly. Carl was on the phone to his work buddy, Frank Tuttle. He'd never called Frank at home before, but Carl had to tell someone. "All on his own," he said. "Without any coaching . . ."

"Well, that's—terrific, Carl," Frank replied.

"Oh, you should have seen it. . . ."

"Well, that's really something," Frank said. "So— um, what's going on?"

Carl laughed. "Sam walked! He really can walk now."

"Oh, then you're not calling about work?"

"No, I just wanted you to be the first to know about Sam." Carl suddenly felt very foolish. Why, he wondered, should Frank Tuttle give a rat's ass about Sam taking his first steps? He wished he knew someone else to call. There was only one other person who would care as much as him that Sam had walked for the first time. And he couldn't phone her. He'd have to tell her in another letter.

"Anyway, nothing else is new," Carl managed to say. "Just thought I'd give you a buzz. See you Monday?"

"Sure thing. 'Bye, Carl," he replied. "Oh, and congratulations again."

"Thanks," he said, frowning. Then he hung up the phone.

"Do you think Paul has any idea you're doing this?" Dr. Amberg asked.

"I'm sure he doesn't suspect a thing," Amy said. It was her fourth appointment with Dr. Amberg, and the second session that Paul had managed to miss. "I'm very careful, only during lunch hours. I never give my real name or phone number. So there's no way it could get back to Paul. You know, I've been doing this behind his back for a couple of months now. I started out just thinking about it, and then I—" Amy shook her head and laughed. "The funny thing is I've yet to find one that really satisfied me—at least, not enough that

I'd move out on Paul. I guess that must say something. They're always wrong for me."

"When was the last time?"

Amy slumped lower on the tan sofa seat. "Day before yesterday," she answered, frowning. "It was awful."

"What exactly. was wrong with it?"

"Too small—and dark. I want an apartment that has some sunlight. This place was like a tomb. If I get my own place, I ought to be thrilled with it, don't you think? Anyway, like I said, maybe I'm not ready to move out. Maybe I'm just stringing myself along. Otherwise I'd tell Paul that I'm looking for an apartment of my own—instead of being so sneaky about it."

Dr. Amberg just nodded. She was perched beside Amy in the matching sofa seat, a notebook in her lap.

Amy got up and moved to the window. Dr. Amberg's office was on the second floor of a small office building near the Lloyd Center. There was a lot of pedestrian traffic on the sidewalk below, and Amy watched through the slats of the venetian blinds as a shirtless young man climbed inside a beat-up Mustang. Apartments weren't the only thing she'd been looking at on the sly lately. She'd notice men—in the store or on the street—checking her out too. Some of them were young and cute, and they'd smile at her. But she never had the nerve to smile back.

She still shopped at the old Safeway, and her former coworkers complimented her on the designer dresses she wore from Frederick and Nelson (the employee discount helped Amy expand her wardrobe and upgrade her taste). One of the girls down in Cosmetics had done her colors (she was a fall), and shown her how to accent her eyes and cheekbones. With her shoulder-length hair wavy and shimmering—thanks to an expensive auburn tint—Amy had never looked so close to beautiful in all her life. Yet Paul wouldn't have known the difference if it were the Bride of Frankenstein crawling into bed with him every night.

"Our sex life—or lack thereof—is the same," she said, turning away from the window.

"Have you and Paul tried what I suggested during our last session?" Dr. Amberg asked.

"Paul wasn't exactly gung ho on the idea," Amy replied. In an effort to reactivate their sex lives, Dr. Amberg had suggested fifteen minutes of touching, kissing, and caressing—without intercourse. Amy called it foreplay therapy. Paul called it an experiment in prick-teasing and a waste of time. "To tell you the truth, Dr. Amberg, he doesn't put much stock into any kind of therapy. I really don't think he minds that we haven't had sex in eons. If it were up to him, we'd go on living like nonsexual roommates until the cows come home."

Amy wandered behind Dr. Amberg's desk and gave the empty chair a little spin. "When I think about it now, I realize I got married for all the wrong reasons," she said. "I mean, he was the first guy I'd ever been to bed with. And when my parents found out we were living together . . . Well, I guess I married him to fix things with my family."

"Is that the only reason?"

Amy picked up a letter opener, then put it down. "Well, I felt I should." She uttered a pathetic laugh. "Those *shoulds* get you every time. There's a world of difference between doing something you *want* to do and doing something because you think you *should*. I let those *shoulds* guide me into this miserable marriage. I thought I *should* make my parents happy, I *should* be like my brother and sister. . . ."

"Yet from what you've told me, you don't seem very close to anyone in your family except for your mother."

"That's right," Amy said, swinging the empty chair from side to side. "My brother and sister are so—respectable, squeaky clean. I've always felt as if I didn't measure up. See, they're pretty judgmental. I feel like the family fuck-up around them." Amy got to her feet. "I haven't talked to either one in months. My mom fills me in on what they're doing. How am I on time?"

"We still have a few minutes left."

Amy moved to the window again. She checked the scenery on the street below. No hunks. "I'm supposed to look at another apartment at one-fifteen," she said. "I'm not sure I'm ready to go out in that heat again." A bank sign across the way flashed the time, date, and temperature: *12:42 PM; TUES, 8-20; 93°*.

"A minute ago you said the 'shoulds' guided you into a 'miserable marriage,"' Dr, Amberg remarked. "Have you always felt this way about your relationship with Paul?"

"First couple of months, the marriage was great," Amy said, twirling the cord to the venetian blind around her finger. "Then I found myself having to invent reasons for staying with him. I guess the best reason came with the baby. I felt that I really should make the marriage work. Huh, there I go with the stupid 'shoulds' again. . . ."

"And after you lost the baby?" Dr. Amberg asked soberly. "What's kept you together this last year and a half?"

"This last sexless year and a half?" Amy said. "I don't know. Maybe that's why I wanted us to come to you. I've run out of excuses for staying together. I'm hoping you'll give us one."

"You don't have a reason of your own? Think, Amy. Why do you want to save your marriage?"

"Well, I feel I should."

The doctor smiled a bit condescendingly. "There you go with those 'shoulds' again. I asked why you *wanted* to stay with Paul."

"I don't know," she answered edgily.

"Do you want to stay married to Paul? Do you love him?"

Amy checked her wristwatch, even with the bank sign across the way in clear view. "Our time's almost over, isn't it?"

"It's all right," she heard Dr. Amberg say.

"Well, I should go." Amy returned to the sofa seat and grabbed her purse. "I told this landlord I'd be there at one-fifteen, and it's eight blocks from here. I think it was a good session, don't you? See you next Tuesday, okay? I'll make sure Paul comes, too." She headed for the door, but the doctor's voice stopped her.

"Amy," she said. "Give some thought to what I asked you."

"I will," she said, nodding. Then Amy hurried out of the office.

SPACIOUS ONE-BEDROOM in newly renovated, classic brownstone; Old World charmer w/hardwood floors, view, ample closet space. Parking avail. Convenient to buses; walk to Lloyd Center. No pets. $305 . . .

Amy had copied it down. She never circled the classified ads, because Paul sometimes read the morning paper when he came home from work. She liked the building, although there seemed room for more renovations. The courtyard garden was overgrown, and brown paint flaked and peeled around the three stories of windows. She checked the names by the door and buzzed the manager. No answer. She tried again.

"Whoizzit?" came a voice on the fuzzy intercom.

"Is this Terry?" she called into the speaker.

"Yes. . . ."

"I'm Jennifer Russell. I called about the apartment. . . ."

"Come on in. Be right down."

The door buzzed. Amy gave it a push and stepped inside. The lobby seemed hotter than outside. She pulled a Kleenex from her purse and dabbed her forehead. The teal wraparound dress she wore was damp and sticky against her skin.

It was such a waste of time. She'd already given the guy a fake name; she couldn't very well change it if she wanted to fill out an application. She thought about just leaving now, but she heard someone on the stairway.

Amy caught a glimpse of his broad, hairy chest. He was pulling on a green Izod sport shirt as he came down the stairs. He was barefoot, and it was obvious by the loose movement at his crotch that he wore nothing beneath his grey sweatpants. He smiled at her, all shiny with sweat. His long brown hair fell over his brow in damp clumps. He needed a shave.

"I'm Terry Harlowe," he said, jingling a set of keys in his hand. "You caught me lifting weights. Excuse my appearance."

"It's okay." She liked his eyes—green, with long lashes, shadowed under dark, heavy eyebrows. He was about thirty years old. The thick bulging arms, his tapered waist and V-shaped torso all attested to his weight-lifting ritual. He stood only an inch or two above her. She liked her men taller. Amy tried to find something else about him that would diminish his attractiveness, the same way she'd always find fault in all the apartments she'd seen. Then she could go on searching—window-shopping.

Why do you want to stay with Paul?

"The place is ready for occupancy now," he said. He gave her a crooked smile. "It's on the third floor and there's no elevator. That's the one drawback. Are you still game?"

Amy nodded, and followed him up the darkened stairway. She checked his buns. He kept glancing back to grin at her as if he knew where her eyes were looking. "You new to Portland?"

"No. I just want to get out of my old place. It's a little noisy, and the rent's going up." She gave the same story to every apartment manager. "Plus," she said, "I'm living with this guy and we're breaking up." That was a new angle, and she'd just blurted it out.

Again, he grinned at her. He had a sexy smile, knew it, too. "He's crazy to let a girl like you go without a fight."

She managed to smile back at him. "Well, there have been a few too many fights. That's why we're breaking up." She laughed nervously and wondered if this was how people talked when they met in bars. Pickup conversation. The last time she'd even attempted something like this, the line had been, *"What's your major?,"* and the evening together had never gone beyond necking in the guy's car. She hadn't gotten many opportunities to flirt lately. Sure, sometimes she'd flirt with customers in the store. Harmless stuff. She wasn't even about to contemplate having an affair with any of them. They'd always know where to find her five days a week. And it could so easily get back to Paul.

But this hunky stranger beside her now didn't even know her real name. The no-risk possibilities suddenly terrified her.

"Me, I'm a lover, not a fighter," he said.

Amy laughed cordially, even though the line was pretty stupid. Then again, with his looks and that body, he probably never had to rely much on sweet talk to get a girl into bed. She wondered how many airheads he'd laid during her two years of enforced celibacy. It would be so easy with him. She'd let him do everything. She shouldn't be afraid. All she had to do was respond when he made his move.

But Terry Harlowe was talking about the washers and dryers in the basement, the storage lockers, and the parking facilities. Amy pretended to listen and eyed the bulge in his sweatpants as he unlocked the door marked 301.

"I just repainted in here a couple of days ago," he said, opening the door for her.

"Looks wonderful." Amy dared to touch him on the shoulder for a moment, as if congratulating him on a nice paint job.

The living room was large, vacant, and hot. Sunlight streamed through the open windows. There was an echo as she wandered across the hardwood floor in her high heels. Unlike her other apartment inspections, she wasn't counting electrical outlets or checking the view out the window. She was looking at the young landlord as he closed the front door and stepped toward her. He swept back the sweaty tufts of hair that hung over his forehead. "This eastern exposure means it'll be a lot cooler at night when you get back from work," he said.

"Yes, it is awfully hot in here, isn't it?" Amy pulled at the V neck of her dress and fluttered the jerseylike material to fan herself. She stepped into the kitchen, careful to avoid a low-hanging light fixture that was meant to hover above a breakfast table. She moved toward the oven and range. It was quiet, and she could hear bees buzzing outside the window screen.

"We've got steam heat here, which is cheaper—" She turned and saw him walk into the light fixture. He hit his head against the copper shade. "Ouch! God, that's the second time I've done that in here—" A hand went up to his forehead. "Hurts like a son of a—"

"You cut yourself," Amy said. She searched through her purse until she found a clean handkerchief.

"I'll live," he said sheepishly. Then he lifted his front shirttail and dabbed his forehead. Amy glimpsed his taut, rippled stomach, the trail of hair that grew below his navel. The sweatpants rode low around his trim hips, and she could see his tan line.

She busied herself at the sink, dampening the handkerchief. "You're bleeding," she said. "Come here. Let's fix that."

"Yes, nurse." The sexy grin again, and his green eyes stared into hers. He stood so close, she could feel the warmth of his body, and smell a musky cologne mingled with his sweat. She brushed aside the damp bangs from his forehead, then applied the handkerchief to the tiny cut. Amy tried to keep from trembling. She listened to the bees outside, and a steady drip from the faucet behind her. He wouldn't stop staring or smiling. She wanted him to say something. Amy let one hand slide down to his whisker-stubbled cheek.

His pelvis brushed against her. She glanced down at the bulge in his sweatpants. The material was so flimsy, she could see the mushroom-shaped head of his penis as it stirred. She looked back into his thick-lashed, green eyes.

He gently touched Amy's lips with one finger.

"Don't," she whispered. But she took the finger in her mouth. She nibbled and sucked on it. He rubbed against her, and she felt the hardness of his erection. Amy dropped the handkerchief. He pulled his finger away and replaced it with his mouth. The whiskers were rough, like sandpaper, but his lips against hers were so soft and wet. His tongue probed her mouth.

It had been so long since she'd kissed like this. Amy couldn't believe it was happening to her now. She moved her hands up and down his hot body, so firm and brawny. She tugged at his shirt, pulling it up to his neck. He broke away for a second, then shucked it over his head and tossed it on the floor. Frantically, she kissed the hairy chest and gnawed at his nipples. She'd never done this to Paul.

His hands were under her dress, peeling down her panties. She felt the same finger she'd sucked on— now entering her. Amy quivered at the sensations that were awakened after so many, many months.

She feverishly pulled at the sweatpants until his erection was freed. The brown pubic hair was a shock against the untanned section of his torso. She squeezed his taut, manly buttocks. A moment later, his finger slipped out of her as she fell to her knees. Amy took his swollen penis in her mouth. She listened to him groan with pleasure. His fingers roamed through the tangles of her hair. Finally, he buckled down on the linoleum floor as if his legs had given out. He pulled Amy on top of him and kissed her. "God, you're beautiful," he said, between kisses.

"No, I'm not," she replied weakly.

"Beautiful," he whispered, clawing at her dress until it was up over her waist. The panties imprisoned her thighs. Amy wanted to take them off, but he rolled on top of her. The sweatpants were still bunched around his knees, and their legs remained trapped by clothing. She wanted to be totally naked with him, see every inch of his toned, tanned, muscular body. Yet his erection was gliding up the soft inside of her thigh and he penetrated her.

The linoleum floor somehow felt cool against her buttocks as he rhythmically moved deeper inside her. It was so animal-like and alien. She kissed this stranger, and tightly clung to his broad, sweaty shoulders. His thighs were hard and hairy against her own. He kissed her neck, the beard chafing the tender skin there. But she liked it. Amy felt herself overpowered by ecstasy, all the pleasure coming alive inside her.

Yet she did not surrender to it entirely. She thought of Paul as this other man rocked and shuddered on top of her. She'd never done this with anyone else but Paul. He was the father of her child, and together they'd suffered his loss. She remembered Paul in college, and the first time they'd made love. She'd broken curfew to spend the night with him in his dingy little apartment. How she'd loved him then. It had been new and sinful and passionate. She'd never known such happiness.

For a moment, when Terry Harlowe had pulled her to the linoleum floor, she'd almost felt that passion again. But the pleasure was just discomfort and muted pain now. She wanted him to finish. When he did, she kissed his whiskered cheek one last time and gave his shoulders a gentle push. "Oh, that was nice," she managed to say. "Real nice. I'm—a little squashed here. . . ."

Finally, he rolled off her.

Amy found the handkerchief and wiped her thighs. "I'm going to be late for work," she said, pulling her panties back on. "See, I'm on my lunch hour. How's your forehead?"

He chuckled. "I don't feel a thing."

The muscular torso was marred with scratch marks she'd made. Amy picked a piece of hair out of her mouth, then handed him his sport shirt. Unsteadily, she got to her feet. "I hate to run off like this," she said. "I had a—a wonderful time. . . ."

He stood and pulled up his sweatpants, a baffled smile on his handsome face. "You haven't seen the bedroom yet," he joked.

Amy's dress was wrinkled and soiled with sweat. She wanted to shower and change. Most of all, she wanted to get out of there. "Sorry," she said. "My boss has it in for me as it is. I'm going to catch hell. It—was fun. Better put some iodine on that cut." She hurried to the door, ran down the stairs, and then outside. But she couldn't run away from what had just happened. His semen was still inside her. Suddenly she worried about venereal diseases, or herpes. She felt like damaged goods. It would be another five hours at work before she could take off this dress and stand under the cleansing spray of a hot shower.

She wasn't worrying about Paul finding out. He wouldn't. What disturbed her most was that for a few reckless moments, she'd almost allowed herself to feel happy again.

CHAPTER NINE

"The date on this is almost two years old," the pharmacist said, examining the empty prescription bottle.

Amy had taken out the eleven pills and wrapped them in a Kleenex—now in her purse. The sedatives had probably lost their potency since her doctor had first prescribed them the night Eddie had been taken; but she was saving them as backups—in case a new bottle of eighteen didn't do the trick.

"I only use them when absolutely necessary," she told the pharmacist. He looked Arabic, and about fifty years old. The ugly, pale blue polyester shirt-jacket made him appear stupid—easy to fool. "Sleeping pills scare me," she said. "That's why it took me so long to get through the bottle. But I do need them from time to time. If there's any problem, you can call my doctor. The number's there on the bottle."

The bluff worked. He moved away from the window and reached for a canister of white pills on the shelf behind him.

She'd phoned in sick that morning—after Paul had

gone off to work. He never called her at the store, and he wouldn't be home until six. By then, it would be over.

She'd been walking around in a blue stupor for the last two weeks—ever since that sweaty encounter on the kitchen floor with Terry Harlowe. Lately, she'd just start crying without really knowing why. Sometimes, Paul would say something to her, and she wouldn't respond—often on purpose. She practically flaunted her listlessness, waiting for him to notice, perversely wanting him to suspect she'd *done* something. But Paul didn't care enough to worry. He took no notice.

She drove home and went into the bedroom. When they found her, she'd have on clean underwear and a nice dress. Amy spent fifteen minutes in front of the mirror, making up her face. She kept glancing at the bottle full of pills—and the others wrapped in the tissue—on her dressing table. She filled a tumbler with water, forced down three of the old pills, then returned to her mirror to brush her hair. Amy swallowed two more pills. Already she was feeling a bit tired—and bloated from the water. She gagged on the seventh pill, and it lodged in her throat. Refilling the tumbler, she forced down the rest of the old pills. Her mouth was full of their powdery bitter taste.

Amy carried the tumbler and the unopened bottle of pills into the nursery. This is where they'd find her.

Eddie's teddy bear stared back at her with vacant button eyes. He'd loved that thing. He was clutching it in the studio portrait that hung in their bedroom. She should have given away the toy bear last year—along with everything else in this room. What were they saving all this stuff for anyway? They certainly weren't going to have another baby. And the child who had occupied this room had outgrown everything in it. He was two years old now, not a baby anymore. Even if she got him back, those precious months with him were lost forever.

Amy started to empty all the baby clothes from Eddie's dresser drawers, repeatedly reminding herself of their practical uselessness. There was a girl at the store who was pregnant, her first, and she needed baby things. Amy figured she'd give it all to her. She'd pack everything in boxes and label them "For Suzy," a last generous act. They'd find her in the stripped nursery— everything in boxes. Then they could just put her in a box, too, and be done with it.

The old pills must have lost their potency, because she no longer felt tired. She got some empty boxes and bags from the cellar. As she shoved his toys into a Frederick and Nelson box, Amy didn't stop to examine any of them. She lumped all his clothes together and shoved them in bags, not lingering over any of the cartoon emblems or washed-in baby food stains. It was as if someone else were packing Eddie's things away, and she stood by, helpless, watching.

Amy unscrewed the mobile of little wooden airplanes and round-faced smiling pilots that dangled over Eddie's crib. She dumped tiny sneakers and saddle shoes in another box. One slipper—with tiny pictures of Mickey Mouse, Goofy, and Pluto decorating it—fell to the floor.

A terrible emptiness swelled in her stomach as she looked down at the little slipper. Amy crumpled to the floor. All the pent-up sorrow came out in dark, inconsolable sobs. She curled up on the floor and wept, cradling the slipper as if it were a precious doll.

She had no idea how long she remained there at the foot of Eddie's crib, but she'd used up all her tears. The carefully applied mascara streaked down her face. She had an awful headache and felt dizzy when she got to her feet. She glanced over at Eddie's changing table and remembered what she'd come in here to do. Had she been stalling with all this packing? She smiled. Didn't matter. In a few minutes, she'd be unconscious— the long, trouble-free sleep. No pain or misery or tears.

Amy wiped her eyes, then opened the bottle of pills. She poured them out on the table, and reached for the tumbler.

Just then, she heard the front door open. "Shit," she said, under her breath. It couldn't be six already. "Paul, is that you?" she called.

"Yeah . . ."

Amy quickly opened the top drawer of the changing table and swept the pills and the bottle inside it. Paul came to the doorway just as she closed the drawer. Loosening his tie, he frowned at the boxes and bags she'd filled. "What the hell are you doing in here?"

"What's it look like I'm doing?" Amy replied. She scooped the Mickey Mouse slipper off the floor and tossed it into a box. She resented the interruption to her glorious exit. "I'm giving all this stuff away," she said. "A friend at work is having her first baby. I'm giving her the crib, the changing table, the whole works."

"Think you might have discussed this with me first?"

Amy shrugged. "Well, we don't need this stuff. It certainly doesn't look like we'll have another baby— not the way it's been lately. I don't see why you should care. You're the one who wants to put it all behind us." Amy busied herself closing up the boxes.

"So you're just giving all this away? Ever stop to think that we could get a nice chunk of change if we sold this junk to a secondhand shop?"

Amy glared at him. "No, I didn't, you insensitive, cheap son of a bitch."

"Hey, if I'm acting like a son of a bitch, it's because work bit the big one today and ten seconds after I come through the door, you start talking in this snotty tone to me."

Amy smiled. She'd succeeded in making him angry. At least that was something. It had been a while since they'd even had a good fight. "Sorry," she said. "I've got this doozie of a headache." She glanced around the nursery—at the cartoon jungle animals on the wallpaper. "Anyway, with a couple of coats of paint, this would make a good study for you, Paul."

"Maybe, whatever," he grumbled. "I'm too tired to give a shit right now."

Amy set a box aside and went to him. "So it was a cruddy day at work, huh?" she asked. Then she kissed Paul on the lips.

"What'd you do that for?" he asked.

"Apology kiss. Can I get you a beer, hon?"

He turned away and started for the kitchen. "I'll get it."

Amy trailed behind him, rubbing his shoulders. "God, I can feel how tense you are," she said. "What happened at work?"

"I don't want to talk about it," he sighed. Paul kept trying to wiggle away from her. "C'mon, cut that out. Okay?" He bent down at the refrigerator to grab his beer.

Amy ran her hands up and down his back. She felt him shudder, and knew his resistance was beginning to wane. "Why don't you take off your shirt and let me give you a rubdown?"

"Amy, I'm hungry. I'd like dinner more than anything else. "

"We'll order pizza. Come to the bedroom first. Lie down and let me rub those aching muscles. . . ."

Laughing nervously, he broke away from her. "God, what's gotten into you?"

In a week, Amy would be alone for another session with Dr. Amberg, and she'd discuss why she suddenly got affectionate with Paul—in the midst of their bickering. *My timing was lousy,* she would admit. *"Neither one of us was in a romantic mood. I guess, deep inside, I didn't want it to work out well."*

Amy took the beer out of his hand, and sipped it. "C'mon. Let me give you a massage. It'll do you a world of good." She led him to the bedroom, then set the beer aside on his dresser and pulled off his tie. She started to unbutton his shirt.

"This is stupid," he said weakly. "Cut it out. . . ."

Yet he let her continue. She unbuckled his belt and zipped down his fly. "Relax," she whispered. "Enjoy life." Amy slowly peeled off his shirt, then worked her mouth down the center of his hairy chest. Paul shivered again. His body was rather flabby and dilapidated compared to her memory of that stranger she'd been with two weeks before. Still, she ran her tongue over one of Paul's nipples.

He laughed and gently pushed her away. "What are you doing? Christ Almighty . . ."

"Don't you like it?" she asked. Amy climbed out of her pretty dress, performing a little striptease for him. The underwear she'd chosen to die in was a champagne-tone bra with delicate embroidery and a pair of matching panties; an expensive ensemble and pretty damn sexy, too. At least, she felt sexy in it now. She sauntered toward Paul and lowered one thin bra strap.

"Wait a minute," he said. "Is this that stupid foreplay therapy your shrink recommended?"

Amy kissed his shoulder, then stepped behind him. Her hand slid around to his soft stomach, her fingers inching under the elastic band at the front of his undershorts. "Not quite," she whispered in his ear. "If I remember correctly, we weren't supposed to go beyond kissing and caressing. Right now, I'd like you to fuck me."

She enjoyed this role as the seductress, and the use of some dirty words made her feel even sexier. Amy rubbed her breasts against his back. Her hand moved deeper into his shorts, and she fondled his penis. It was flaccid, but grew heavy and firm with her caresses. "Your body's so nice, honey." She nibbled at his ear. "I've really missed it. Hmmm, you're getting hard. . . ."

"C'mon, Amy, this is stupid," he said with a nervous laugh. "You're making a fool out of yourself."

"Let me suck you off," she whispered.

He tore away from her and laughed again. "Jesus! Listen to you. Do you know how ridiculous you sound?"

"Then I won't talk. I'll do something else with my mouth." Amy got on her knees in front of him. He looked down at her, and momentarily touched the bra strap that dangled off her shoulder. Amy imagined that the champagne lingerie and her subservient position must have perked his interest—even if he was frowning a bit. She kissed him on the stomach. Then she shucked down his trousers and shorts. But he was flaccid again.

Embarrassed, Paul yanked his shorts back up. "Shit, give me a break," he snickered. "One minute you're bitching at me and the next you're giving this bad Linda Lovelace impersonation. What are you, nuts?" Laughing again, he zipped up his trousers.

But Amy's hands fumbled over his. "No, don't get dressed, honey," she pleaded, still on her knees in front of him. "At least let me give you a massage—"

Paul backed away from her. "For God's sake, turn it off, Amy. You're not even good at it."

She looked up. "I'm not good at what?"

He chuckled. "This asinine sex-goddess act."

She thought if he laughed at her once more, she'd kill him. How much humiliation could a person take? She was actually down on her knees, begging for him to desire her. Amy reached for her blouse and covered herself. The sexy bra and panties might as well have been some tacky ensemble from Frederick's of Hollywood; she felt worse than naked there on the floor in front of him. He'd made her feel silly and vulgar.

Tears stung her eyes and she glared up at him. "You bastard," she whispered. "God, I hate you. I hate you so much. . . ."

"Hello. Is Connie there, please?"

"This is Connie."

"Hi, Connie. This is Carl Jorgenson. We met—"

"Who?"

"Carl Jorgenson. You gave me your phone number at the Red Robin about five weeks ago. You waited on me. I was there for lunch . . ." Carl rolled his eyes, and he tossed the Red Robin matchbook on the kitchen counter. Way back in his pre-Eve days, he'd always dated by the rules—the first being that once he got a woman's phone number, he had better call her within three days or forget it.

Obviously, Connie had forgotten him. "I—I'm kind of tall," he explained. "With light brown hair. I was there on a Thursday with a coworker from Allstate. . . ."

"Oh, Carl!" she said. "Yeah, I remember you now. Hi. How've you been?"

"Fine, now that we've gotten that out of the way."

"How come you haven't been by for so long?" she asked.

"Well, I have a little boy, and I usually eat lunch with him at his day-care center. Stuff like that comes with the territory when you're a single parent."

He figured this revelation would be the kiss of death. He'd tagged Connie as a free spirit who wasn't about to get involved with a widower-father. Just as well. He hadn't been with a woman for so long, the prospect of dating again was scary. But the guys at work had been pressuring him to ask Connie out, and he'd been pressuring himself, too. He was lonely.

Well, fine. So he'll ask her out now, and she'll say "no, thanks." He could pat himself on the back for trying, and look each of his work buddies in the eye and tell them that Connie wasn't interested. And he'd go on being lonely.

"Anyway," he said, "I've been brown-bagging it with my son at the day-care center."

"Oh, that's sweet," she replied. "Are you divorced?"

"I'm a widower."

"Is it just you and your son?"

"That's right. Anyway—"

"Listen. Do you usually have dinner with your son, too?"

"Yes—"

"Well, you think some night this week you could find a sitter and have dinner with me? I'm free Saturday."

Saturday? But *North by Northwest* was on Saturday night! Pizza with Cary Grant, Eva Marie Saint, Mount Rushmore, and only three commercial interruptions. He'd been looking forward to it all week. . . .

"Carl? You still there?"

"Um, yes. Saturday's fine," he said. "It's just—we'll have to make it early in the evening, because I usually save Saturdays for my boy, and I'm pretty tuckered out by nighttime. I won't be much fun. Is six-thirtyish okay with you?"

"Sounds great."

Carl knew nothing of Seattle's finer restaurants. So he asked Frank Tuttle for advice on where to wine and dine Connie.

"Ray's," Frank told him. "Great food, terrific view. Get a window table. She'll be Play-Doh in your hands after that."

Word got around the office about the date with Connie. He was very popular for the remainder of the week.

Carl called her Friday night and they talked for almost an hour—a good sign. He found out that she'd spent a while backpacking through Europe with her boyfriend, with whom she'd had a messy breakup a few months ago. Talking with her was effortless, because he didn't have to talk. In fact, she hardly asked him a thing about himself. Still, he enjoyed having a woman open up to him, and Carl could have spent another hour on the phone with her—if Sam hadn't gotten into his record collection and started mangling a James Taylor album. Then Carl had to hang up.

Sam sort of mangled his Saturday morning, too, waking him at six-fifteen with cries of boredom and hunger. After breakfast, Carl tried to grab some shut-eye on the living room sofa while Sam watched cartoons, but he never managed to drift off. He was too nervous about his date that night.

He took Sam to the zoo. It was hot out. They must have walked four miles within the maze of cages, wildlife settings, insect, reptile and monkey houses—and Sam wanted to be carried half the time. Carl's worst mistake was eating what must have been a bad *jumbo* hot dog at the snack shack.

He cut the zoo trip short as soon as the first wave of nausea hit him. He sped home in the car, thinking, *This must be what labor pains are like.* If he didn't get to a bathroom soon, he'd die.

As Carl sprinted up the apartment stairs, carrying Sam in his arms, he thought he might shit in his pants.

"I got to go potty," Sam announced.

"So does Daddy," he said, out of breath. "Real bad. Which way do you have to go? Tinkle or grunt?" Carl fumbled with the key to unlock the door.

"Tinkle."

"Okay, okay, just be quick. C'mon . . ." He burst into the apartment, carried Sam to the toilet, then yanked down his shorts and training pants.

Sam just stood there, staring at the clear toilet water,

his shorts around his knees. Carl hovered over him. He had tears in his eyes from the stomach cramps. "I know it's tough to rush these things, Sammy," he gasped. "But please. Go on three. One . . . two . . . three . . ."

Carl counted to himself—in agony—for fifty seconds until Sam sprang a leak. It wasn't much of a leak either. Naturally, Sam insisted on flushing and watching the water fill up the bowl again.

Then Carl hurriedly pulled up Sam's pants and steered him out of the bathroom. "Go watch TV. I'll be out in a minute." He shut the door.

Even after he'd finished in the bathroom, Carl still felt queasy. Three gulps of Pepto-Bismol didn't help much. And he had only a couple of hours until he was supposed to pick up Connie for their big romantic evening together.

"Hi," she said, answering the door in a pair of tight Calvin Klein jeans and a frilly, white, scooped-neck camisole that accentuated her ripe breasts. Blond hair fell over her shoulders in soft curls. Around her neck was a thin gold choker. Apparently, Connie never wore makeup on the job, because Carl hadn't recalled her eyes as this dark and intriguing; and he would have remembered her lush, red lips against the pale, cream-colored skin. "You're right on time," she said, showing him inside the apartment. "You can open the wine for me."

It was a large studio, and she had at least twenty candles flickering around the place. The overhead in the kitchen was the only source of strong light. A waterbed occupied one far corner of the room, and there were brick-and-board bookshelves, travel posters on the walls, and a large sectional sofa that looked secondhand. Early postcollege decor. Carl didn't recognize—or much like—the music on her stereo, and he noticed a Pink Floyd album resting beside it. "I like your place," he said.

"I'm kind of a candle freak, as you can see." She giggled and touched his arm.

She wants it, Carl thought; but it was more like Frank Tuttle's voice than his own speaking inside him. He was still nauseous and depleted. When he'd dropped Sam off at Mrs. Kern's, she'd said he looked "a bit peaked." Why he hadn't rescheduled with Connie he didn't know. He planned to eat very little at Ray's, and maybe by the time they finished dinner, he'd feel better. For now, his lust for this blond vision was squelched by worry and sour stomach.

"You look terrific," he said.

"You too. I like your shirt. Hmmm, Polo, expensive." Her hand lingered on his chest as she stroked the material.

"Where's your bathroom?"

Carl wished she'd turned up the volume on Pink Floyd, because as he sat on her toilet, he was afraid she'd hear him. He didn't even try. He got up, washed his hands, checked the medicine chest, and stole two tablets of Rolaids. He winced at his pasty reflection in the mirror. *God, please, get me through this night,* he thought. He'd be happy just to feel normal again. All he wanted was to make a good impression on her, maybe hold and kiss her a little. He wasn't asking to get laid . . . at least, not tonight.

He rode out another wave of nausea, took a few

deep breaths, then went back to the living room. She was ensconced on the sofa. A bottle of wine, two glasses, and a tray of cheese and crackers sat on the coffee table in front of her.

"I opened the wine myself," she said, patting the empty space beside her on the sofa.

Carl sat down next to her. Connie poured the wine. "Only a little for me, please," he said. "I'm not much of a drinker."

"Oh, would you rather do a bong instead?" she asked, setting the bottle down.

"Do a what?"

"I've got some really terrific Colombian stuff. . . ."

A sickly smile froze on Carl's face. "No, thank you, Connie," he managed to say.

"Now, don't pig out and load up on cheese and crackers, because din-din will be ready in twenty minutes."

"But I was going to take you out to dinner," he said. "We have seven-thirty reservations at Ray's."

"Too late. The lasagna's in the oven."

"Well, I didn't expect you to cook for me. You wait on people all week. I thought you should be waited on for a change."

Connie reached over and squeezed his knee. "God, you're sweet, you really are, Carl."

"I just don't want you going to all this trouble," he said.

Her hand inched up his thigh now, and it aroused him. The combination of a hard-on and sour stomach was unsettling—just another part of his body working beyond his control. He shifted a little, hoping to camouflage the bulge in his pants.

"It's no trouble," Connie was saying. "I love to cook. I make a mean lasagna."

"I bet it's real rich," he said, trying not to wince.

She nodded, then got to her feet. "Lots of spices. I don't use ground beef either. Hot Italian sausage, ground up. And there's salad, and French bread dripping in butter and garlic."

"Sounds wonderful," Carl said weakly.

She hunted through some books on her brick-and-board shelves. "Now, don't worry about the garlic either," she said with a giggle. "We're having crème de menthe cordials for dessert, so our breath will be 'kissingly fresh.'"

"That's thinking ahead," he replied. She was kind of a dip really. Of course, he probably made her nervous. He was acting like such a zombie. Carl watched her as she bent over the bookcase, the twin orbs stretching her Calvin Kleins to their fiber limit. He forgot about his stomach for a few moments.

"I found it," she announced, waving a photo album. "Picture time!" Connie sank down beside him and opened the photo album across their laps. Her shoulder was pressed against his, and the view of her cleavage was unavoidable. He tried not to gawk. "This is our trip to Europe," she said. "Y'know, the one I told you about? Have you ever been? I forgot if I asked you or not."

He smiled at her. "No. I'd like to, though."

"Oh, you should—on your very next vacation."

"I'm afraid it's Disney World for my next vacation," he chuckled. "In fact, tonight is like a vacation for me. It's been a long time since I've enjoyed the company of a sweet, attractive—"

"This is Wayne, of course." Connie was pointing to

a photo of some tan, muscular, grinning moron with a brown, afro hairdo.

"Wayne," he said. "Is that your ex-boyfriend?"

"Yeah. This is my favorite of him. I took it in Greece."

"Um, yes, it's very nice," Carl said. "Good color. . . ."

"He's a massage therapist. I fell in love with his hands. I think the sun was hurting his eyes in this one. Hmm, I fell in love with his buns, too." She turned the page and giggled.

Carl was staring at a photo of Wayne, looking over his shoulder with his back to the camera. He was naked. Carl couldn't believe she was showing him nude photos of her ex-boyfriend. Below another bare-assed shot of Wayne lying facedown on a beach towel was a photo of Connie taken from a side angle. She sat, slouched forward on the sand, her arm blocking any view of her bare breasts. Hardly a flattering picture. Connie was squinting, and she looked sunburned and peeling. There were about five folds in her stomach, and her long blond hair looked limp, and dark at the roots.

She let out a screech of protest and slapped her hand over the picture. "Oh, no fair peeking at this one," she giggled. "I look terrible! My hair was so greasy that day." But Connie kept taking her hand away anyway, then covering up the photo again. "We were at this nude beach in Greece. You wouldn't believe all the guys who came on to me. Oh, now, don't look. Half the pictures didn't come back from the film place. I guess some guy at the store still has them and he's getting his jollies. . . ."

Fortunately, Wayne and Connie had their clothes

back on during their trip through Italy for the next eight pages.

She talked all during dinner—mostly about Wayne and a bunch of her friends: Vicki, Simone, Randy, Donny, and Jo-Jo. The names tripped off her tongue with no explanation of who they were or how she knew them. It was as if she expected Carl to automatically know them himself. She'd mentioned Jo-Jo eleven times before Carl finally caught on that Jo-Jo was Wayne's stupid cat. "Wayne got custody of Jo-Jo," she said.

Carl listened to a half hour of cat stories while they sipped their crème de menthes. It struck him as ironic, since he'd decided earlier that day not to bore her with talk about his son. His stomach problems had vanished sometime back when she'd been showing him a second photo album (her and Wayne "at home"). Apathy had chased away the nausea, and he'd managed to eat her lasagna without a hitch. She was a good cook. He'd told her so a couple of times—between Wayne and Jo-Jo stories.

Connie put her hand over his. "Why don't we go back to the couch, where it's more comfy?"

Carl took to the sofa while she changed a record on the stereo. He was disappointed that she'd turned out to be a flake. The strange part was, he still wanted her. Before Eve, back when he'd been sowing his wild oats, he'd bedded a few women like Connie—dull, even irritating—yet the sex had been great. Hell, he thought he'd grown out of that callow stage. But it had been two years since he'd even necked with a woman; and Connie, despite what she lacked in personality, had three things going for her: she was gorgeous, alone with him right now, and she wanted him, too. The voice inside Carl's head was not Frank Tuttle's, but his own.

"Would you like to do that bong now?" she asked, once she had Joe Cocker groaning over the stereo.

"No thanks," he said, stretching one arm across the top of the sofa. "But you go ahead and indulge if you want."

She sauntered toward him. "Party pooper." She bumped her knee against his as she stood in front of him.

"But the party hasn't even begun yet," he said. A corny line, but she seemed to go for it. Carl reached for her hand and pulled her down into his lap.

"What do you think you're doing?" Connie asked, giggling. Her arms slid around him.

"Just this," he whispered. Then Carl pressed his mouth to her lips for only a moment. She looked like she wanted more. He smoothed back her blond curls, then he kissed her again, his tongue sliding past her red lips. He caressed her bare shoulders. Her skin was smooth and delicate. Carl felt himself growing hard as she rocked in his lap. He knew she could feel it too, pressing against her ass. His hand moved across the ruffly chemise, then he cupped her breast, gently pinching the nipple. The material was fine and flimsy—like a second skin.

Connie ran her fingernails through his hair as Carl kissed her hungrily. His mouth slid down her neck, and she shivered as he breathed into the hollow at the base of her throat. He buried his face between her breasts— so warm, silky, and firm. It had been so long since he'd done this, he was hoping that his movements weren't too clumsy. And he wished he really liked her.

Carl felt her kissing the top of his head. He started to unfasten the pearl buttons of her chemise. His hands trembled as he brushed against the soft skin of her breasts.

"God, don't rip it!"

The chemise hung off her shoulder, and one breast, with its rose-brown nipple, was fully exposed. Still, the harpy tone of her voice made Carl pull his hands away.

"I didn't tear anything," he murmured, looking up at her. "Was I being too rough? I'm sorry. . . ."

The lipstick was smeared around her mouth, and when she gave him a limp smile, she almost looked like a clown. Connie buttoned up the camisole. "You're just going a little too fast," she said. "Don't get me wrong. I like you a lot. In fact, I want to sleep with you tonight. We could cuddle and kiss and cuddle some more. But I don't want to do anything else—beyond that."

Carl squinted at her. "Um, you want me to spend the night, but you don't want to make love?"

Connie nodded, then kissed him. "I even have an extra toothbrush. Of course, it's early yet. . . ."

Carl's arms were still around her, but he didn't respond to her kisses along the side of his neck. They wouldn't lead to anything. She wiggled on his lap, rubbing his erection with her buns. He was ready to burst. He couldn't imagine another hour of this luscious torture without any release—no less an entire night of it in bed with her.

"Can I ask," he said, "if there's any particular reason why you don't want to make love with me, Connie?"

"Oh, but I do," she replied, between kisses. "But tonight, all I want to do is cuddle and sleep together. You understand, don't you? That big waterbed can get awfully lonesome when you're in it by yourself." She nibbled at his ear.

Suddenly, he felt sorry for her. She probably had scores of men ready to lay her; but half-wits like Wayne—the ones who stuck around, slept with her, and made her feel loved for more than a couple of hours— were probably very rare. "Connie, I can't stay the night," he said finally. "I promised the babysitter I'd be back by eleven-thirty."

"Oh, shit, I forgot. You have a kid." She sighed. "Well, can't you just call and tell them you'll be back in the morning? I'll cook you breakfast. . . ."

She started to kiss him again, but Carl gently pulled away. "I wish I could, but—"

"Listen," she said. "If you really want to—you know, do it, that's okay. But you'll have to spend the night if you do."

"I'm sorry, I can't." Carl pried her hands off his shoulders and squirmed out from under her. "I feel like a real jerk," he said. "You fixed me a wonderful dinner and I—" He shook his head. "I should be going, I really should."

"But it's not even ten yet," she grumbled.

"I know," he said, getting to his feet. "But I'm a little worried about my son. He had a stomachache when I left. I really should be with him. I'm sorry." Carl kept one hand in his pocket to camouflage his hard-on, "You've been terrific."

She looked at him dubiously. Her lipstick was still smeared. "You'll call me?"

"Of course," he lied. "Sometime . . . soon . . ."

Connie smiled. "You will," she cooed, giving him a long kiss at the door. It left him dangling with its false promise of more; but then, he'd just made a false promise to her. He wasn't going to call her, and he'd avoid having lunch at the Red Robin for a while. The guys at work would be pumping him for details of this dismal night's activities. He'd tell them that they'd kissed a little until she got a long-distance call from her boyfriend, and that had been that. He'd tell them no more.

Carl kept thanking her and apologizing as he inched out the doorway.

After putting Sam to bed tonight, he'd catch the end of his movie, then pull out a girlie magazine and release his pent-up desires. He'd go to bed himself, and fantasize he was holding a girl in his arms instead of the spare pillow. Then he wouldn't feel so lonely by himself in the big double bed.

Amy carefully folded up the sweater and set it in the box with all the others. She'd already filled another box with shoes, and two more with books. Standing in the bedroom doorway, Paul silently watched, his hands in his pockets.

"If it's okay with you," she said, taping the box shut, "I'll take the negatives, and you can keep the photo albums. Then I'll get prints made of the pictures I want. We have duplicates of Eddie's portraits from Sears, don't we?"

"You can take all the pictures. I don't care."

"Don't be silly," she muttered, returning to the closet for more sweaters. "Even if you don't want any pictures of me, there are dozens of you alone or with Ed, the ones from college—"

"Fine," he said. "Take the negatives. Take anything you want."

Amy just nodded, then resumed packing. After only one session with Dr. Amberg, Amy had realized something about her aborted suicide and the botched seduction of Paul that night. She didn't want to die; she just wanted a second chance at life. And Paul's cruel rejection of her advances had only given Amy what she'd really sought—a reason for leaving him.

Her new apartment was a fifteen-minute drive away, and she'd been making trips back and forth like this all week, trying to time it right so not to catch Paul in. Sometimes, she'd leave him a note on the kitchen table:

Dear Paul,
 No, you haven't been robbed. It's just me again. I hope you don't mind, but I took the lamp from the living room. It was my grand-mother's before my mom gave it to us, and I want to have it. If that's a problem, give me a call.

 A.

She took only a few furnishings. Thanks to her employee discount at Frederick and Nelson, Amy had bought a sofa, a bed, a TV, a stereo—practically all the essentials. The decor was far classier than all the secondhand furnishings they'd accrued during their struggling newlywed days. She'd even spent sixty dollars on a lamp—for him—to replace the one she'd taken.

"You haven't said anything about the lamp. Do you like it?" She'd set it on the end table by the sofa, where the old lamp had been. They hadn't spoken—or seen each other—in over a week. "Anyway," she said, taping up another box, "I hope it's okay."

"Do you like the lamp?" he asked.

"No, Paul. I hate it. That's why I bought it for you." Amy rolled her eyes. "C'mon, don't be this way. Of course I like it."

"Then take the lamp. I don't want it."

"Tell you what," Amy growled, lifting the box. "Bring it back to the goddamn store and exchange it for one you like." She brushed past him as she carried the box outside.

When she returned to the bedroom for a second load, Paul was rummaging through a pile of work papers in a box on his closet floor. "You might as well take these, too," he said. He tossed a thin stack of postcards, held together by a rubber band, onto the bed. "They're all addressed to you. . . ."

"What are you talking about?" She picked up the postcards. They were the blank, generic kind, no pictures—just the stamp and her name and address scribbled on the front of each one. The handwriting was distinctly masculine. Amy took off the rubber band. "What are these?" She read one of the cards. There was no salutation or signature:

> *12/2/78*
> *Said his first word today—"dog." Had a cold last week, but very healthy now. 27 lbs., 31 inches.*

"What is this?" Amy murmured, frowning. She read the postcard again, and its message became more clear to her. Anxiously, she read the next card:

7/13/79

Wonderful news. Finally walked yesterday—
all on his own. Bathroom-training going well.
Seems very bright. 34 lbs., 32 inches.

Amy sank down on the edge of the bed. Tears brimmed her eyes, but she was smiling. Eddie was still alive. Someone had her little boy, and he was safe . . . loved. How she wished she'd been there to see him take those first steps, to hug and kiss him proudly. She missed him more than ever now. Yet beyond her frustration and wanting, Amy felt grateful. The notes verified what she'd somehow known all along: Eddie was alive. "My God, he's okay," she whispered. "Oh, Paul, he's all right. How—how long have you known?"

"The first card came over a year and a half ago," she heard Paul say. "It was a Saturday. You were at work."

"Which one is it?" she asked, riffling through the cards. There were seven of them.

"It's not there. I thought it was a crank, so I threw it out."

"You threw it out? God, how could you? We stopped getting crank mail a couple of months after it happened. Look at the dates on these! Look at what he says. They're genuine. What did the first card say?"

Paul shrugged. "I don't know. Something about him being healthy, then the weight and height. I don't remember. Second one came a few weeks later—on a Saturday again."

"That's pretty damn convenient," she replied, her eyes narrowing at him. "Did all these cards just happen to arrive on Saturdays while I was at work?"

He shook his head. "Just the first two. I gave the

second card to the police, and they forwarded it to some crime lab in California. All they could tell from the handwriting was that it was from a male in his thirties or forties. The postmark was Vancouver, Washington."

"He's just across the river in Vancouver?" she asked.

"Look at the other postmarks," Paul said glumly.

Amy examined them: *Portland, OR.; Longview, WA.; Castle Rock, WA.; Olympia* . . .

"All up and down Oregon and Washington," Paul said. "He's a foxy son of a bitch, isn't he?"

Amy clutched the postcards to her chest. They were her only connection to Eddie. Dazed, she looked up at Paul. He turned and walked out of the bedroom. She followed him into the kitchen. "How could you keep these from me?" she asked. "All this time not knowing for sure if he was alive or dead. I'm his mother, for God's sakes! How could you? How *did* you? These cards are addressed to *me*!"

Paul grabbed a beer out of the refrigerator, then sat down at the breakfast table.

"Paul?"

He sighed. "After the second card came, I promised the mailman twenty bucks if he'd hold any more like it whenever they came, then give them to me on Saturdays while you were at work."

She gazed at Paul as if she didn't know him. She never imagined he could be so devious and scheming; he didn't seem shrewd enough for that; no, not her thoughtless husband.

Sipping his beer, he stared back at her, almost shamelessly, but not quite. "I thought you were better off not knowing," he said. "When the cops couldn't trace the second note, all I felt was frustrated and pissed off. He's torturing us, and I spared you from that."

"Oh, how noble of you," she snapped. "So why did you think I should know about these letters now? Why did you spring them on me today? To see me fall apart? So you could hurt me?"

"If you move out, they're not going to deliver the notes here anymore."

"No, they'll deliver them to me at my new place. I filled out a change of address form last week, Paul." She glanced at the postcards in her hand. "Jesus, I can't believe this. For over a year, you've known he was alive. Yet you kept me in the dark. Why?"

Amy stood by the kitchen table, staring down at him. Paul's eyes avoided hers, and he glumly stared over toward the kitchen sink as if she wasn't there. "I felt you were better off not knowing," he mumbled.

She shook her head. "If that's true, you're even more stupid than I thought. And if it's a lie, then you're a sick and hateful person. Either way, any second thoughts I've had about leaving you just flew out the window." She started for the door.

"What about the rest of your stuff?" he said, frowning.

"I'll come by after work tomorrow. Try not to be home." She opened the door.

"Wait a sec," he said, rising from his chair. "What if you get any more cards about him? Are you going to tell me?"

Amy smiled coldly at him. "Would you feel better off not knowing, Paul?"

He said nothing for a moment, then sank back down

in the kitchen chair. "I guess I'll take the few crumbs this asshole tosses us," he muttered.

"I'll let you know," she replied.

Inside the car, Amy sat behind the wheel and pored over every card again. The most recent was dated six weeks before:

8/20/79

Can recite the alphabet now, and counts to ten. But doesn't know what it means yet. Talkative and energetic—almost to excess. But a good boy. 36 lbs., 34 inches.

Amy wished she could hear what he sounded like as he spoke the alphabet. She didn't know his voice. Was his hair still that golden blond shade? His eyes had changed from blue to hazel green after the first couple of months. Were they still that same misty color of the sea or had they changed again? She wondered if she'd even recognize him now.

She would. And the day would come when she'd see her son again. Amy knew that—as surely as she'd known he was alive all this time.

Amy slipped the postcards inside her purse. She looked forward to receiving the next note. After nearly two years of misery, she finally had something she could look forward to.

Turning the key in the ignition, she glanced back at the town house, then started for home.

CHAPTER TEN

The woman in the framed, blown-up photograph was a striking brunette, wearing a floor-length, ruffly white dress. She sat in a wicker chair and held a boy in her lap. He looked about Sam's age—four and a half—and wore a little suit with shorts, knee socks, and a bow tie. He had his father's red hair, and a sweet, puzzled expression. The father, decked out in a blue suit, stood at his wife's side, one hand on her shoulder.

Sam couldn't take his eyes off the picture, which was displayed in the window of a photo store at Southcenter Shopping Mall. Carl tugged at his hand. "C'mon, Sammy, there's nothing in here we want."

He knew why the photograph fascinated his son. Lately, whenever he picked up Sam at the day-care center, he'd notice his boy looking at all the *mommies* there to take his classmates home. Most of the time, Carl was the only father there, and he knew Sam felt different from the other kids.

"Am I a norfin?" he'd asked, early one evening the week before. They were driving home from Sunnyside Day Care.

"No, you're not. An *orphan* is a child whose mom and dad are *both* dead. As long as I'm still alive, you're not an orphan."

"Larry Westhead said I'm a norfin."

Larry Westhead is full of shit, Carl wanted to say. "Well, you're not, sport."

"Is my mommy really dead?"

"Yep, I'm afraid so, Sammy. I told you, she died in a car accident shortly after you were born. She's buried near where we used to live in Santa Rosa."

"But you said she's in heaven."

"She is. But her body is buried in the ground in Santa Rosa. Hey, tiger, whaddaya say we go to McDonald's for dinner tonight? Won't that be neat? Dinner with Ronald?"

Carl knew how to get Sam's mind off such things. As he pulled Sam away from the photography store window, he promised to buy him a helium balloon at the toy store. The ploy didn't seem to excite Sam much. He let go of Carl's hand while they strolled through the crowded mall. "Did my mommy look like that?" he asked, wiggling his finger inside his nose.

"Look like what? Stop that."

"Like the lady in the pitcher."

"No, but she was very pretty. Do you want a hand-kerchief?"

Sam finally pulled his finger out of his nose and wiped it on his khaki shorts. "Do we have any pitchers of her?"

Carl hesitated. "Yes. But I'm not sure where they are. What color balloon do you want?"

"Gween." Then he was quiet for a while. Carl welcomed the silence. Sam was going through a talkative phase lately. He was constantly asking questions, and his new favorite word seemed to be "why?" Yet he'd never hold his tongue long enough to hear an explanation. When Sam wasn't talking to him, he talked to himself or to the TV. He even talked in his sleep. Carl did his best to listen when the never-ending chatter was directed at him, but sometimes even *pretending* to listen wore him out.

The problem with Sam when he was blessedly quiet was that it indicated there was a problem. He walked alongside Carl, frowning down at the floor.

"What's wrong, tiger?"

He took a deep breath, then squinted up at him. "Did it hurt when they cut off her head?"

"What? Cut off whose head?"

"Mommy's. You said her body's in the ground and the rest of her's in heaven. I don't want them to chop off my head."

Carl laughed. "Oh, no, Sammy. They bury you all in one piece—everything attached. Your head stays with your body when you die. The part of you that goes to heaven is your spirit."

"Like a ghost?"

"Not quite. See . . . well, okay, when somebody dies, it's like they go to sleep forever. But you know how you dream when you're asleep? You can still see and feel and think even though your body's asleep? Well, the part of you that feels and thinks and sees goes to heaven when you die. Then your body sleeps in the ground while you see and feel everything in heaven."

Carl was proud of himself for what he thought was a

clever explanation. His own father wouldn't have bothered. Hell, the old man wouldn't have wasted a Sunday afternoon taking him shopping.

He reached down and mussed Sam's blond hair. "You understand a little better now?" he asked.

"Fred Flintstone saw a ghost yesterday, but it was Barney under some sheets, trying to scare him."

"That Barney's a real cutup." Carl sighed. "There's the toy store up ahead. See?"

Sam ran ahead of him. Carl smiled and shook his head. He thought about the young mothers he'd sometimes notice during his strolls through the Volunteer Park Art Museum with Sam, the ones who tried to educate their toddlers in the fine arts: *"Now, the man who painted this painting was named Picasso. Can you say Picasso?"* Then in the same breath: *"Do you have to go potty?"* Sometimes, trying to explain things to Sam was just as futile.

Sam slowed down several feet ahead to gaze at a toy in Woolworth's window. Carl wasn't close enough to see what had captured Sam's attention, but Sam was looking back at him now. He gave an excited, little jump and pointed to the toy.

All at once, a woman stepped between them, her back to Carl. She was plump, wearing a cheap red wig, sunglasses, and a flowered jumper. She seemed to come out of nowhere, and she grabbed Sam's arm.

For a moment, Carl didn't know what was happening. He was still several feet away. But then he heard her as she started to pull Sam toward the mall exit doors: *"Your mommy sent me to get you, honey. Come with me outside. She's waiting in my car."*

"HEY!" Carl yelled, racing toward them. He felt a rush of anger and panic. *"That's my son!"*

The woman saw him, and her pudgy face froze. Then suddenly, she gave Sam a hard shove. He toppled to the floor and let out a startled cry. The woman barreled through the crowd for the exit door, never looking back.

Carl reached Sam and scooped him into his arms. "You okay, Sammy?" he asked, out of breath. He looked over toward the glass exit doors. The woman ducked inside the front seat of a beat-up, beige Cadillac that had been waiting outside for her. She'd left in her path a dozen curious onlookers. The car sped away.

Carl and Sam had drawn the attention of the crowd too. "You okay, Sammy?" he asked again.

Sam nodded, then buried his face in Carl's shoulder. He was embarrassed by the crowd. Carl stood up, clutching him to his chest. He patted Sam on the back, then looked around for a pay phone to call the police. He wanted to take Sam away from all these people. No one stepped forward to offer help— or to ask if his boy was hurt. They just stared. Carl noticed one woman eating an ice-cream cone as she gaped at him.

He turned away and carried Sam toward a pay phone. "You're okay now, Sammy, aren't you? Did she scare you?"

He felt Sam nod against his shoulder. "She said my mommy was looking for me," he whispered. "She knew where Mommy was."

Carl phoned the police again. It was seven o'clock, and he stood at the kitchen counter, fixing dinner. The cop on the other end of the line told him that they still didn't have anything. Carl wasn't surprised. He hadn't given them much to go on—a fat lady in sunglasses and a wig. He hadn't even gotten the license plate off the Cadillac. He'd been too worried about Sam at the time. It had all happened so fast that he'd phoned the police from the mall without a thought about the risk of involving Sam and himself with the law. He just wanted to get that sleazy bitch who tried to steal his son away.

The idea of her taking possession of little Sammy made Carl's stomach turn. He still felt a little shaky— as if he'd cheated death. He couldn't help thinking about how Amy McMurray must have felt when it had happened to her four years ago. Strange, how he still felt connected to her, even though they'd never met. In a way, Sam was their little boy—his and Amy's. With every minor and significant event of Sam's life, Carl thought about Amy McMurray. Then he'd write to her, take Sam for a long drive, and mail the card. No one else could have cared as much as he did about the milestones in Sam's childhood—except her.

He wouldn't write to her about what had happened at the mall that afternoon. With a little detective work, she could trace him through the police report on the incident.

The cop said they'd call if they found anything. Carl knew they wouldn't. But he thanked him anyway, then hung up.

He set the kitchen table, made a glass of chocolate milk for Sam, and got dinner ready: meat loaf, green beans, and Tater Tots.

Thanks to a helium balloon, a G.I. Joe doll, and a

stop at 31 Flavors on the way back from the police station, Sam seemed to recover from any traumas. In fact, all the kid-gloves handling had put him in a bratty mood. Funny, how he picked up on the fact that old dad wasn't about to scold him for anything right now.

Calling him to dinner, Carl found Sam standing on the living room sofa—his shoes on, no less. He was playing with his new G.I. Joe doll as he gazed at the arrangement of framed photos on the wall—pictures of him and his father. He mimicked machine gun noises and death cries.

"C'mon, Sammy," Carl said. "You know better than that. Get down from there."

"How come there aren't no pitchers of my mommy here?" he asked, bouncing on the sofa cushion.

"Most of the pictures were lost when we moved from Santa Rosa. Did you hear me, Sam? I said climb down from there. You're getting the couch all dirty. Dinner's ready. Come on now." Carl retreated into the kitchen.

"Don't we have *any* pitchers of her?" Sam asked midway through the meal. He'd already eaten all of his Tater Tots, but nothing else. He walked G.I. Joe across the place mat.

"I might have one or two photos tucked away someplace," Carl said. "I'll have to check. Now, c'mon, put G.I. Joe down and eat your dinner. You haven't touched your meat loaf or beans."

He maneuvered Joe around his plate. "When can I see her pitcher?"

"Picture," Carl said patiently. "We'll talk about it after you finish eating. Now, would you please—"

Sam knocked G.I. Joe against his milk glass.

"Oh, Jesus, Sammy!"

Chocolate milk splashed across the table and dripped onto the floor. Carl got to his feet. "Okay, that's it, that's it. G.I. Joe goes into the living room until you finish dinner. Look at this mess. For cryin' out loud, Sam."

Sam was a champ at milk-spilling, both chocolate and white; he wasn't picky. But usually he was apologetic. Not tonight. He seemed downright resentful as Carl snatched the doll out of his hand and tossed it into the living room. Carl wiped up the mess with a sponge. His food was getting cold, and Sam glared at him, lips turned down in a pout.

"I'm sorry I yelled at you," Carl said calmly. "Accidents can happen. Now, just three bites of your meat loaf, and three of your beans, then you can have a chocolate chip cookie for dessert and play with G.I. Joe all you want. Okay?" Just once, he wished he could get through a meal without having to plead and bribe Sam into eating.

"I want another glass of chocolate milk."

"Put a dent in your meat loaf first, okay?" Carl dropped the sponge in the sink, then returned to the table. He picked up his fork.

"But I want some chocolate milk! I'm thirsty!"

"Don't use that tone with me, Sam. Now, eat, or you can go straight to bed, no cookies, no G.I. Joe. Do not pass go, do not collect two hundred dollars. You're making me very angry." His own father wouldn't have stood for this.

Sam idly pushed the food around his plate with his fork, frowning at it. "I'm not hungry," he grumbled.

Carl swallowed some cold meat loaf. "Then you can be excused from the table and go to bed."

"You're mean."

Carl put down his fork. "Did you hear me?"

Sam sneered down at his plate.

"I said you can eat or go to bed—"

"I don't wanna eat this," he shot back.

"All right," Carl said. "Then slide your little butt off that chair and move it into your room before I make it a *sore* little butt. Get moving."

"Mean," Sam grunted. He shoved himself away from the table. But he hadn't quite lifted his hands from the place mat, and it moved from the table with him. The place mat, silverware, and his plate—full of food—toppled onto the kitchen floor.

Carl jumped up from his chair. "You little brat—"

"I didn't mean it!" Sam yelled back.

Carl took his napkin and grabbed Sam's arm. "Dammit," he hissed. "Keep still." He bent down and brushed the food off Sam's shoes and pants.

"You're hurting," Sam cried, wiggling his arm against Carl's grip. "Ouch . . . stop it, Daddy . . . I didn't do it on purpose . . ."

Carl released him, only to point toward the general direction of Sam's bedroom. "In bed, this instant! Or I'll really give you something to cry about."

Sobbing, Sam ran out of the kitchen. "I hate you! I hate you! I wish you'd die!" he screamed.

"And leave the damn G.I. Joe where it is!" Carl called back. He heard Sam's bedroom door slam shut and the muffled crying.

Carl cleaned up the mess. He couldn't stop shaking.

He felt so defeated—angry more at himself than his son. He kept replaying in his mind the moment that awful woman had knocked Sam onto the mall floor. How close he'd come to losing him. Yet he let this happen tonight—of all nights, when he should be thanking God he still had him.

His dinner was cold, and he threw it out. He didn't even save the remaining meat loaf for leftovers. Everything got hurled into the garbage. He scrubbed the dishes, letting the hot water nearly scald his hands.

At least once every couple of weeks something like this would happen and make Carl sorry he'd ever snatched Sam from Amy McMurray's car. "What have I got?" he muttered as he worked the Brillo pad over a casserole dish. "Shit job, no love life at all, no real friends, and a kid who hates my guts right now. Don't get a moment of peace or privacy and yet I'm lonely as hell. . . ."

The only woman in his life at the moment lived in the building across the way, one floor down. He'd checked the names by the front door, and figured she was probably B. Kramer in 203. He imagined her name was Belinda. From his living room window, Carl had a good view of her apartment, very neat and nicely furnished—considering that the building itself was kind of dumpy. She didn't go out or entertain much. Practically every night, Carl would spy her, writing at a desk by her window. He wondered if she were a student, or an aspiring novelist. She wrote by candlelight, always wearing the same pink terry cloth robe, her light brown hair pulled back in a ponytail. Carl never got a good look at her face, but she seemed beautiful. He hadn't seen her in anything less than her street clothes or that pink robe. In a strange way, he was glad his watching her was chaste—without any vulgar Peeping Tomism. Belinda would write late into the night, and sometimes, Carl would look out his living room window just before going to bed. She'd be there, the candlelight glowing around her. And like him, she'd be alone. Somehow, it made him feel better about himself.

Carl dried the dishes and put them away. Then he went into the living room and picked up Sam's toys. He glanced out the window. Belinda wasn't home tonight. But then, it was only eight-thirty. He'd check again later.

Carl brought the toys into Sam's bedroom. Sam was asleep—still dressed—on top of his bed. Carl roused him and got his clothes off. Asleep on his feet, Sam let his father dress him in his Spider-Man pajamas. Carl gave him the G.I. Joe doll and tucked him in bed. "I love you, Sammy," he whispered, kissing him goodnight. But Sam was already asleep again, hugging G.I. Joe as he once had his yellow blanky years before.

Carl would spend the rest of the evening trying to find a mother for him.

There was a tiny crawl space in the front closet. Its little door was warped and the latch often stuck; the damn thing always took some prolonged tugging—sometimes even a screwdriver—to pry open. That made it a perfect place to hide things from Sam.

There, under boxes of Christmas ornaments, loose pads of steel wool, by cans of paint thinner, wood stain, and other rarely used poisonous cleaners, was a large box that held Carl's past.

He dragged it into the living room, put a Dan Fogelberg album on the stereo, and opened a beer.

He'd saved two news clippings about the kidnapping. Looking at the yellowed, fuzzy news photo of Amy McMurray with the baby, Carl saw that Sam had her smile and her eyes. *"Looks like you,"* he imagined telling her in the next note.

But of course, he'd have to find another woman amid all the old papers and photographs.

He shuffled through the papers—the divorce decree, his birth certificate, diplomas—until he found pictures taken during his college years. He'd had a lot of dates, and someone always had a camera—especially for formal dances. But the photos only made him feel old, and they'd never do: him, with his crew cut and dumb-jock smile; the girls' dresses and hairstyles were straight out of 1962, Jackie Kennedy, and Sandra Dee clones—every one of them. Sure, Sam might accept one of these girls as his mother now, but in a few years, he'd know better.

Carl kept looking. There were many pictures of Eve, which he'd saved despite himself. But he would never use them, and he refused to linger over any one. It was getting late, and he could see the bottom of the box.

Then he found it—a five-by-seven, black-and-white in a cardboard frame. The picture had been taken sometime in the early seventies, before he'd met Eve, when he'd had that coaching job at the grade school. He'd been a groomsman at the wedding of a faculty friend. He posed with a pretty, blond bridesmaid, who looked a little like Candice Bergen. He'd necked with her in a pantry at the reception hall, but he'd forgotten her name.

But it was a splendid picture, not bad of him either—even with those god-awful sideburns and the Sundance Kid hair. The woman's bridesmaid's dress was pale enough to pass as white, and she held a small bouquet. It could be their wedding portrait. He'd show the picture to Sam in the morning, then have it framed and hang it above the couch.

It was past midnight by the time he got the box of junk put away. Carl turned off the living room lights, then paused at the window to see if his girlfriend was home.

Two candles flickered on her writing desk, and the kitchen light was on. Carl kept waiting to see her in that pink robe. After a few minutes, she appeared in the kitchen, wearing a pretty green dress. She pulled a bottle of wine from the refrigerator, then moved out of Carl's line of vision. It was another moment before he saw her again—by the writing desk. She set down the bottle and started to open it with a corkscrew.

That was when Carl noticed the man in the apartment with her. He wore a suit and tie, and looked much closer to her twenty-something years than Carl was. The man took the corkscrew and bottle, then kissed her on the cheek. She kissed him back—on the lips, it looked like. Then she turned toward the window. Carl stepped back. She glared at him, shaking her head in disgust. Then she lowered the blinds.

CHAPTER ELEVEN

"I've already rung these up. She's taking them with her." Tiffany shoved a set of plates toward Amy's register, then handed her a copper teakettle. "But she's sending this out of state."

Tiffany was her boss. Word around the store had it that Tiffany was either related to or sleeping with some bigwig. There seemed no other explanation for her tenurelike position in management. Personnel had a stack of complaints from employees who had worked for Tiffany, yet she remained at the Housewares helm, continuing to treat her saleswomen like incompetent serfs.

Amy recalled how impressed and intimidated she'd been back when Tiffany had first interviewed her for the sales job. That was four years ago, when she was married to Paul, dressing in J.C. Penney rack specials, struggling to lose weight and wishing she were as sophisticated-looking as this woman named Tiffany. Amy felt like a fashion flunky in the company of the thirty-six-year-old, with her wavy black perm, oversize glasses and designer dress. She didn't resent Tiffany's condescending manner or her bossiness when she'd started at the store.

Amy knew better now. Had she strolled into that interview today, she never would have gotten hired. No, not the 1983-model Amy Sheehan (she'd shed the Mc-Murray once she'd shed Paul): trim and sporty in Liz Claiborne blouse and skirt ensemble. She was damn good at her job, and every month, averaged about five customer compliment cards. Yet Tiffany only got more cold and critical toward her. Amy might have given a shit, except no one in the store liked Tiffany—that included most of the customers.

The lady buying the teakettle was no exception. She frowned a tiny bit at Tiffany, who acted as if she wasn't there. "She wants the kettle gift wrapped," Tiffany said. "Ring it up, code 17." The code was Tiffany's, so she'd get the commission.

Amy made some small talk with the customer and the lady instantly warmed up to her. "You know," she said, "I bet you could help me. I'm looking for this retractable makeup mirror that was in your catalogue, but they don't have it at the bath department. And that snooty woman waiting on me just now wasn't any help. Do you know where I can get one?"

Amy hid a smile as she finished ringing up the sale. "Tell you what," she said. "I'll make some calls. They might have the mirror in another one of our stores, or somewhere else in the mall. Why don't you browse a bit while I check it out for you?"

Ten minutes later, Amy gave her the name of another store in the Lloyd Center, Rosemary's Bed & Bath Boutique. They had the mirror. The lady thanked her about five times.

The woman would probably ask for her the next time she came into the store. That drove Tiffany crazy—people passing her over so Amy could wait on them. And oh, if the customer was a handsome guy, it really burned her. "I'll thank you not to flirt with the customers," Tiffany had whispered to her, after a certain cute guy had returned to ask for Amy's assistance last week.

Amy had just laughed. "Oh, Tiffany. I sold him a microwave yesterday. I wasn't flirting, for goodness sakes . . ."

He had dark chestnut hair and brown eyes like Al Pacino. Amy wrote her home phone number on a business card and gave it to him. Perhaps Tiffany had seen her do it.

The woman was such a snoop. Amy wasn't about to tell her that Mr. Microwave (his real name was Joe D'Angelo) had already taken her out. And she had a date with him tomorrow, the zoo.

There wasn't exactly a swarm of single, heterosexual males coming through Housewares, but she got asked out on occasion. Guys like Joe gave her their business cards, or asked for hers. Among her single and divorced girlfriends at the store, dating was the big thing to do. At least, they all said she should be out there dating. So she dated. Most of the guys were nice, but Amy never got serious with any of them. Divorced three years now, and of her hundred-plus dates, she'd had sex with only two. There was the widower with the toddler son and baby daughter. Instant Family. She almost convinced herself that she loved him just to be a mother to those kids. But he was boring and kept sending the kids to his sister's every time Amy came over—

so they could be alone. That lasted three weeks. The other guy was a *Looking for Mr. Goodbar* stint from loneliness. The dark, wiry naked stranger in her bed was sexy and nice, but he terrified her. Amy asked that he not spend the night. After he left, she threw up. So much for her life as a swinging divorcée. Yet for every man she shut out of her life, there would be another to come into the store and give her his business card.

There was a lull, and Amy replenished the sales table with some stoneware. Flo, the other saleswoman, was helping her. She liked Flo, a cheery, fiftyish widow with three grown children. She had a wonderful, blond bubble hairdo, and spoke in a gravelly, yet daffy voice. "That new guy in Men's—the cute one? I have it on good authority that he's got a crush on you, hon."

Amy busied herself arranging some plates. She shrugged.

"Or are things heating up with the Microwave Man?"

"I'm seeing him tomorrow," Amy replied listlessly.

"You don't sound too excited about it. What's wrong, hon? Last few weeks, you haven't seemed too excited about *anything*. You've been in a real rut ever since . . ." Flo shook her head.

"Ever since I found out that Paul got remarried," Amy said, frowning.

"Yeah," Flo said.

"I don't know what it is," Amy sighed. "I certainly don't miss him or envy his new wife."

"The poor girl," Flo interjected.

Amy managed a weak chuckle. Flo had been there during the divorce, and she knew everything—except about Ed. She'd made several friends at the store, but none of them knew she had a son. On an end table in her living room, she kept a framed photograph of her mother, herself, and Ed. She told everyone it was her godchild she was holding in the photograph. She loved that picture, and the explanation seemed easier than trying to hide the photo every time someone came over.

"I guess it's just strange to know he's getting settled again," Amy admitted. "Going on with his life." Meanwhile, she still clung to the past—and to Eddie. Knowing he was out there somewhere kept her from moving on. She'd been in a holding pattern ever since the divorce.

"Well, cheer up," Flo said. "Your ex is someone else's headache now."

Amy artfully arranged some coffee mugs on the display table. "I don't know why it makes me blue," she said. "I suppose I should be happy for him."

"Who can't you be happy for?" It was Tiffany. She appeared from behind a tall display rack. Amy wondered how long she'd been eavesdropping on their conversation.

"Oh, nothing, Tiffany," she said, trying to look busy.

"No, what is it?" she pressed, with a phony look of concern.

Amy didn't like confiding things to Tiffany, especially something personal and painful; but she'd been caught in a weak moment. She shrugged. "Oh, my ex-husband got remarried, and I was telling Flo that I feel a little funny about it, that's all."

"Oh, that's too bad," Tiffany chirped. Yet a bright smile lit up her face, and her eyes widened with delight behind the designer glasses. "Really too bad. . . ."

"Then why are you smiling, Tiffany?" Amy asked.

"Well, I was just thinking you might buy him and his bride something nice here in Housewares. You know, we could always use the business." With a bounce in her step, she walked away.

"Meow," Flo said, under her breath.

"God, what a creep," Amy muttered, going back to work on the display table. She glanced at Tiffany, a few sales tables away. Amy studied the superior expression on Tiffany as she waited on an old black lady. "You know," she said, "I'll never figure out what I did to make her dislike me so much."

"Oh, that's easy," Flo said. "You're younger and prettier than her. Plus I have it on good authority that if it weren't for her upstairs connections, you'd have had her job ages ago."

Amy had heard the same thing. She'd applied for positions in several other departments, but never got a transfer. Tiffany was always the one to tell her: *"I'm not supposed to know, but that job in Linens? They found someone else. So our happy family here in Housewares won't be breaking up after all. Isn't that nice?"* It was as if Tiffany wanted to keep Amy under her thumb until she found an excuse to fire her.

"Oh, miss?"

Amy looked up. It was the teakettle woman, bypassing Tiffany to talk to her.

"Well, hello again," Amy said.

Laden with shopping bags, the woman patted the only one not from Frederick and Nelson. "I just want to thank you," she said. "They had the mirror at that Rosemary's Bath place. And can you believe? It was two dollars less than the one in your catalogue."

"Well, then you got a bargain. Good."

"And I'm ever so grateful," the woman said.

Tiffany stared at them. She waited until the lady walked away, then asked in a hushed voice: "What was that all about?"

Amy explained how she'd helped the woman find the mirror, downplaying it so Tiffany wouldn't feel threatened by her superior finesse with customers. Tiffany's ego was already bruised since the woman had completely ignored her. "I didn't do any more for her than you'd have done, Tiffany," Amy concluded.

"You're right about that," Tiffany shot back. "I certainly wouldn't have sent one of *our* customers to another store—for an item in *our* catalogue no less."

"Tiffany, I checked. We don't have the mirror in stock yet. I even phoned our store at Vancouver Mall, and nothing."

"So you made calls to other stores on company time?"

"Well, yes," Amy said. "But it's not like we were *real* busy. I don't see why you're so upset. The customer was happy, and it's good PR for us."

Tiffany swiveled around and stalked into the back room.

"Score one for our side," Flo whispered.

But Amy wasn't sure. Maybe Tiffany would use this business with the mirror and twist it around so she could get rid of her.

Sure enough, a few minutes later, Tiffany pulled Amy away from a customer. "I called the stockroom about that mirror," she whispered. "They expect a shipment of them tomorrow afternoon."

"Tiffany, I'm with a customer. . . ."

"We have an appointment in Mr. Ballentine's office

in twenty minutes. I've covered up a lot for you in the past, but I'm afraid you've gone just a little too far this time, Amy."

"What?"

Ballentine was the store manager, and—if rumors were correct—the bigwig Tiffany had on a leash.

Hadn't these people seen *Miracle on 34th Street*? Didn't they know how much business Macy's generated in that movie when they sent shoppers to Gimbels for items not in their store? This "customer first" approach seemed totally alien to Ballentine. He was in his forties, skinny, with red hair, and an ugly mustache. He dressed nicely though—some dark, designer suit and a flashy tie. The image of him and Tiffany naked, doing things to each other in bed, popped into Amy's mind and made her stomach turn.

Her stomach was already a mess of knots, as she stood there in front of Ballentine's desk like a soldier ready for court-martial. Tiffany was ensconced in a chair at Amy's side, enjoying the show. Ballentine hadn't said much. Amy did all the talking: "And while I made those calls, the lady bought two more items—at a cost of twenty-seven dollars." She hadn't told Tiffany that part, and she revealed it now as sort of a trump card to win her case.

But Ballentine's passive expression didn't change. He just scratched his ugly red mustache and kept staring at her as if he expected more. She hadn't won him over. How could she? He was Tiffany's boyfriend. They were going to fire her—and for making a customer happy, no less. It was so insane and unfair.

"Mr. Ballentine," she said, "I'm a good employee. You can check with anyone in the store. Personnel has a whole stack of cards from satisfied customers thanking me for helping them—"

"She works harder to get those customer compliment cards than she does trying to sell merchandise," Tiffany remarked.

"You know that's not true," Amy replied in a low voice.

"The point is," Tiffany said, shaking a finger at her, "you have an attitude problem. You went off on your own with this. Had you consulted me, we might not have lost that customer."

"But we didn't lose the customer! She came back just to thank me!" She turned toward Ballentine and tried to bring some control to her voice. "And correct me if I'm wrong, but I think that lady will come back to Frederick and Nelson next time she needs something—anything, because she knows we'll help her."

"How?" Tiffany asked smugly. "By sending her to another store to shop?"

"Listen," Amy said. She felt her whole body tingling. "This is crazy. I should be getting a pat on the back instead of this—interrogation. That customer was grateful." She glared down at her boss. "I didn't see her thanking you for anything, Tiffany. In fact, she told me you were 'snooty.' Maybe if you learned how to deal with people better, they might actually like you. I don't know one person in this store—customer or employee—who likes you at all."

"Now, hold on," Ballentine said.

But Amy couldn't stop now. She'd suffered in silence too long. Tiffany's nasty smile when she'd made that crack about buying Paul a wedding present was still fresh in Amy's mind. "I tried to be your friend," she said, shaking her head at Tiffany. "God knows why, but I tried—for four years! Well, want to know something? You aren't worth the effort, you insufferable creep!"

"That's enough!" Ballentine said.

"I'm sorry!" Amy hissed, her heart pounding. "But this is ridiculous. She's a lousy manager and a nasty person, and I'm about to get fired for helping a customer find something she needed—"

"I said that's quite enough," he barked. His face was almost the color of his hair. "Please, wait outside, Ms. Sheehan."

Tiffany wasn't looking at her. She had a stony, slightly pained expression on her face, like someone getting a tetanus shot from the doctor and pretending it didn't hurt.

Amy took the long walk out of Ballentine's office. She sank down in a chair outside his door. His secretary had stepped away from her desk; for that, Amy was grateful, because she could barely hold back the tears.

What the hell was she going to do for a living? She didn't have a college degree or any secretarial skills. There went her employee discount. No more bargains on clothes and furniture. She'd have to move; the rent was too high. And the only friends she had were at that store. In one reckless moment, she lost everything that had made her meaningless life bearable.

"I can't believe I called Tiffany a 'creep' to her face," she whispered to herself. She started to laugh. It was worth it. At least she'd stood up for herself; she

would try to remember that when the goddamn unemployment office denied her application.

The door to Ballentine's office opened. Tiffany strutted past her without a glance, then disappeared around the corridor. Amy had expected some snide good-bye. It was a good thing the bitch sailed by, too. Had she stopped for even a moment, Amy would have punched her lights out. Perhaps Tiffany knew a little bit about people after all.

Ballentine poked his head out the doorway. "Ms. Sheehan?" He motioned for her to come inside his office.

Amy followed him in. She'd never been fired from a job before—a new experience in her lifetime of screwing up.

Ballentine told her to sit down, and she took the chair Tiffany had vacated. "I'm afraid you've made it impossible for me to keep you on at this store any longer," he said, sitting on the edge of the desk.

"Yes, I know," she murmured. "I'm sorry for that outburst. It was very unprofessional. But Tiffany had it coming—"

"That's enough," he said, holding up a hand. "I don't want to hear another word about Ms. Kimbler."

"I just want you to know before you fire me that I've been a good employee. And I don't like telling people off. I'm not the shiftless jerk she's probably made me out to be."

"Yes, you have been a good employee," Ballentine said. "I read some of those customer cards you talked about, and I was very impressed. I hate having to let you go, Ms. Sheehan."

"That makes two of us." She tried to smile. "Huh, maybe you'd write me a letter of recommendation . . ."

He shook his head. "I'll just make a call. There's an opening for manager of Bathwares at our Southcenter Mall store in Seattle. The job's yours if you'll relocate. You'd be making more money, and you wouldn't have to deal with Ms. Kimbler."

Amy stared at him. "You mean, you aren't firing me?"

"I'm asking if you can relocate to Seattle. It's either that or yes, I'll have to dismiss you. After what just happened, I can't very well allow you to stay on here." He glanced at an open file folder on his desk. "It says here you're divorced . . . no children . . . next of kin is a mother in Chicago. Is there any reason why you'd be unwilling to move to Seattle?"

Amy shrugged. "I don't know. This is all so sudden . . ." She still couldn't believe he hadn't fired her. "Do I have to give you an answer now?"

"Tomorrow's Saturday. Were you working this weekend?"

"Yes, on Sunday."

"Not anymore. You can clear out anything that's yours downstairs. As of now, you're no longer working at this store. Call me Monday and let me know if you want the Seattle job."

With uncertainty, Amy nodded and got to her feet. "Well . . . thank you, Mr. Ballentine . . ."

"By the way," he said. "If you should run into Ms. Kimbler between here and the exit door, I'll thank you not to say anything to her."

"All right," Amy said. She winced a little. "But you

know, if I take that Seattle job, Tiffany's bound to find out eventually anyway, won't she?"

"Oh, I already told her, and she was livid. I just don't want you giving her another speech. See, you showed remarkably good judgment in helping that customer find her mirror. I told Tiffany so, too. But that little speech you made did you in, remarkably bad judgment on your part. That's why you're the one who has to relocate or lose her job. Between you and me, I'm sorry it wasn't the other way around."

Amy dared to crack a smile. "You mean you . . . ?"

He nodded. "I can't stand that woman either. Now, go on. I want your decision on Monday morning. In the meantime, you can sleep on it."

Amy couldn't sleep. The clock on her nightstand said 2:20. "Shit," she grumbled, climbing out of bed. She put on her plaid flannel robe, padded down the hall to the kitchen and poured a glass of wine. From the bottom drawer of her antique desk in the living room she pulled out a stack of postcards. Amy curled up on the couch with her glass of wine and read them again. She lingered over the most recent one:

9/1/81

Fell down in the park playground and cut his chin this morning. 4 stitches, but the doctor says it won't show much. Didn't cry at all at the doctor's office. A very good boy. Energetic, bright. Can hardly wait to show off the bandage to his friends. 49 lbs.; 3'8".

That was the last, almost two years ago. She wondered if the stitches had left Eddie with a scar. On the street and in the store, she found herself staring at blond-haired boys, and each time, she'd look for a mark on his chin.

When Ballentine had asked if there was any reason why she couldn't move to Seattle, she'd thought about Eddie and these postcards. If she left Portland, her son's keeper would never be able to reach her; she couldn't hope to get Eddie back.

Yet in recent months, she'd given up even hoping for another card about him. Only on her really dismal days at work did Amy dare wish for some comforting news about Ed when she returned home. Even then, she knew she was stringing herself along.

Today, she'd found herself doing it again. She'd put off her zoo date with Joe D'Angelo until tomorrow, then spent the day scouting want ads and inquiring at stores. No jobs. Nothing. Even if there were something, it couldn't have compared to the Seattle job: management position; a salary increase; the employee discount. Yet by the end of the afternoon, she was picking up an application at her old Safeway. She'd prayed for a new postcard in her mailbox—something to make her staying in Portland seem worthwhile. But she was no closer to finding Ed than she had been five years ago.

In fact, she was farther away. The first couple of years, her son's keeper had sent several postcards. But he seemed to have forgotten her. Ed should have started kindergarten by now. All the little landmarks in his life that she was missing: his learning to read and tie his shoes, riding a two-wheel bike; losing his front teeth and growing new ones; his first report card. Why hadn't there been a note about these things? For all she knew, this postcard about the stitches would be the last she'd ever get.

Amy turned over the card and glanced at the post-mark: *SEPT 2 81, SEATTLE, WA.* She needed more than that before she'd move to Seattle. The other cards were postmarked from all over the Pacific Northwest.

Paul had thrown away the first, and given the second to the police. Amy had noted their unspectacular conclusion from the handwriting analysis: the writer was a male in his forties. The notes told Amy a bit more about this man who had taken her son.

Except for her baby, this guy lived alone. He probably didn't have any family, close friends, or love interest. If he was close to anyone, he wouldn't need to write to her about all these events in her baby's life. This guy was a loner.

12/2/78
Said his first word today—"dog." Had a cold
last week, but very healthy now. 27 lbs., 31
inches.

He was educated, maybe even a college graduate. The quotes around the word "dog," and his correct grammar and spelling in all the cards were an indication that he wasn't some illiterate slimeball with about eight teeth missing. The guy was smart.

For a while, she'd imagined that he was a widower, living on a farm somewhere. But the next postcard helped her realize that Ed was in a major city, or at least close to one:

8/20/79

A very smart boy. At the zoo today, he pointed to a young giraffe, and said, "Look at the baby giraffe!" Not walking yet, but can stand up if there's something to grab onto. 32 lbs., 32 inches.

"At the zoo today," he wrote. The tone implied— she hoped, unintentionally—that zoo trips were a pretty regular thing for him and her little boy. The card about him cutting his chin in the *park playground* seemed to corroborate her theory that this man was an urban dweller, close to parks and zoos.

Then again, what if these postcards were full of lies?

No, she had to believe that the man who took her son had a spark of decency, that he wasn't abusing Eddie in any way. She had to believe, or she wouldn't have been able to bear it.

Amy got to her feet and put the postcards back in her desk. She frowned at the Safeway application, there on the desktop. She'd fill it out tomorrow, before her date with Joe. "You can't leave Portland," she muttered to herself as she plodded back to bed. "Not until you have a better idea of where he is."

That Halloween nearly five years ago, they'd forced her to go home from the bank. She kept thinking that Eddie would be returned to the place she'd lost him, and she didn't want to leave. She felt the same way about Portland. She couldn't move.

* * *

Joe was a nice guy. He'd kissed her good-night the last time they'd been together. She didn't know what to expect with him once this afternoon's zoo trip was finished—maybe dinner, maybe even sex. They walked through the monkey house. Joe wore a pink Polo sport shirt that complemented his olive complexion. He held Amy's hand and talked about his job with a consulting firm. Amy pretended to listen. She was still thinking about her own job, and Seattle.

When they came out of the monkey house, she saw the giraffes in their wildlife setting. Amy stopped dead. Joe kept walking a couple of feet before realizing he was alone.

Like a mesmerized, wide-eyed child, Amy stared at the giraffes on the other side of the moat. *"At the zoo today, he pointed to a young giraffe, and said, 'Look at the baby giraffe!' "*

Joe D'Angelo didn't understand Amy's urgent need to visit the zoo's administrative office. Behind the counter, the white-haired woman with a hearing aid wasn't very understanding either. She'd merely stopped by the office for an hour that Sunday; but for the anxious, teary-eyed young woman, she looked back into their records for 1978 and 1979. "We only had one giraffe that summer, a full-grown male." She read from a folder, which she'd set on the counter. "But I have a clipping someone stuck in here from the *Seattle Times,* dated May 3, 1979. *'Seattle's Woodland Park Zoo announces the arrival of a healthy baby giraffe, Toby, born Sunday evening . . .'* Is that what you're looking for?"

Amy nodded. "Yes. Thank you."

"I'd offer to make you a copy," the lady said. "But the Xerox is broken."

"It's all right," Amy murmured. "You've been more help than you'll ever know. Thank you very much."

Joe nudged her. "I don't get it. What does all this mean?"

"It means I'm moving to Seattle."

"Seattle? Really?" He sounded disappointed. "Why?"

"Job offer—too good to resist."

"Do you know anyone in Seattle?"

"I might," Amy said. "I just might. . . ."

CHAPTER TWELVE

The Mariners led by two runs in the last inning. Carl had gotten excellent seats—above the third base bullpen in the Kingdome. In addition to ticket costs, he'd shelled out a small fortune on popcorn, hot dogs, and soda pop for Sam and his two friends. No special occasion—just another Saturday Carl was spending with his son—now eleven years old. He prided himself as one of those fathers who made time for his son's friends, too. Though he wasn't exactly crazy over Sam's choice of buddies.

Sitting beside him was Craig, a painfully skinny boy with glasses and adolescence in bloom all over his face. He was very smart and polite, but Carl figured poor Craig was something of an outcast at school; and he wondered if Sam was considered a loser too—since he and Craig were best friends. Carl couldn't help wishing that Sam made friends with kids more athletic and—well, normal-looking. But the only other boy who sometimes hung around with Sam was Earl Gleason, a squinty-eyed, future juvenile delinquent. He was short and wiry, with straight black hair and the snake-

like charm of Eddie Haskell. The evening Carl had
come home from work to find the apartment smelling
of cigarette smoke—and an unflushed butt floating in
the toilet—had been after Earl Gleason had come over
to play. Although Sam was catching on that Earl got
him into more trouble than he was worth, he hadn't
quite shaken him off yet. During the eighth inning,
Carl had overheard Earl whisper to Sam: "Check out
the lady with the big tits in the pink dress behind us.
She's got her legs apart. I thought I saw beaver."

Seated between the young nerd and the preteen
hood was Sam. His little boy, angelic beauty had been
replaced by an awkward handsomeness. He had a
solid, athletic build, and his hair was curly and dark
gold. He tried to comb it straight, but it was full of
cowlicks and bumps. He had better success—thanks to
nightly applications of Clearasil—keeping his complexion smooth. His eyes already seemed to belong to
an adult—so beautiful and serious, an enchanting blue-
green color, thick-lashed, under dark heavy brows that
nearly—but not quite—grew together. He'd be a real
heartbreaker when the rest of him caught up with those
eyes. But then, Carl wasn't very anxious for that to
happen. Sam was growing up fast enough already.

He wasn't watching the game. His head was turned
ever so casually as he tried to peek up the dress of the
woman behind him. Carl reached across Craig's lap
and tapped Sam on the knee. "Cut that out," he whispered. "It's rude, Sam."

"Sorry, Dad," he mumbled, once again focusing his
attention on the game.

He was a good kid. Oh, sure, sometimes it was like
pulling teeth getting him to empty the garbage or clean

his room. A week before, he'd thrown a fit when Carl refused to let him go see *Fatal Attraction*. But Sam always kissed him hello when Carl got back from work, and again at night before going to bed. He was smart enough most of the time not to fall under Earl's influence, and sincere enough to remain friends with an obviously unpopular, nice boy like Craig. There were times while Carl was washing the dinner dishes that—for no apparent reason—Sam would come up behind him, slide his arms around his waist and say: "I love you, Dad."

Yet Carl never stopped worrying about him. Even those sweet hugs raised some concern. Was Sam too affectionate for his age? Overly protected? Left alone in the apartment too much? Was the absence of a mother going to warp him? Did he need more time with just his friends? Did he even have any other friends besides these two?

Carl glanced over at Craig, who was blowing his nose on a long string of toilet paper that came from his pants pocket like an umbilical cord. "You're so lucky to have a dad who does stuff with you," Craig said to Sam. He shoved the toilet paper back in his pocket. "Mine never takes me anyplace."

Sam was watching the game. "Yeah. He's okay, I guess," he replied, yawning.

Carl almost dropped his beer. He was kissing off close to sixty bucks so Sam and his friends could have a fun afternoon. And that was all Sam had to say on his behalf? Of course, what did he expect him to say? *"Oh, I'm the luckiest kid alive! I love my dad."* Sam had to act cool in front of his friends.

They dropped off Earl first. The words "thank you"

weren't in his vocabulary. He just got out of the car and slammed the door, then ran into his house.

"Oh-oh!" Sam said lightly. "Earl didn't thank Dad again. We're gonna hear about it all the way to your house, Craig."

"Would it kill him just to say two simple words?" Carl asked, stepping on the gas. "Why do you hang around with that kid anyway?"

"He hasn't got any other friends but us," Sam said.

"Small wonder."

"Listen, Dad. Is it okay if I spend the night at Craig's?"

"Tonight?"

"It's okay with my folks," Craig piped in from the backseat. "I asked this morning. Sam's invited to dinner, too."

Carl hesitated. He stared at the road ahead. "Why don't I drop you first, Craig? Then Sam will call and let you know."

"Why can't I?' Sam asked.

"I didn't say you couldn't. We'll discuss it later."

"What's to discuss?"

"The key word here is 'later,' Sammy. We'll talk about it, okay?" He glanced at Craig in the rearview mirror. "We might have other plans, Craig. Sam will call you."

"Okay, Mr. Jorgenson."

Craig thanked him—as always—when Carl let him off in front of his house. Then Sam slouched lower in the front seat, his arms folded. The breeze through the open window whipped his golden hair into a disarray. "So why can't I spend the night at Craig's?" he asked. "You mad 'cuz of Earl? He won't be there. . . ."

"I'm not mad," Carl said. "I just want to get our

schedules in order. I mean, you and I had plans to go to the beach tomorrow—early, before the crowds get there. Remember?"

"That's no problem," Sam said. "I can go with Craig. His mom won't mind driving us. Is that all?"

Carl said nothing for a moment. He tried to smile. "Listen, why not invite Craig to spend the night at our place? Then I'll take you guys to the beach." He glanced over at Sam, who was frowning. "What's wrong? On the beach, I'll go sit somewhere else—if it's uncool to be seen there with your dad. You know, you've slept over at Craig's at least a dozen times, and we've yet to reciprocate."

"To *what*?"

"Invite him over to our place for the night."

"Oh."

"*'Oh.'* Well, how about it? Don't you think it's time we had him at *our* place for an overnight?"

"But there's nothing to *do* at our place," Sam groaned.

"And what's Craig's house? Disneyland?"

"Well, at least they got a backyard, *and* a tree house, *and* a basement rec room, *and* a VCR, *and* a dog . . ."

"Sam, for the umpteenth time, we cannot have a dog. They don't allow pets in our building."

"Well, it's no fun living in a stupid apartment. Everybody else lives in houses."

Carl couldn't blame him for wanting to be like other kids. Sam had been out of after-school day care for two years. Since then, he'd been returning from school every day to an empty apartment, where TV was his only diversion. No wonder he wanted a VCR. How many "Partridge Family" reruns could a kid take? If not for day camp and Little League during the summer, Sam would have gone crazy cooped up in the apartment all day. He really seemed to enjoy spending the night at Craig's house—as if it were some kind of liberty leave.

But for Carl, those nights without Sam were dull, lonely, and long. He often told himself he should take advantage of the time alone—go to a movie, or perhaps even a bar, where he could meet someone. Hell, with Sam gone, he was free to take a girl home. He was free to spend the entire night with her.

Yet those nights of "freedom" were spent alone, belting back a few too many bourbon and waters and eating leftovers in front of the TV. Then he, too, would wish for a VCR, a dog, a house, and a yard. He knew what it must be like for Sam, alone in the apartment so much.

"Listen," he said. "It's okay for tonight, sport. But next time, let's have Craig over. We owe him."

"Hot damn! Great! Thanks, Dad."

That night alone, Carl bought an early Sunday paper and went through the real estate section. He started pricing houses in the area.

"You had a cost-of-living increase just four months ago, Carl. You're not due for another raise until next year."

He sat across from the desk of his boss, Glen Enright. They were the same age, forty-nine, but Enright seemed older—with his thick glasses, the sparse, Grecian Formula black hair, and the pompous way he smoked a pipe. He had a private office. After eight years as a claims adjuster, stuck in a cubicle, Carl felt overdue for the same kind of setup. Until now, he'd been reluctant to ask for a raise. He didn't want to come off as disgruntled about his job or salary—the squeaky wheel that gets replaced.

But he wanted to buy a house for Sam and himself —a place Sam could have his friends over and not feel ashamed, a home like normal families had. Fat chance on his current income. And he deserved more money. Hell, to replace him they'd need three people. Everyone in the department came to him for help. Good old Glen was just a figurehead, who spent most of his time bullshitting, playing computer games on his desktop terminal, and taking every business trip he could—so long as it included a day of executive golf. Things at the office went very smoothly in his absence. But when Carl was out sick, the place went to pot. They needed him. Didn't Enright realize how valuable he was?

"Well, I was thinking about a raise based on my performance, Glen," Carl said. "I've worked very hard—"

"Yes, yes, of course, Carl." Enright lit his pipe and waved out the match. The sickeningly sweet aroma filled the room. He was studying some papers on his desk. "I've got your record here," he said. "I didn't know this, but you missed a whole week while I was on vacation last month."

Carl nodded. "My boy was sick. German measles."

"You couldn't get a sitter?"

"Well, my usual sitter is my landlady, Mrs. Kern. But she fell down and broke her hip last July. I'm afraid she's getting up in years . . ." *Besides, asshole,* Carl thought, *you have kids, don't you know how serious German measles can be?*

Enright puffed on his pipe and nodded impatiently.

"I see here that you've used up most of your sick leave, Carl. You've left early quite a bit, too."

"Yes, I know," Carl replied quietly. Could he help it if Sam got sick a lot? Enright had written on his last employee evaluation form: *"Carl Jorgenson is very capable. He carries out his duties efficiently and writes excellent reports. However, his frequent absences and an unwillingness to take out-of-town trips makes him less than dependable for a management position."*

"That week I missed," Carl said. "I caught up on all the work by the middle of the following week. I did it at home."

Through the curtain of smoke, Enright nodded. "Yes, well, these sick days and early quits, they don't *look* good, Carl."

Carl said nothing. He glanced at the framed fake *Golf Digest* cover on the credenza behind Enright's desk. A grinning Enright was on the cover, with "GOLFER OF THE YEAR," across his Munsingwear shirt.

Enright put down his pipe, and gave him a phony, concerned-big-brother look. "Are you happy here at Allstate, Carl?"

"Why, yes, I'm very happy. I like working here." Carl squirmed in the chair. He wondered if everyone who asked for a raise had to go through this grilling. He wished Enright would simply say "no," instead of questioning his dedication to the company. If he didn't have Sam to support, he'd have said "Fuck you very much," and walked. But Carl managed to smile at Enright. "Listen," he said. "About the raise. I was just asking on account of I'm thinking of buying a house. I understand if it's a problem. Just thought I'd ask." He stood up.

"Well, I'm afraid it's not in the budget right now, Carl."

When he returned to his cubicle, Carl flopped down at his desk and yanked open the bottom drawer. He took out a folder, which the real estate lady had given him, and he dumped it in the wastebasket. The telephone rang.

"Claims," he said into the receiver. "This is Carl Jorgenson." He slumped back in his chair.

"Mr. Jorgenson?" It was a woman's voice.

"Yes, this is Carl Jorgenson. Can I help you?"

"Mr. Jorgenson, I'm Margo Hopper, Sam's sixth grade homeroom teacher—"

Carl sat up. "What's wrong? Is he sick?"

"Well, he had a little fainting spell after recess. He seems all right now, but I thought you might want to come take him home—just to be on the safe side."

"He *fainted*? Did he hurt himself?"

"He bumped his head on the floor a little. We've got him resting in the nurse's office. As I said, he seems fine now—"

"I'll be right there," Carl said.

He passed Enright's office on his way to the elevator. It didn't occur to him until he'd pressed the "down" button for the fifth time that he should tell his boss he needed the rest of the afternoon off. He was too frazzled to care what Enright thought as he ran back and poked his head past the office door. "I'm sorry," he said, out of breath. "There's an emergency at my son's school. I may be gone the rest of the day. I'm sorry."

Enright gave Carl the sickly smile of someone who didn't especially like being proved right. "Go ahead, Carl," he said.

"I feel fine, Dad. Honest," Sam said. He sat on a cot in the nurse's office, squirming as Carl felt his forehead.

"I took his temperature," the nurse offered. She was an emaciated old blonde who wore Keds sneakers with her nurse uniform. "It's normal," she said.

Carl examined the red mark above Sam's right eye.

"He's going to have a goose egg tonight," the nurse said. "We put some ice on it earlier."

Carl took the discarded ice bag from the foot of the cot and gave it to Sam. "Here, keep that on your head. Lie back. You look pale. You feel sick to your stomach?"

Sam sighed. "I feel fine. Jeez, Dad . . ."

"Oh, stop fussing," Carl whispered. "There's no one here to see. You have nothing to be embarrassed about."

"No? I only passed out in front of the whole class. I wish I was dead."

Carl turned to the nurse. "Excuse me, where can I find his teacher? She's the one who called me."

"Ms. Hopper? She's in 602, down the hall on your left."

Carl found Room 602, and knocked on the windowed door. The teacher was a busty, plump brunette in her late thirties. She wore a stylish navy blue dress and big, white earrings. She had a kind face. She looked over at Carl, said something to her students, then came to the door. "Yes?" she whispered to Carl.

"Hi, I'm Sam's father—"

"Oh, Mr. Jorgenson . . ." She peeked back in the classroom. "Earl Gleason, I swear I'm going to beat the tar out of you if you don't get back in your seat this instant! Not a peep out of anyone!" She stepped out to the hallway and closed the door. "Sorry. I'm Margo Hopper. Sam's in the nurse's office . . ."

"Yes, I know. I saw him. Can you tell me what happened?"

"Well, um, the children were coming in from recess, taking their seats. And I noticed Sam stagger a little as he started toward his desk. Then all of a sudden, he just keeled over. Scared the—lunch out of me. Luckily, he didn't hit himself against one of the desks, but he bumped his head on the floor. . . ."

"Yes, I saw," Carl said.

"I got one of the boys to help me carry him to the nurse's office, and he came to on the way. He seemed fine by the time I called you. In fact, he kept saying he wanted to go back to class. But I thought you should be notified."

"Oh, I'm glad you called," Carl said. "Thank you."

"Threw me for a loop. Has he ever fainted like that before?"

"No, never . . ." Beyond the window, he noticed Craig, in the third row staring back, a worried look on his acne-ridden face.

"Well, maybe he just overexerted himself at recess," Ms. Hopper said. "That can happen. Did you want to take Sam home?"

Carl nodded. "After a visit to our doctor, yes."

"I hope he's all right. Last time a student fainted on

me, I was teaching junior high. It was an eighth grade girl. Turned out she was pregnant."

Carl grinned. "Well, I don't think that's Sam's problem."

She shook her head. "No. Ha, what a stupid thing to say. Dumb. Anyway, nice to have met you." She extended her hand.

Carl shook it. "Thanks, Ms. Hopper."

"Margo," she said, blushing a little. "You know, Sam's my favorite student. See you in a couple of weeks, Mr. Jorgenson."

"A couple of weeks?"

She smiled. "Parent-teacher conferences on the twenty-second. 'Bye now." She ducked back into the classroom.

Dr. Durkee, the Humming M.D., had agreed with Margo Hopper's diagnosis. "He seems all right. Have him take it easy tonight. Unless he has any problems like nausea or headaches, I see no reason why he shouldn't go to school tomorrow—so long as he doesn't try to run the decathlon during recess. . . ."

But Carl wasn't taking any chances. He insisted that Sam spend the rest of the day in bed. At the moment, however, Sam was sitting at the foot of his father's bed and talking on the phone to Craig: "I know, my dad saw you, too. He said you looked worried . . ."

He watched his dad struggle to reach the portable television's plug, which was stuck in an outlet behind the big dresser. After much grunting, Carl finally got the TV unplugged.

"Anyway, I'm fine, except I got a bump on my forehead that looks like a humongous zit . . . Yeah, we just got back. He says I can go to school tomorrow. So— was everybody talking about it?"

Carl carried the TV into Sam's bedroom. He could barely hear him talking now, because Sam's voice dropped to a whisper. He set the portable TV on the desk, then plugged it in.

The bedroom walls were covered with movie posters: *Top Gun, Raiders of the Lost Ark,* and *Aliens*; and there was a Christie Brinkley calendar; a University of Washington pennant; a stop sign someone had knocked down; and several grisly looking pictures of movie creatures clipped from some sci-fi magazine.

Carl turned down the bedsheets. He heard Sam say good-bye to Craig, then, after a moment, he plodded into the room. "We've gotta move to another town, so I can go to a school where no one knows me," he announced, unbuttoning his shirt.

"So you're the news of the day, huh?" Carl said.

"You kidding? This is worse than when Cindy Levenson barfed in the middle of fourth grade math class. That was two years ago, and people are still talking about it. I'll never live this down." He kicked off his shoes. "Craig said that Earl was making fag jokes about me for fainting like that."

"I can't believe you still consider that little weasel a friend," Carl said, swiping a discarded sweatshirt off the floor. "Last week, he tries to cheat off you during a test, and today he's calling you a. . . ."

"Fag," Sam said, frowning.

"I don't like you using that word, Sammy."

"He said it, not me." Sam climbed out of his pants, then crawled into bed. "Y'know, Dad, I really feel fine. Do I gotta stay in bed tonight?"

"Doctor's orders," Carl said, folding up the sweat-shirt.

"I was there, remember? I should take it easy, he said."

"So humor me." Carl put the sweatshirt away, then moved over to the TV. "What channel do you want?"

"Five, I guess." Sam sighed and tugged the bed-sheets. "God, I can't face them at school tomorrow. Earl making jokes, everybody laughing at me. What am I gonna do, Dad?"

Carl sat on the edge of the bed. "Well, make jokes about it yourself. Act like you think it was really funny. Get them laughing with you instead of at you."

Sam rolled his eyes, then looked away.

"Okay," Carl said. "You sit next to Earl, right?"

"Yeah . . ."

"So when he starts in with the jokes, tell him—tell him—don't know—that his BO made you pass out."

"Ha! That ought to shut him up!"

"Well, don't start unless he provokes you," Carl said soberly. "And save it for the playground. I don't want you disrupting class or getting into a fight over this. Promise me."

"I won't pick a fight, Dad," he said, a grin tugging at the corners of his mouth.

"I mean it, kiddo."

"I promise," Sam said, more seriously.

Leaning over, Carl kissed him on the forehead. "I'll bring dinner to you in an hour."

In the kitchen, Carl pulled some chicken out of the freezer and set it under the faucet. Then he fixed himself a much needed drink.

Sam considered the school cafeteria's fish sticks a total grossout, so he'd brought his lunch today. While most other brownbaggers settled for their mothers' bland sandwiches, Sam would feast on hot macaroni and cheese, SpaghettiOs, or corned beef hash that his father cooked and spooned into his thermos. Today, the thermos held a hot dog, which Sam plucked out of the steaming water. He set it on a bun, then squeezed out a McDonald's packet of mustard.

"Trade ya?" Craig asked, holding up his peanut butter and jelly sandwich. The jelly had bled through the white bread.

"Know the meaning of 'fat chance'?" Sam replied. He opened a small bag of potato chips, then set his orange in front of him. "Y'know, I can't believe nobody's said anything about yesterday."

But then, almost as if on cue, Earl Gleason plopped his tray directly across from Sam. "So, Jorgenson," he announced loudly. All the kids seated at the long table looked up at him. "Why'd you faint yesterday? You pregnant?"

A couple of guys laughed. Sam tried to laugh, too.

"Maybe you got your period," Earl said, snickering. He sat down and munched on a fish stick. Everyone was staring.

"Shut up, Earl," Craig mumbled. He sipped his milk through a straw.

"Maybe your panty hose were too tight," Earl went on.

"It's because YOU FARTED!" Sam shot back. "I PASSED OUT BECAUSE ONE OF YOUR ROTTEN-EGG FARTS POLLUTED THE ATMOSPHERE, EARL!"

Craig lurched forward, coughing. Milk dripped out of his nose and mouth as he laughed hysterically.

Sam glanced down at the other guys seated at the table. They were laughing too—not at him, not with him, but at Earl.

"I did not fart yesterday," Earl grumbled, his eyes narrowed at Sam.

"Oh, God, you didn't?" Sam cried. "THEN WE'RE IN FOR A BIG, MEAN ONE ANY SECOND NOW! WOMEN AND CHILDREN FIRST!"

Sam heard someone howl, and the table shook. But he kept his eyes fixed on Earl, whose face had turned blush red. "Real funny, Jorgenson," he whispered. "So shut up already."

"I'll shut up if you shut up," Sam replied in a low voice.

Earl just nodded, then bit into a fish stick. For the rest of the day, Earl didn't say another word about Sam's fainting spell. Nor did anyone else. But a few jokes circulated regarding Earl Gleason's lethal, rotten-egg farts. Sam could hardly wait to tell his dad all about it tonight.

"I gather from Sam's perfect attendance these last two weeks that there haven't been any more fainting spells."

Margo Hopper wore a crisp, ivory-colored blouse and sat with her hands folded on the desktop. Carl, seated across from her in one of two hard, wooden chairs, noticed she wore no wedding ring. He'd thought about Margo Hopper a lot since their meeting two weeks before. He had a feeling she liked him. And he was attracted to her, which was something new. He usually went for cool, svelte, long-haired beauties. Margo Hopper didn't fit that mold at all: Botticelli plump, and pale, with straight, close-cropped black hair. She didn't exactly light a fire in his loins, but she was a woman he could easily love—intelligent, warm, and obviously good with kids. He wondered when those attributes had replaced passion in his want for a companion.

"So—Sam's all right, isn't he?" she asked.

"Oh, he's great," Carl said. "I want to thank you for taking care of him that day, Ms. Hopper."

"Margo," she said.

He nodded. "Margo . . ."

"You know, I've been a teacher for almost twenty years." She let out a wry laugh. "Whew! Makes me feel ancient to hear myself say that. Anyway, I always end up with a favorite student every year. This year, it's your Sam."

Carl couldn't contain a proud smile. "That's music to my ears," he said. "I had my favorites too—back when I was coaching grammar school."

"A fellow teacher? My God. Where did you coach?"

"Oh, not around here. In Portland." Carl immediately regretted letting that slip out. Santa Rosa was supposed to be the only place he'd lived before Seattle. "It was a long time ago," he said. "But I know what you mean about having favorites."

She leaned forward. "And isn't it usually the one

who puts you to the test? The one without any friends—
or he disrupts class, because he's starved for love and
attention. I'm such a sucker for hard luck cases.'"

Carl cleared his throat. "Well, I hope Sam isn't a
'hard luck case.'"

"Oh, no, no. On the contrary. Sam's unique in my
Favorite Students' Hall of Fame. He's a good student,
well behaved. His homework's always in on time.
He's very conscientious. . . ."

Carl nodded and kept waiting for her to name the
flaw that made Sam her favorite.

"He's very mature for his age," she continued.
"Like a little adult."

"Are you saying that he doesn't fit in with the other
kids?"

"No, he seems to fit in fine." She laughed. "Listen,
will you forget what I said about hard luck cases? You
don't have to worry about Sam, Mr. Jorgenson. He's a
fine boy."

Carl laughed a little, too. "I'm sorry. These conferences scare the hell out of me. I'm always afraid I'll
hear the worst—some big surprise like he's a bully, or
he's being bullied, or he's friendless, or he hasn't
shown up for school in over a month." Carl nodded to
the empty chair beside him. "And there's no one else
here to share the blame with me."

"Well. Sam's a wonderful boy. So I'd say that you
deserve all the *credit,* Mr. Jorgenson."

He smiled. "Carl."

She nodded. "Carl." Margo picked up a pencil and
tapped it against her desk. "No, what makes Sam stand
out from the others is—Well, don't take this the wrong

way. But I know you're a widower, and it's just you and Sam at home. Forgive me for speaking so candidly."

"No, it's okay, really."

"See, I'm divorced and I have two teenage daughters of my own. I couldn't love them more. But I always wanted a son. I've got a soft spot for little boys. Sam's a very handsome and sweet kid. How could I resist him?" She shrugged and started to gather up some papers on her desk. "Anyway, there's not much else to tell you. Sam's a trifle weak in math and science, but I wouldn't lose any sleep over it. He really excels in history and English—especially creative writing. Has quite an imagination. Last week, I had the class write a short story about a boy and girl who find something in the woods. The students had to determine what it was. Well, about ten kids had them discover a chest full of money; a couple more came up with a space ship; one had Bigfoot. But Sam had them find a classmate's decomposing body. It was very gruesome, and for the next eight pages—three more than the required length, mind you—he had the boy and girl stalked by some homicidal maniac."

Carl nodded. "Sam's a bit preoccupied with horror movies."

"Well, he read it to the class, and they ate it up. I think you have a budding Stephen King on your hands. He's a very talented young man." She took a deep breath. "Anyway, that's about it."

Carl glanced at the clock above the blackboard. "Do you have any more parents waiting to see you?"

"Nope. Saved the best for last. I enjoyed talking with

you, Mr. Jorgenson." She caught herself and smiled. "I mean, *Carl.*"

He stood up. "Listen, would you like to go out for a cup of coffee or something?"

She stuffed her papers in a briefcase, but hesitated before closing it. "You mean now?"

He nodded. "I just thought—"

"Oh, no. I mean, I'd enjoy that. But I have a stack of English compositions to grade tonight." she shut her briefcase. "Any other night, I'd jump at the chance."

"It's all right," Carl said, a little disappointed.

"Would you mind walking me to my car?" she asked. "The parking lot's very dark. . . ."

"Not at all. Here"—he reached for her briefcase—"let me take that."

Margo smiled shyly. "Now I know where Sam gets his good manners—and his good looks." She flicked off the overhead lights in the classroom. They walked down the dark, empty corridor together. "I've a confession," she said. "I scheduled you for last so we'd have some more time to talk. I'm just sorry I have all this work tonight; otherwise, I'd take you up on your offer."

"Maybe some other night?" Carl asked, as they stepped outside. "Or are you already seeing somebody or something?"

"Oh, I'm not seeing anybody," she said, glancing down at the pavement. "The cupboard is disgustingly bare." She rubbed her arms from the chilly night's breeze.

"So what do you think?" Carl said. "Could I see you again?"

"You mean, like a date?"

Carl shrugged. "Yes . . ."

Margo laughed. "I'm sorry. God, what a klutz. It's been so long since . . . Forgive me." She opened her purse and dug out the keys. "This is me, the blue Volvo."

"It's been a long time since I've had a date, too—if that's what you were going to say. I'm afraid I've lost my touch."

"No, you haven't," Margo said. She smiled, then unlocked her car door. "I'm deeply flattered—and tempted. But I can't help thinking that it would go over like a pregnant pole-vaulter with Sam—I mean, you dating his teacher."

Carl handed her the briefcase. "Well, if it isn't a problem with Sam, would you have any objections to seeing me again? I understand if the answer's 'no.'"

"Are you kidding? This is the best offer I've had in over a year," She threw her briefcase inside the car, then climbed behind the wheel and rolled down her window. "Talk to Sam and call me with the verdict. I'm in the book. Margo Hopper on East Kirkland Place. Okay?"

Carl smiled. "Okay."

"I think you're pretty terrific, Carl," she said. Then Margo rolled up the window, started the car, and drove away.

"Oh, God, gross! You gotta be kidding, Dad. Please, tell me you're kidding. . . ."

Carl set the last of the dinner dishes aside to dry, then he turned off the water at the kitchen sink. "I don't understand," he said. "You like her, don't you?"

"But she's my *teacher*! She's not even that pretty . . ."

"I think she's nice," Carl said, drying his hands.

"I can't believe this," Sam moaned. He sat on the countertop. "Why Ms. Hopper?"

"Because I enjoyed talking to her tonight. And she likes you very much. I just want to take her out to dinner. I'm not planning to marry her, for God's sakes. Would it kill you to see your old man have a friend—maybe a girlfriend?"

Sam stuck his finger in his mouth and mimicked throwing up.

"Funny," Carl grunted, tossing the dish towel in Sam's lap.

"You aren't really going to ask her out, are you?" He climbed off the counter. "I mean, God, what if the guys at school found out? My father, Ms. Hopper's boyfriend. Everyone will think I'm a total geek. C'mon, Dad, anybody but her . . ."

Carl didn't look at him as he reached into the cabinet for the bourbon. "That's for me to decide," he said.

"What does that mean exactly?"

"It means I can go out with whomever I want, and I don't need any lip from you, thanks." He dropped some ice into his glass. "Ms. Hopper said you're not doing so hot in science and math. You better go study, kiddo. You don't want to have to repeat any of those subjects with Ms. Hopper next year—not when you disapprove of her so much."

"I didn't say that, Dad. I just—"

"Go study, Sam." He sighed.

Frowning, Sam rolled his eyes. "Excuse me for living," he mumbled. Then he turned and walked toward his bedroom.

Carl sipped his bourbon and water. He left the bottle

on the counter, because he'd probably have another drink before the night was over.

Carl had stretched out on the sofa to watch TV after dinner, and the next thing he knew, Sam was shaking him. "C'mon, Dad. Wake up. You promised to help with this . . ."

"What is it? Can't it wait, sport?"

"No. I gotta hand this in day after tomorrow." He shook him again. "C'mon, Dad. You promised."

"Sammy, I'm tired. . . ."

"But it isn't even eight-thirty yet," Sam said. Carl saw him sneer at the half-emptied glass of bourbon on the coffee table. Sam clicked his tongue against his teeth.

"All right, all right," Carl grumbled. He sat up. "What do you need help with?"

"My autobiography for English class. It's got to be at least a thousand words, and include a family tree. I've only told you about it a million times, Dad. Geez." He sat down on the floor, set his spiral notebook on the coffee table, and took a Bic pen from behind his ear. "Jimmy Cadwell's family tree goes all the way back to his great-great-grandfather, who fought in the Civil War. . . ."

"Bully for Jimmy Cadwell," Carl said, rubbing his eyes. "I can't tell you stuff that far back, Sammy. I'm sorry."

"Well, all *I* got so far is: 'Father: Carl Jorgenson, born, 1939. Mother: Anne Brewster.' When was Mom born?"

Carl reached for his drink. Most of the ice had melted.

"Um, she was five years younger than me. Nineteen . . . forty . . ."

"Forty-four?"

"Right."

"Nineteen forty-four till nineteen seventy-seven. Right?"

Carl nodded and sipped his drink.

"I said you work for Allstate Insurance. What did Mom do?"

"What do you mean?"

"Like a job," Sam said. "Did she have a job?"

Carl shook his head. "She quit after we got married."

"Well, what did she do before that?"

He hadn't prepared himself for all these questions. He was too tired, and yes, perhaps he'd had too much to drink. The lies weren't coming easily. He remembered now that Sam had indeed mentioned several times about having to write his autobiography for Ms. Hopper's English class. *Margo Hopper.* It had been a month since the parent-teacher conference. He'd never called her. It had seemed stupid, phoning to say that Sam had vehemently objected to his dad dating his teacher.

"Dad?" Sam was raising his voice. "What was Mom's job?"

"She was a—teacher. Put down that she was a teacher."

"You don't sound too sure," he said.

"Of course I'm sure. She taught third grade—in Santa Rosa." Carl took another sip of his drink.

Sam jotted it down in his notebook. "What year did you guys get married?"

"Th-the year before you were born."

"Nineteen seventy-six?"

"Yeah, right, right. Seventy-six." Carl rubbed his forehead. "Sammy, can't this wait until morning? I'm bushed."

"Dad, it isn't even eight-thirty yet!" he wailed. "Want me to get an 'F' on this? C'mon!" He wrote something in his notebook. "You and Mom didn't have any brothers or sisters, right?"

"Right."

"What were Mom's parents' names?"

Carl hesitated. "Walter and Teresa."

"That's *your* parents. I want Mom's."

Carl drew a blank. He reached for his drink again.

"God, Dad. Can't you remember?"

"They were dead before I met her," he answered, exasperated. "I never knew them."

"How did they die?"

"Um, they were in a car accident."

"That's how *Mom* died, Dad. How did *they* die?"

"Old age. They were very old."

Sam dropped the notebook in his lap and stared up at him. "Dad, are you making all this up?"

"Of course not! I—I just . . ." Carl shook his head. "I'm just tired. Isn't there some other homework you can do tonight? I'll help you tomorrow, when I'm not so tired."

"Huh," Sam mumbled. "When you're not so drunk, you mean." He grabbed his notebook and got to his feet.

"What did you say?" Carl asked, suddenly alert and angry.

"Nothing. Go back to sleep." He stomped toward his bedroom.

But Carl reached over and grabbed his arm. "Wait a minute, young man . . ."

"Let go!" Sam yelled.

"Who do you think you're talking to?"

"Let go of me! You're drunk!"

Carl slapped him across the face. It was as if he couldn't stop himself, and he didn't realize what he'd done until he heard the smack. His hand stung. He saw the hatred and hurt in Sam's eyes. Sam rubbed his cheek. Carl waited for him to cry, because he wanted to hug him and say he was sorry. He wanted to erase the hurt—and that defiant look of contempt on his son's face. He reached out to him.

But Sam lurched back. He ran into his bedroom and slammed the door. He hadn't cried at all.

Sam ripped a picture off the bulletin board above his bed. The photo was of him and his father, taken on a ferry ride last summer. Sam remembered how embarrassed he'd been when his dad had stopped some total stranger on the deck, handed him the camera, and asked him to snap their picture. He was always doing weird stuff like that.

"Fuck you," Sam whispered to the smiling image of his father. He hated him so much right now. He spit on the picture—right on his father's face. The slap hadn't hurt very badly. But he wanted to hurt his father back for it.

Sam found a pencil compass in the top drawer of his

desk. He wiped the spit off the photo, then with the pointed end of the compass, he slashed a line across his father's face—from his hair down to his shirt collar. With another angry stroke, he made a jagged line across his eyes. He wondered if by some kind of voodoo, this would cause his father to go blind.

Frowning, Sam put down the compass. He wished he could run away. He'd tried that a few times when he was little, and his dad had always let him go without an argument. " 'Bye," he'd say. "Take care of yourself. Write now and then to let me know how you're doing." *What an asshole.* His father had seemed to know he'd crawl back after a couple of hours—or at least before dark. Running away wouldn't do any good now. It was already dark, and besides, his father was too drunk to even notice he'd gone.

He *did* drink too much. Oh, he wasn't a stumbling, loud drunk like the ones on TV; and he wasn't mean either. He'd never, ever hit him—until tonight. Usually, he'd just dump the dinner dishes in the sink to wash in the morning, then, drink in hand, he'd plod over to the sofa and conk out before the first commercial of whatever show was on TV. He wasn't that way all the time; but the thing was, he never used to be like that.

At least, he didn't get drunk in front of anyone else. All of Sam's friends thought he had a cool dad. But they didn't have to live with him. They didn't have to see him passed out, or listen to his stupid lectures: *"Why, if I talked to my old man the way you talk to me, he'd have knocked me across the room! You don't know how lucky you are . . ."* And blah, blah, blah. Yeah, he was a really neat dad, all right.

Sam picked up the compass again and put another

gash through his father's image. At that moment, he would have gladly traded parents with any kid in his class. Then at least he'd be like everybody else.

When Ms. Hopper had assigned them the autobiography, she suggested a lot of things everyone could write about—everyone but him. "I'm sure your parents have stories about the day you were born," she'd said. "You can write about your brothers and sisters. Maybe you have household pets, and you can include them in your autobiography. Stories about dogs and cats are always fun. A lot of you have moved from other cities—or from one house to another. You can write about that. Maybe you can remember a special day you spent with a grandparent or an aunt or uncle. A favorite Christmas or holiday you remember . . ."

Sam had glanced around the classroom at all the other kids, jotting notes. He couldn't think of a thing to write about.

They'd lived in the same, stupid apartment ever since he could remember. Every Christmas and holiday, it was just his father and him. No aunts or uncles or grandparents. No cats or dogs. No fun. And it was all his father's fault.

Sam absently drew another scratch through his father's picture, and he tried to remember what they did last Christmas. He'd gotten the electronic football game set that he wanted so badly. They spent all morning in their pajamas, assembling the pieces, then playing with the game. It was somewhere in the back of his closet now, half the pieces lost long ago. Everyone else probably had a lot more interesting Christmas.

He stared at the mangled photo of his father—the proud smile on his face. What had he given him last

Christmas? Soap on a Rope. And his dad had given him the money. Ten bucks. The soap only cost six. He should have gotten him something else, but he didn't. It was the only present his dad received last Christmas. And Sam had raked in about a dozen other gifts in addition to the football game.

Sam remembered how they won the father-son relay race at the school picnic last year. His father had lifted him up and carried him on his shoulders afterward. And Sam remembered he hadn't been embarrassed at all . . . back then.

Biting his lip, Sam found some Scotch tape in the desk, and tried to mend the picture best he could. But lightning bolt scratches still obscured his father's kind face. He felt awful.

There was a knock on his door. Sam stashed the ruined photo in his desk drawer, then turned around.

His father opened the door, but hesitated before coming inside. He was holding a cup of coffee. "I'm sorry I hit you, Sammy," he said.

Sam didn't say anything.

His father stepped toward him. "I didn't hurt you, did I?"

"I'll live," Sam murmured.

His father gave him an awkward smile. "About that family tree, I'll work on it at the office tomorrow. Okay?"

Sam shrugged, then looked away. "If you want . . ."

"I'm sorry I wasn't very much help, Sam. It's—difficult for me to talk about your mom. I still miss her. But I'm ready to help now. What is it you wanted to know?"

"Nothing," Sam mumbled. "It's okay. You're tired . . ."

"Not anymore. This is my second cup of coffee. I really want to help you with this autobiography. A lot of stuff has happened to you that I'm sure you don't remember. Interesting stuff, too . . ."

Sam frowned. "Like what?"

His father took a sip of coffee. "Well, did I ever tell you about the time when you were four, and you almost got kidnapped in Southcenter Shopping Mall?"

The adventure at Southcenter Mall took up two pages in Sam's seven-page autobiography, which he entitled—at his father's suggestion—"Sam, I Am." The facts were slightly overembellished by Sam's young imagination. His would-be abductress was now a *"6-foot, 2-inch blond lady with a Russian accent. She threatened to shoot me right there in the mall if I didn't go with her. She grabbed me. and I fought to escape . . ."*

He vividly described the scene: the horrified, screaming shoppers; his father's brave attempt to chase after the armed villainess, and the screeching tires of the big, black getaway car. *"The police never found the woman,"* Sam wrote. *"She is still at large."*

Sam's playground accident that resulted in four stitches to his chin also got a lot of coverage. He'd received ten stitches in his own telling, and he graphically recounted the bloodspilling—on his clothes, his father's clothes, the seat of the car, and in the doctor's office. Sam was careful to point out: *"I never cried the whole time. My father said I was very brave."*

Of the day he was born, Sam didn't add many details to his father's version:

On June 7, 1977, my mother and father went to see a movie. His name is Carl Jorgenson, and her name was Anne. They lived in Santa Rosa, California. The doctor said I was due to be born any day now. During the movie, my mother got pregnant and went into labor and my father took her to the hospital. It was on the other side of town and traffic was very bad and they thought I might be born in the car. Luckily, they reached the hospital in time. I was born there at 9:30. My father gave out cigars to everyone, even the nurses! They named me Sam after nobody.

Having a parent who had died made Sam rather unique in his sixth grade class. But he did not dwell on it—probably because his mother's death was one thing that seemed to have happened outside his lifetime. The framed photograph above the couch—of a pretty, blond bride with his father—was the only evidence that she ever existed. Even then, he didn't feel much attachment to that woman in the picture.

When I was five months old, my mother got killed in a car accident. She was killed instantly. She was thirty-three years old. I don't remember her at all. She is berried [sicl in Santa Rosa. I have not seen her grave. But my father says there is an angel on her tombstone.

CHAPTER THIRTEEN

"**W**ow," Amy murmured. She closed the register drawer. It was impossible not to gawk at him. He stood over at the counter in Bedwares, weighed down by two large shopping bags. He was gorgeous; tall, with wavy brown hair and beautiful eyes that seemed to dazzle even in the distance between them. He smiled at her. Automatically, she turned away, and feigned interest in some charge forms on the register counter.

One of her saleswomen, Veronica, slid up beside her. "Hunk alert," she whispered. "Catch the three-piece suit over in Beds."

"Yes, ma'am, I'm catching him," Amy mumbled, peeking at the handsome stranger. He was talking to Lila, the sixtyish saleslady in the Bedding department. He seemed to be charming the ruffled panties off her. She was all smiles and giggles

"Any eye contact yet?" Veronica asked.

"A little."

Veronica put on her glasses to get a better look at him. The glasses were new, and Veronica, who had just turned forty, didn't like needing—or wearing—them. But she looked cute with them on. Veronica had frosted blond hair and a pale, somewhat mousy face. The glasses camouflaged her tiny, tired-looking eyes. "So what do you think?" she whispered. "Married or gay?"

"I don't know. But if he comes over here, he's mine."

"That's not fair," Veronica said. "You always wait on the good-looking guys."

"Why should you care? You're married."

"So are you," Veronica snorted. "To your job."

After three years at Frederick and Nelson, Amy had taken a job offer from the Bon Marché in downtown Seattle. She became buyer and manager for the Bath department. The job took her to New York and Hong Kong twice a year on buying excursions. She pampered herself: a beautifully furnished two-bedroom apartment in West Seattle with a fireplace and a panoramic view of Puget Sound; a designer wardrobe, and first-class airline tickets she'd send to her mother so she'd come visit.

But these luxuries didn't compensate for what Amy really wanted. During her first year in Seattle, she must have visited Woodland Park Zoo about thirty times, walking along the paths he walked. She wandered around parks and playgrounds, the places he had been; and maybe he came back to from time to time.

She was thirty-five now, and yearned to have another baby. After ten years in a holding pattern, she was ready for a man to love, someone to give her a child.

The man in Bedwares was the perfect age for her— mid to late thirties. From the suit, she guessed he was a lawyer, possibly an advertising executive. He played racquetball during his lunch hour; and on weekends, he went sailing. Yes, definitely the type who owned a boat. Very Kennedy-looking.

He moved away from Lila's counter.

"Oh, he's headed this way!" Veronica whispered, scurrying out from behind the counter. "He's yours, honey. Go for it!"

Amy adjusted the shoulder padding to her Evan-Picone blouse, but kept her eyes averted from him as he approached her. He was so handsome, it made her nervous just to look at him. She reached into the depths of her professional resources and gave him a cool smile. "Can I help you?" she asked. God, his eyes were beautiful—the brilliant blue color of a chlorine pool.

He slumped against the counter, and gave her a tired, lopsided grin that was incredibly cute. "I need bathroom stuff. I'm furnishing a new apartment from scratch, and I'm brain-dead."

Amy laughed, then stole a glance at his left hand. No wedding ring. Probably gay.

"Let's put your bags behind the counter here, and I'll show you some towels we have on sale." She helped him with the bags. "Is there a particular color or pattern you have in mind?"

"Um, well, the tiles in the bathroom are green."

"Sort of a deep forest green or more of a mint?" she asked as they approached the towel display.

He chuckled. "I don't know. Light green, I guess. Whatever you think goes with that is fine. I trust you."

Amy smiled. In her sales experience, gay men usually knew colors and exactly what they wanted; but this man didn't seem to care at all. And if he were married, his wife would be the one shopping for linen and bathroom accessories. Maybe he was recently divorced. That would explain the new apartment.

She picked out a jade-colored set of towels. He seemed happy with the selection. She noticed that when she looked at him, he was looking at the towels; but the moment she turned her eyes away, she felt him glancing at her face and her body. "You just moved to Seattle?" she asked, showing him shower curtains.

"I live in Spokane, but my job takes me here two weeks every month. The company figured it would be cheaper if I got a studio apartment here. So from now on, I'll have to buy my own soap and shampoo instead of stealing it from the Westin every other week. What do you think of this clear one with the watermelons on it?"

"I think it's cute," Amy said. *And so are you.* She gazed at his profile. "Must be hard on you, traveling so much."

"Oh, it's not so bad," he said, absently turning the shower curtains on the tall rack—like so many pages of a magazine he wasn't really reading. "I like Seattle, but don't know anyone here. I keep telling myself, 'See a show while you're here, check out the Space Needle, go to a restaurant.' But who wants to go out alone? So I always end up staying in my hotel room, watching the tube and eating room service. Crazy, isn't it?"

"No, not really," Amy said. "I know what it's like. I take a lot of business trips. They can be awfully lonely."

The blue eyes studied her. "Somehow, I just can't picture you sitting alone in some hotel room all night. You must have guys constantly asking you out wherever you go."

Amy shrugged. "Oh, most of my dates on the road

are business-related and boring." She laughed. "For that matter, so are most of my dates at home."

He suddenly looked interested in the watermelon shower curtain again. "I think I'll take this one."

Amy found the boxed model in a drawer beneath the display. She kept telling herself: *"Ask him out, stupid!"*

He gave her his VISA card. The name on the card was Barry Horton. "Promise me something, Mr. Horton," Amy said as she rang up the items. "Don't sit alone in your hotel room tonight. Seattle's a great city. You should go out and have some fun."

"What's your name?" he asked.

She stole another glance at him as she totaled up the sale. "Amy—Amy Sheehan."

"I'll take it under advisement, Amy Sheehan."

She handed him a pen, then watched him sign the sales slip. "I guess I'm not one to talk," she said casually. "I'll probably just sit at home tonight myself. . . ."

Her words hung in the air for a few seconds. He said nothing. He gave her back the pen and the charge slip. Amy managed to work up a polite smile, then she started loading the shower curtain and towels into a bag.

"I was wondering . . ." he said.

She looked up. "Yes?"

"When do you finish up around here?"

"Six."

"Um, there's a movie at seven, one of my all-time favorites. But I don't know where the theater is. Anyway, I figured in turn for giving me directions, I'd treat you to the movie and perhaps dinner afterward." His

shy smile was very endearing. "Do you know where
the Neptune Theater is?"

"Sure. It's a revival house in the University District.
What's playing?"

"*West Side Story.*"

Barry picked her up in front of the store at six-
fifteen. On their way to the theater, Amy learned that
he had a house in Spokane, which he'd shared for two
years with his fiancée, Gretchen. But they'd broken
up, and she'd moved out. A friendly parting, he said.
Gretchen hadn't liked him traveling so much. He was a
sales manager for a computer software company. For
fun, he played racquetball; he loved old movies, and
despite an indifference toward spectator football and
baseball, he read the sports pages every morning so
he'd come off as "one of the guys" with clients and
coworkers.

Amy was already imagining pictures of them together in a photo album. He looked photogenic—with
those chiseled, Northern European features. He dressed
so fine, too. He'd changed from his suit into an expen-
sive-looking sweater and pleated khakis. Amy remembered how she'd practically had to dress Paul, the
Polyester King, for every social outing.

During the movie, Barry didn't put his arm around
her, but they shared a bucket of popcorn. Amy remembered trying to watch this same movie on a black-and-
white portable TV in the kitchen, while Paul and his
buddies had booed and cheered to some stupid football
game in the next room. She glanced at Barry beside her,
the light from the movie screen flickering across his

handsome face. He was so much better-looking than Paul.

Amy wondered why she kept comparing them. On other dates, she'd never thought about her ex-husband. Why was it different with Barry Horton? Maybe because for the first time since her divorce, she found herself with a man she could easily marry.

He was smiling, but not up at Natalie Wood. At her. Barry then took her hand in his.

The movie ended at 9:45, and, as the lights came on, Amy wiped the tears from her eyes. She felt embarrassed for crying. But Barry put his arm around her and kissed her on the lips. It was a romantic, yet chaste kiss—and over with much too quickly.

They headed up the theater aisle, and he asked where she'd like to go for dinner. "What I'd really like to do," Amy said, "is go home and change out of these work clothes. Then we could order a pizza—if that's okay with you."

It was okay with him. Barry uncorked a bottle of red wine while Amy telephoned Domino's. He helped her build a fire in the fireplace. Then Amy changed into a pullover and designer jeans that were both comfortable and attractive. When she emerged from the bedroom, Barry was sitting on the sofa. He studied the framed photograph of her with Eddie and her mother. He held it up. "Is this you in this picture?" he asked.

Amy took her glass of wine. She nodded. "That was taken eleven years and several excess pounds ago. I was twenty-four at the time." She wished he'd put the picture down.

"Is this your mother?"

"Yes."

"She's lovely. Who's the baby?"

"My nephew. I'm his godmother. It's my sister's baby. He—" Amy quickly shook her head. "No, that's a lie. . . ."

Barry looked up at her, confused.

Amy took a gulp of wine. "It's my son. His name's Eddie."

He put the picture down. "Your son. Is he—still around?"

"No," Amy whispered. "He's been gone a long time."

The door buzzer rang. It was the pizza man. Barry paid for it. They sat on the thick, white shag rug and ate in front of the fireplace. With Nat King Cole on the stereo and the lights turned down low, it might have been very romantic if Amy hadn't felt compelled to give Barry an explanation about her failed marriage and her missing child.

"I'm sorry," Amy said, refilling her wineglass a third time. "I shouldn't be going on like this, Barry. God, not on our first date. I'm not the morose type." She toasted him with her wineglass. "Huh, I usually don't drink like this either. Honest. I don't go around pouring out my tales of woe to people. In fact, I haven't told a soul about Eddie since I moved to Seattle five years ago. None of my Seattle friends know. You're the first one I've told."

"Well, then I'm flattered, Amy," he said, his beautiful eyes full of kindness and understanding.

"The thing is," she said, "I know my son's still alive. And that's kept me from finding someone new and starting a family. I still have a son out there somewhere, and *he's* my family."

The wine must have caught up with her, because for the second time that evening, she found herself crying in front of him. Once again, her tears prompted Barry to reach out to her. He rested a long, graceful hand on the back of Amy's neck. She looked into his blue eyes and felt so weak.

"It's all right," he whispered. Then he kissed her.

Amy melted inside. She wrapped her arms around him, and they gently tumbled onto the shag rug together. He kissed her tears, and when his lips met hers again, they were wet, soft, and warm. Amy took comfort in his strong arms. For a moment, she almost panicked as she thought he was about to pull away. She clung to his shoulders and kissed him more deeply. She didn't want him to stop.

But suddenly he did draw back. He sat up. "I'm sorry," he muttered. "This isn't right. . . ."

Amy touched her mouth, where his lips had been just a moment before. Numbly, she stared up at him.

He turned away. "It's no good." He rubbed his forehead. "You're very vulnerable right now."

Amy sat up. "I know what I'm doing, Barry," she whispered in a voice still throaty from crying. "I like you . . . very much."

He got to his feet. "I like you too, Amy," he said.

"Are you leaving?"

"I think I better." He glanced toward the door. "I've got a breakfast meeting at seven-thirty tomorrow."

Amy smoothed back her hair. Her face was still flushed and moist from his kisses. Unsteadily, she got up and followed him to the door. "Will I see you again?" she heard herself ask.

"I leave for Spokane day after tomorrow. I'm not sure. I'll call you."

Amy frowned. "You don't have to say that. In fact, I'd rather know now if tonight was it for us. Otherwise, I'll spend the next few days in limbo, waiting and hoping for you to call." Before he could answer, Amy buried her face in her hands. "God, listen to me, what an ass." She took a deep breath and managed to smile at him. "If you call, you call. If you don't, fine, I understand. Anyway, I think you're a wonderful guy, and thanks for the movie."

He smiled back—almost regretfully. Barry gave her a quick kiss on the cheek. "I'll call you," he whispered. Then he left.

The next day, Amy returned home from work, and before even taking off her coat, she checked her phone answering machine. There was a call from her mother, and another message from this self-involved drip who had taken her to dinner two weeks before: *"Hi. This is Christopher. Why haven't you returned any of my calls? Are you away on vacation or something?"* There were also two hang-ups. Amy was convinced the hang-ups were from Barry. But more likely, it was someone trying to sell her something.

"Oh. he's not going to call," Amy lamented to her mother over the phone an hour later. "I was such a twit. Our first date, and I spill my guts to him about Paul and Eddie and everything. I even cried, for God's sakes."

"Well, what's so terrible about that?" her mother asked.

"Pouring out your personal problems isn't exactly

recommended first-date procedure, Mom. It puts a guy off. I may as well have told him about my last Pap test." She couldn't very well tell her mother about the most humiliating event of the evening—the incomplete pass.

"Who's to say he won't call?" her mother offered. "It's only eight o'clock there. He might be trying to call you right now."

"He would have beeped in," Amy said, frowning.

Barry didn't call, beep in, or leave a message for the next nine days. And typical—that jerk Christopher called three times. By Monday, Amy figured Barry was back in town. But he didn't call that day. There wasn't even a hang-up on the machine; so she couldn't fool herself into thinking he'd tried.

Then on Tuesday, something happened at the store that made her stop thinking about Barry Horton—for a short while anyway. A smartly dressed, tawny-haired woman in her twenties came into Bathwares, pushing a baby in a stroller-chair. As Amy helped her shop for towels, she asked how old the baby was.

"He's going to be a year old next month."

The little boy had dark hair and brown eyes like his mother. He kicked his legs and seemed to babble baby talk to her.

Amy grinned. "What's his name?" she asked.

"Eddie."

"Eddie?" Amy repeated. Her hand went to her heart. "Could I—hold him?" she whispered. "Would it be okay?"

The young mother smiled and nodded. She unfastened the straps harnessing him in the stroller. Amy reached down and gathered the baby boy in her arms. The tiny hand came up to fondle her mouth and nose;

and Amy pretended to bite at it. The baby laughed. She found herself smiling and holding back the tears at the same time. The boy's large brown eyes stared at her with wonder. She kissed him on the cheek.

"Oh, he's drooling all over your beautiful blouse," the woman said. "I better take him."

Amy continued to bounce him in her arms. "Hey ya, little Eddie," she whispered. "Hey, handsome." She rubbed her nose against his, and he giggled.

"Miss . . ."

Amy kissed him again. His cheek was so warm and smooth.

"Miss?"

Amy glanced at the woman. She'd forgotten that she was there.

The young mother gave her a strained smile. "I think I better take him now," she said, holding out her arms.

Amy felt so foolish as she handed the baby back to his mother—foolish and empty. She watched the young mother push her own little Eddie in his stroller toward the elevators.

Once again, Amy thought about Barry Horton. She would have adored having a child by him—a little boy with Barry's dimples, that golden brown hair, and those blue eyes.

Why are you doing this to yourself? She was picking out their kids' names, and they'd had only one bomb-of-a-date, then he'd walked out of her life forever.

When she returned home that night, she deliberately ignored the blinking light on her answering machine until after she'd changed her clothes, opened up a Diet

Coke, and read her mail. Then she played back her messages. There was only one: *"Well, hello. It's Christopher. I got tickets to a play on Thursday—"*

"OH, CAN'T YOU TAKE A HINT?" Amy screamed. She realized, despite the odds, she still hoped to hear from Barry again.

As she watched "Moonlighting," and ate her Lean Cuisine, the telephone rang. Amy let the machine answer it. She heard his voice, over a car chase scene on TV: *"Um, hi. This is Barry Horton, y'know, from a couple of weeks ago almost? From Spokane? I just got back into town yesterday . . ."*

Amy put aside her dinner and got up from the couch. She stared at the telephone, not quite sure she should pick up the receiver. He'd made her wait so long for this.

"I'd like to see you this week. My number is 555-0820. Give me a call if you feel like getting together . . ."

Amy's hand hovered over the receiver. She let him go on talking: *"If you don't call back, I understand. Just wanted to let you know I was thinking about you. Oh, by the way, it's Tuesday night at—um, nine twenty. Hope you're—"*

Amy grabbed the receiver. "Hello?"

"Oh, hi . . ."

"Just a sec," she said hurriedly. "I just got in the door. Let me turn off this machine. There. Hi, this is Amy."

"Hi, Amy. This is Barry Horton."

"Barry Horton?" she repeated.

"Yes, from a couple of weeks ago. Um, *West Side Story*?"

"Oh, sure, Hi, Barry. How are you?"

* * *

Naked, they lay together in front of the fireplace. The fire was dying, and they held each other tighter to fight off the chill. Neither she nor Barry wanted to move. It was as if they couldn't bear separating—if only for the minute it would take to get a blanket or throw another log on the fire.

It had been a perfect evening. With a single yellow rose, he'd appeared at her door, dressed elegantly in a Giorgio Armani grey suit. He was even more handsome than she'd remembered. At McCormick's Restaurant, they put away a bottle of vintage wine, a plate of mussels swimming in butter, and two melt-in-your-mouth baked salmon fillets. Outside the restaurant, they got caught in the rain, a glorious downpour. Barry took off his suit coat and placed it over her shoulders. While he ran for the car, Amy stood beneath the restaurant awning, wrapped in his coat. She could smell his cologne on it, a spicy, masculine fragrance.

They started kissing as soon as they got into the front seat of his car. She didn't say anything, and neither did Barry. But their breath steamed the windows, while rain hammered at the car roof. Their faces were wet and warm. Yet they both couldn't stop trembling.

Inside the lobby of her apartment building, they started kissing again. Along the row of mailboxes, he hungrily kissed her neck and ran his fingers through her damp hair. "Oh, God," he whispered, between kisses. "God, I didn't plan on this."

Through the layers of clothes, she felt his erection pressing against her. "You're coming upstairs, aren't you?" she asked, clinging to him.

His hands were on her breasts now. He licked her ear. "I didn't bring anything, Amy. I didn't—"

"Shut up," she whispered, kissing him again. She held him tightly and looked over his shoulder at the rain outside. "We're okay, Barry," she heard herself say. "You've got nothing to worry about. I'm—fully insured." She couldn't say how—IUD, the pill, the sponge—because she had none of those things. Nor had she had any use for them in the last few months. She was lying to him.

She couldn't bear it if he walked out on her again. She wanted to make love with him, and the notion of his seed inside her suddenly made the act even more desirable. A baby. His baby. She wanted that.

Barry Horton smiled, kissed her once more, then they started up the stairs together.

At first, their lovemaking had been so urgent—almost selfish; but then he'd become tender and warm, endearingly conscious about pleasing her. Barry was a wonderful lover; and he would give her a beautiful child.

A few glowing embers were all that remained of the fire now. The soft shag rug beneath them had left little white fibers in Barry's chest hair and Amy picked them out. He kissed her and lazily stroked the curve of her hip. "Do you know how much I missed you last week?" Amy confessed. "I was so afraid I'd never see you again. After the way I acted on our last date—"

"Oh, no, no," he murmured, brushing his fingertips against the side of her face.

She kissed his hand. "What I mean is, I thought about you a lot. I usually don't let this" —she gave him a squeeze—"well, *this* sort of thing happen so soon after I meet a guy. But you're the exception. I had a special feeling for you the first time I set eyes on you, Barry."

For a moment, she thought she detected a darkness in Barry's eyes, a brief look of doubt and pain; Amy immediately regretted her candor. Too honest, too soon.

"I think I'm hung up on you already," he whispered.

She laughed, then kissed his nose. "Well, the feeling's mutual, honey. So what's the problem?"

"You know my schedule. I'm in town one week and out the next. That's not very fair to you."

"I'd be happy just to see you next time you're in town."

"What about later?"

"We'll see," she replied, kissing him on the chin. Amy figured he was probably thinking about his ex-fiancée. "Don't worry," she said. "I'm not Gretchen."

"Gretchen?"

"Yeah. Didn't you say she broke off the engagement because of all your traveling?"

"That's right. I couldn't be there for her as often as she wanted. That was her biggest gripe."

Amy kissed him again. "Well, you don't have to worry about that with me."

During the ten days Barry was gone, Amy was never so happy being miserable. At last, she'd found a man she truly loved, and he loved her back. He sent her a dozen red roses that Saturday, and called from his office in Spokane. They talked for an hour. He said that he'd have to work late every night that week. There was a pile of homework he'd neglected while in Seattle—with her. "And I wouldn't have it any other way," he said. He phoned every night that week, usually around six. Amy always rushed home from work so she wouldn't miss his call. It was like having someone to come home to. She hadn't experienced that since her time with Eddie, when she'd been working at the Safeway. There was that same feeling of being missed, loved, and wanted by someone again. She could hardly wait for Monday, when Barry would come back. At last, she had something to look forward to.

The stove clock said it was 2:20. Barry was a light sleeper, and Amy didn't want to wake him—as she had during last night's bout with insomnia. Clad only in her robe, she poured a glass of wine and sat down at the kitchen table.

They'd had three wonderful nights together since his return. Tomorrow would be their last for another ten days, and yet, she almost looked forward to his leaving. He was around all the time, and she didn't want to risk buying one of those kits for fear he'd find it. But once he went back to Spokane, she could get one, do the test, and finally know for sure.

It had been just two weeks ago since they'd first made love. Could it happen that quickly? She should have gotten her period Monday, today at the latest. She'd never been this late before.

Of course, she couldn't breathe a word to Barry, not when she'd convinced him that she was "fully insured." What a stupid way to have put it. Yet that night, she'd wanted so much to make a child with him. She hadn't thought about his traveling schedule, or her own job. Somehow, she'd imagined getting pregnant some time further into their relationship. How could she tell him she might be carrying his child *now*?

Amy sipped her wine and glanced at the beads of rain on the kitchen window. For all she knew, this was her last chance to indulge in alcohol for a while. She still wanted Barry's child and wanted it to be healthy.

She imagined herself fully blown under a maternity smock by Christmastime, decorating the tree with Barry as carols played on the stereo. But that pretty picture had them married, and him working full-time in Seattle. More likely, she'd still be single, and he'd still be spending every other week away. She couldn't really blame him if he wanted her to get an abortion— or if he dumped her completely

But Barry wasn't like that. He'd stay on with her. She had no intention of making him feel trapped into a marriage. Having a wedding ring didn't seem all that important, so long as her child knew his father.

She'd thought she knew Barry really well, but now, she wasn't quite so sure. Amy wondered how he'd take the news.

She sipped her wine. There was no use telling him until she knew for certain.

"What do you think the chances are of you working full-time in Seattle?" she asked over dinner the next evening. They sat at a window table in an expensive restaurant overlooking Lake Union. They had a view of the city lights and boats parked at the dock.

"Maybe in a couple of years, " he said, cutting into his trout. "They're talking about opening an office here—just talk. Why the long face? Thinking about tomorrow?"

She nodded. "And the next ten days without you."

"Sure you don't want to try any of this wine, honey?"

"No, thanks," she said. "I'll stick with 7Up tonight."

Barry reached across the table and took her hand in his. "Don't be blue, sweetheart," he whispered.

"Listen," she said. "Week after next, why don't you come in on Friday night, and stay through the following weekend? That would give us eleven days together. Think of it . . ."

He let go of her hand, picked up his knife and fork, and started cutting into his dinner again. "I usually have to work in the Spokane office on Saturday mornings. You know that, honey. Sometimes Sundays too."

She frowned. "Well, what is it with this stupid job of yours? Don't you get any time off?" What kind of father would he be if he couldn't even spend weekends with his child?

"It's my job, Amy, my career. I told you what a pain in the ass it would be that first night we got together."

She sighed. "Yes, you've been honest from the start."

He sipped his wine, then glanced out the window at the sailboats. For a moment, he seemed so far away.

Amy moved her plate aside and straightened up in her chair. "Hey, listen," she said. "I'm long overdue for a vacation. Maybe I can come to Spokane in a couple of weeks."

He wiped his mouth with his napkin. "Well, that's—an idea. I'd—I'll have to check my itinerary."

"You don't seem too enthusiastic."

"Oh, no, no. I am. I just need to make sure I don't have any commitments. I'll have to get back to you." He set his crumpled napkin on the table, then glanced out the window.

Amy stared at him, but he wouldn't look at her. *"I'll have to get back to you."* That was something she'd say to a pain-in-the-ass vendor. He hated the whole idea.

"Barry, if you're worried about me wanting to spend every waking hour with you in Spokane, no problem. If you need time for work or friends—"

"Really, it sounds great," he cut in. He pushed his plate away. "I'm not pooh-poohing the idea. I just don't feel too sharp right now. Maybe I'm coming down with something . . ." He looked over his shoulder. "Have you seen our waiter?"

"What's wrong? Your stomach? Your head?"

"I just feel kind of clammy all of a sudden," he said, rubbing his forehead. "Maybe it's work catching up with me."

"You're stressed out, that's what's wrong. All this traveling and working weekends . . ." Every night this past week, he'd brought his briefcase to her place and done homework there. "Whatever they pay you, it's not enough. I thought my job was stressful, but yours is absolutely nuts."

Barry shifted restlessly in his chair. "Honey, I can't quit. Try to understand . . ."

But Amy wasn't listening. He looked so pale, it frightened her. She remembered Paul and his epilepsy. *"Did you take your pill today?"* she'd ask; and he'd always answer: *"Yeah. Don't worry, I took it."* Barry had that same sickly, white look, and she wished he could take some kind of pill to make it go away.

"You look awful," she murmured. "And you're perspiring . . ."

"I think I need some fresh air," he whispered. Then he glanced over his shoulder. "Where the hell's our waiter?"

Amy reached for her purse. "Don't worry. I'll pay the check. You go outside, darling. Go. I'll be out in a minute."

He nodded and got to his feet. "I'm sorry, honey—"

"It's okay. Go, Barry."

Quickly, he threaded around the tables toward the exit. Some of the customers glanced up from their dinners, looking at him as if he were drunk. Amy flagged down their waiter and asked if he could hurry with the check.

Two minutes later, she was outside. She saw Barry in the parking lot, sagging against his car. It was a beautiful, clear night; she hoped the crisp, lakeside air had done him some good. The way he'd left the restaurant, she was grateful to see him still standing.

Amy hurried toward him, but hesitated when Barry looked up. Maybe he wanted to be left alone. He'd been fine until she'd started talking about spending more time together.

He waved feebly. She noticed a handkerchief clenched in his other hand. Amy stepped toward him. Under the streetlight, she saw his face was wet and shiny. Had he been crying? Strange, she might be carrying his baby; yet he was the one suddenly stricken by physical and emotional attacks. "Are you okay, honey?" she asked, afraid to get too close.

He nodded and took a few deep breaths. "Better," he replied, still leaning against the car as if it were the only thing holding him up. "I'm sorry, Amy," he said, in a voice that was low and strained. His shoulders began to shake. He wiped his eyes with the handkerchief. "Please, don't hate me."

He turned away from her. Amy stroked his back. "I couldn't hate you, darling. What is it? What's wrong?"

"I don't want to lose you. I love you . . ."

She tried to laugh. "Well, I'm not going anywhere, And I love you, too," She massaged his shoulders. "Everything's going to be all right. You're not going to lose me . . . not this easily. I'm not going to do what Gretchen did to you. So we only have ten days a month together, I understand. Maybe we can work something out later. Don't feel pressured. I was just thinking out loud back there in the restaurant."

Barry turned around, but didn't look at her. His nose was running, and he stared down at the pavement. "Amy, I'm married."

She told herself that she hadn't heard him right. Her hands slid off his shoulders. She stepped back. "What?" she murmured.

His sorry, tear-filled eyes finally met hers. "Gretchen's my wife. We've been married three years. I've never done anything like this. I didn't expect to fall in love with you. Gretchen's a wonderful woman. So are you. Both of you deserve better. I'm sorry, Amy—"

She slapped him across the face. She didn't want to hear any more. Yet all at once, everything became so repulsively clear: how he'd pulled away from her that first night; and the phone calls—always from his office.

Hunched over, her arms crossed in front of her, Amy

backed away from him. It was as if he'd just kicked her in the stomach. Barry reached out to her, but she reeled back. Amy staggered over to the streetlight post. Clutching it, she bent forward and vomited.

She hardly remembered Barry holding her head while she was sick, or him driving her home. His incessant apologies and I-love-you's during the car ride only made her feel sicker. "Oh, would you just shut the fuck up?" she screamed.

He was quiet all the rest of the way. When he pulled up in front of her building, Amy hurried out of the car and ran inside. His car was still there, two hours later. Amy looked down at it from her window, before staggering into her bedroom. She fell asleep crying—for herself and her poor, poor bastard child.

The next morning, Friday, his car was gone. He was on his way back to Spokane, back to his wife.

"Amy, there's a call for you on 9-2," Veronica said. "It's Barry."

Amy went on ringing up a sale, bagged the items, and handed the plastic sack to the old man she'd been waiting on. "Thanks a lot," she said. "Have a nice day."

She gazed at the blinking light on the telephone until both the customer and Veronica had wandered away from the counter. Amy lifted up the receiver and pressed the lighted button. "Bathwares. This is Amy."

"Hi, honey. It's me . . ."

Amy said nothing. Slowly she lowered the receiver back on its cradle. The light went out.

She got her period that day. It was June 6, 1989, the eve of her Eddie's twelfth birthday.

CHAPTER FOURTEEN

Saturday, June 7, 1989—11:15 P.M.

I'm tired and depressed. How's that for a cheery opener? If I had a dollar for every entry in this journal starting this way, I could retire & write mystery novels or something.

Sam's birthday party at the Seattle Center fairgrounds got rained out. So I took him & 4 of his friends bowling instead. No one was too thrilled about it. I treated them to lunch at the greasy spoon connected to the bowling alley. Moron that I am, I decided to do the birthday cake bit there. So I snuck out to the car & got the cake from the trunk. It was in perfect condition when I gave it to our waitress (a real bimbo, and rude too).

When I got back to the table, Sam knew something was up. He gave me a look like, "Please, don't humiliate me here."

Just then, our charming hostess came out of

*the kitchen with the cake. But it was a goddamn
mess! She must have dropped it in the kitchen,
because one whole side was smashed in. She
didn't seem to give a shit either, and I wanted to
strangle her. I thought Sam would crawl under
the table while we sang "Happy Birthday."
Craig & I were the only ones singing. The others
must have been in shock. "God, it looks like she
picked that cake out of the garbage," Earl announced (for once, I had to agree with the little
asshole). No one wanted to touch it. So I left the
cake at our table in lieu of a tip (God knows why
I feel guilty about it, that waitress was such a
jerk—plus since the cake set me back $16.00,
she did all right).*

    *Anyway, the whole ordeal makes me realize
how lucky I am. Any other kid would have been
pissed. But not my Sam. In fact, by dinner
tonight, we were already laughing about it.*

    *One good thing, the CD player was well
worth the $250. He went crazy. Craig is spend-
ing the night. Right now, they're in Sam's room,
listening to Bruce Springsteen. The music is re-
verberating through the apartment, and I'm sure
the neighbors will be phoning or pounding on
the door with complaints.*

Carl put down the pen and sipped his bourbon and
water—heavy on the water. He was at his desk in
his bedroom, the only place where he wrote in his private journal. He refused to call it a *diary,* because that
smacked of teenage girls writing in leather-bound books

with flap locks on the outside. Carl's *journal* was just a spiral notebook. He'd started it seven months before, because he'd needed someone to talk to. That had been a low point for him, last November.

He'd been drinking too much, too often, and had hit bottom that night he'd struck Sam. He considered counseling. But a journal was cheaper and less risky than having someone probe into his past. The journal even helped him keep tabs on his drinking. Most nights, he'd limit himself to a couple of beers.

Sam noticed the change too—as Carl had reported in a journal entry on February 8:

> *I felt wound-up tonight, and fixed a bourbon and water, hoping it would relax me. Sam was about to go to bed, and said to me something like, "Wow, Dad, this is the first time I've seen you with a regular drink-drink in a couple of months." I told him that I've been trying to taper off, and about his grandmother dying of serosas (sp?) of the liver and a little bit about his grandfather's violent temper. Sam took it well. He's so mature for his eleven years. I'm not sure if this is the kind of stuff you should discuss with your young son, but we talked until midnight (an hour ago). It was like I was talking to my best friend, and I think Sam felt the same way. I waver between thinking we're terrifically close for a father and son, and thinking I'm setting him up for years of psychoanalysis.*

Keeping a journal wasn't entirely risk-free. There was always a chance Sam might find the blue spiral notebook hidden under a pile of sweaters on Carl's closet shelf. Carl referred to Amy and Paul McMurray only by their initials, and he never mentioned who "A.M." or "P.M." were or how they were related to Sam. He was equally cryptic about his sexual fantasies and frustrations. A memorable one-night stand (he'd met the woman in a bar one evening when Sam had been sleeping over at Craig's) was never reported. It was frustrating to conceal some truths from his own journal, but Carl didn't want to risk having his son discover certain secrets.

Another source of secrets that made him nervous was the box of memorabilia, still hidden in the front closet crawl space. What would happen if Sam ever found that box—with the pictures of Eve, the divorce papers, and news clippings about a kidnapping in Portland? The "evidence" was buried under a layer of old bills and bank statements. Risky as it seemed, Carl held on to that box. His past was in there, his uncensored past.

Bruce Springsteen was interrupted mid-song, then the TV came on. "Saturday Night Live." Sam and Craig were watching it on the portable in his room.

Carl picked up his pen and wrote:

The weatherman promised a nice day for tomorrow. So I'll be taking Sam and Craig to the fairgrounds at the Seattle Center. It should make up for today's birthday debacle.

It's strange, but I keep thinking this is my last time with him on his birthday. Call it a hunch or a premonition or whatever. I felt so horribly sad all day. Maybe I just hate to see him grow up

*and not need me so much anymore. Shit, maybe
it's just my male menopause. I worry too much.*

Sam and Craig yelled in loud, prolonged unison.
They sat in the front cart of the Wild Mouse, and, as it
careened downward, they splayed their arms crazily.
Then they broke up laughing. It was all an act. They'd
pretty much outgrown the skimpy Wild Mouse. Still,
they were having fun. When the ride ended, they staggered over to Carl, laughing and breathless. "Are you
going on the Tilt-O-Whirl with us, Mr. Jorgenson?"
Craig asked.

"No way." He dug into his pocket for more ticket
money.

"Go for it, Dad." Sam took the five dollars. "C'mon!"

"Sammy, I'm fifty years old. Want me to have a heart
attack?" He looked over at the Tilt-O-Whirl. "Besides,
that damn thing turns you upside down. I'll probably
lose everything out of my pockets—and my stomach."

"Barf-o-rama!" Sam yelled. He nudged his father.
"You're gonna *Tilt-O-Hurl!*"

"Funny guy." Carl smiled at Sam. He and Craig
were laughing as they strolled past the booths, toward the
Tilt-O-Whirl. "Having a good time?" he whispered.

Sam was still laughing. But then the smile sort of
froze on his face. His eyes rolled back.

"Sam?"

It happened so fast. Suddenly, Sam's legs sank from
under him, and he fell toward the pavement. It was as
if he'd been struck down by a bullet. Somehow, Carl
managed to grab him before his body hit the concrete.
"Oh, Jesus," Carl whispered. Sam felt so heavy and
lifeless in his arms.

Carl hoisted him up, and started running toward the Pavilion offices. "Do you see a phone?" he yelled back at Craig, who was following them. "Look for a phone!"

"He'll be okay, Mr. Jorgenson. . . ."

Carl heard Sam groan a little. The heavy, limp body stirred. Carl stopped and laid him on a park bench. He pulled off his jacket, balled it up, then placed it under Sam's feet. "Sam?" he whispered. "Sammy?"

"Oh . . . God . . ." Sam moaned, his eyes still closed.

Carl glanced over his shoulder at Craig. "Get a cup of water from one of the vendors. Okay?"

"He'll be all right in a minute," Craig said, hovering over him. "This happened at my house twice last week."

Carl swiveled around. *"What?"*

"He was okay right afterward—both times," Craig explained. "Didn't he tell you he fainted last week?"

Carl frowned. "No, Craig. He didn't."

With half-slit eyes, Sam looked at his father—and then at his friend, as if betrayed by him. "Oh, God," he murmured.

"Dad, if it's okay with you, I'd rather go into the examination room by myself."

They sat on the long sectional sofa in the waiting room to the doctor's office. Two toddlers played in the kiddie area, and a pregnant woman sat across from them, jotting in a notebook.

"Why?" Carl asked. "Don't you want me in there with you?"

Sam picked up a copy of *Highlights,* sneered at the

cover, then tossed it back on the end table. "I'm old enough to go in by myself, Dad," he muttered. "It's bad enough that I'm still going to a *baby* doctor."

"He's my doctor too, Sam. He's a general practitioner. You have nothing to be embarrassed about."

"Just the same, Dad, would you mind staying out here while I go in? I don't want to feel like a total spaz."

Carl unfolded the newspaper in his lap. "Suit yourself."

"Now you're ticked off," Sam said.

He studied his newspaper. "No, you're right," he said coolly. "You're not a baby anymore."

Sam knew his father's feelings were hurt. But he really hated waiting in that outer room with babies, kids, and pregnant ladies. Sure, his dad wasn't embarrassed going to the Humming M.D. He was already grown-up.

Sam had thought turning twelve would somehow suddenly make him more "adult." But he was still a kid and hated it. His father continued to tower over him by a foot. But worse, he didn't have any pubic hair yet. In junior high, most of the guys who hadn't reached puberty were pip-squeaks and wimps. He didn't want to be considered one of them.

It was kind of tough feeling grown-up while a baby doctor examined his hairless body with his *daddy* in the room.

There was another reason why Sam didn't want his father with him now. They were peeved at each other.

Driving back from the fairgrounds yesterday, his

dad had waited until they'd dropped off Craig, then he'd bawled him out: *"What do you mean not telling me that you fainted twice last week? I have to find out from Craig? God, Sammy, you let me put you on all those rides when you could be sick! You practically gave me a heart attack . . . "* And blah, blah, blah. Then more of the same after his father's call to Dr. Durkee. Outside of a headache, Sam had felt fine, but his dad had made him spend the rest of the day in bed—as if he were really sick or something.

Begrudgingly, Sam had to admit—at least to himself—that he should have told his dad after fainting last week for the second time. Even Craig had bugged him about it: *"God, Sam, twice in one week. You should get a checkup or something. Aren't you worried?"*

He was, but said he wasn't. He didn't like to think he might be sick, and he hated going to the doctor.

Yet that was where he sat now—on the edge of the examination table, nervous and alone, feeling the sweat trickle down from his hairless armpits.

The nurse came in. Her name was Judy. She was thin and pretty, with shoulder-length brown hair; and she'd been Dr. Durkee's nurse for as long as he could remember. "Hi ya, Sam," she said, tossing a clipboard on the examining table. She had a friendly smile that helped put him at ease. "So you passed out on us yesterday, huh?"

He nodded.

"How's about losing the shoes and stepping over to the scale here so I can get your height and weight?"

Sam pulled off his shoes, then got on the scale.

"By the way," she said, fiddling with the measuring rod attached to the scale. "Happy birthday tomorrow."

"Thanks. But my birthday was Saturday."

"Sixty-two inches, 131 pounds," she announced, writing on her clipboard. "You can step down now. What's that you said? You had a party on Saturday?"

"I said my *birthday* was Saturday."

"But isn't tomorrow the tenth?" she asked.

"Yeah. But my birthday's June seventh."

She glanced at the clipboard again. "You sure?"

"Positive," he chuckled. Sam sat back down on the table.

"Well, that's strange. I got it down here as '6-10-77'" She went to the cabinet and got out a disposable thermometer. "June seventh, huh? I must be losing my mind. Open up." Sam opened his mouth and she slipped the thermometer under his tongue. He watched her adjust the birthdate on his medical form, scratching out the zero and making the one into a seven. "All this time, I thought we had the same birthday," she said. "See, mine's tomorrow."

"Habby birday," Sam said, the thermometer in his mouth.

Judy frowned as she chewed on the top of her pen. "I remember telling your dad that my birthday was the tenth, too. I was here the day he first brought you in. You were just a baby then. I think you had roseola. Your dad was so worried. I felt so sorry for him. And wow, what a handsome guy. You'd just moved here, and we had to send away for your medical records . . ." She frowned again, then shook her head. "No, I remember now. We never got any early medical records on you. Your dad said they were lost or something. That's right. I remember now."

Sam wondered how his father, who had saved all of his report cards since kindergarten, could have lost his early medical records. It just didn't make sense.

"So—you've fainted three times within the last ten days. Is that right?" Dr. Durkee stared at him from behind his thick, black-rimmed glasses.

Sam was sitting on the examining table in his BVDs. He nodded. "What do you think? Am I really sick or something?"

Dr. Durkee pulled a chair over to the table and sat down. "Sam . . ." He took a deep breath, then ran a hand through his curly grey hair. "I want you to be totally honest with me. Have you been—doing some things you shouldn't?"

Sam gulped. *Uh-oh,* he thought, *he wants to know if I've been masturbating, that's what this is all about— I'm fainting because I whack off too much.* Sam gave him a pale smile. "What do you mean, Doc?" he asked innocently.

"Have you been experimenting with drugs, Sam?"

An astonished laugh escaped him. "What? God, no . . ."

Sam endured the next fifteen minutes of Dr. Durkee's poking, prodding, and grilling. "No," Sam told him, he'd never tried coke, or crack. No, the only pills he ever took were aspirin if he had a headache. Once the Humming M.D. was convinced that Sam wasn't a dope fiend, he flashed a penlight in his ear. "Do you remember hearing anything—or a hearing loss just before you fainted?"

Sam bit his lip. "Last couple of times, I thought I heard music, like the radio, but it was fuzzy. Plus I'd try to talk, but I couldn't get any words out. And I know you'll think this is weird, but I also got a funny taste in my mouth—like St. Joseph's Aspirin, an orange-ish taste. That and the music, then I conk out. Does it mean anything?"

"It might," Dr. Durkee said, still gazing into his ear.

"I feel perfectly okay," Sam said. He was afraid they'd put him in the hospital or something. He couldn't really be sick.

After more poking and peeking, Dr. Durkee said: "Count Dracula time. Judy's going to take some blood. Just sit tight, put your pants on, and I'll be back in a bit."

"What?" Carl said, not sure he'd heard him right.

Dr. Durkee was seated beside him on the sectional sofa. "That's just an educated guess. This Dr. Kinsella I'm sending you to, he's the specialist. He can tell you for sure. It's not as bad as it sounds, Carl. There are medications he can take—pills to retard the seizures."

Carl kept shaking his head.

"Some forms of epilepsy are hereditary," the doctor said. "Is there any history of that in your family?"

"No, not at all."

"Well, maybe I'm wrong . . ."

"No one in my family—" Carl choked on his words. *His family.* But what about Paul and Amy McMurray? He suddenly felt very sick. "Um, I shouldn't say that," he muttered, rubbing his forehead. "I'll—have to double-check. Yes, yes, I'll do that."

"Good," Dr. Durkee said. "The more you can dig up for us, the better chance we have of pinpointing this thing without having to stick Sam in the hospital for a night or two. It might spare him from a lot of needless tests, some of which, I assure you, are not pleasant."

"So does he know what's wrong with me?" Sam asked as they pulled out of the parking lot to Dr. Durkee's office. He rolled down the car window.

"We're not sure yet, sport," Carl said. "That's why we're seeing this Dr. Kinsella on Friday. He's going to do some tests."

"Tests?" Sam's eyes widened with dread. "What kind of tests?"

" . . . *a lot of needless tests, some of which, I assure you, are not pleasant.*" Possibly a couple of nights in the hospital, too. He couldn't allow Sammy to go through that hell just to save his own skin. He'd have to contact the McMurrays—somehow. If Sam's problem was hereditary, they could tell him. He hoped to God that the McMurrays still lived in Portland, and that their phone number wasn't unlisted. What would he say to them? And how could he get Sam out of the apartment while he made the call? What was he going to do? Send him to the store for something—so that he'd have a seizure on the way?

"Dad? What kind of tests are they gonna do on me? Are they gonna stick me in some hospital for this or what?"

Carl glanced at him and tried to smile. "No one said you have to go to the hospital, Sam. It's probably going to be just another checkup—no worse than today. Don't sweat it. We'll see what they say on Friday."

Frowning, Sam started to examine the Band-Aid on his arm, from where they'd taken blood. "Want to hear something weird?" he asked. "When Judy was checking me out, she said she had my birthday down as June tenth."

"Well, that's crazy," Carl said, without thinking. "It's the seventh."

"I told her that," Sam replied, pushing down his sleeve. "But she was sure you told her the day you first brought me in that my birthday was the tenth. She said you didn't have my medical records or anything . . ."

Carl tightened his grip on the steering wheel.

"She said they never got them at all," Sam continued. "Said you lost them or something."

Carl nodded. "Yes, a lot of things got lost when we moved up from Santa Rosa," he replied stiffly. "I told you that, Sam."

"Along with most of Mom's pictures, right?"

"That's right," Carl said, staring straight ahead.

"I can't believe that," he heard Sam say.

"What do you mean?"

"All that stuff getting lost, it's unbelievable. You should have sued the movers. That's what you should have done . . . *Hey, up ahead, Dad . . . Dad . . .*" He plastered his hand against the dashboard. *"DAD, THE STOP SIGN!"*

But already the blaring sound of another car's horn drowned him out.

Carl slammed on the brake. They screeched to a halt at the intersection, and the other car weaved in front of them. The other driver yelled out his window at Carl and flipped him the bird.

Carl caught his breath and looked at Sam. "Sorry."

Sam still had one hand braced against the dashboard. He rolled his eyes, then sat back. "Jeez, Dad, didn't you see it?"

"No, I didn't," he replied. It felt as if his heart had stopped for a moment. "You—are you okay?"

Sam laughed a little. "Yeah, fine. How are you?"

Carl gently stepped on the gas. "Okay," he sighed.

"What were we talking about?" Sam asked. "I can't remember."

"Um, neither can I," Carl lied. "Couldn't have been very important."

Carl was making a casserole from leftover chicken when Sam asked if he had time for a shower before dinner. All afternoon, Carl had been wondering how to get Sammy out of earshot so he could telephone the McMurrays, and here was his chance. "You want to take a shower? Oh, that's a great idea," he said.

Sam blinked at him. "Why is it such a great idea? Do I got BO or something?"

Carl laughed nervously. "No. Dinner won't be ready for a while. I was just worried that you were really hungry. Take your time."

Sam gave him a look, then wandered toward the bathroom.

When he heard the shower start, Carl put down the Campbell's cream of chicken soup can, picked up the phone and dialed.

"I'm sorry," the operator for Portland directory assistance told him a minute later. "I don't have a Paul McMurray listed at that address."

"Well, he may have moved," Carl whispered into the phone. He leaned over the kitchen counter, a pen in his hand. "It's very important I get in touch with him. Is there another address for a Paul McMurray? Or just a P. McMurray?"

"There's a Paul and Sheila McMurray on Southwest Fifty-ninth," the operator said. "Nothing else."

Grimacing, Carl imagined all the awful tests Sam would have to endure. He had a feeling he'd come to a dead end, but asked for the phone number anyway. His only hope was that McMurray had divorced Amy and married this Sheila.

He thanked the recorded voice that recited the number, pressed down the phone cradle, then dialed the couple on Southwest Fifty-ninth. He counted two ring tones.

"WHAT?" It was a child, a girl, and she practically screamed the poor excuse for a greeting into the phone.

"Um, hello," Carl said, unnerved. "May I speak with Mr. McMurray, please?"

"WHO'S THIS?" she demanded to know. Her voice was abrasive, and Carl imagined it belonged to a six-year-old urchin with a chubby face and stringy, dark hair. He hoped someone would snatch the receiver from her fat little hand before she screamed something else at him. He heard a TV blaring in the background.

"This is Frank Baxter from the accounting department at—"

"WHO?"

"Frank Baxter," Carl said.

"Whaddaya want?"

"I'd like to speak to your father," Carl said patiently.

"WHO ARE YOU?" she shouted—almost angrily.

"My name is Frank Baxter. Is your father there?"

Silence from the other end of the line.

"Hello?" Carl said.

"DADDY!!!" She yelled it right into the phone. Then there was a loud thud, like she'd thrown down the receiver.

Carl could hear the TV still blaring.

"Yeah. Hello?"

"Mr. McMurray?" Carl asked.

"Who's this?" he grunted.

Carl knew where the little girl got her phone manners. "My name is Frank Baxter," he said. "I'm with the accounting department at Portland General Hospital. We may owe you some money due to a billing error from several years back."

"Oh, yeah?" he asked. "How much?"

Carl smiled. He knew the money ploy would keep him on the line. "Ninety-seven dollars and eighteen cents," he said. "I'd like to verify that we have the right Paul McMurray. Are you employed by the Hallmark Company?"

"No," he said.

Carl closed his eyes. *Shit.*

"No, that was a while ago," he said. "I work for Del Monte now. Do I still get the money?"

"Oh, yes. Yes, sir," Carl replied brightly. Then he glanced over at the closed bathroom door and remembered to keep his voice down. Hot damn, he had the right guy. Suddenly, he realized that the rude little brat on the phone earlier was Sam's half sister: *"There but for the grace of God goes Sam"* He recalled how formal and polite Sammy had been as a little boy whenever he answered the telephone—as if each call might have been from the Pope.

"Hey, bub, you still there?" McMurray asked.

"Yes. Um, have you ever been a patient at Portland General, Mr. McMurray?"

"Well, my first wife had a baby there. But that was nine or ten years ago . . ."

Try twelve, Carl thought. "Were you ever treated at Portland General for epilepsy?" he asked.

"No. I'm epileptic, but I haven't had any bad seizures for a long time. I'm on medication—takes care of it."

Carl grabbed a pencil. "What's the name of the medication that you're taking?"

"Depakene," McMurray answered. "What does this have to do with the ninety-seven dollars you owe me?"

Carl was writing down "Depakene," unsure about the spelling. "Um, what particular form of epilepsy do you suffer from? Does it have a name?"

"I don't remember offhand. It's been years since I've had to think about it. You'd have to ask my doctor."

"Could you give me his name and telephone number, please?"

"Wait a minute," McMurray said hotly. "I already told you, I was never treated at Portland General for epilepsy. What's going on here? Am I getting the ninety-seven bucks or what?"

Carl put down his pencil. He'd gotten as much as he could from McMurray. Still, he had to ask one more question, and the businesslike tone left his voice for a moment: "Your first wife, is she—still alive?"

"Yeah, she's still alive. And don't ask me for her address, because I don't have it. Now, about the money . . ."

"Oh, yes," Carl said. "I'm giving you the opportunity to save up to ninety-seven dollars a year if you buy your medication from"—he glanced around the kitchen—"Kettle Pharmaceuticals."

"You said you were from Portland General—"

"If you sign up today," Carl continued, "you're eligible for our Super-Saver Discount Club. All it requires is a simple three-hundred-dollar down payment—"

"Hey," McMurray said. "Pound sand up your ass, buddy." Then he hung up.

Carl smiled. "Have a nice day," he said to no one.

Sam got a boner in the shower. But he wasn't sure he should whack off now; after all, maybe excessive masturbation caused his fainting spells. Still, he was so horny. He hadn't done it in five whole days.

He left the shower running and stepped out of the tub. Pressing an ear to the door, Sam listened for his dad. The door had no lock. His dad never barged in there while he was taking a shower; but just his luck, he'd walk in now and catch him flogging his dolphin. Sam didn't hear footsteps. His dad was talking to somebody. It sounded like he was on the phone.

"—think you're right, Dr. Durkee . . ."

His head against the crack of the door, Sam blindly reached for a towel and wrapped it around his waist.

"Turns out my father had epilepsy," his dad was

saying. *"I phoned our old family doctor just now—in Santa Rosa—and he told me. I had no idea, because my father never mentioned it. He was on this medication. It stopped the seizures. Maybe we could get the same stuff for Sam . . ."*

The noise from the shower was drowning him out. Sam quickly turned off the water and tiptoed back to the door. Still wet, he started to shiver. A puddle formed around his feet.

"Of course, I realize that," his father was saying. His voice had dropped to a whisper. *"But it helps, doesn't it? I mean, all those tests you referred to, Sam won't have to go through them now, will he?"*

Tests? There was that word again. Sam remembered the hospital scene early on in *The Exorcist,* when they didn't know what was wrong with Linda Blair. They'd stuck that long needle in her throat and blood spurted all over the goddamn place while she writhed in pain on the table; they'd taken X-rays of her head, and watched her on closed-circuit TV as she spazzed out, strapped in her hospital bed. Sam imagined all that being done to him—and worse, the stuff they couldn't show in the movie: tubes up his pee hole, a periscope up his ass to look inside him, shots, and bedpans, and hospital gowns that were open in back.

"Well, okay," his father said. *"Thanks, Dr. Durkee. Sorry to bother you at home . . . Yes, okay. I'll call Dr. Kinsella tomorrow. Thanks again. 'Bye."*

Sam quickly dried off, then got dressed—the same clothes he'd been wearing before. He picked up his socks and stepped out of the bathroom. His dad was in the kitchen, putting the casserole in the oven.

"Were you talking to Dr. Durkee just now?"

His father shut the oven door. "Were you eaves-dropping?"

"No," Sam lied. "I just heard you thank him for something." He sat down at the breakfast table, sniffed his socks, then pulled them on. "Does he know what's wrong with me yet?"

His father sighed and sat down at the table with him. He rested a hand on his shoulder. "Dr. Durkee isn't positive. But it looks like you might have a mild form of epilepsy, sport. Now, it's not as scary as it sounds."

Sam frowned. "Is epilepsy that disease that makes you spaz out all of a sudden, and somebody's got to grab your tongue so you don't swallow it?"

"That hasn't happened to you yet, has it?"

"No, but the fainting . . ."

His dad smiled and squeezed his shoulder. "If Dr. Durkee's right; there's some medication you can take that will help prevent you from fainting."

"Shots?" he asked, wincing.

"No, pills. Don't worry, kiddo. My father was epileptic, and I didn't even know it until I did some checking around just now. He was on the same medication we might get for you, and it didn't slow him down any. We'll know for sure after this Dr. Kinsella takes a look at you on Friday."

Sam shifted restlessly in the kitchen chair. "He's going to do a lot of weird tests on me, isn't he?"

"I suppose he'll do some poking around. It shouldn't be too bad, Sam."

"Will you be there?" he asked.

"Of course. You think I'm going to send you off to some strange new doctor by yourself?"

"No, I mean, are you going to be there in the examining room while he's doing all this stuff to me?"

His father shrugged. "Not if you don't want me in there."

"But I do," Sam insisted.

A smile came to his father's face, and he kissed Sam on the forehead. "Then I'll be there with you, Sammy."

Saturday, June 21, 1989—11:40 P.M.

You can measure the emotional wear & tear on me lately by the few drops of Canadian Club left in the bottle I bought last week. Yes, I fell off the wagon a few nights—turning to the booze to combat insomnia. But at least I can stop worrying about Sam's epilepsy. Tuesday, Dr. Kinsella put him on medication, the same pills P.M. is taking, so my calling the jerk paid off. Anyway, knock wood, there haven't been any more fainting spells or side effects. I've just got to keep on Sam's case about taking his pill every day.

Guess things are finally getting back to normal around here. We had French bread pizza for dinner tonight & I burned the roof of my mouth something fierce. Sam's in the living room right now, watching "Psycho" for the umpteenth time.

Work has been heinous, with Enright on my ass for missing so many days this month. I hear they're thinking about moving the SOB to Denver, because he's outlived his uselessness here. Despite my absences, two people have told me so far that I'm being considered as his replacement. I refuse to get my hopes up. Besides, I really don't give that much of a rat's ass about climbing up the corporate ladder. The extra money would be good. But hell, just let me win the lottery (would help if I ever played), and I'd quit that job and return to coaching grade school kids. There was a lot of fulfillment in that.

Sam's getting at that age in which he doesn't need me for much—except to chauffeur him back and forth from Little League, Craig's house, the movies, & the bowling alley. He's growing up.

And I'm growing old. In five years, he'll be going away to college. Then what will I do? Hell, I'll be fifty-five, and alone here.

Well, I lived alone & liked it for 12 years before I got married. I'll do okay. The funny thing is, I was prepared to have my son needing & depending on me, but I never thought I'd come to depend on him so much.

God, it's too depressing to think about right now. Another word on this subject & I'll be sucking up the last drops of Canadian Club & boiling the bottle for extra. Think I'll go join Sam and catch Janet Leigh before she takes her shower. Adios.

Sam stood at the far end of the hallway. The tune, "Sweet Baby James" still played inside his head—even after his father had gone inside the apartment and closed the door. He couldn't hear the whistling anymore. But from other apartments, there was a TV turned up too loud, someone coughing, and a baby crying. He wondered if the apartment itself was like the one they'd shared in Seattle. Most of their furniture had gone into storage. His father had probably picked up everything and carted it to Eugene when they'd released him from jail. Yeah, it'll look like home, Sam thought.

He walked toward the end of the corridor, past the loud TV, and the old woman coughing. The muffled noises faded as he approached his dad's place—all except for the crying baby.

It's not coming from his apartment, it's not, Sam told himself.

But it was.

PART THREE
THE ONLY SON

CHAPTER FIFTEEN

"**H**i, how are you tonight?" Amy asked.

"Good, thanks," the customer replied. "How about you?"

"Oh, I'm pooped. One of my salesgirls took sick and I'm filling in. Been on my feet since eight this morning." She always got a bit gabby with customers on slow nights. Besides, this customer was handsome; a tad too old for her, mid-forties, but his smile was youthful, and he had a full head of neatly groomed light brown hair and beguiling green eyes. He looked a little like Paul, but more handsome and fit—and, obviously, with better taste in clothes. He wore a navy blue blazer, grey pleated trousers, a crisp white shirt, and a striped tie. He looked as if he'd just stepped out of a J.Crew catalogue.

"So what can I help you with?" she asked.

"I need a new shower curtain."

"Something plain or jazzy?" she asked, leading him to the display rack. "We've got flamingos, and this one with the fish and the sea horses."

He seemed to favor a model with a map of the world

on it. "Well, this would belp my son with his geography," he said.

"Oh, is this for his bathroom?"

"His and mine. One-bathroom household. I'm a widower." He studied the shower curtain. "I think you have a sale here."

Amy found the boxed shower curtain in a drawer below the display rack. "Anything else I can help you find?"

"Just my son," he said. "We split up a half hour ago, and he was supposed to meet me here. You haven't seen a twelve-year-old boy in a red jacket wandering around here, have you?"

"No. But I can have him paged if you want."

He followed her to the register counter. "Thanks anyway. That would only embarrass him. I'll wait." He paid in cash. As he laid the money on the counter, Amy caught him staring at her. A puzzled half smile came to his face. "This sounds like a line. But I think we've met before. You look very familiar."

Amy grinned. "No. I think I'd remember you."

"Well, I know I've seen you someplace before," he insisted.

"I've worked here three years," she said. "You probably saw me here." Amy counted out the change for him. Then, over his shoulder, she saw a sweet, gangly looking boy step off the escalator with a shopping bag. He had wavy, golden-colored hair and wore a red jacket. "I think we found our missing person," she said, pulling out a shopping bag. "Is this him?"

He turned, then waved at his son. "That's him. Thanks."

Amy couldn't help notice the boy's beautiful eyes

as he hurried toward them. He had the eyes of an adult, and she recalled seeing photographs of her mother as a child—with those same serious, grown-up eyes.

"Sorry I'm late, Dad," the boy said.

"You look a little pale, sport. You all right?"

"I'm fine."

The man took the shopping bag from Amy. "Thanks a lot."

"Thank you. Have a nice day." She began to straighten out the counter.

"You still look pale to me," the man was saying. "Did you take your pill today?"

"Yeah. Don't worry. I took it. I'm fine."

Amy looked up. It was as if she'd just heard Paul talking to her. She stared at the golden-haired boy with her mother's eyes. He had a tiny scar on his chin.

He and his father turned to walk away.

"Eddie?" she whispered.

They kept walking.

She called to him: *"Eddie?"*

But only the father stopped to look over his shoulder. He stared back at her. The shopping bag fell out of his hand, and he quickly stooped down to retrieve it. His eyes were locked on her face. But it was only for a moment. He turned and hurried to catch up with the boy, taking his arm. They disappeared around the corner.

On the escalator, Sam pried his arm out of Carl's grasp. "Jeez, Dad. You want people to think I'm retarded?"

"Sorry," Carl muttered. "Keep moving. There's no one in front of us. Come on."

"What's the rush?" Sam asked.

Carl just nudged him to move faster. Then he glanced back to see if she was following them. *"You look familiar,"* he'd said. How could he have been so stupid? Of course, she looked familiar. How could he fail to recognize Amy McMurray?

"They got the leather bomber jacket I want on the first floor," Sam was saying as they stepped onto the next escalator down. "But it's two hundred bucks . . ."

Carl was still looking over his shoulder, still wishing Sam would hurry. His heart pounded. How in God's name had she recognized Sam? Was there something in his face—or his voice? Carl told himself to relax. She would have caught up with them by now—unless she was calling store security.

". . . really need a new jacket, Dad. And if we get it a size too big, I can grow into it and keep it a few years."

"C'mon, Sammy. Pick up your feet."

"Okay, okay. Anyway, you can just *look* at it with me."

"Look at what?" Carl asked, glancing around for the nearest exit as they reached the ground floor.

"The jacket. Geez! What do you think I've been talking about? It's right over there—"

"Not now." He pulled Sam toward the exit.

"Jeez, what's the rush?"

"I just don't want to miss our bus," Carl managed to say. "We'll look for a jacket at Nordstrom this weekend, I promise. For now, I just want to get out of here."

"Maybe I'd have made a fool out of myself if I chased after them. But I wish I had. It was eerie." Amy drummed her fingers on the dinner table. "He had Paul's features and my mom's eyes. Of course, the guy he was with looked a bit like Paul. But that scar on the boy's chin, it's too much of a coincidence." She sipped her wine. "Do you think I should have run after them?"

"I'm not sure, Amy."

"The boy was twelve. That's how old Eddie would be now." She picked up her fork, then put it down again and shoved her plate away. "Damn, if only that guy had used a credit card, I could trace him through that."

"Aren't you having any more dinner?"

"I'm sorry. You're a sweetheart to have it ready for me when I came in, Barry. I'm just not hungry."

He nodded. "It's all right, honey."

She took another swallow of her wine. "Not much of a last night together, is it?" she said, smiling sadly. "I'm sorry."

"Quit apologizing," Barry said. "I understand."

"You don't think it was Eddie I saw today, do you?"

Barry took his wineglass and sat back in his chair. "I think the chances are slim. You said so yourself, the father and son looked like each other, seemed right together. Somehow, I can't picture this guy as a kidnapper, not from the way you described him. He sounds too friendly and—well, *ordinary*—to be a suspicious character." He sipped his wine and shrugged. "But hell, that's just my opinion. If it'll make you feel better, you should phone the police and explain it to them."

"They'd think I was crazy," Amy sighed. "And maybe I am."

Barry got up from the table, took his plate, and then hers. "C'mon, I'll wash. You dry."

Amy gathered up the silverware and bowls, then followed him into the kitchen. At the sink, he tucked a dish towel around the waist of his jeans. He looked cute and Amy could almost fool herself into thinking they were married. But she wouldn't. "Do you cook and wash dishes for Gretchen, too?" she asked.

"I help with the dishes sometimes," he replied.

"Did you call her today?" She cleared the stove of pots and pans. "It's getting late. You better."

"I'll see her tomorrow, Amy. Besides, I called last night."

"You ought to call her every day. I mean, maybe she thinks you don't care. Maybe that's why she has the weight problem. She's frustrated and insecure, so she eats."

"What? Are you quoting Jenny Craig to me or something?"

Amy walked up behind him and massaged his shoulders. "I know what it's like to be married to a guy who doesn't seem to give a shit about you anymore," she said. "I couldn't like you very much if you treated your wife like that, Barry." She patted his butt, then bumped against him at the sink. "I'll finish here," she said, taking the sponge out of his hand. "Go call Gretchen."

Barry sighed. "All right, if it'll make you happy." He dried his hands and lumbered out to the living room.

"I want you to make *her* happy!" Amy called. She scrubbed a pan and tried not to listen to Barry on the living room phone.

She wasn't suited to play the mistress role. But she'd fallen in love with a married man. Of course, that had happened before she knew he was married. Strange, even then, she'd been drawn to a man who spent most of his time in another city. Had she felt she didn't deserve someone entirely hers? Is that why she'd chosen Barry—of all the men who came into the store?

Then he'd told her that he was married. That would have ended it. But he'd sent her flowers and notes, and kept calling to apologize, begging to see her again. She never picked up the phone. She let the machine take his calls, and she played the tape over and over again, crying as she listened to his pleas, still wanting him—maybe even more in love with him than before. He was in town the following week, and she agreed to see him—as "friends." They were together every night, and they didn't so much as kiss each other. She learned all about Gretchen and Amy liked her, admired her. Most of all, she envied her.

That Thursday night four months ago, before Barry left her apartment to pack for Spokane, they'd made the all-too-convenient and unavoidable mistake of kissing good-bye. The following morning in bed, they resolved that it wouldn't happen again when he came back to town.

But by the Wednesday morning during Barry's next trip to Seattle, they'd stopped making resolutions in bed, and Amy had resigned herself to becoming "the other woman."

Barry was the one good thing in her life right now. And it was perverse that "the one good thing" she had made her feel ashamed, guilty—and bad.

"You got the toothpaste in there again?" Amy called past the shower curtain. She rubbed the sleep out of her eyes.

The curtain opened on one end, and Barry poked his hand out, holding a tube of Crest. Amy took it and squeezed some onto her toothbrush. "Just heard on the radio," she called. "Snow on the mountain passes. Be careful driving back to Spokane, okay, babe?"

"I'll be fine," he replied from the other side of the curtain. "Get any sleep last night?"

Her mouth full of toothpaste, Amy mumbled, "A little."

The shower went off with a surrendering squeak. Barry stepped out of the tub, grabbed a towel, and started drying himself. He kissed Amy on the back of the neck. "All the tossing and turning last night," he said. "Still wondering about that boy you saw in the store?"

Amy rinsed out her mouth and wiped the steam off the mirror. "I've decided," she said. "I'm reporting it to the police. Who gives a damn if they think I'm crazy?" She opened the medicine chest, put away her toothbrush, and took out a jar of Noxema. "Another thing, I'm going to hire a private investigator. If that was Ed last night, I don't want to let him slip away."

Barry stepped into his undershorts. "I happen to know someone here in town who's good."

"A private eye? How do you know a private eye?"

"Remember I told you about my oldest niece?"

"The one who ran away and became a Moonie or something like that for a while?"

"Yeah. That was here in Seattle—three years ago when my brother's family lived in Kirkland. They hired a guy named Sharkey, Milo Sharkey. He's the one who found her. Got her back in ten days. Didn't cost an arm and a leg either."

Amy looked at Barry in the mirror. "Think he'll help me?"

"I'll try to set up an appointment for today—that is, if he's still in Seattle."

Milo Sharkey was still in Seattle. Barry phoned Amy at the store to tell her they'd see him at noon. She tried to keep busy all morning, because thinking about it only got her hopes up. But think about it she did. At the first lull, she left Veronica in charge and hurried down to Young Men's Apparel.

"Sorry, Amy," Brian said, running a hand over his moussed black hair. He'd been working in Young Men's Sportswear last night. "I don't recall any blond kid in a red jacket. But we were pretty swamped last night. I can't say for sure."

"Well, he might have been carrying the jacket. Could have been next door in Men's, too." Amy knew the boy had bought something in the store; he'd been carrying a Bon Marché bag. "Like I say, this was around six o'clock."

Shrugging, Brian shook his head. "Sorry, Amy."

"Thanks anyway," she said. "Could you do me a favor and ask around? Somebody else might remember him."

Amy asked around, too.

"Ted, he's the salesman in TVs," Amy explained to Barry as they drove to the Smith Tower, where Milo Sharkey had his office. "Ted saw him looking at the big-screen TVs last night. If we can only find someone who sold him something, we might get his father's name off a credit card receipt."

"Honey, the credit card idea is a stretch. And it's still a long shot that this kid and your Eddie are one and the same. I don't want you setting yourself up for a big disappointment."

But Amy couldn't help feeling excited. Eddie might be within her reach once again.

The ninth floor of the Smith Tower seemed stuck in a time warp from the early thirties, when the Tower had been built. Barry and Amy walked down the tall, narrow hallway, her high heels clicking loudly against the tiled floor. The doors had windows of fogged glass with names and agencies painted on them: MILO SHARKEY—INVESTIGATIONS—903.

Amy almost expected to find Humphrey Bogart inside the old office, his feet up on a battered desk. Instead, a plump blonde in her late forties sat at the keyboard of a computer terminal. She offered them coffee and explained that Mr. Sharkey was due back shortly. "I talked to him after we spoke," she told Barry while pouring coffee into two Styrofoam cups. "And Mr. Sharkey said he'll see you. Hope you like it black. I don't know where he keeps the cream and sugar. I'm just a temp, filling in today."

Amy and Barry sat quietly and sipped the bitter coffee while watching the secretary struggle with a computer that was obviously unfamiliar to her. Amy felt some of her enthusiasm wane during the long wait in the cramped, ugly little room.

She and Barry were starting their third round of rancid coffee when Milo Sharkey finally stepped inside the office. He was a tall, formidably built black man. The blue, three-piece suit almost seemed too small for his broad shoulders. There were flecks of grey in his close-cropped hair; Amy couldn't tell if he was closer to thirty or fifty. One thing was apparent. He seemed very surprised to see them—and a bit annoyed.

Barry stood up and extended his hand. "Mr. Sharkey?"

"Are you my noon appointment?" Sharkey shook his hand. Amy noticed his eyes darting back and forth from her to Barry.

"This is Mr. Horton and Ms. Sheehan," the secretary said.

With a slightly dazed smile, Milo Sharkey opened his office door. "Have a seat," he said. "Sorry you had to wait so long. I'll only be another minute." Once they were inside his office, he closed the door.

The room was cluttered with grey file cabinets, Sharkey's desk and chair, and two ugly metal and pea-green vinyl chairs. Barry and Amy sank down in them. They stared out the plate glass window at the view of the Puget Sound. In the outer office, they could hear Sharkey whispering to the secretary.

"Well, you didn't ask me what their names were," Amy heard the woman say indignantly. Then more whispering.

"I don't know about this guy," Amy said. "Something's wrong. Was he expecting somebody else?"

Finally, Sharkey came back inside the office, a cup of coffee in his large hand. He sat behind his desk. "Now, I understand you're looking for a teenage boy who may or may not be your son, Ms. Sheehan. Is that the story you gave my secretary?"

"I'm the one who talked with her," Barry explained. "I'm a friend of Ms. Sheehan's. A couple of years back, you helped locate my niece, Lisa Horton—"

"And I need you to help find my son," Amy cut in. Barry quickly clammed up and let her talk. She explained how Eddie had been kidnapped twelve years ago. She told Milo Sharkey about the postcard "updates" from his abductor—all of them postmarked from cities between Portland and Seattle. She described the twelve-year-old boy she'd seen the night before, his resemblance to Paul, the telltale scar on his chin, the medication his "father" had referred to. "My ex-husband took daily medication for epilepsy—which he inherited from *his* father," she said. "We might be able to trace him through local doctors' or pharmacists' records for epilepsy medication. That shouldn't be too tough." All the while she talked, Milo Sharkey just nodded. It bothered Amy that he wasn't writing anything down. And he was looking at Barry half the time—his eyes narrowed.

"Anyway," she continued, "I think this boy I saw last night could be my son. I talked to a couple of salespeople who saw him. He bought something in the store. He was carrying one of our shopping bags. We're hoping he used a credit card. But even if he paid in cash, we might get a name or some clue . . ."

"Ms. Sheehan, you work at the store, right?"

She nodded. "I've been there five years."

"Well, then you're better acquainted with the store and the salespeople than I am. I don't think I'd be much use to you."

"But that's crazy," Amy said. "I mean, okay. If I find the man's name on a credit card receipt, then I wouldn't need you. But what if that doesn't happen? I mean, you're the pro. You know how to look for missing persons." She reached into her purse. "This morning, I wrote down descriptions of both the man and the boy—"

Milo Sharkey held up one hand. "I'm sorry," he

said, shaking his head. "If you're sincere about this search for a missing son, I—"

"Of course I'm sincere!" she replied, the folded piece of notebook paper in her hand. "What kind of thing is that to say?"

"Forgive me. I just don't think it's plausible that this boy you saw last night is your son. It's just too much of a coincidence." He glanced at Barry. "Not that I don't believe in coincidences. In any event, you'd be wasting my time—and your money—trying to track down this customer and his boy."

"Listen," Amy said. "If you're too busy to take this case, just say so."

Then Barry piped in: "If money's a problem, between Ms. Sheehan and me, I'm sure we could handle it."

Amy patted his arm. "Oh, no, honey, I won't have you spending any money on this."

"I don't want to take money from either one of you," Milo Sharkey said. "And I don't want to take this case. It's not because I'm too busy either. I just don't like the odds. Of course, you could get yourselves another private investigator."

"Maybe we should," Amy sighed, frowning at him.

"He'll tell you that the odds are wonderful," Sharkey continued. "He'll tell you everything you want to hear. He'll also charge you at least a hundred a day—plus expenses. Then he'll take a week to find this father and son. For that, he'll demand a five-thousand-dollar bonus. About six thousand dollars later, you'll discover that this boy isn't yours. A lot of PIs would be happy to do that for you, but I don't like charging people for an investigation that leads to a dead end."

Amy said nothing for a moment. Finally, she stood

up. "I get your point, Mr. Sharkey," she murmured. "Thank you."

"Why couldn't he have just told us he was too busy to take the case? Why did he have to shoot down my hopes like that?" Amy was shaking her head. She and Barry sat in his car, parked outside the Bon Marche employee entrance.

"Want to try another private investigator?" Barry asked.

"Yes." But then Amy frowned. "Oh, crap, I don't know."

He stroked her shoulder. "I just don't want to see you setting yourself up for another heartbreak. Maybe Milo Sharkey's right. It might be a wild-goose chase."

Amy said nothing.

"I know how depressed you are, honey." Barry leaned over and kissed her. "I wish I didn't have to go back to Spokane today. I hate leaving you alone now like this."

"Oh, I'll be fine," she replied with a pale smile. She opened the car door. "I'll buy a bag of Pepperidge Farm cookies and eat them all in one sitting. I'll be fine."

"Call you Monday night."

Amy climbed out of the car. "Be careful driving back," she said. Then she shut the car door. She watched Barry drive away.

Later, Gayle, who worked with Brian in Young Men's Sportswear, came up to Amy's department. Gayle was a bit chubby, with dark lipstick, exotic eyes, and short, styled dark auburn hair. She was a flashy, smart dresser and very gregarious. She'd heard Amy had been asking about a teenager in a red jacket. "I waited on him," she said, leaning against Amy's sales counter. "Cute kid, polite, too."

Amy felt her heart leap. "Oh, God, you're kidding. Did he buy anything?"

Gayle squinted at her, then twisted her mouth up.

"Try to remember," Amy pleaded. "I need to know who he is. I'm hoping to get his name off a credit card receipt. Please, Gayle . . ."

She snapped her fingers. "I remember now. He bought a Huskies sweatshirt—fourteen bucks." Then she frowned. "Oh, but he paid in cash. I remember, because it was a five and a bunch of singles."

A hopeful smile still clung to Amy's face. "You said that he was polite?"

"Oh, a doll. He asked to try on one of the leather jackets locked to the display rack. I helped him with a few, and he kept thanking me all over the place. Sweet kid. Who is he?"

Amy shrugged. She felt her throat tightening. "I think I might know his parents. Did he seem to you— like he was happy?"

Gayle chuckled. "I guess so. Most kids I can't stand. This one was sweet. But that's all there is to it, Amy. He told me that he'd bring his dad back in a few minutes to show him the jacket he liked. But he never came back. Listen, if he does show up today, do you want me to give you a call?"

"Thanks." Amy was barely able to get the word out. She nodded and tried to smile. But her heart ached, because she knew: neither the boy nor his father would be coming back to this store.

CHAPTER SIXTEEN

Football practice had been canceled on account of heavy rains that Tuesday in November. But it didn't stop Sam from playing football.

"Largent turns on the ten-yard line. He's clear! Bosworth pulls back . . . hesitates . . ." Sam pivoted around the ottoman to his father's favorite chair and leapt up on the sofa. "He passes!"

Craig threw the football. Too late. Sam had already run the length of the sofa and was jumping off the other end as the ball spun in the air—a few feet behind him. He tumbled on the carpeted floor. "Oh, Jesus!" he heard Craig cry. The football smashed one of the framed pictures on the wall behind the couch. Glass shattered. Both the picture and the football bounced off the wall. Another crash as the picture hit the floor, and more glass broke. "Oh, Jesus!" Craig said again. "I told ya we shouldn't be doing this inside!"

"I was way the hell over here!" Sam yelled. "What are you passing it there for? God, my dad's gonna shit." In his stocking feet, he threaded around bits of broken glass to the picture frame, lying facedown beside the coffee table. Sam glanced up at the wall and the blank spot amid several framed photographs that had been knocked askew. He knew the casualty among them: his parents' wedding portrait. It was the only picture they had of his mother. "Oh, crap . . ." he murmured. If the photograph was ruined, his father would kill him. Sam turned over the picture frame to assess the damages. Only a small white scratch at the hem of her wedding gown, practically unnoticeable. The frame had survived, too.

"I didn't even want to do this in the first place," Craig whined.

"It wasn't your fault," Sam said. He carefully picked a sharp triangle of glass out of the frame.

"What are you gonna do?"

"I don't know. But we got an hour and a half before my dad gets back from work. Help me clean this up, will ya?"

They'd disposed of all the broken glass when Sam got a brainstorm. If he could find another piece of glass to fit the frame, his dad would never know the difference. There was a framed photo of Mel Gibson as Mad Max hanging above Sam's desk. Sam took the photo from his bedroom wall. He compared it to the frame holding his parents' wedding portrait. Too small.

He tried several others until he found that the frame to his Brian Bosworth picture was a perfect fit. Sam pried out Brian, then removed the glass. With a scissors, he cut the brown paper sealed against the frame backing to his parents' wedding picture. "Won't he notice?" Craig asked.

"Not for a few months at least—I hope." He was about to replace the glass when he saw some writing on the back of the wedding portrait. It looked as if someone had tried to erase the words, written in blue ink. The faded penmanship belonged to his father. His dad always labeled the backs of pictures with the date, the occasion, and the locale. It seemed funny that he'd found it necessary to scribble such information on the back of *this* picture. Like he'd ever forget his own wedding day . . .

But that wasn't what it said.

Sam saw it, in his father's handwriting: *Tom Welshons Wedding—Groomsman, 1970.*

He frowned. It didn't make any sense. This was supposed to be his parents' wedding—in 1976. His mother and father. He wasn't a *groomsman* in this picture, he was the *groom*.

Sam checked the photo again, and read his father's caption once more. How could his dad make a mistake like that? Or was it really a photograph from someone else's wedding?

"What's that say on the back?" Craig asked, pulling his glasses out of the breast pocket of his shirt.

"Nothing," Sam said. He quickly turned the picture over, then reached for the glass. "Just the date, that's all."

Sam had never seen another photograph of his mother besides the one he now held in his hands. The pretty blond lady in the picture had always been a stranger to him, and now he wondered if she was really his mother.

"Hey, your hand's shaking," Craig said.

"No, it's not." Sam set the glass in the frame, then placed the matted photograph on top of it. He didn't want Craig to see what his father had written. He didn't want his friend thinking something was wrong. He cov-

ered the back of the picture with cardboard and stuck
the tiny nails in place. Hurriedly, he taped the brown
paper to the back of the frame, then hung the picture on
the wall. He straightened out all the pictures around it.

"Looks good," Craig said. "I don't see any difference."

But to Sam, the wedding portrait of his parents suddenly seemed very different indeed.

Sam glanced at the picture he'd drawn in first grade:
a gruesome G.I. Joe battle scene. He must have worn a
fresh red crayon down to a pebble with all the blood. It
was a horrible picture. Yet his father had saved it—
along with all the other pictures, watercolors, finger
paintings, and homemade birthday cards Sam had ever
given him. They were stowed away in a liquor store box
that sat on the floor in his father's closet. The box also
held Sam's old report cards, photos that hadn't made
the family album, and negatives. Sam had been through
the memento box at least half a dozen times in the past,
but then, he'd only been browsing out of boredom,
never really looking for anything.

Now he wanted to find some proof of who his
mother was—another photo of her that his dad might
have overlooked; their marriage license; or her death
certificate. He'd settle for just her name on his own
birth certificate. But Sam couldn't find any of these
things in the old liquor store box.

He checked the desk drawers. He'd been through
them several times before, too. His dad kept some *Playboys* under his bed, and Sam often sneaked a peek at

them. Routinely, while his dad was at work, he'd check the desk and dresser drawers, hoping to uncover similar hidden treasures. But he'd never found anything.

And he didn't find anything now: nothing about his mother, and no birth certificate either. He *had* to have one, and her name would be on it.

He didn't like to think that his dad had been lying to him all these years about the wedding picture—and about his mother.

If he had to turn the bedroom inside out, he'd find something—just to prove to himself how silly the whole idea was. Under the bed: just the *Playboys* and one sock. In his father's dresser: clothes, nothing else; the closet shelf: sweaters.

Then he found something—under one of the sweaters.

Sam dug out the blue spiral notebook. Frowning, he flipped through it. The back pages were blank; but the first fifty or more sheets were filled with his father's handwriting.

He stopped on one page and noticed it was dated about six weeks before:

Thursday, Sept. 14, 1989—11:20 P.M.

I'm a wreck. Sam met me downtown at work so we could shop for back-to-school clothes. The evening started out great. Everyone in the office (especially the women) made such a fuss over Sam. It wasn't just because he's the new boss's son either. He seemed impressed with my new office, too. Later, we had burgers at the Bon's restaurant. Everything was swell.

Then I gave Sam some money to buy clothes, and I went up to look for a shower curtain. The girl waiting on us—

The telephone rang. Startled, Sam dropped the notebook and reached for the phone on his father's nightstand. "Hello?"

"I just got home, and I'm drenched."

"Oh, hi, Craig." He glanced at the notebook on the foot of his father's bed.

"Listen, are you pissed at me?" Craig asked.

"No, of course not. Whaddaya mean?"

"Well, you kicked me out in such a hurry, I figured you were ticked off at me for breaking the picture."

"It wasn't your fault," Sam said. "Don't sweat it."

"Well, what was the big rush? Why'd you make me leave all of a sudden?"

Sam looked over at the notebook again, then at the clock on the nightstand. His dad would be home in a half hour. "I just had a lot of stuff I remembered I had to do," he said. "In fact, I'm right in the middle of something now. So I can't talk."

"You sound funny, Sam. You sure you're not pissed off?"

"Positive! Jeez! I'll see you in school tomorrow. I gotta go. Okay?"

"Well . . . okay . . . 'bye."

"'Bye." Sam hung up the phone. He sat down on his father's bed and reached for the spiral notebook. His heart was racing.

So his dad kept a diary—all his secrets and personal thoughts in this notebook. It was different from sneaking a peek at his dad's *Playboys*; it seemed far more private and forbidding. And he was a little scared. But he picked it up anyway, and found the passage he'd been reading before:

—and I went to look for a shower curtain. The girl waiting on me was attractive & something about her was familiar. I couldn't place her though. Sam showed up & just as we were walking away, I heard her say, "Eddie." I turned around, and God, it all came together. I must have looked guilty as sin when I recognized A.M. I went into a panic, and ran for the escalator. Thank God, Sam just kept walking the whole time.

I was sure she'd follow us. I couldn't get out of there fast enough. Anyway, we made it out of the store and home OK, but I still feel wired, like I've just narrowly missed getting killed in a car accident or something. I keep waiting for the phone to ring, or a knock on the door. I'm a wreck. And yes, I've had a couple of drinks tonight.

What gets me too is how lovely A.M. turned out. I'd always thought she and P.M. were a couple of greaser lowlifes and he'd do better with me. I hadn't counted on A.M. turning out so lovely. And she hasn't forgotten. She's still searching. How could I be so stupid to think that wound had healed long ago?

It's crazy, but I almost want to write to her again. Just to tell her, yes, it was us, and we're happy. I wish she could understand and forget what happened. But that's wishing for the moon. For a long time, I felt very close to her. Strange, I know, but I still feel that way.

I looked her up in the phone book. She said she's worked at the Bon Marché 3 years. I've been in that store with Sam dozens of times. We could be neighbors, passing one another on the street every day. Anyway, I couldn't find her in the book at first, then I remembered her maiden name and tried that. She lives in West Seattle.

So now I'm wondering if we should move. God knows, I don't want to—not after the promotion & raise at work. Plus Sam is doing so well in school, and I don't want to take him away from his friends. But it's inviting trouble if we remain here in the same city as her.

Well, it's late. My hand's tired & I'm slightly shitfaced. Although I probably won't sleep a wink tonight, I should make an attempt. Tomorrow, I'll weigh over the risks of staying in Seattle. Good night.

Sam frowned. He didn't know what to make of it. His dad had written this seven whole weeks ago; so obviously he'd decided not to move. But why had the saleslady at the Bon Marché thrown him into such a panic? Was A.M. an old girlfriend or something? And who the hell was P.M.? Her husband? Did his dad have an affair with a married lady? And who was Eddie?

Flipping through the pages of the spiral, notebook, Sam shook his head. "Jesus," he murmured. "What's going on here?" Just two hours before, everything had been fine. And now, he wasn't sure who his mother was, and his dad seemed to be living some kind of double life.

If he expected to understand any of it, he'd have to read the journal—from beginning to end.

He couldn't ask his father anything. He'd gone around that corner when he'd covered up his own little crime, then invaded his father's bedroom and read his diary. Besides that, all of a sudden, for the first time in his life, Sam wasn't sure he could trust his dad to tell him the truth.

Sam read a little bit more of the diary every chance he got—usually during that hour alone after football practice and before his father came home. He didn't like himself very much for what he was doing.

His dad didn't write one mean word about him in the whole book. It was very clear that in his father's eyes, he could do no wrong. And here he was, doing wrong.

If his dad was mean to anyone, it was himself. *"Moron that I am,"* seemed to be one of his favorite expressions. Using swearwords Sam had never heard him say out loud, he ruthlessly criticized himself for drinking too much. He kept writing about how he wished he could be a better father; and once, for two whole pages, he beat himself up for missing one of Sam's Little League games last summer. He hated his job (something Sam never knew), and felt bad that on his salary, he couldn't afford to give Sam the things he wanted— a house with a backyard and a dog. He was so hard on himself.

After reading those passages, Sam almost wanted to hug his father when he came home, then assure him that he was a terrific dad and he loved him very much.

But there were other things in the diary that made Sam shrink back whenever his father tried to embrace him.

Portions of the journal reminded him of events last summer that he'd practically forgotten. The day after he'd fainted at the Seattle Center fairgrounds was one such time. He'd been in Dr. Durkee's office, scared about the fainting spells and concerned that he was the hairless wonder. Well, he was showering in the locker room after football practice now, and he had no cause for embarrassment. Puberty had come at last. And his epilepsy was under control, too.

But his father's account of that day, June 9, 1989, ripped the lid off a whole new can of worries:

As if I weren't enough of a wreck, I guess Durkee's nurse told Sam about the 1st time I brought him in, and the missing medical records from his infancy. I never expected that to come back & haunt me. He mentioned it in the car, and I ran a stop sign, almost had an accident. Nothing happened, and thank God, Sam seems to have forgotten about the damn medical records . . .

Sam had forgotten about them completely—until he read that passage in his father's journal.

He also caught his father in a lie. The story his dad had given him was that he'd called an "old family doc-

tor" to find out about Grandfather Jorgenson's epilepsy.
But the journal didn't mention anything about an old
family doctor or Sam's grandfather.

That night, his dad had called "P.M." to ask about
the epilepsy:

*I got what I needed. I was so afraid I wouldn't
get him to tell me, but he did. He hung up just as
soon as I made out like I was trying to sell him
pharmaceuticals. I felt kind of proud & very
clever the way I handled it. And now, I've got a
pretty good idea what's wrong with Sam. He
should be OK now.*

   *It was strange talking to P.M. He sounded
like an asshole. I wonder when he and A.M. split
up. It's been so long since I've written to her.
I guess A.M. probably moved years ago. She
might have even left Portland. I hope she's all
right, remarried & with a tribe of kids by now,
wherever she is . . .*

Sam knew where she was, because in a diary entry
four months later, his father would write about meeting her at the Bon Marché. She sold him a shower curtain. Funny, they didn't use that shower curtain with
the map of the world on it. His dad never even took it
out of the box. It just disappeared; and later, he bought
a plain white one and hung it up in the bathroom.

On the Tuesday before Thanksgiving, exactly one
week since he'd found the diary, Sam read the last passage. It wasn't like the final chapter of a regular book,
where everything comes together, and all the questions
are answered. The last page was dated three days ago:

I don't know what's gotten into Sam lately. He's been so withdrawn. He spends most of the time holed up in his bedroom, like he's avoiding me. He used to be so affectionate, but he hasn't so much as hugged me in over a week. And when I try to reach out to him, he stiffens up like a board and pulls away. I keep telling myself it's just an adolescent phase, the hate-your-parents bit. But on the contrary, he's been very coopera- tive about doing his chores, emptying the garbage, etc. In fact, too cooperative, too polite. He hasn't even gotten sarcastic or wised off to me at all lately—and that's totally unlike the Sam I know & love. I haven't seen him laugh in a while either.

I think he's been through my things. Not just the Playboys either. No, it's much worse. Some- thing's tearing him up inside, and I've almost been afraid to ask what's wrong, fearing the worst. But I have asked, several times, and he just shrugs, says he's fine, and looks at me as if I were a total stranger.

God, please, let this just be a phase, and let it pass quickly.

Sam closed the notebook. The rest of it was blank.

"What's wrong with you, Jorgenson? Get with the program!"

It was the Monday after Thanksgiving. They were having a scrimmage game, and Sam had dropped three passes. On defense, he'd performed miserably. Coach

Geara had already bawled him out in front of the team. Finally, he called Sam to the sideline and sent someone else to take his place in the practice game.

"So what's the problem?" Coach Geara asked, his hands on his hips. He was a big, burly man—covered with hair everywhere except on the top of his head. Sometimes, he took a shower with the team after practice, and the guys joked about his hairy back, his hairy butt, and his hairless head. But everyone liked him—including Sam. He hated disappointing Coach Geara.

"I'm sorry," he muttered, holding his football helmet under his arm. "I think I'm coming down with a cold or something."

"I'm not just talking about today. The West Seattle game on Saturday, you weren't concentrating at all. I should have benched you after the first quarter. Last couple of weeks, your mind hasn't been on the game, Jorgenson. What's the matter?"

"Nothing's wrong," he said. "I'm sorry. I'll try harder."

Coach Geara sighed. "Well, you look tired. That—ah, condition of yours, it's okay? You taking those pills?"

"Yeah, I'm fine. It's just a cold or something."

"Well, if you're sick, you ought to be home in bed. No use infecting the whole team. Shower up and go home. I don't want to see you for a couple of days, Jorgenson. Not until you're well and you have your mind on the game."

"I'm sorry, Coach," he murmured. Sam took the long, lonely walk to the locker room, showered, then caught a bus for home.

He'd succeeded in pissing off practically everyone.

Most of the team was still mad at him for screwing up against West Seattle on Saturday. Now Coach Geara was mad at him too. He'd been avoiding Craig, who, of course, was confused and hurt. He kept asking Sam if anything was wrong. But Sam just wanted to be left alone until he figured out exactly what his father was hiding. There was some awful secret about his mother or how he'd been born. And he felt ashamed, even though he didn't know the secret yet. He couldn't tell Craig what was troubling him. It was easier just to shut out his best friend completely.

But it wasn't easy.

Nor had the last four days been easy at home. His father had gotten an extended weekend, because of Thanksgiving, and Sam couldn't avoid him. But the TV was on most of the time, bowl games and videos. Sam asked to watch a game during Thanksgiving dinner. He didn't want to talk. It was just the two of them, of course—as it had been on every holiday he could remember. Suddenly, this Thanksgiving, it didn't seem right.

He and his father had no other family. They never got any visits or calls from old friends. Sam didn't know anybody who had even met his mother. His dad was the only one.

If Sam couldn't trust his father to tell him the truth, at least he could believe what he read in the diary. In the last four days, he hadn't had a chance to look at it. Riding the bus home from football practice, Sam wondered if his dad had written anything new in his journal during the long holiday weekend.

Sam's hair was still damp from his shower, and he was still wearing his leather aviator's jacket when he headed straight into his father's bedroom. He dumped his schoolbooks on the bed, then opened the closet door. He reached under the blue V-neck sweater. But the journal was gone. Panicking, he tried the next stack of sweaters, then the next.

Nothing.

He went through the whole closet, the desk and dresser drawers. It was no use. His dad had found a new hiding place for the diary.

Sam couldn't help feeling betrayed and vulnerable. His only connection to the truth was gone. And his father was on to him.

Now he had no other choice. For a week he'd procrastinated. He even had his jacket on. He could take a bus downtown. The department store where *A.M.* worked was only fifteen minutes away.

BATHS—5th FLOOR, said the directory sign by the foot of the escalator.

Sam hadn't been inside this store since that evening his father had been in such a hurry to leave it. That wasn't the first time his dad had mentioned "A.M." in the diary. Those cryptic initials came up again and again—often linked with "P.M." He'd written about a lot of people in the journal, but A.M. and P.M. were the only ones he referred to only by their initials. The diary was full of names—except for one very important name: *Anne.* He wrote about his dead father and his dead mother, but not a word for the dead wife.

Maybe she wasn't really dead. Maybe Anne Jorgenson had deserted her husband and baby, taking with her a box full of photos and documents—including their baby's medical records and birth certificate. Then later, she married "P.M." *"A.M. and P.M."* Now Anne Jorgenson-Whatever-Her-New-Last-Name-Was worked at the fifth floor of this store.

Christmas music churned over a speaker. Shoppers brushed past him onto the escalator. They kept bumping against him, knocking him with their umbrellas, bags or gift boxes, and no one said "excuse me." Sam stepped onto the escalator. He hadn't lied to the coach earlier; he really was coming down with a bad cold or flu. His head ached, and his throat felt scratchy and raw.

Stepping off the escalator at the fifth floor, he noticed tables stacked with bath towels. Over at the register, the saleswoman waited on a customer. Sam didn't recognize her. He'd barely glanced at her that time with his father. He couldn't even remember if she'd been a blonde or brunette.

He approached the counter. The saleslady was busy with another customer, and she had two more women waiting in line. Sam got behind them. He guessed the saleslady was a little younger than his dad—about forty or forty-five years old. It was hard to tell with adults.

Another lady got behind him in line. He glanced at his wristwatch: 5:20. His dad would be home soon, wondering where he was. *"I went looking for my mother,"* he imagined telling him.

Finally, he was at the front of the line.

"Can I help you?" the saleslady asked. She took off her glasses and rubbed the bridge of her nose. She smiled without really looking at him. She had tiny, dark eyes.

"Um, is your name Anne?" he asked nervously.

"No. I'm Veronica. We don't have anyone named Anne working in this department. Is there something *I* can do for you?" She put her glasses back on.

"Do you sell shower curtains here?"

"We sure do." She pointed. "There's a whole rack of them on the other side of that post. Why don't you have a look-see? I'll be over just as soon as I take care of these folks here."

Sam glanced over his shoulder. Now there were two ladies behind him, each with an armload of towels. He looked back at the squinty-eyed saleswoman. "I'm sorry," he said. "You sure a lady named *Anne*—her last name begins with M, A.M.—you sure she doesn't work here? I know she was here back in September."

"Well, I've worked here two years. And I'm sorry, but we haven't had anyone named Anne in this department. Maybe it was some other store you saw her."

"But I know it was this store, and she sold me a shower curtain." Sam heard the lady behind him clearing her throat.

Now the saleswoman looked annoyed. "Do you have the shower curtain with you? Do you have the receipt?"

"No . . ."

"Well, bring them in next time, and then I might be able to help you. I'm sorry, but you'll have to step aside and let me help these folks."

"I'm sorry," Sam murmured. "Thanks. I'm sorry to bother you." He turned away and wandered toward the escalator. He wasn't going to cry—no matter how frustrated, scared, and tired he was. People kept bumping into him again, then hurrying along as if he wasn't even there.

He didn't know who A.M. was, who his mother was, and without a birth certificate, he didn't even know who he was. He just knew he felt sick and very lost.

"This isn't my room. I didn't know this room was here. What are all these boxes?"

Across the hall from Sam's bedroom, Carl gathered dirty towels for the wash. He never used to pay attention to Sam's sleep-talking. Now he listened, hanging on each word and hoping he'd hear something to explain what was troubling him lately.

What troubled Sam this morning and most of last night was probably the same flu bug going around the office. Carl had called in sick himself to look after him. He'd let Sam sleep past ten, then brought him a tray of toast, juice, two aspirin, a vitamin C tablet, and his epilepsy pill. Afterward, he'd taken Sam's breakfast tray away and told him to go back to sleep.

Now it was one o'clock, and Sam's incoherent mumbling turned into anguished cries. Carl dropped the dirty laundry and hurried into the bedroom. "Hey, Sam . . . Sam . . ."

He lay on his stomach, the bedsheets twisted around him. Carl had plugged in the old vaporizer at his bedside, and the dim room smelled of Vicks VapoRub. He sat on the bed and shook Sam awake. "Hey, Sammy. Hey, you're having a bad dream."

He came to, then pulled away from Carl and sat up. He started coughing. His complexion had a grey tinge to it, and his eyes were bloodshot half slits.

Carl handed him a tumbler of water from the night table. "Sounded like you were having a bad dream."

Sam nodded over the water glass. "Someone tried to get in the apartment. They were breaking the chain lock." He coughed again, then gulped down some more water.

"You had some trouble finding your bedroom, too," Carl said. "At least, you said something to that effect."

Sam looked at him warily. "I say anything else?"

"Something about a room you didn't know was there and some boxes. Very mysterious." He felt Sam's forehead. "Pretty warm there, sport. How do you feel?"

"Like five trucks ran over me. My back's killing me." He fingered his undershirt. "Plus I'm sweating like a pig."

"Good. Your fever's breaking. Lose the shirt. I'll give you one of mine. All yours are in the wash." Carl tried to help him pull the damp T-shirt over his head, but Sam drew back.

"I got it, thanks." He handed the undershirt to him.

Tossing it aside, Carl rolled up his sleeves. "Turn over. I'll rub your back for you."

"It's okay," Sam replied, shaking his head.

"Don't be silly. I know it aches."

With a sigh, Sam rolled over on his stomach. Carl started massaging his shoulders. It felt like his skin was on fire. Sam shuddered gratefully. "Sorry I made you miss work," he muttered, half his face pressed against the pillow.

"No sweat. But you're on your own tomorrow. Big meeting I can't miss." Carl worked his fingers down Sam's spine. "So—tell me about your dream."

"It was stupid, really. I don't even remember."

"You've had a lot of bad dreams lately, haven't

you? I can hear you at night. You talk in your sleep, you know. You have—ever since you were a little kid. So what's bothering you?"

He felt Sam's body stiffen. "Nothing's bothering me."

"Oh, it's gotta be something, Sammy. Maybe you don't even want to think about it—like that stranger in your dream just now, the one you wouldn't let come inside."

Sam turned over and sat up. "It was just a stupid dream, Dad. Doesn't mean anything." He coughed again.

"Something *is* bothering you, Sam. It's been bothering you the last couple of weeks now. Why don't you tell me what it is?"

"I'm cold. Could you get that T-shirt, please?"

Carl pulled the sheet up to Sam's chin. "I want to hear what's wrong first."

Sam turned away and rubbed his forehead.

"Come on," Carl said. "There isn't anything too personal or embarrassing that you can't tell me. Maybe I can help. Are you in some kind of trouble at school?"

"No, Dad." He sighed, "School's fine."

"We don't have to talk about *drugs,* do we?"

"God, no. Of course not." Sam rolled his eyes. "You know me better than that."

"Yeah, well, I don't know what's bothering you, Sam. Does it have to do with sex? Whatever it is, I'll understand."

"It's not sex," he mumbled.

"Well, we've eliminated sex, drugs, and rock 'n' roll. That means the problem must be here at home . . . with me maybe." Carl waited. He tried not to look nervous as Sam let a few moments pass without responding.

"It's got to do with me, doesn't it?" Carl whispered, the understanding smile frozen on his face. Sam had seen the journal, or perhaps he'd found that box in the crawl space. Carl wondered how he could lie his way out of this. A sickly emptiness swelled in his stomach. Twelve years of hiding the truth from him, and now Sam knew. He kept smiling, but felt his whole world about to crumble. He wished he hadn't pushed him this far. Right now, if Sam said nothing was troubling him, Carl would gladly let it go.

"It's kind of weird," Sam said, frowning. "See, a couple of weeks ago, Craig and I were tossing the football—in the living room. It was my idea, not his. And I know I shouldn't have been—y'know, doing that inside."

"Go on," Carl said.

Sam wouldn't look at him. "Anyway, I knocked over th-the wedding picture, and the glass in the frame broke."

"The *wedding* picture?" Carl murmured. Then he cleared his throat. "I—didn't notice the glass was missing from that."

"I replaced it."

"Wait a minute," Carl said steadily. He got to his feet, then went into the living room and took the wedding picture off the wall. The back of it was hastily taped up. Was this what had been troubling Sam these past two weeks? A stupid little accident he'd covered up?

If only it were that easy. Carl bit down on his lip. Of all the pictures Sam could have broken, it had to be this one. Sam knew something—or at least, thought he did.

Just deny it, Carl told himself; *whatever he says, deny it.* He didn't want to go back into that bedroom and face him. But he'd have to give Sam a lecture for playing football in the living room, breaking the picture, then covering it up. *Shit.*

Carl took a deep breath, then he brought the picture back into Sam's bedroom. "Lesson number one," he said, showing him the back side of the frame. "A sloppy repair job like this will get you busted every time—eventually." He sat down on the bed and Sam moved away from him a little.

"There's writing on the back of the picture," he mumbled, his eyes downcast. "Take a look."

"What are you talking about?" Carl peeled off the tape, then pried out the tiny nails that held the cardboard backing in place. His hands were shaking. He lifted out the cardboard. Then he saw his own faded handwriting on the back of the photograph: *Tom Welshons Wedding—Groomsman, 1970.*

"You and Mom were married in 1976, right?"

"That's right," Carl heard himself answer.

"Well, what does that writing mean?"

Carl tried to smile: "What did you think it meant, Sam?"

Now Sam was staring at him. "I think it's a picture from somebody else's wedding in 1970," he replied steadily. "And maybe that's not my mother."

"Sam, that's crazy."

"Is it?"

"Yes! I've never heard anything so ridiculous. If you'd come to me about breaking the glass in the first place, I could have told you, saved you a lot of worry." He shook his head and tried to laugh. " *'Not my mother.'* Of course, this is your mother. Good God, Sammy. What an imagination."

"Then what's that writing mean? Who's Tom Welshon?"

"Tom *Welshons*." Carl pointed to the faded, incriminating note. "He was my groomsman, just like it says. In fact, he—he took this picture, see? Tom took a lot of pictures at the wedding. Did you think this was *his* wedding?"

Sam just shrugged. But his mouth was still twisted in a skeptical frown.

"Sammy, why would I be posing with the bride if this wasn't my own wedding? What do you think your mother is in this picture? The flower girl?"

"Why does it say 1970? You were married in seventy-six."

"Well, nineteen-seventy certainly isn't the date," Carl said. "I know I paid Tom for the pictures. It was around twenty bucks. I guess it's how much the pictures cost." One look at Sam, and Carl knew he wasn't buying it.

But a childhood of keeping his own father's abuse a secret, and the last twelve years of shielding the truth from Sam and others had made Carl a master at fabrication. He needed details here, something real Sam could latch onto.

"Y'know, Tom wouldn't even let me pay him back. He said the pictures were a wedding present. But he'd already given us one. That lamp in the corner of the living room, it was Tom's wedding present to your mom and me. You know the lamp I'm talking about?"

Sam nodded.

"That's from Tom Welshons, the guy who took this picture."

"How come you never talked about him before?"

"Well, after your mom died and we moved up here, Tom and I just lost track of each other. It happens when friends move away." Carl set the cardboard back inside the frame, then started pushing the tiny nails in place.

Sam was quiet for a few moments. Putting the frame back together, Carl glanced at him only briefly; but he detected an inner struggle behind Sam's tired, blood-shot eyes. Sam shivered and he pulled the sheet back up around his neck. "Dad?"

"Hmmm?" Carl pushed in the last nail.

"I have a birth certificate, don't I?"

"Of course you do," Carl said, for there was no other answer he could give. "Do you think you were adopted or something? Is that what's bothering you?"

He shrugged and looked away.

Carl set the picture down on the night table. "Sam, practically every kid at one time or another wonders if he was adopted. Heck, I used to think the same thing way back when."

Now Sam looked directly at him. "So where is it?"

"Where's what?"

"My birth certificate. You said I have one. I know it's weird, but I'd really like to see it."

"Well . . ." Carl hesitated. "That won't be so easy. It's not here. See, it got lost in the move up from Santa Rosa."

Nodding, Sam sighed and reached for his water glass. "Along with all the other pictures of my mother and the early medical records from when I was a baby. I figured you'd say that."

There was no defiance or sarcasm in his tone, just disappointment.

"I'm sorry, Sam." He tried to smile. "Look, if it's any consolation, my birth certificate got lost in the move, too."

"At least you got to see yours," he grumbled.

One small solace: Sam didn't catch his lie. He must not have discovered that box in the crawl space, because Carl's birth certificate was in there. The wheels started spinning again. He could take his own birth certificate to work, Xerox it, white out all the names and dates, then type in the information about Sam. He'd have the proof he needed. The idea was so simple, he wished he'd thought of it years ago, when some immunization records and a lot of evasive smooth talk had gotten Sam enrolled in school without a birth certificate.

"Listen," Carl said. "If you don't believe me, would seeing a copy of your birth certificate make you feel any better?"

"You said it was lost."

"I'll write the county clerk in Santa Rosa and see if they can send us a copy. I know it's on file in the county records."

Sam's tired eyes lit up. "You could do that?"

Carl nodded. "Seeing that you won't take my word for it."

"Well, you don't have to," Sam said. "I believe you, Dad. I only wanted to—y'know—see for myself. But if it's a lot of trouble for you . . ."

"I'll write them." Smiling, Carl reached over and smoothed back his hair. "No problem. Remind me Monday, and I'll get right on it. In the meantime, stop worrying about this nonsense. It's bad for your complexion."

Sam chuckled, a bit relieved, it seemed. "Yeah," he

said. "Yeah, I will." He slouched down until his head rested against the pillow.

Climbing off the bed, Carl grabbed the framed wedding picture. He took it back to the living room and set it down on the coffee table. Carl decided he must be an alcoholic, because it wasn't even two o'clock in the afternoon and he very much wanted a drink. Instead, he got a clean undershirt from his bedroom dresser and took it in to Sam. This time, Sam didn't pull away when Carl helped him put it on.

Sam settled back again and watched him check the water level in the vaporizer. "Huh, small wonder that thing doesn't blow up. It's older than I am."

"Correction," Carl said, moving to the portable TV that sat on top of Sam's bookcase. "It's eleven years old. I bought it when you were thirteen months and had the croup."

"What are you doing, Dad?"

Carl unplugged the TV and picked it up. "I'm taking this out of here, kiddo. Sorry."

"But there are a lot of good shows on tonight."

"I know. Too bad." Holding the TV, Carl paused at Sam's bedside. "What do you expect when you play football in the living room, bust a picture, and cover it up for two weeks?"

"But that's not fair!" Sam protested.

"You're right. 'Fair' would be no TV for a week. But since you're sick, you can have the TV back tomorrow." He bent down and kissed Sam's forehead. "Get some rest."

"Thanks a lot," Sam snorted. "I hope you get a hernia carrying that."

"I love you, too." Carl started for the door.

"Dad?"

"Yeah?" He looked back at him.

"I'm sorry about earlier—for y'know, thinking all that stuff. I musta' been nuts or something."

Carl smiled. "Yeah, well, you've always been a pretty weird kid." He carried the television out of Sam's bedroom.

CHAPTER SEVENTEEN

"**S**o tell me the truth," Amy said, setting the gift box on the register counter. She opened it and carefully peeled back the tissue paper. "What do you think?"

"It's gorgeous," Veronica said. The object of her approval was a Ralph Lauren navy blue crew neck sweater with tiny V-shaped cream and burgundy designs symmetrically woven throughout it. "Let me take a wild guess. Christmas present for Barry?"

Amy nodded. "I'm giving it to him next Thursday. It's our last week together before the holidays."

"How much did it set you back?"

"Ronnie, you can't put a price tag on love. Two hundred forty-one bucks including employee discount and tax."

"I hope his wife likes it."

Amy frowned at Veronica, then put the top back on the gift box. "So he'll wear it here for a while," she said. Amy glanced around for a customer so she could get Veronica off her back. But the Christmas rush didn't include the Bath department today.

"I'll bet my next paycheck whatever he gets you won't be half the cost of that sweater."

"Well, I don't expect him to be extravagant," Amy replied.

"Flowers and dinner out," Veronica said, leaning against the counter.

"What?"

"That's what he's giving you for Christmas, flowers and dinner out. Maybe expensive. But that's all you get."

It had been exactly what he'd given her on her birthday—well, not *on* her birthday; he'd been in Spokane then. But the following week, he'd treated her to a post-birthday dinner at the Space Needle and a dozen coral roses. It certainly hadn't been a cheap birthday present; yet Amy had been disappointed. She would have preferred an inexpensive locket or bracelet, something she could have *kept.* She never should have told Veronica about her secret disappointment after the roses and the Space Needle dinner.

"Sometimes, I don't think you like Barry," she said, tidying up the register counter. "You don't know him. I've never had a guy treat me so nice—so caring and considerate."

"Yeah, but you deserve someone like that who is all yours, Amy. I mean, look at the setup. You'll go out, buy a tree, and have your Christmas with him two weeks early. Then come Christmas Day, you're stuck alone in your apartment with the damn tree, which by then is a dried-up, needle-shedding fire hazard."

"Thanks for the cheery thought," Amy muttered. She stuffed the sweater box inside a shopping bag. "You just don't like Barry, that's all."

"I think he's real cute, honey, and awfully sweet. But what he's doing to you makes him a real creep."

Amy sighed. "Guess it doesn't make me Mother Teresa either."

"He's the one who's cheating . . . and stringing you along."

"If you found out Bill had been involved with a woman for the past six months, who would you blame more—him or the slut he was seeing?"

Veronica shrugged evasively.

"I rest my case," Amy said. "So Barry and I are a couple of sleazeballs." It hurt to say that out loud. For she knew they were both nice people. They had fallen into a routine of dining out at a favorite Italian restaurant every Thursday night he was in town. All the waiters and waitresses knew them by name, and most of them assumed Barry and she were married. They'd come by the table, even when it wasn't their station, just to chat. Barry learned their names quickly, long before Amy did. There was Marilyn, the pretty, struggling law student; Debbie, the thin, neurotic one who sometimes read them snippets of poison-pen poems dedicated to ex-boyfriends; and Justin, the gay waiter with a terminally ill roommate. Barry remembered all their problems, and after stopping by the table, they'd always walk away smiling.

It was like that wherever she and Barry went. People just seemed drawn to them. During walks, he never failed to smile and say hello to old people—lonely, withered old men, and bent-over skeletons of ladies walking alone. Their faces lit up at the friendly words. Often, they'd become the patient audience to some senior citizen's tales of woe or past glories. What really got her was that Barry genuinely enjoyed listening to these people. If Barry taught her anything, it was how to be truly nice to people—not just to friends or customers in the store. Everyone. It was starting to rub off on her, too. Amy found herself being nice to people who weren't even there. Hell, now whenever she took a load of laundry out of the dryer, she automatically cleaned the lint trap for the next person. She'd seen Barry do it once.

They were two very nice people. Damn nice. They loved each other, and it was beautiful. And for that, these two nice people were a couple of sleazeballs.

Amy rode home on the bus that night, her purse and Barry's present in her lap. Her mood had perked up. It was Thursday and TV was good tonight. She'd fix herself a salad, address some Christmas cards, watch the tube. Veronica had insisted she come over for Christmas dinner. Some neighbors—a few of them single—would be there too, so Amy need not feel like she was imposing on some family celebration. At least she wouldn't have to be alone on Christmas night.

She got off at her stop. A light, wet snow drifted down from the dark sky and melted as it reached the ground. Definitely a Duraflame night.

Stepping into the lobby of her apartment building, Amy saw a woman there. She sat on the carpeted stairs, eating a Nestlé's Crunch bar. She was pretty, with wavy, shoulder-length red hair; smartly dressed in a tan polo coat. She was around Amy's age, maybe younger; and heavier—by about seventy pounds.

"Hi," Amy said, checking her mailbox. "Ugly night

out, isn't it?" She pulled out her letters: a bill, what looked like two Christmas cards, and some stupid sweepstakes thing saying on the envelope that she was eligible to win fifty thousand dollars.

"Are you in apartment 306?" the woman asked, tossing the half-eaten candy bar inside her purse.

Amy looked up from her mail. "Yes. Are we neighbors?"

The woman grabbed hold of the banister and pulled herself up. "You're Amy Sheehan?" she asked.

Amy dropped her letters in the shopping bag, then hugged the package against her breasts. *Oh, Jesus,* she thought. *I've seen your picture. Why didn't I recognize you?*

"Are you Amy Sheehan?" she asked again.

Trying not to wince, Amy stepped back and bumped into the mailboxes. She nodded. "Can I—help you?"

"Yes. You can help by staying away from my husband."

Numbly she stared at Barry's wife. She'd dreaded this moment, had nightmares about it. Amy almost wanted to throw herself at Gretchen's feet and beg for her forgiveness. But all she could say was: "Are you Gretchen Horton?"

"Yes. Why do you need to ask? Are you screwing someone else's husband, too?"

Stunned, Amy just shook her head. "I'm so sorry."

"I'm sure you are," Gretchen replied.

Amy dared to take a step toward her. "Please . . . listen, would you like to come up to my apartment and sit for a while? We can talk. You'll be warmer and more comfortable."

Gretchen looked at her as if she were insane. "No, I

don't want to come up to your apartment! I want you to stop seeing my husband."

It was just as well Gretchen refused to come up; Amy suddenly remembered the framed photo on the table by her sofa: her and Barry at a restaurant, very cozy, very much in love. Gretchen didn't need to see that now. "Listen," Amy said meekly. "I never wanted to break up your marriage or anything. It's not like that. I started seeing him before I knew about you."

One hand on the newel post, Gretchen glared down at her.

"I fell in love with him before I knew," Amy continued. "I never wanted you to get hurt. And you mustn't blame Barry. He was just lonely and . . . He loves you very much."

Gretchen folded her arms. "Of course he loves me, *stupid*. You don't mean a thing to him. He's just killing time with you."

"Did Barry tell you that?" Amy murmured.

Gretchen just smiled—as if she knew her remark had hit a vulnerable nerve.

"You two discussed this?" Amy asked. "He—he told you? Is that how you found out about me?"

"That's not your concern."

"I think it concerns me very much."

"No. What you should be concerned about is finding yourself another guy to fuck. Because it's over between you and Barry." Gretchen came down from the steps and brushed past her as she headed for the door.

"If you only knew how bad I've felt about all this." Amy reached out for her. "Please, try to understand—"

Gretchen swiveled around and slapped her hard across the face. The sound echoed in the cold hallway.

It stung, and took Amy by such surprise that she dropped her bag. She hadn't been slapped like that since the nuns in grammar school. It was fierce and brutal. Mean.

"Goddamn you," Gretchen whispered. Then she pushed open the door and hurried outside.

Amy touched her mouth. Numbly, she gazed at her fingertips. Blood. She picked up the shopping bag and ran up the stairs, three flights. She felt sick and ashamed. The side of her face still throbbed from Gretchen's slap. Yet something inside her wanted to turn, run back down, and try to explain things to her again. It wasn't supposed to happen this way. It was not how she wanted it to end.

She didn't buy a Christmas tree that weekend. But she didn't return Barry's sweater either. Amy put everything on hold, waiting for Monday, when he'd call. No matter what Gretchen had said, nothing would keep Barry from at least phoning her.

She felt sorry for Gretchen Horton one minute and hated her the next. Amy now regretted all her self-sacrificing speeches to Barry about not wanting to ruin his marriage. The idea of him leaving Gretchen for her didn't seem so wrong anymore. Barry deserved better. He couldn't possibly love that woman.

On Sunday, she was writing out Christmas cards— the ones she'd put off for last—to long-lost college friends. They all had husbands and families. Amy saved their cards from year to year so she could keep track of the kids' and spouses' names. It got so writing out Christmas cards was like an open-book exam.

"Dear Mary Lou," she wrote. *"Once again, I've let too much time slip by without writing or calling. I loved your card last year. The girls are beautiful."*

She studied Mary Lou's card from last year again, then wrote: *"You were going back to work when you last wrote. How's the job? Give me all the scoops. Me, I'm still working for the Bon Marché & loving it. Haven't heard from Paul in ages, but Lynn Davis wrote & told me his wife had another baby last year."*

Amy hesitated for a moment, then scribbled: *"Met a wonderful guy in May. Despite a job that keeps him on the road a lot, we're still going strong. His name is Barry . . ."*

By the fourth card to another college friend, she wrote that she and Barry were *"practically engaged,"* and somehow, she'd convinced herself that it was almost the truth.

She was addressing envelopes when the phone rang. Amy jumped up and answered it before the machine went on. "Hello?"

"Hi, it's me."

"Where are you?" she asked. "I didn't think you'd call until tomorrow."

"I'm at a pay phone, not far from our place."

"You're here?"

"No, I mean, Gretchen's and my house," he said.

Amy suddenly felt very silly, assuming "our place" meant her apartment. "You sound funny. I guess Gretchen has told you then."

"Yeah. She lowered the boom this morning—after church."

"Something tells me you've been forgiven so long

as you don't see me again," Amy said, a slight tremor in her voice. "Am I right?"

There was silence on the other end of the line.

"How did she find out?" Amy asked. "She wouldn't tell me."

"A few weeks ago, while I was away, she stopped by my office. Something about an electric bill she wasn't sure got paid. Anyway, she went through my desk and found receipts from the flower shop next door. Your name and address were on them."

Amy sat down on the sofa. "She tell you about her visiting me on Thursday?"

"Yeah. I thought she was spending the day with her sister in Kettle Falls."

"And you believed her. Well, I guess she's a better liar than either of us."

Barry said nothing for a moment. "Listen," he muttered finally. "I can't talk long. I'm standing in this phone booth with five dollars' worth of quarters in my hand. I just wanted to let you know, I probably won't be coming to Seattle tomorrow."

"Later in the week then?" she asked. But she already knew the answer.

"I'm sorry. I don't think so."

"In other words, you're not going to see or call me again," Amy said, tugging at the receiver cord. "Am I right, honey?"

"Well, see, I won't be coming to Seattle much anymore," he said. "Something more—grounded has opened up here in the Spokane office. Actually, it's a promotion."

"Congratulations," she murmured.

"The truth is, Amy, I've known about this job opening for a couple of months. They approached me a while back. But I've been stalling them. Now, I think I better take the offer. I don't see any other way."

"It's the practical thing to do," Amy said listlessly. "I hope the job works out for you, Barry." She glanced at the framed black-and-white photograph on the end table—beside the one of her mom, Eddie, and herself. She had her head on Barry's shoulder, both of them smiling and starry-eyed. They looked so beautiful in the candlelight of the restaurant, dressed to the nines, champagne glasses on the table in front of them.

"I'll miss you, honey," he whispered.

"I suppose this is my cue to say, 'It was nice knowing you, Barry Horton.'" Her voice cracked a little. "But you know, it was hell most of the time. All the guilt and worry and shame. Still, I wouldn't take back a single minute. I loved you, Barry."

"Oh, Amy, I'm so sorry . . . for everything. I hate losing you. I think this is the worst—the saddest day of my life."

Past the tears, she let out a weak laugh. "Honey, you haven't lived." She gazed at his picture—beside the one of Eddie. She would never see either of them again. They each belonged to someone else. Somehow, she missed her baby boy more than ever right now. "I've got to go," she managed to say.

He was crying, too. "I still love you . . ."

Amy hung up the phone, then whispered, "Goodbye, Barry."

Dec. 17th

Dear Amy,
　　This is my sixth letter to you since our goodbye on the phone Sunday. The others ended up

in my wastebasket at work. They were love notes, asking for forgiveness, saying how much I miss you and still love you. I think you already know that.

But there's something else you should know. I just found out about it last night.

As you can imagine, things between Gretchen and myself have been pretty tense lately. She's still blowing off steam and I've taken some well-deserved flak. In last night's installment, she informed me that she'd been wise to us since August. That's when she found the receipts from the florist. Rather than confront me, she'd hired a private investigator in Seattle to check up on us. Three guesses who she hired.

Gretchen and I were newlyweds back when my niece, Lisa, ran away. We were both on the phone with my brother every day back then. I guess that's how Gretchen remembered Milo Sharkey.

Anyway, that day we went to see Sharkey, he already knew who we were. I remember the peculiar way he stared at me most of the time, and how he didn't seem to believe your story about Ed. Now I see why he refused to take your case. He couldn't very well take on as clients two people he was already investigating.

Sharkey had pictures of us. Gretchen showed them to me last night. No Peeping-Tom shots, thank God. But there were photos of us holding hands and kissing—all taken while we were outside, in public. I know it sounds strange, but when Gretchen ripped them up in front of me, it was like she was destroying something precious. Some of the shots were very romantic, and you looked beautiful in them. It made me remember that I don't have any pictures of you. The dates on those photographs were all in late September, around the time you and I went to see Sharkey. I'll never know why Gretchen waited three months to confront us.

Anyway, I don't want you hating me, though you have every reason to. I lied to you, then pestered you into seeing me again, and wasted six months of your life. But I think the worst thing I did was come between you and a chance of finding your son. Because of me, Milo Sharkey refused to help you locate that boy you saw in the store. Any other private investigator would have taken the case, and today, maybe you'd have your son with you. I think back and in the six months we were together, that was the only time you ever saw someone you thought could be Ed.

Maybe I shouldn't be telling you this, but I think the boy you saw could have been your son. We just let my wife's "spy" talk us out of pursuing it any further.

Anyway, I hope you keep pursuing it, Amy. I hope you find your son. I also hope you find yourself a nice, unmarried guy, who will love you as much as I do. You deserve someone who belongs to you and only you—whether it's a son or a lover.

It's hard to say this, but I don't want to hear

from you again, and I won't try to contact you anymore either. While I don't think I'll ever forget you, Amy, it's best you pull the plug on this two-timing rat and forget me.

Maybe you already have.

Anyway, again, I'm sorry. I miss you and love you, Amy. Take care.

> *Love,*
> *Me.*

CHAPTER EIGHTEEN

Sam had recovered from the flu, but recurring doubts about his mother lingered like a bad cough. He still didn't know who A.M. was; and despite everything his dad had told him, he didn't feel any connection to that woman in the wedding picture. It had been two weeks since he'd talked to his dad, and he'd yet to see his birth certificate. He tried not to think about it. Like the fainting spells he'd chosen to ignore back in June, he could go on as if nothing was wrong for long stretches of time. But there were other times—alone on the bus from school; in bed at night; or now, bored to smithereens in Mrs. Hull's algebra class, last period—and the worries came back.

He had no idea what Mrs. Hull was talking about and prayed to God that she wouldn't call on him for anything.

He never found his father's new hiding place for the diary. But then, he hadn't looked very hard for it in the last two weeks. Plenty of other things occupied him: football play-offs, exams, and Christmas vacation, which began the day after tomorrow. His Christmas list grew longer each day: a skateboard, a Bruce Springsteen book, several videos, and a basketball. Sam figured he could go piss up a rope for the skateboard. His dad considered them dangerous, and often complained about having to dodge "the little creeps racing down the sidewalk on those things." Sam's only sure bet was the basketball: a sole, square gift-wrapped box that had been sitting on the bedroom floor beside his father's desk for the last few days.

"Sam Jorgenson?"

He sat up and looked at Mrs. Hull. "Yes?"

The bell rang, and she smiled at him. "Saved by the bell. Class dismissed."

Sam thanked God, grabbed his books, and hurried out of the classroom.

"So who are you Secret Santa for?" Craig asked. He leaned against the lockers while Sam worked his padlock combination.

"Mitzi Bateman," Sam answered .

"Gag me. What are you gonna get her? A personality?"

Shrugging, Sam opened his locker and pulled out his jacket. "I'll trade ya. You take Mitzi, and I'll take Beth Hadwell."

"Huh, you wish."

Sam had a crush on Beth Hadwell, the prettiest, shapeliest, most popular girl in the seventh grade. Naturally, she was going with the most popular guy, Jim Collier. But rumor had it that they'd split up during Thanksgiving. Sam had no idea what his chances were with Beth. She seemed to *like* him enough. If only he were her Secret Santa, he'd go over the five-dollar limit and buy something that would really knock her out. "So what are you going to get Beth anyway?" Sam asked, throwing on his jacket.

"Perfume, I think," Craig said.

Perfume for under five bucks. Beth's family was loaded. She'd never wear perfume that cheap. Didn't Craig know anything?

"I'm gonna have my mom help me pick it out."

Then Beth definitely wouldn't use the perfume. Craig's mom wore some stuff that smelled like Raid bug repellant. It stank up their whole house. Sam nodded. "Good idea." He grabbed his schoolbooks and shut the locker.

"We're going to Northgate Mall tonight. I figure I'll get Beth's present there. Want to come with us?"

"Thanks, but my dad and I are buying a tree tonight."

"God, you're so lucky. A real tree. We've had our fake one for practically like forever, and it looks like shit."

On the bus, Sam continued to listen to his friend talk about how lucky he was. In Craig's opinion, Sam's dad pissed perfume (probably better smelling than the stuff Craig would buy for Beth). Craig pointed out that every Christmas, Sam received a ton of great presents. "I know it sounds creepy, but if you had a mother, she'd make sure eighty percent of your Christmas presents were clothes. And if you had any brothers or sisters, you'd have to share the other twenty percent of good stuff with them. You don't know how lucky you are."

Sam got off the bus at Broadway, the main shopping drag of his neighborhood. He wanted to buy something nice for Mitzi Bateman. While Mitzi suffered from a mild case of acne, she wasn't ugly. She wasn't particularly dumb, nor obnoxiously smart. In fact, there seemed no real explanation for why tall, quiet, plain-faced Mitzi Bateman was considered a major loser by most of her classmates. But she was. And Sam felt sorry for her.

He spent a half hour in an expensive knickknack shop until he finally bought her a large glass angel ornament. It cost seven bucks—two over the limit; but the ornament was the kind of thing girls got all mushy about. Mitzi would like it. Last year, Earl Gleason had been her Secret Santa, and he'd given her a gift-wrapped box of Milk-Bone. Mitzi had laughed louder than anyone else over it.

At least this year she wouldn't need to laugh.

Sam got home at four-fifteen, opened a Coke and a bag of barbecue potato chips, then switched on a "Gilligan's Island" rerun. It was the one in which Ginger's look-alike showed up on the island; he'd already seen the episode about a kijillion times.

They were getting the tree tonight, so Sam decided to pull out the ornaments, lights, and other Christmas junk. He needed a screwdriver to pry open the crawl space door in the front closet. It had always been uncharted territory to Sam; there wasn't anything in the crawl space he'd ever wanted. When he was little, he'd been afraid of it, thinking that monsters lived in there amid the moldy boxes and cans of old paint.

It smelled musty and dank. His hands got dirty just taking out the first box. He opened it up in the living room, and found the nonbreakable ornaments—a lot of hideous Styrofoam and papier-mâché figures he'd created back in kindergarten. Only God knew why his dad was still saving them. Another carton, from Nordstrom, held the breakable ornaments.

Toward the back of the crawl space, a box slightly larger than the others lay askew on top of some paint cans, varnish, and bags of steel wool. The other boxes had been covered with dust, but this one wasn't—although the top flaps were marked with drops and rings of wood stain. Unlike the other cartons, which bore the names of Seattle department stores, Sam had never heard of the store advertised on this box. *"Meier & Frank,"* it said in fancy script. He figured it was some store in Santa Rosa. The box was heavier than all the rest. He found the tree stand underneath it and carried them both into the living room.

He heard the front door opening. "Sam?" his father called.

"Hi, Dad," he called back. Sam sat down on the floor.

His dad stepped into the living room and dropped his briefcase. *"My God, what are you doing?"*

Sam looked up, startled. Then he gave him a dazed smile. "I'm just getting the Christmas junk out, that's all. Aren't we buying the tree tonight?" He reached for the Meier & Frank box. "I thought I'd—"

"Leave that alone!"

Sam drew back. "Jeez, what's the matter?"

"Don't open that." He grabbed the box out from under Sam's hands. "There's nothing in here you want. You have no business prying into these things. You shouldn't . . ." Frowning, his father shook his head. He hoisted the box up to his chest.

Dumbfounded, Sam stared up at him.

"There aren't any ornaments in here," his father said. "Just work papers . . . important documents. I don't want you to get them out of order, that's all. I—I'm sorry to snap at you."

"Why do you have work stuff in the store space?" Sam asked. "If it's so important, what's it doing in that dirty old box?"

"They're old records, that's all. Nothing that concerns you." His father started to carry the box toward his bedroom.

Sam knew he was lying. The contents of that box concerned him very much. "I think I know what's really inside there," he said loudly. "You were hiding it from me, weren't you?"

His father turned around. His face was red. "There's *nothing* in here . . ."

"Then why don't you let me take a look?" Sam was grinning. He got to his feet. "You've got a Christmas present in there for me, don't you, Dad? Maybe even a couple? You can't fool me . . ."

A tiny smile flickered across his father's mouth. "Listen, wise guy," he said. "From now until Christmas, my bedroom is off limits. Understand?"

His dad gave him a look—like he meant business—then he carried the Meier & Frank box into his bedroom.

Thursday, Dec. 18, 1989—1:55 A.M.

This won't take long. I'm hoping that by writing here, I'll calm down. I can't go into details. The gist of it is, Sam found the box in the crawl space tonight. Thank God I caught him before he

opened it. He was simply getting out the Christ-
mas decorations. But I lost it & started yelling
at him. Then I apologized. Fortunately, Sam
thought he'd found my hiding place for his
Christmas presents, and I let him believe that.
Of course, now he's curious as hell about what's
inside this box.

Putting down his pen, Carl glanced at the Meier &
Frank carton on the floor beside his desk. The bedroom door was closed and locked—as it always was
when Carl wrote in his journal. He'd found a new
place to hide the blue spiral notebook back around
Thanksgiving, when Sam had been acting so peculiar.
There was a loose corner in the bedroom carpet—behind the rocking chair he never sat in. The notebook
left a small, square bump in the carpet that was practically unnoticeable. Now Carl wished he could find a
similarly ideal hiding place for this box.

He should have gotten rid of the damn thing a couple of Saturdays ago, when he'd had the chance. Sam,
over his flu, had been spending the night at Craig's
house. Carl was alone. He dragged the Meier & Frank
box from the crawl space and sorted through the old
letters, photographs, diplomas, and documents. There
was a fire going in the fireplace, and when he un-
earthed the news clipping about a baby boy abducted
in Portland, Carl thought about burning it. The box contained so many incriminating things: pictures of Eve;
their marriage license; the divorce papers, and another
news clipping about the disappearance of Eddie Mc-
Murray. Although everything was hidden under a layer
of old bills, it was risky to hold on to these souvenirs of

his unspoken past. Yet Carl burned only three not-so-flattering pictures of Eve, nothing else. He couldn't part with the rest of those memories—just as he couldn't part with his journal. It would have been like destroying his past—everything that led up to his life with Sam.

He found his birth certificate amid the keepsakes; it was what he'd been looking for that Saturday night. He wanted to take the certificate to work, where he could forge one for Sam. But Sam hadn't mentioned the birth certificate since that day he'd been sick. Carl wasn't about to open that can of worms again—not until Sam said something.

He picked up his pen again.

God, it's late. I've got work in five hours. We bought the tree tonight & decorated it. I'm exhausted, but still jittery & wired up. A couple of shots of bourbon would really help me relax, maybe even sleep. But I can't afford that right now. I've got to figure out what to do with all the stuff inside this damn box. It's too late to throw it away & I still really don't want to. Shit. I'll never get to sleep tonight . . .

Mitzi Bateman started to open the beautifully wrapped present with visible apprehension. Sam hadn't quite yet dissociated himself from her previous Secret Santa, Earl Gleason, and she must have figured the gift was another cruel joke. But when she saw the crystal angel and held it up to the light, her plain face became beautiful for a moment. She smiled with relief, gratitude, and genuine delight. Sam felt good.

All the other girls made a fuss over it, too. While Mitzi gushed her thank-you to Sam, he heard Earl remark that the glass angel was "pretty faggy."

But it was Sam's crush, Beth Hadwell, who had the last word. He trembled inside when—after the bell— Beth approached him at his locker. She wore a tiny spray of fake holly in her blond hair. Beth was so popular she could get away with corny stuff like that. "Hi, Sam," she said.

"Hey, Beth," he said. Very cool.

"Y'know, all the girls think that was really neat, what you did for Mitzi. You're like super-nice, you really are."

Blushing, he could only shrug and smile back at her.

"I mean it," she said. "I wish you'd been *my* Secret Santa."

They stood in the hallway talking for ten whole minutes, and Sam was elated. One moment, he wished everyone in the school saw them there together; and the next, he wanted to be all alone with her. He missed his bus home, and had to wait twenty-five minutes for another. He didn't mind a bit.

That morning in school, he'd been eager to get back home for something; but Beth made him forget what it was. Sam didn't remember until he opened the front door at four-fifteen.

"My bedroom is off limits," his dad had said, carrying the mysterious box in there. He may as well have told him about a nude beach nearby and said "I don't want you going around there." How could he resist? The box had been too shallow for a skateboard. But it could have held several videos, compact discs, books, and other treasures.

They'd gotten the tree last night and decorated it while eating Arby's. Sam had kept hoping his dad would need to go out for something—so he could check the box in the bedroom. But just his luck, an unprecedented tree-trimming: they hadn't run out of ornament hooks and all the Christmas lights worked.

So Sam had to wait until now—with only an hour until his dad came home—to peek inside that box. He hung up his coat, plugged in the tree lights, and headed into his father's "off-limits" bedroom.

The box sat there in the open, by his father's desk—with the gift-wrapped basketball. His dad hadn't even bothered to hide it or tape up the top flaps. That was how much he trusted him. Sam felt a pang of conscience. Maybe he shouldn't be in here, sneaking around like this. Maybe he should wait until Christmas morning—eight days from now—to see his presents.

No way.

He sat on the floor and stared at the box. He lifted it. Heavy. If everything inside was already gift-wrapped, he'd shit.

Sam opened the top flaps—covered with droplets of wood stain. Inside was a bag from a Waldenbooks store. He started emptying it and his eyes widened. He enjoyed that special guilty thrill of finding something he really wanted ahead of time. A video gold mine: *Batman, The Birds, Psycho, Big, Alien,* and *Lethal Weapon.* His dad had covered the whole list. But there was more in the bag: the Springsteen book, and even *Pictionary.* God, his dad had gone crazy in the bookstore. There was one more item: *The Sports Illustrated Swimsuit Calendar*! He hadn't even asked for that. Talk about a score!

Unfortunately, everything was individually sealed in clear plastic wrap. He'd have to wait until Christmas morning before he could ogle all twelve calendar girls, read the Springsteen book, and view highlights from the videos. He found the receipt clinging to the plastic wrap around the *Pictionary* game.

"Holy shit," he murmured. The total read $193.88. His dad had spent a fortune—all in one day at that one bookstore.

Then he saw the date on the receipt: *12/18/89— 12:07 PM.* It was today. Noon, today.

"What?" Sam whispered, squinting at the receipt.

After a moment, he glanced over at the empty, old box. If his dad had bought all this stuff today, what had been inside the box last night?

"Hey, Jackie," Carl said. "I want to ask you something."

The secretary was covering her typewriter with its plastic shroud. She was a tiny, thin woman with starved, hardened features and frosted brown hair. Jackie wore too much eye makeup and dresses that had been out of style for at least five years. On the corkboard wall beside her desk were pictures of her three kids and her cats, a postcard of a "jackalope," and a Xerox cartoon of a woman with a large screw in her forehead sitting at a typewriter—the caption read: *You Don't Have to Be Crazy to Work Here, But It Helps!* She was a divorcée, and in the four years she'd worked in the same department as Carl, he'd successfully avoided any contact with her outside the office. She was clearly interested in him, but he pretended to be oblivious and kept things with Jackie on a friendly, businesslike level. It seemed his misfortune that the only women interested in him were like Jackie—desperate, divorced, fuzzy-dice-on-the-rearview-mirror types.

"You were talking a couple of weeks ago about buying"—he had to remember her son's name—"um, Andy a skateboard for his birthday. Do you remember where you got it? I'm thinking about getting one for Sam."

"Kmart," she said, climbing into her coat with the ratty, fur-lined hood. "But I wouldn't bother there, because Andy took it back and bought another at a place near where you live."

"On Capitol Hill?"

She nodded. "Fifteenth Street, I think. Andy said they had the best selection. Weird little store—run by a bunch of those punkers. Really gave me the creeps. I don't know the exact address, but it's on Fifteenth."

"Thanks, Jackie. G'night."

Returning to his office, Carl cleared off the desk, then grabbed his coat and briefcase. He felt his pocket for the parking stub. He'd driven to work this morning. He'd needed the car for his lunchtime shopping spree and the trip home to make the switch inside the Meier & Frank box. He figured Sam had already sneaked a peek at the presents by now.

Though in hock up to his ass to Waldenbooks, he still wanted to get Sam something else. After all, what fun would Christmas morning be if there were no surprises? So he'd reluctantly decided on the skateboard. That way, at least Sam could unwrap something he didn't expect to find.

*   *   *

A musty, oblong box with varnish stains on the top flaps. It must have been in the back of the crawl space for a long, long time. Sam had never really noticed it before. What had his father been hiding in there? *"Leave that alone!"* he'd practically shouted at him last night. *"Don't open that!"*

Now, as he set the presents back inside the Walden-books bag, they seemed shabby and fake—$193.88 worth of junk to cover up some secret.

"I'm on to you," Sam whispered. He shoved the bag inside the Meier & Frank box, then closed the top flaps. That long talk he'd had last month with his father, none of his questions were really answered. He didn't really know anything more than he'd known back at Thanksgiving time. He'd just let his father convince him that there was nothing to worry about.

"Fuck!" He whacked the side of his father's desk, "Where is it? What are you hiding? C'mon . . ." He marched to the closet and threw open the door. With one angry swing of his arm, the sweaters on the shelf toppled to the floor. Several bundles of old bills and bank statements—all bound together by rubber bands—remained on the back of the shelf. Sam took no notice.

He kicked one of the sweaters aside as he made his way to the dresser. He yanked out three drawers. Clothes flew across the room. "Goddamn it!" he cried.

He rifled through his father's desk. A couple of drawers fell out completely. Hopping down on the hard-backed chair, he leaned over the desk and cried. How he hated his father right now. And yet he was mad at himself for hating him.

He glanced around the room at the mess he'd created. "Oh, shit," he muttered tiredly. He took a deep breath, got to his feet and started gathering up the sweaters. He refolded them and placed them back on the closet shelf. If his father kept the sweaters in some sort of order and he noticed a difference, it didn't matter anymore. Let him ask.

Sam put all the clothes back inside the dresser drawers.

His father would be home soon. But Sam didn't care. So what if he caught him in the bedroom? *"Sure, I'm in here,"* Sam imagined telling him. *"I don't give a shit about my Christmas presents. I want to know what you were hiding in that box last night. I want to know the truth about my mother and who I really am. I want to know . . . what you don't want me to know."*

He sank back down in the desk chair and started closing the drawers. Then he noticed something was different inside the bottom double drawer. He'd searched the desk several times a few weeks before, and the bottom drawer had always been full of old bills and bank statements—bundled up by rubber bands. The same kind of junk was in there now, but it was loose and messy— no rubber bands holding the papers together.

He picked up an old American Express bill. There were a couple of drops of wood stain on it. And he recognized the musty odor from the crawl space.

ZAP SKATEBOARDS & USED LP'S was practically hidden between two secondhand stores that appeared to be closed. The dark, grimy little shop was just as Jackie had described it. Carl imagined that he was probably the first guy wearing a suit and tie to enter the place in months. But the two teenagers behind the counter ignored him. The girl, about seventeen, was a short, dumpy creature with a pug face and magenta crew cut. She wore an oversize, studded, black leather jacket. Carl figured her parents couldn't have been too broken up when she'd first adopted the punk look, because she seemed pretty homely to begin with.

"So we're outside the 7-Eleven, just hanging out, y'know?" she was saying to her boyfriend. "It's around three in the morning and Sharon's got her radio. And this stupid derelict, some Indian, he comes over and tries to pick me up . . ."

He must have been very, very drunk, Carl thought, half-listening as he examined the skateboards fixed to the wall. The store's prices were almost as ridiculous as its employees.

The girl was talking to a tall, emaciated boy not much older than she. He had blond hair with dark roots and chartreuse tips that hung over his eyes. He leaned on the old-fashioned, hand-crank cash register. His torn black T-shirt allowed him to display a thunderbolt tattooed on his skinny upper arm.

"Then he tries to hit on Sharon," the girl went on. "Finally, Mark came over and made him leave. We asked Mark if he had any, but he didn't. So we just hung out till four, when the cops came, 'cuz we were making too much noise or something."

Carl wondered what the hell was wrong with her parents. Weren't they at all concerned about their teenage daughter, leaving the house dressed like a cosmic prostitute and not returning until after four in the morning? They had to be complete jerks. Even if her parents were divorced, it was no excuse. After all, he was a single parent, and his son turned out all right. Was that on account of sheer luck? Carl liked to think he had something to do with it. Maybe Sam was a good kid because his dad was there for him.

Loudly he cleared his throat, then he glanced back at the register counter. The girl was still talking. Carl approached the counter and cleared his throat again. Without looking at him, the guy held up one finger—as if to indicate he'd acknowledge Carl's existence in a minute.

Carl waited patiently as the couple behind the counter discussed buying tickets for a concert on New Year's Eve. The things he did for Sam's sake. He recalled all the headache-inducing trips through Toys-R-Us years back. Things hadn't changed much. He was getting a headache now.

Finally, the girl said she had to go. She waddled out from behind the counter and smiled at Carl. "I like your tie."

"Thanks," he said. "I like your—jacket."

She stepped outside.

"So—lookin' for a skateboard?" the boy asked. He appeared as if helping Carl was the last thing on earth he wanted to do.

Carl tolerated his almost-rude apathy—so Sam could have his precious skateboard. He was friendly and even managed to get the clerk from hell to show him the best buy for a twelve-year-old boy who wasn't looking to compete in the Skateboard Olympics.

Ten minutes and forty-two dollars later, Carl loaded the skateboard in the trunk of his car. He wrapped it in an old blanket to keep it from moving around. He'd leave the skateboard there until Christmas. Sam wouldn't be looking in the trunk for anything. It was a good hiding place.

Sam dug into the bottom double drawer, scooping out the old bills and papers, then dumping them on the floor. The stale moldy smell from the crawl space seemed to fill the bedroom. Somehow, he knew this wouldn't be another dead end. He felt his heart fluttering against his chest, and it was hard to breathe. He shoveled out another handful of papers and saw the top of a small grocery bag, folded over and sealed with packing tape.

He grabbed the bag from under the top folds. The tape started to give way. "Shit," he muttered, pulling at it. He gave it another tug and heard it rip. Hoisting the bag out of the drawer over to his father's bed, he held on to one side, where photos and papers started to leak out.

Now he'd done it. He'd torn a big hole in the bag, and the place was a mess, and his dad might be home at any minute. . . .

He thought he heard footsteps in the outside hallway.

Sam left the torn bag on the bed and raced to the front door. With a shaky hand, he fixed the chain lock in place. He listened to the footsteps—coming closer. Then he hurried into the bathroom and turned the shower on full blast. His father would figure that he was in there—unable to hear the doorbell.

Any minute now, he expected the sound of the key in the front door. He waited, his feet rooted to the carpet at the threshold of his father's bedroom.

Nothing. False alarm.

Still, he felt wary as he crept back into the bedroom. The chain lock and the roaring shower could keep his dad waiting outside—and buy him time to clean up. But the shower noise also drowned out any sounds *he* might hear from the outside corridor. His earlier bravado about getting caught in his father's bedroom suddenly vanished. Now he knew where the secrets were hidden. If his dad found him snooping in there, he'd only hide everything again—or destroy it completely. Sam didn't want a confrontation. He just wanted to know what his father was hiding.

He kept imagining that he heard someone in the outside hallway. He didn't know what to do. The torn bag sat on the bed, and a trail of photos and letters that had spilled out of it lay on the floor—from the desk to the bed. Old bills were scattered over the carpet, too. He had to put everything back the way it was. He couldn't check inside the bag. No time.

Sam started gathering up what had fallen out of the bag. He knew his father would be knocking on the front door any minute, but he couldn't help noticing the photographs. There were four of them, all of his father and a pretty, long-haired brunette. His father had his arm around her in every picture, and he looked so young. Was this the lady from the Bon Marché?

He found a letter, the envelope addressed to his father, but not in Seattle or Santa Rosa. In Portland.

Sam pulled the letter out and read it. The date was May 18, 1975:

Dear Carl,
After five years on the faculty of Portland's sorriest grammar school, you deserve a medal

or possibly intense psychotherapy! You will be sorely missed. We never had a better P.E. teacher. Our loss will be the business world's gain.

Best of luck on your new job. Best wishes also to you and Eve. The two of you brought a touch of glamour to the last few faculty picnics. You make quite an attractive pair. Let me know when you both decide to tie the knot, and all your faculty friends will dig into their thin purses and come up with a wedding gift. This is my way of saying "keep in touch." All of us here consider you a valued friend.

> *All the Best,*
> *Shirley Goldberg,*
> *Principal/Spinster/Racketeer*

Sam read the letter again. His dad never told him that he'd coached for a grammar school. He'd never told him about living in Portland either. And who was this Eve?

He slipped the letter inside its envelope, then glanced once more at the photos of his dad and the pretty brunette: *"quite an attractive pair."* He checked the back to one of the photos. *"Cannon Beach, May, 1976,"* it said, in his dad's handwriting.

His dad was supposed to have married his mom in 1976.

Click.

Sam froze for a second. Then he heard it again—the key in the front door. *Oh, shit, he's home. . . .*

Shoving the photos and letter in the back pocket of his jeans, he grabbed the grocery bag and hauled it over to the desk. The rip along the side widened and more junk spilled out. But he crammed the bag inside his father's desk anyway. The top was still taped up. He'd replace the bag tomorrow, while his dad was at work. And if his dad pulled out the bag between now and then, maybe he'd think he ripped it himself.

The chain lock rattled. *He's trying to get in.*

Frantically, Sam picked up everything that had fallen out of the bag: a postcard; more photographs; and the folded-up page from some newspaper. He stuffed them inside his shirt.

The doorbell.

He shoveled the old bills on top of the bag. There was no time to care if they were in any special kind of order.

He heard the doorbell again, then knocking.

Sam shut the drawer. Turning, he smoothed out the wrinkles on his father's bedspread. A photo fell out of his shirt. He scooped it up, and, on his tiptoes, hurried into his own bedroom.

"Sam?" his father called from the other side of the front door. He rang the bell again.

Emptying out his shirt, Sam threw everything under his bed. He quickly undressed, and heard the chain lock rattling again.

The shower water was cold, but he stood under it for only a moment. Turning off the water, he grabbed a towel and wrapped it around himself. He was dripping wet when he opened the door for his father. "God, I'm sorry," he said, still a little out of breath. He clutched the towel around his waist. "I didn't hear you. Were you out here long?"

His father smiled tightly. "Only about ten minutes,"

he said, brushing past him. He set down his briefcase. "For God's sakes, Sammy, I'm not going to let you see *Psycho* again if you're this worried about taking a shower in the apartment alone. The dead bolt is more than enough security. You don't need the chain lock. I was about ready to break the door down."

"Sorry," he mumbled.

"Well, no harm done, I guess," his father said, hanging up his trench coat in the front closet. He strolled into the kitchen and examined the mail Sam had left on the breakfast table for him. "So how was the last day of school?" he asked. "Did Mitzi like her present?"

Sam shrugged. "Yeah. She liked it okay." He held on to the towel and stared at his father.

"Who was your Secret Santa? What'd you get?"

"Ellen Shriver. She gave me a paperback, *The Catcher in the Rye.*"

"You've read that already, haven't you?" His father loosened his tie, then opened the cupboard.

"Yeah, but it was your copy. Now I've got my own."

He grabbed the aspirin from the shelf and shook a couple of pills into his hand. Then he looked at Sam. "What is it?" he asked. "Why are you looking at me like that?"

Sam blinked. "Like what?"

"Like I'm sprouting horns or something. Is anything wrong?"

"No, of course not," Sam replied.

"Don't you think you ought to dry off and get dressed?"

"Oh." He glanced down at the puddle he'd made on the floor. "Oh, yeah, sure."

Sam retreated to his bedroom and dried himself off. The corner to one of the photographs stuck out from under his bed, and he pushed it beneath the dust ruffle with his toe. As he stepped into his undershorts, his father passed by the open door and went into his own bedroom.

"I hope you haven't been in here today," he called.

It took a moment for Sam to answer. "No, I haven't, Dad." He put on his shirt and listened. His father was opening the closet door. Hangers rattled.

Sam reached for his pants. He heard a drawer squeak open.

"Sam?"

"Yes?" he called back nervously.

"How's about doing your tired old dad a big favor and running to the video store for me? I feel like *It's a Wonderful Life* tonight. How about you? Or do you already have something cooked up with Craig?"

"No, the movie sounds great, Dad," he called.

Wandering into his bedroom in a T-shirt and baggy striped undershorts, his father handed him a five-dollar bill. "Thanks. Don't go out until after your hair's dry." He kissed Sam on the forehead, then went into the bathroom and shut the door. A minute later, Sam heard the shower start up.

The video store was just two blocks away, and when Sam returned with the movie, his dad was getting dressed. If he suspected something, he certainly didn't act like it. They phoned for pizza and ate in front of the TV. Sam had seen the movie so many times, he knew most of the lines by heart. His father said some of them out loud with the actors. But Sam was quiet. He kept wondering why his father never told him that he'd been a gym teacher in Portland. And then there was that brunette woman in the photographs. Was she his real mother? Was she Eve or maybe A.M.?

James Stewart and Donna Reed stared dreamy-eyed at each other during the school dance. "He never really dates anybody except her," Sam said. They sat on the couch, their feet up on the coffee table. "You'd think he'd at least give Violet Bick a tumble while Mary's away at school."

His dad chuckled. "Too busy with the Building and Loan, I guess."

"You ever have any girlfriends before Mom?" Sam asked, with a sidelong glance at his father.

"No one serious."

"What'd you wish, George?" Donna Reed asked. She wore an oversize bathrobe, and James Stewart sported an undersize Number 3 football jersey and padded pants.

"Well, not just one wish. A whole hatful, Mary . . . I'm shaking the dust of this crummy little town off my feet, and I'm going to see the world. Italy, Greece, the Parthenon . . ."

"But he never gets out of Bedford Falls," Sam remarked. "You ever feel that way about Santa Rosa? Getting out, I mean."

"Sometimes," his father said, staring at the screen.

"But you didn't move away until after I was born?" Sam asked—ever so casually.

"Mm-hmm, except for a couple of years away at college."

"You went to school in Portland, right?"

"Uh-huh."

"And you went back to Santa Rosa after you graduated?"

"That's right."

"And you didn't ever move away again?"

His father sighed. "No, not until I came up here with you. Sammy, what's with the questions? Don't you want to watch the movie?"

"Yeah, sure. Sorry," he muttered. But instead of looking at the TV, he glanced back at the picture on the wall behind them. Now Sam knew that the "wedding portrait" was just one of many, many lies.

Friday, Dec. 19, 1989—12:35 A.M.

A god-awful morning, but tonight made up for it. I'm dog-tired. Sam's still up, watching David Letterman in his room. Details about this morning's "Operation Cover-Up" will have to wait until a later installment, because I've got to hit the hay soon. But my efforts weren't wasted. I checked the drawer a few minutes ago. The bag is still there & taped up. I'm almost positive Sam peeked at the presents. He acted so guilty when I got home tonight. He could hardly look me in the eye.

After tomorrow (or today, rather), I'm on vacation for 10 days. Thank God! First opportunity, I'm throwing out everything in that bag. Last night's close call showed me that I can't afford to be so sentimental. But now, I refuse to worry about it.

Before I wrap up, a word about tonight. The last few Christmases, I never really got into the

*holiday spirit. I was lucky just to cop a moment
or two of a "Christmas feeling." Tonight, I had
my "Christmas moment," watching "It's a Wonderful Life" with Sam. The tree was all lit up,
and it looked beautiful, plus we had a fire going
in the fireplace. There I was, watching that terrific old movie with my son, and I felt really
great.*

  Well, anyway, "and to all, a good-night."

At one-thirty, Sam switched off the portable TV in
his room. Suddenly, everything seemed so quiet; all he
heard was the wind howling outside, and tree branches
scraping against the living room windows. The bedroom was dark, except for a small oasis of light around
his bed from the nightstand lamp.

He crept out to the dim hallway and glanced at the
closed door to his father's room. He was asleep. Sam
felt as if the whole city was asleep right now—and he
was the only one awake.

Ducking back inside his room, he quietly closed the
door. He pulled out what he'd stashed under the bed—
some photographs, a folded-up page from a newspaper, a couple of postcards, and the letter he'd already
read. He set everything on top of his pillow—under the
light.

Most of the photos were of his father and the brunette woman—or just her alone. Sitting on his bed, Sam
examined the date his father had scribbled on the back
of each one. The earliest was August, 1973; the most
recent was dated May, 1977—just a month before Sam
was born. Sam turned the photo over: the lady was stand-

ing by a tennis net, a racket in her hand. The skimpy
white dress she wore displayed her trim, very unpreg-
nant figure.

Sam sighed. Well, she wasn't his mother; that much
he knew. But obviously, the dark-haired lady was involved with his dad for several years, right up until the
time he was born.

More than just involved. One of the postcards was
almost definitely from her. *ALOHA,* it said on the front,
across the belly of a homely Hawaiian lady in a grass
skirt and lei. The card was addressed to his father—in
Portland again:

Dear Husband,
   You said you wanted a tacky postcard. Will
this do? The tournament got rained out today.
But the monsoons didn't keep me from shopping.
I hope to be far away on another tennis trip
when you get the American Express bill! Miss
you. I'm being good & you better too! See you
Monday, probably before you get this. Aloha!

                    Love, Guess Who.

The second postcard was to *"Mr. & Mrs. C.D. Jorgenson,"* at the same Portland address. The front of it
bore a picture of the Leaning Tower of Pisa. *"Dear
Carl & Eve,"* it said in tiny print. Sam didn't read the
whole thing. He got halfway through the day-by-day
description of a tour through Europe, before he realized that the postcard did nothing but confirm that his
father and *Eve,* the tennis lady, were indeed married—

right up until a month before he was born. Yet if the date on that tennis picture was correct, Eve was not his mother.

Then who was his mother? And what had his father done to her?

Sam became aware of the faraway cry of a siren. Then it got louder. Closer. He sat up straight on the bed. The siren's volume was blaring now, and it seemed to pass just below his bedroom window. Then the sound faded away again—as quickly as it had come. Holding his breath, Sam listened for any noise next door in his father's room. Had the siren waked him? He stared down at the stolen "evidence" in the pool of light around his pillow. Sam wondered if he should pull the bedspread over it. But he waited, afraid the tiniest movement would carry into the next room and tell his father that he was up. He listened to the branches, still rubbing against the windowpanes in the living room. No other sounds. Even the wind was silent.

After a few minutes, Sam finally decided it was safe. He reached for the folded-up news clipping. It was worn and yellowed. The creases seemed ready to tear as he carefully unfolded a whole page from the *Seattle Times*. He read the date along the top: *"Saturday, November 1, 1977"*—a few months after he'd been born.

Sam scanned over the headlines, but he didn't see his father's name. There were two pictures—one of a slimy-looking man, the defendant in a murder-rape case. The other photograph was larger: a somewhat frumpy woman and her baby. *"BEFORE THE NIGHT-MARE,"* the caption read. *"Paul McMurray took this photo of his wife, Amy, and their son, Edward, two weeks ago.*"

He looked at the headline: *INFANT BOY AB-DUCTED IN PORTlAND*. For a moment, he couldn't breathe. He thought of his father, asleep in the next room. And he glanced at the photo caption once again.

Paul McMurray . . . Amy McMurray . . . P.M. . . . A.M. . . .

Sam read the article. His father's name wasn't mentioned. They suspected a black man who had been seen leaving the bank's parking lot with a white infant. At the end of the story, there was a description of the abducted baby. Sam didn't read beyond the first two lines:

EDWARD ANTHONY McMURRAY
Born: 6/7/77.

His own birthday.

CHAPTER NINETEEN

*You were four, and you had the stomach flu. I
had you in bed with me—in case you woke up
sick in the middle of the night. Anyway, you
jostle me awake around midnight. I was really
beat, too, up all night with you the night before.
You say you're going to throw up. So real quick,
I steer you into the bathroom—and nothing.
We're in there twenty minutes, and you don't
throw up. So we go back to bed, and I'm drifting
off when you tell me again that you have to
throw up. Another trip to the bathroom, another
false alarm. Then you pull it on me a third time.
We must have been in there a half hour. My back
was starting to ache from standing hunched
over the toilet with you, and meanwhile, you're
playing with the toilet water, poking your fingers
in it. By now, it's two in the morning. FINALLY,
you say you're okay and we go back to bed. I
start to settle down, and without a word, you
lean over and BARF RIGHT ON ME! It's the*

closest I ever came to killing you. And you were
so sick, poor little guy, and I had absolutely no
compassion for you . . .

His father had told that story at least five times, and he'd always laugh when he told it. Sam would laugh, too. But thinking about it now, as he rode the bus downtown, he wanted to cry. He stared out the rain-beaded window, his head turned away from the old man with BO seated beside him. In the breast pocket of his jacket, Sam kept the newspaper clipping.

He'd feigned sleep when his father went off to work three hours ago. But in fact, Sam hadn't slept at all last night.

Even if he could fool himself into believing that the kidnapper had been the black man they'd suspected, Sam couldn't explain away how Eddie McMurray had the same birthday as him. He couldn't account for his missing birth certificate and medical records—or why a chance meeting with Amy McMurray had sent his father into such a panic that he'd even considered moving away from Seattle just to avoid her. He'd called Paul McMurray and tricked him to get information about epilepsy. And how could he explain the lies about his mother? Why else would his dad not want him to know that he'd lived in Portland?

Sam felt his throat tighten up, and tears stung his eyes. The only way any of it made sense was if he'd been the kidnapped baby in that newspaper photograph—and his dad, the kidnapper. Sam started to cry, and he couldn't stop—even though he felt everyone on the bus staring at him.

"Fifth and Pine," the bus driver announced. "Nord-strom, the Bon Marché, and Westlake Center. This stop."

Sam wiped his eyes and nose. Saying "excuse me," to the old man, he got to his feet and moved toward the door. It whooshed open and he stepped off the bus. The store windows were full of Christmas scenes: Santa and Mrs. Claus; the elves at work in the toy factory; children around a Christmas tree. His father used to take him every year around Christmastime to look at the moving mannequins, the holiday scenes, and all the lights. He remembered holding on to his father's hand the whole time so he wouldn't get lost amid all the strangers.

"Frosty the Snowman" chirped over the Muzak system inside the crowded store. Sam got on the escalator. He hadn't eaten any breakfast, yet even with an empty stomach, he felt nauseous. He almost hoped for another dead end like his last visit to this store. Better yet, he'd meet Amy McMurray and she'd laugh at his story and tell him how wrong he was.

He pulled the folded news clipping from his pocket and stepped off the escalator at the fifth floor. His legs felt unsteady. As he neared the tables stacked with bath towels, he ducked behind a pillar and leaned against it. Sam studied the news photograph for what must have been the hundredth time. He was scared. He didn't want to see this dark-haired, frumpy woman in the picture behind a cash register now—the blurry photo coming to life. He didn't want to be her son.

Sam glanced over at the sales counter. The woman behind the register handed a shopping bag to a black man, then smiled. She had a nice smile. It wasn't the same saleslady as last time. Sam noticed a resemblance to Amy McMurray—only the saleswoman was prettier; slim with long, reddish brown hair. *"I hadn't counted on her turning out so lovely,"* his father had written.

She rang up some bathroom supplies for another customer, a middle-aged woman in a fur coat. Suddenly, she looked up for a moment. Her eyes met his.

Sam backed into the pillar and looked away. He wanted to run out of there. But he remained frozen where he was. After a few moments, he folded up the news clipping and tucked it inside his pocket. Then he peeked over his shoulder at the saleswoman again. She was talking to the lady in the fur coat. Amy McMurray wasn't looking at him anymore.

It had been a busy, hell-bent morning so far, and the last thing Amy needed was a teenage shoplifter. Let the kid over by the post steal whatever he wanted; she was too depressed to give a damn. The week Barry had originally been scheduled to arrive in town had come and gone without him. There had been no more calls or letters. The last one had given her such hope—not about Barry, but about tracking down Eddie.

She'd hired another private investigator. At her urging, he'd made the rounds at dozens of doctors' offices, asking about a twelve-year-old boy on epilepsy medication. He'd made several inquiries at Seattle junior high schools, searching for a blond boy with a scar on his chin and a widower father.

Milo Sharkey had been wrong: it wasn't a six-thousand-dollar dead end. Only thirty-two hundred was spent before the investigator gave up. For a while there, Amy had such high hopes.

Now she had nothing to look forward to—except a Christmas alone.

"Do you have any towels in this shade of green?" the woman asked, pointing to a leaf painted on a tissue dispenser.

"I'm sorry," Amy said. "Sort of a jade green is the closest we have. But we'll get some new colors in next month, so try us again." She piled everything into a shopping bag and handed it to the lady. "There you go," she said, making an effort to sound cheery. "Thanks very much. Happy holidays."

As the woman in the fur coat turned away, Amy's eyes strayed over to the boy again. He hadn't moved. He seemed nervous and scared. He didn't look like the shoplifter type after all; and something about him was vaguely familiar. Maybe he was lost. Maybe he was looking for his mother.

He stuck by the pillar as if it were holding him up. He caught her gazing, and he quickly looked away, then shrugged his shoulders.

He's staring at you, Amy told herself.

Amy stepped out from behind the counter. Suddenly, she was trembling. For one breathless moment, she thought she was looking at the same sweet-faced boy she'd seen back in September. But the jacket was different—and this boy seemed older. Still, she couldn't take her eyes off him. *Don't do this to yourself,* she thought; *He's not the same one as last time . . . He's not Eddie. Don't set yourself up for another heartbreak . . .*

He seemed to hesitate, then shuffled toward her. His eyes were downcast.

Amy couldn't move. *He's not Eddie,* she kept having to tell herself. A hand over her heart, she tried to smile at the boy.

"Are you Amy McMurray?" he whispered.

She was still holding herself back, even as she recognized the beautiful, serious eyes, the same tiny scar on his chin, and the golden color of his hair. He was a very handsome boy. *God, let this be him, please . . .*

"Can I—help you?" she managed to say. Tears came to her eyes and she was shaking. The boy was almost as tall as her, yet Amy wanted to sink to her knees and embrace him.

"Do you know a man named Carl Jorgenson?" he asked.

"No, I don't. But I think I might know you." Then she whispered, *"Eddie?"*

Biting his lip, he stepped back. "Are you my mother?"

"Oh, God," she murmured. "Please . . . please, let me hold you . . ." Amy thought she would die if she didn't have her baby in her arms once again. "Oh, my sweet little guy-guy. Please, I know you're scared. So am I . . ."

He didn't move, but he didn't shrink back either. Amy let out a grateful cry as she embraced him. She cradled his head to her shoulder, kissed his golden hair, and brushed her tears against the soft curls. After twelve years, she finally had her Eddie back.

Sam became rigid in her arms. He wondered if she'd ever let go. It was all so strange. She was crying and almost laughing at the same time. He felt too awkward putting his arms around the stranger, so he just patted her back. He'd never had a lady hug him like this. It was odd to feel the bra strap beneath her blouse, stretched across her back. She smelled nice. Yet he wanted her to let go of him.

"Oh, I can't believe it," she cried. "My sweet boy, my Eddie—"

"My name's Sam," he murmured. Gently he tried to pull away.

She let him step back, but one hand firmly grasped his arm. "Look at you," she gasped, smiling. She wiped the tears from her face. "Oh, you've grown up so handsome. You—you've got my mother's eyes. I still can't believe it. You don't know how many times I've pictured this . . . so many years." She smoothed back his hair and started to cry all over again. Yet a smile still stretched across her tear-stained face. Sam glanced past her shoulder and noticed a couple of shoppers staring at her.

"I'm sorry," she said, her grip easing on his arm. "This must be so confusing for you."

Sam just nodded. He wanted to go home.

"How did you find me?" she asked. "All these years, I've been looking for you, and here, you find me. How did you?"

Sam dug into the pocket of his jacket, then handed her the news clipping. "I found this in my father's desk."

Finally, she let go of him and looked at the clipping.

Another saleslady approached them. It was the same beady-eyed woman from the last time Sam had come to the store. "Are you okay, Amy?"

Without looking at her, she nodded. "Yes. Oh, yes, fine . . . wonderful. Can you take over for a while, Ronnie?" Then she took hold of Sam's arm again. "Come on," she said, and the smile she gave him was almost reassuring. "Let's—let's go back here so we can talk. Okay, honey? I know how strange all this is for you. Don't worry. Everything's all right now."

Sam let her lead him behind a curtain into a storage room. Amid the shelves of boxes and items wrapped in plastic, there were a couple of folding chairs and a stepladder. Amy McMurray laughed nervously and said something about how she must look a mess, then she asked him to sit down. She looked at the newspaper clipping again. A sad smile came to her face. "Your dad took this picture of us when you were five months old," she said. Then she glanced at him. "You're still not sure, are you? But I'm your mother. I know I am.

"That scar on your chin. The man who took you, he used to write me little updates about you on postcards. One of the last ones I got was when you were four. You fell on the playground and cut your chin. Four stitches, right? He said you didn't cry at all in the doctor's office."

Sam stared at her and nodded.

She grinned, but her eyes were still watery. "Did you take your medication today?"

"How did you know about that?" he murmured.

"You were here three months ago, and the man you were with asked you the same thing. I heard—"

"That was my father," Sam said.

She shook her head. "No. Your *real* father lives in Portland. You have the same color hair he has. And he's an epileptic. The medication you take is for epilepsy, isn't it?"

Sam couldn't answer her.

She took hold of his hands. "I know how you must

feel," she said. "I can hardly believe it myself. Tell me how I can prove it to you, and I will. I'm your mother." She brought his hands up to her face and kissed them. "You must have thought so, too. Why else would you come to me?"

He shrugged. "I just wasn't sure. I'm still not. I'm sorry."

Her red-rimmed eyes were full of pain. "I'm just a stranger, aren't I?" she asked. Letting go of his hands, Amy stood up. She scooped the news clipping off the floor and folded it up. She wasn't quite looking at him. "You said your name is Sam?"

"Sam Jorgenson," he said.

"You haven't got someone else who's—supposed to be your mother, do you?"

"No. It's just my dad and me."

"But he isn't your—" She stopped herself, then smiled awkwardly, as if it hurt to swallow the words. "Does he treat you well?"

"Yes."

"He seemed nice when I met him—back in September, I mean."

"He is nice," Sam said.

"And you love him, don't you?"

Sam looked at her steadily. "Yes, I do."

"You love him, and you don't even know me," she said. "I guess right now, I hate him for that more than anything else." She was silent for a moment, then gave Sam back the news clipping. She touched his shoulder. "You hungry?"

He shrugged.

"I'll take you to my apartment. I've got dozens of

your baby pictures there, pictures you've never seen. I'll fix you some lunch. Will that be okay?"

"Is that his handwriting?" she asked.

Sam stared at the postcards she'd saved. "I think so," he murmured. But he didn't just think, he *knew*.

She'd shown him his baby pictures and fixed him a grilled cheese sandwich. They sat at her dinner table. Her apartment was bigger than theirs, with a terrific view of the city, and furniture that looked very expensive—the type he wouldn't dare put his feet on. Her Christmas tree seemed stolen from the department store, perfect; all white lights, blue ribbons, and blue ornaments. Sam still liked their tree at home better.

She was trying hard to make him feel like her son. But he only felt sorry for her. She was still a stranger. He wanted to be in his own room at home. The only things he felt close to in this place were the postcards, because they were from his dad.

She sat beside him at the dinner table, describing the awful period of waiting, hoping, and praying after he'd been abducted. Everything she said made his dad out a criminal. Sam felt as if she were his kidnapper now. He knew Amy McMurray wouldn't let him go home. Since she'd first embraced him at the store, she was never more than a reach away. She didn't give him a moment alone. It was hard to breathe around her. If only he were home, he could breathe right again.

"Can I use your bathroom, please?" he asked.

She sprang up from the dining room table—almost as if she planned to go with him. "Oh, of course. Let me show you." She held out her hand for a moment, then seemed to think better of it, and scratched behind her neck instead. "It's right over there," she said, pointing down the hall.

"Thanks," Sam said. He started toward the bathroom.

"I'm sorry if I seem nervous," she called, her voice quivering.

"It's okay," he called back, closing the bathroom door.

Amy had always hoped for this day, but never prepared for it. The calendar suddenly seemed to whirl back twelve and a half years, and she was giving birth to him all over again; the same joy mixed with terror; the sudden, huge responsibility. All at once, she had someone who mattered more than herself.

She knew her son, holed up in the bathroom, was in a state of shock and confusion. Amy didn't dare curse his abductor out loud, because her son still loved the SOB. And she held back from smothering her boy with affection, too. *Let him get used to you,* she told herself. *Take it slow. Don't push, Amy. Don't push.* The Lamaze method all over again. She wanted her baby to feel loved and safe as he saw the light.

But she could tell, he just wanted to get away. He'd been in her apartment for nearly an hour and still hadn't taken off his jacket.

She gathered up his old baby pictures from the table. Amy glanced at the framed photo of Eddie with her and her mother. She set it back on the end table in the living room. Her mom would be so happy, and Amy could lean on her a little, the same way she'd come to her for help when Eddie was just an infant. She reached for the telephone.

The bathroom door opened down the hall. "Excuse me!" he called, running toward her. "What are you doing?"

Quickly, she put down the receiver. "What's wrong?"

"Are you calling the police?"

"No. I just wanted to tell my mom the good news."

He seemed relieved when she stepped away from the phone. But Amy noticed his eyes were puffy and bloodshot; and she realized that he'd been crying in her bathroom. "Oh, what's wrong?" she whispered. She started to reach out to him.

But Sam stepped back.

Letting her arm drop to her side, Amy shrugged. "'What's wrong?' Huh, talk about your stupid questions."

Wiping his nose with the back of his hand, Sam looked down at the carpet. "I miss my home," he said, his voice cracking. "I just want to be back there right now. I'm sorry. You can come with me if you want. Please, just let me go back home . . ."

They didn't say much to each other in the car, except when she asked for directions. She found a parking spot about half a block from the building. Sam was so happy to see it again. The hours away had seemed like days.

In the lobby, Sam opened the mailbox and fished out a couple of bills. "We're okay. My dad isn't home. Otherwise, he'd have gotten the mail. Follow me."

In the back of his mind, Sam hoped that once she saw where he lived, she'd allow him to stay there. She wouldn't call the police on his dad, and maybe they could work out some kind of arrangement for her to visit from time to time. Divorced couples did it. Why couldn't she and his dad work something out?

He showed her into the living room, and all at once, he saw the place through her critical eyes. Until now, he'd never cared about the water rings he'd made on the coffee table, or the food stains on the sofa. "We're getting the couch reupholstered after New Year's," Sam felt compelled to say. "I guess your place is a lot nicer. But I like it here a lot. It's real comfortable."

She just nodded.

Sam plugged in the Christmas lights for her.

A look of pain and regret ran across her face as she touched one of the dilapidated ornaments he'd made in kindergarten. "It's a very pretty tree," she said.

Sam draped his jacket over the back of his father's favorite chair. "We put it up night before last."

"You took off your jacket," she said.

"Yeah. Oh, I'm sorry. Can I hang yours up for you?"

"No thanks—Sam." She glanced at one of the framed photos hanging on the wall behind the couch. "Huh, you look just like my brother in this one of you on the swing." Her smile waned as she gazed at another photo—of him and his father at a Little League game. "He's very handsome," she said, her voice cracking.

"He's real nice, too," Sam replied. "I mean, he never hit me or beat me up or anything like that. He's a good father."

She kept studying the pictures of him through the

years. She began to weep, and she rubbed the back of her neck as if she had a sharp pain there. "Damn it!" she cried. "Damn it, I hate him! The son of a bitch! Look what he stole from me." She waved a hand in front of the pictures on the wall. "I didn't get to see you grow up. Those ornaments should be on *my* tree. This couch, this stupid couch, mine should look like this! Every stain on the carpet, every smudge on the walls, they should be in *my* house! And I'd yell at you for making a mess, and worry about you, and nurse your bruises and cuts, and love you. Goddamn him for taking that away from me! He's a monster—"

"He isn't," Sam said, backing away from her.

"That's the worst part," she retorted, shaking her finger at him. "He's got you sticking up for him! You were the love of my life, my baby, and he tore you away from me. He may as well have cut out my heart. Oh, damn it."

She dug a handkerchief out of her purse, then wiped her eyes and blew her nose. She seemed calmer now, but Sam still kept a distance. "I'm sorry," she muttered. "I know you love him. I know it's hard for you to believe he did what he did."

"It is," Sam replied, staring at her.

She stuffed the handkerchief back in her purse. "Are you still unsure about who I am?"

"No. I think you're my real mother," Sam heard himself say. He nodded toward the pictures on the wall. "But to me, he's still my father, y'know? It doesn't matter what he's done. I mean, I'm sorry he hurt you. But he's always treated me nice. He's a good guy. He doesn't deserve . . ."

"Deserve what?" she asked.

Sam frowned at her. "I don't want you to tell the police."

"I'll have to," she whispered. "I'm sorry—"

"But they'll put him in jail. I don't want to do that to him. He's my father. This is my home. I don't want to live anywhere else. If I thought all this was going to happen, I never would have come to you."

She reached out to him. "Listen, Eddie—"

"Sam!" He pulled away. "My name's Sam."

"Okay, *Sam.* Believe me, I understand what you must be going through. I know you don't want your whole life turned around. But that man did a horrible thing. And he could do it again. He could turn around and steal someone else's baby."

"He wouldn't do that. You don't know him like I do."

"Do you really know him?" she asked. "After all this, do you think you know him? Could you ever trust him again?"

Sam couldn't answer her.

Amy McMurray glanced at the telephone over on the kitchen wall, then her eyes met his. She took a deep breath. "I'm sorry. Now, I'll call you Sam, because it's the name you grew up with. And anything here that's yours you can take . . ."

"No!" Sam yelled. "I don't want to live with you!"

"You'll have to give me a chance," she said. "You'll have to." She moved toward the kitchen.

"You can't!" he cried. "Jesus! Who do you think you are, coming in and—"

"I'm your mother," Amy McMurray said. She picked up the receiver. "That's who I am. I'm your mother, Sam. And I'm going to make everything all right again."

Then she dialed for the police.

* * *

Carl left work early. On his way home, he stopped by the supermarket, then the video store. He rented *A Christmas Story.* The clerk reminded him that he still hadn't returned *It's a Wonderful Life* from last night. Carl walked away, wondering why Sam hadn't returned the video yet. He'd called home from work three times today and never got an answer.

All day long, he'd been fighting an eerie premonition that something had happened at home. He'd told himself he was imagining things. But now he was worried again.

"Nothing's wrong," he whispered to himself. "You're being ridiculous, Carl. You always get this way when you leave him alone. He's okay, stupid. Probably at Craig's . . ." But Carl's hands kept a white-knuckle grip on the steering wheel as he drove home. There was a light rain, and beyond the windshield wipers, he saw a couple of police cars parked in front of the apartment building. His heart stopped for a moment. He told himself that if something were really wrong, there would be an ambulance.

Still, Carl pulled over to the curb, a few spaces behind the squad cars. A cop stood in the doorway of the building, talking to two men in trench coats. They looked like police.

Carl hurried out of the car. They all stared at him, and one of the plainclothesmen nudged the policeman. Carl stopped suddenly in front of them.

"Carl Jorgenson?" the policeman asked.

"Yes?" he replied, a little out of breath. He sensed someone coming up behind him, and he glanced over his shoulder. Another cop. All of them looked so grim.

He knew something had happened to Sam, something awful.

"Seattle Police," one of them said, flashing his badge.

Carl shook his head. "Oh, no, God," he murmured. "Is he all right? Tell me my son's all right . . ."

The cop behind him grabbed his arm.

"Is my boy okay? Please, tell me what happened!" Carl struggled with the cop who had ahold of him. Tears stung his eyes. "Good God, where's my boy?"

"He's all right. Mr. Jorgenson," the plainclothes cop said. "He's with his mother."

CHAPTER TWENTY

Sunday, Dec. 21st

Dear Dad,
  It's really weird writing to you like this. I've never been away from you long enough that I've had to send you a letter. I know it's only been a couple of days, but it seems a lot longer.

From his desk, Sam looked at the clock on the nightstand. It was past midnight. He thought about changing the date at the top of the letter to December 22nd, but that meant scratching out the old date or starting all over again. He'd already ripped up four letters he'd started. He put down his pen and idly glanced around the room.

His new bedroom was an odd mix of Amy McMurray's tasteful guest quarter furnishings and his old posters, pictures, and artifacts. Like him, they didn't seem to belong in the room. She'd insisted he take anything from the old apartment that he wanted. It was her attempt to make him feel more at home in her place. But everything just clashed with what had been there

already, cluttering up her elegant decor. Even her "perfect" tree, with its blue-and-white theme, was spoiled
by the addition of a dozen ornaments he'd grown up
with. She'd insisted. And now, it was the ugliest Christmas tree he'd ever seen.

Sam picked up his pen.

*I'm still not used to it here. Today I kept track
and 7 reporters called and another 4 buzzed
from the lobby, but she keeps turning them
away. On Friday and Saturday it was a lot
worse. The cops have been here too of course,
asking a ton of questions. Mostly they want to
know if you molested me or if you were a pervert
or something. Of course I told them no. But it's
weird. I talked to Craig finally today & he said
the police came to his house & asked if you ever
tried to molest him. It really got me mad. Craig
said they kept asking, even after he told them
you were OK and never tried anything.*

*My real grandmother is staying here until
after Christmas. She's from Chicago. I like her
OK. Right away she told me to call her
Grandma. It seemed weird at first, but I'm kind
of used to it now. It's funny how names are a
problem all of a sudden. I don't think they like
calling me Sam, but I won't answer to "Eddie,"
so they're going to let me keep my name. Meanwhile, I never know what to call her. She said I
can call her Amy for the time being. It beats
calling her Mom. Most of the time I don't call
her anything.*

I talked to my real father last night on the

telephone. It was strange. He's coming up from
Portland tomorrow to take me to lunch & spend
the afternoon. I wish it were you instead.

I guess you must hate me. I'm sorry. She's the
one who called the police. I didn't want her to. If
I knew it would turn out like this, I would have
talked to you first. I still don't understand why
you took me when I was a baby, & I can't
believe you did it, though I guess it's true. I try
not to think about it too much. I miss you some-
thing awful, but sometimes I get mad at you,
because—

Sam slapped the pen down on his desk, then crumpled up the letter and threw it in the wastebasket. It
was too late to start another, and he wasn't going to
think about it.

Sam undressed, but then remembered. He had to put
his pants back on before going to use her bathroom
down the hall. No more walking around in his underwear; no more peeing with the door open; and now, he
always had to remind himself to put the toilet seat back
down afterward. She was manager of the store's Bath
department, so her own bathroom was like a goddamn
shrine: the towels, rug, shower curtain—everything,
new and perfect. He spent most of his time in there
cleaning up after himself.

When he finally crawled into bed that night, Sam
knew sleep was a long time coming. Even with his old
pillow from home, he didn't sleep well in Amy Mc-
Murray's guest bed.

*   *   *

Someone buzzed from the lobby downstairs. Sam was in the bathroom, trying to shine his loafers with some wadded-up toilet paper. The lunch date with his real father seemed like an important occasion, and Sam dressed for it: a sport jacket and tie. His dad used to make him get all decked out for rare special occasions when they dined out at some fancy restaurant.

He heard Amy open the front door. "Hi," she said. "Hope you didn't have any trouble finding the place."

"No. Why? Am I late?" Sam heard him ask.

"Oh, no. In fact, you're early. Come in, come in. You look good, Paul. You really do."

"You too. God, you've gotten even skinnier. But it—it looks good, I mean. And your hair, you—"

"Yeah, I know. It's a henna rinse I use. Lightens it up."

Sam had his ear to the bathroom door and one hand on the doorknob. They sounded so nervous—like a couple of strangers.

"Hi, Lauraine," Sam heard him say. "Boy, you don't look any older than when I first met Amy."

"Thank you, Paul. You're sweet to say that. How are you?"

"How's your family?" Amy asked.

"Fine. We're all fine. So where is he?"

"In the bathroom," Amy said. Then she called out: "Sam!"

"What's this 'Sam' shit? Um, excuse me, Lauraine."

"We figured he's adjusting to enough changes as it is," Amy whispered. "Least we can do is let him keep the name he grew up with. Besides, he prefers 'Sam.' I told you that on the phone yesterday." She called out again: "Sam! Your father's here!"

Sam straightened his tie one last time. Then he opened the door and started down the hallway to the living room. Paul McMurray was grinning at him, his arms spread open like a singer belting out the last, long note of a song. It was as if he expected Sam to run and embrace him.

But Sam stopped just a few feet away from his real father. He felt stupid, all dressed up for this special occasion. Meanwhile, Paul McMurray wore jeans, a flannel shirt, and a goosedown vest. He looked like a lumberjack. "Well, howdy, stranger!" he said, his arms still sticking out.

Sam extended his hand. "Hello."

"Well, well, real grown-up, I see," McMurray said, shaking his hand. He laughed. "And dressed so dapper. Look at you. Jesus, wow! I mean, excuse me . . ." Tears brimmed in his eyes. He gently touched Sam on the side of his face. "It's like looking in a mirror. Oh, we won't be strangers for long, old buddy. We're going to get reacquainted real quick. You'll see . . ."

Sam nodded. He glanced over at Amy and his grandmother—the awkward smiles stretched across their faces.

McMurray clapped his hands then rubbed them together. "Well, what do you say we hit the road, son? You hungry?"

"Sure, I guess."

He mussed his hair, which Sam had spent ten minutes combing so all the cowlicks would stay down. "'Sure, I guess'—what?" McMurray said, grinning.

"Pardon?" Sam asked.

"Sure you guess—*what?*"

"Sure, I guess I'm hungry?" Sam replied, though he

had a pretty good idea what McMurray wanted him to say.

"C'mon. Who are you talking to here?"

Amy let out a loud sigh.

McMurray gently punched his arm. "Okay, I'll ask you again, old buddy. Are you hungry?"

Sam gave him a pale smile. "Sure . . . Dad."

Paul McMurray drove a silver Chevrolet Cavalier that had a bumper sticker that said: *IF YOU DON'T LIKE MY DRIVING, CALL 1-800-EAT-SHIT!* From his rearview mirror dangled a flat, cardboard air-freshener that bore the *Playboy* bunny insignia. McMurray told him this was his company car. "I get a brand-new car every two years," he explained as they slowed down for a stoplight. "Last year, I had a Monte Carlo, and next year, we're supposed to get a Corsica."

"That's nice," Sam said.

"My wife, Sheila—you'll like her—she has an old beater station wagon, but she's insured to drive this, too. How long until you get your driver's license?"

"Not for another three and a half years."

"Well, when you do, I'll include you in the coverage."

"My—" Sam stopped himself. He was about to say, "My dad works for an insurance company," but thought better of it.

"That way," McMurray continued, "every time you come down to Portland for a visit, you can use the wheels. How about that? Sound good, old buddy?"

"Great," Sam replied. He hated being called "old buddy," by this stranger. It was what the Skipper called Gilligan. Or was it "Little Buddy"? Either way, it sounded stupid.

McMurray went on about all the options on his Cavalier—V-6, cruise control, miles per gallon, and blah-blah-blah. Sam just nodded and pretended to listen. He stared at his real father. He was handsome, rugged-looking, like some guy in a beer commercial or cigarette ad. Sam couldn't imagine him cooking a pot roast, washing dishes, or folding laundry—all the things he'd seen his dad do so often. He'd never considered his dad a wimp, but there had been times Sam wished he were more like those idols of masculinity, the brawny outdoorsmen from the beer commercials. Now he'd gotten his wish, and he hated it.

As they pulled into the parking lot of a Denny's, Sam took off his tie and stuffed it inside the pocket of his sport coat.

In the restaurant, McMurray flirted a little with the waitress, and she seemed to think he was a pretty hot number. He ordered a cheeseburger, and Sam asked for the chicken strips. The waitress was pretty, but her elbows were dirty, and she snapped her chewing gum while she wrote down their orders. Paul McMurray stared after her as she sauntered away with their menus. Then he turned to grin at Sam. "Not bad, huh?"

Sam nodded. "She seemed to like you, too."

He laughed, then held up his hands. "Hey, I'm a married man."

Sam just nodded again.

"How about you? Got a girlfriend?"

"No, not really."

"Well, give it time. Good-looking kid like you, you'll have the babes chasing you all over pretty soon."

Sam shrugged, then managed a lame chuckle.

"You're on the football team at school, I hear."

"That's right."

"Well, you like football. That's a good sign."

"What's it a good sign of?" Sam asked.

McMurray smiled tightly. "Nothing. Shows you're a normal kid, that's all." He glanced down at the place mat and moved it a little on the green Formica table-top, "I mean, that creep had you for twelve years, I can't help but wonder . . ."

Sam said nothing.

"I know what you told the cops and the story the newspapers gave," McMurray continued. "But here, it's just you and me—you and your old man. Nobody else has to know. You can tell me."

"Tell you what?" Sam asked, frowning a little.

"You know, there's no way he can get at you now. You don't have to protect him. Whatever happened, it's not your fault. I'm not going to blame you for anything that guy made you do."

"He didn't make me do anything," Sam said.

McMurray glanced at him for only a moment, then he fingered the salt shaker and pretended to be inter-ested in it. "You mean this guy never made you go to bed with him?"

"Only when I was little and if I was sick," Sam said angrily. "And that was only so he could get me to the toilet in time if I had to throw up. Sometimes, if I had a nightmare, he'd let me climb into bed with him. But he never tried to do anything to me the way you think."

"Okay, settle down," McMurray said.

"No, really," Sam went on. "You want to know if he touched my dick? Well, he did once, when I was eight or nine. I got it caught in my zipper, and he got me un-stuck. Okay? And he changed my diapers for a couple of years. Maybe you want to count that. But I don't re-member exactly what went on back then."

"You finished?" McMurray asked.

"I'm sorry." Sam took a deep breath. "But every-one's trying to make him out a pervert, and that's just not true. He's a real nice guy."

McMurray frowned at him. "Well, twelve years ago, that 'real nice guy' stole my son away from me. So you'll forgive me if I don't share your high opinion of him. If it were up to me, I'd put that scumbag away for life. Lock the bastard up and throw away the key. Let him rot, that's what I'd do."

Sam didn't say anything.

"I used to change your diapers, too, you know," Mc-Murray whispered.

The gum-snapping waitress returned with their lunches, apparently a little disappointed that McMur-ray didn't flirt with her anymore. They ate quietly. Sam hardly touched his chicken strips. He told Paul Mc-Murray that he wasn't so hungry after all.

"I've been doing most of the talking here," Paul McMurray said, turning onto the West Seattle Free-way. "You've hardly said a word since lunch."

Sam stared at the road ahead. He shrugged. "Sorry."

"You're sore at me, aren't you?" McMurray threw him a condescending smile. "I think I know why, too. You're sore at me because I waited until today to come see you. You think I don't care. I let four days go by—"

"That's okay. I'm not—"

"No, let me explain," he cut in. "I wanted to drive up and see you on Friday night after your mother phoned with the news. I don't mind admitting, I cried like a baby when I heard. I was ready to drop everything and come to see you. But your mother said it was too soon. Said you were tired and confused."

"That's right," Sam nodded. "I was. She—"

"I was dying to see you," McMurray cut in again. "And she tells me to wait a few days until the hubbub dies down with the reporters and cops. Meanwhile, you're wondering where the heck your dad is. I never should have listened to her."

"'No, she was right," Sam said. "I've been kind of out of it the last few days. It's better you waited. Sorry I haven't talked much. It's all kind of strange to me, that's all."

"Well, your mother's the one who made me wait," McMurray said. "I've wanted to see you since Friday night. Hell, old buddy, I've been looking forward to this day for twelve years."

He pulled the car in front of Amy's apartment building, then turned off the ignition and sat back. He said he wanted Sam to come down to Portland before New Year's, and spend a couple of nights at his house. "Your sister and two brothers are dying to meet you. And Sheila, your stepmother, you'll like her."

Sam had one hand on the car door handle. He glanced up at Amy's building, then at McMurray. "Aren't you coming up?"

"No. I've got a three-hour drive home ahead of me."

Sam stared at him for a moment.

"She's got a nice place," McMurray said, his big hand dangling on the steering wheel. "Huh, you should have seen her ten years ago. You wouldn't think it was the same girl. She's done okay for herself." His eyes met Sam's and he smiled sadly. "Y'know, I wasn't sure what to expect from you. But you're a nice kid. You turned out real swell. I guess you and her did all right for yourselves without me, huh?"

Sam didn't know what to say. Suddenly, he felt very sorry for this man.

"Well, I'll call you tonight. Okay, son?"

Sam opened the car door. "Sure, that would be great," he replied. "Thank you for lunch."

Paul McMurray slid across the seat and embraced him. It was so awkward and forced that Sam didn't feel compelled to hug him back. McMurray didn't seem to want that. His arms were stiff, and he held his head as far away from Sam's as possible. Then he quickly let go and slid back behind the steering wheel. "Well, take care," he muttered.

"Thanks," Sam said. He climbed out of the car and almost expected to feel relieved that he was back home. But Amy's apartment wasn't his home. And he didn't think it ever would be.

After a week, he still felt like Amy's houseguest. She and his grandmother were constantly asking about what foods he liked, what his routines were for sleeping, eating, and playing. They were always ready to accommodate him, these two nice strangers.

"Do you like opening your presents on Christmas Eve night or on Christmas morning?" Amy McMurray asked.

They were in the kitchen. She stood at the stove,

cooking his "favorite breakfast," French toast. He'd merely agreed that he'd liked French toast when she'd made it for him a few days ago. Now he was about to eat it for the fourth morning in a row.

Sam shrugged. "We usually opened the presents Christmas morning. But if you want to do it tonight, that's okay."

"Oh, we usually open them Christmas morning, too. Anything special you'd like to do today?"

"Well, I kind of promised my friend, Craig, that I'd get together with him."

"Okay. I'll drive you. Where does Greg live?"

"Craig. Capitol Hill. I can take a bus."

"Don't be silly. You'd have to transfer at least three times. I'll drive you. It's no problem."

"Thanks, Amy," he said. "Breakfast smells good."

"It's French toast, your favorite."

The ten-minute trek to Craig's house was now a three-quarter-hour drive across town via the express-way. Amy said for him to call when he wanted to be picked up.

"It's all so totally weird," Craig said, sitting in his chair, which was turned around and tilted back against his desk.

Sam sat on the bottom bunk bed. Elmo, the family mutt—part cocker spaniel, part Lab—lay curled up beside him, his big head in Sam's lap. Sam scratched him behind the ears. "Can I spend the night here?" he asked. "For the rest of my life?"

"She that bad?" Craig asked, pushing his glasses up the shiny bridge of his nose.

"She's okay. I just don't think I'll ever get used to living there. I keep having to remind myself that my dad isn't ever going to come pick me up and take me home."

"I still can't believe he did it," Craig frowned.

Craig had always idolized Sam's father. Sam had been forever hearing him say how lucky he was, what a "neat dad" he had. The front-page stories must have really shaken him up.

"You haven't talked to him since?"

Sam shook his head. "No. Last thing he said to me was 'don't forget to unplug the tree lights.' That was the night before. She's taking me to see him tomorrow. I asked. But now, I'm not sure I can face him." He hated the idea of seeing his father behind bars in a prison uniform. And if his dad started to cry, he'd really lose it. Sam had never seen him cry before.

"Think he's pissed at you?" Craig asked.

Sam frowned. "I don't know. I'll find out tomorrow."

"So what's the other guy like? You didn't tell me how it went with him."

"That's because when I talked to you on the phone, she and my grandmother were right in the next room. There's no place in her apartment to have a private phone conversation."

"So how did it go? Does the guy look like you?"

Patting the dog's head, Sam shrugged. "A little, I guess. But he's kind of a greaser. He tried real hard to act like we were old buddies or something. In fact, that's what he kept on calling me, 'old buddy.' I'm supposed to go visit him and his family down in Portland next week. He wants me to spend a couple of nights there. I'd rather have all my nose hairs torn out."

Craig shook his head. "Totally weird."

Sam had twenty dollars in his pocket. He figured he ought to buy Christmas presents for his grandmother and Amy. Craig accompanied him to the same expensive knickknack shop where he'd gotten Mitzi Bateman's Secret Santa present. Sam chose an eight-dollar brass pin for his grandmother. It was of a smiling cat. For Amy's present, Sam fell back on the same glass angel ornament he'd given to Mitzi, the girl he felt sorry for.

"Where to now?" Craig asked, zipping up his jacket as they stepped outside the store.

"I kind of want to go home," Sam said.

"Already? It's not even one o'clock. What are you gonna do at her place all afternoon?"

"No," Sam said. "Not her place. Home. I still got the key to the old apartment. Wanna go?"

Through some arrangement by his father's attorney, everything from the Capitol Hill apartment was going into storage. Amy said they'd have to go there before New Year's Day to grab anything else he wanted. The apartment had to be emptied and ready for its new tenant by December 31.

It seemed empty already. He and Amy had been there twice this week. They'd taken down the Christmas tree, and he'd removed the pictures from the walls. They were now in boxes in Amy's basement storage space. Someone had turned off the heat, and it was cold. Most of the plants were dying.

"This is bizarre," Craig whispered. "I feel like we're trespassing or something. I mean, everything's practically just the same, but it *feels* different."

"We're not trespassing," Sam said. Yet Craig was right. This wasn't his home anymore.

He wandered into his old bedroom. The walls and bookshelves had been stripped of everything he treasured. He sat on his bed—without its pillow.

Craig sat beside him. "You coming back to school after New Year's? Or will she make you go someplace in West Seattle?"

"She said I could finish here," Sam replied, staring at the blank walls.

"The commute will be a pain in the ass."

Sam nodded. "Guess everybody's going to treat me like some kind of freak when I get back."

"It'll be a couple of weeks. Maybe they'll forget by then."

"Oh, yeah, right," Sam groaned.

"Well, it beats starting at some new school, doesn't it?"

Sam tried to smile. "You'll still be my friend, won't you?"

"I don't know. Your dad used to pay me twenty bucks a week. How much is What's-Her-Name gonna pay?"

Grinning, Sam punched his shoulder. "Eat shit."

Craig laughed. But then he glanced around the bedroom, and the smile ran away from his face. "God, it's gonna be weird not coming here anymore. All the bullshit sessions we've had in this room . . ."

"Don't get sentimental on me, Craig. Because if you're trying to make me cry, it ain't gonna work."

"Sorry. I'm just going to miss this place, that's all."

"Me too," Sam said. "Listen, would you think I'm a total shit if I kicked you out? I kind of want to be alone right now."

"Of course I think you're a total shit," Craig said, getting to his feet. "But that's nothing new. You coming over later?"

Sam shook his head. "I'll call you tomorrow night."

Craig paused in the doorway. "When you talk to your dad tomorrow, will you say hi to him for me?"

Sam nodded.

"I'll really miss this place," Craig said, giving the room one long, last look. "You gonna be okay here?"

Sam nodded again.

"You gonna cry?"

"Probably," Sam whispered.

For the first time in his life, Sam needed to be awakened at nine on Christmas morning. Another first, he brushed his teeth, washed his face, and got dressed before opening up his presents. He tried to act excited. But he was tired and nervous. He'd been up most of the night thinking about the visit to his dad today.

Craig's prediction from a while back came true. Except for a thirty-dollar gift certificate to Tower Records, all of the presents from "mother" were clothes. "Gosh, this is great," Sam said as he pulled out each new garment. "Thank you, Amy."

His grandmother seemed delighted with the brass cat brooch. She kissed him, and pinned it on the lapel of the robe Amy had given her—the store tags still dangled from her sleeve. "Your mother and I got you something together," she said. "But we're saving that for last."

Sam pretended he was dying of curiosity, and in the meantime, unwrapped a Seattle Seahawks sweatshirt from Paul McMurray. Then Amy opened up her glass angel, and she carried on as if it were the Hope diamond. She hugged and kissed him, then made a big production about hanging it on the tree.

All the presents had been unwrapped. Then, in a sober tone, Amy announced: "There are some other things from—Mr. Jorgenson." She retreated to her bedroom.

Sam looked at his grandmother. She smiled and fingered the cat brooch on her lapel. "His lawyer talked to your mom," she explained. "He wanted you to have these."

Amy carried the Meier & Frank box into the living room. On top of it was the gift-wrapped basketball and another, smaller package. She set the boxes in front of him, but held on to the other gift—obviously the one they were saving for last.

Sitting on the floor, Sam unwrapped the basketball. Then he opened the Meier & Frank box and glanced at the Springsteen book, the videos, the calendar, and *Pictionary*—all the gifts he'd wanted. But he hardly even smiled.

"I'm supposed to tell you that the color TV and the VCR are yours if you want them," Amy said.

Sam just nodded.

"I don't mean to undermine his judgment," he heard her say. "But I don't think the *Lethal Weapon* video is suitable for a boy your age. After all, it's rated 'R.'"

"It's okay," Sam answered quietly. "I've seen the

movie, Amy. Seeing it again isn't going to corrupt me or anything."

"Well, it's bad enough that he gave you *Psycho*. When I was your age, your grandma wouldn't even let me go see it."

"But you sneaked out and saw it anyway," Sam's grandmother interjected.

The three of them laughed, and for a moment, the tension was gone. Then Amy said, "Well, I might as well tell you, he bought you something else. But I don't think you should have it."

"What is it?" Sam asked.

She shrugged. "It's a—a skateboard."

"He got a skateboard for me?" Sam broke into a smile. But then, all of a sudden, he remembered where his father was now. It was like getting a wonderful present from someone who had since died. "Where is it?" he murmured.

"In my bedroom closet. But why even look at it? I don't think it's safe, Sam. I'm sorry. I don't want you to have it."

"But *he* gave it to me, and *he* must have figured it was safe enough."

"Yes, well, worrying about you is my job now," Amy replied. "And I get ulcers thinking about you wiping out on that thing. I have a friend at work. Her son smashed himself up on a skateboard. He's had to have three operations on his knee."

"Jeez, Mom, he could have had the same kind of accident falling off his bike," Sam argued. "I'll be careful on it."

"I'm sorry, Sam—"

"But more than anything, a skateboard's what I

wanted for Christmas. *He* knew how much I wanted one."

"Let's not start in on that. Now, you can take the skateboard back and buy something else with the money."

Sam stood up. "You just don't want me to have it, because *he* gave it to me."

"That's not true. I'm letting you keep the videos and everything else. Now, come on, quit pouting." She held out the gift-wrapped box, "You still haven't opened the present from Grandma and me."

"I don't want it," he grumbled, sneering at her.

"Oh, now, Sammy—"

"No. Why don't you *'take it back and buy something else with the money'?* You can take back the lousy sweaters you got me—and all the rest of this junk, too." He kicked the box that held the Seattle Sea-hawks sweatshirt. "I don't want any of it."

"Stop it."

"I think this is the crummiest Christmas I've ever had."

"And I think," Amy replied steadily, "that you're acting like a brat, because you didn't get what you wanted."

"Yeah? Well, finc, fine. Merry Christmas to you, too, and go to hell while you're at it." He marched into his room, then slammed the door.

Amy squeezed her eyes shut. "Goddamn it," she whispered. She glanced at the gift box in her hands. "I wanted so much for this to go well. Oh, Mom . . ." She sank down beside her mother on the sofa and started to cry. She'd given her son "the crummiest Christmas he'd ever had." He hated her, and he'd never accept her as his mother. "God, he hates my guts. Did you hear him?"

"I did." Lauraine smiled. "I heard every word, honey. And you did everything right."

Amy stared at her mother, and wondered how she could look so happy after everything had just fallen apart in front of her eyes. She was grinning, for God's sakes.

"He called you 'Mom,'" Lauraine whispered. "In the middle of all that, he called you 'Mom.'"

Sam emerged from his bedroom an hour later. Amy and his grandmother had changed from their night-gowns and robes into regular clothes. They were throwing out discarded wrapping paper and trying to set the opened presents in some kind of order beneath the tree. Both of them just smiled at him when he wandered into the living room. Then they went back to what they were doing—as if nothing had happened earlier.

"I'm sorry," Sam mumbled, looking down at the carpet. "You're right. I was acting like a brat. And I'm sorry I told you to go to hell."

Amy crunched up some used wrapping paper and sighed. "Well, it wasn't very bright of me to tell you about the skateboard, then say you couldn't keep it. But I was afraid he'd mention it to you this afternoon. I didn't want you to think I was holding out on you." She gave him a sympathetic smile. "Guess from where you stand, seems like I'm holding out on you anyway. I understand why you don't want to take the skateboard back. Maybe you can give it to Craig—or loan it to him."

Sam frowned. "Naw. Craig's mom won't let him have one."

"What?" Stunned, Amy had to laugh. "Then what are you giving *me* such a hard time for?"

He cracked a smile. "Well, I said I'm sorry—"

"Listen, fella, are we all forgiven or what?" she asked.

He nodded. "Sure, I guess."

"Hallelujah," she said. "Well, don't just stand there. You've still got one more present to open." She grabbed the wrapped box from under the tree and handed it to him. "Here, from Grandma and me."

It was a bit heavy. Sam tore off the paper and gazed at the box from AT&T: a cordless telephone.

"There's a jack in your room," Amy said. "We figured you'd like a little privacy when you talk to your friends—and all the girlfriends you're going to have."

Sam hugged his grandmother and thanked her. Then he went to Amy. Sam kissed her. Amy's arms came around him, and he returned his mother's embrace.

"Nervous?" Amy whispered.

"Kind of," Sam said. He wore one of the new sweaters she'd given him. They sat close together in a couple of dirty, orange plastic chairs. Just as his mother clung to her purse, Sam kept a tight grip on the thin bag that held a present for his dad.

He counted: there were only four other white people among the thirty or so who crowded the visitors' waiting room at King County jail. It felt strange and scary to be a minority all of a sudden. The place smelled of stale cigarette smoke; and most of the smokers just

flicked their ashes onto the floor. Babies screamed, little kids ran around unattended, and women checked
their faces in compacts. Two big, obnoxious, teenage
boys threw around a plastic ornament from the scrawny,
fake tree in the corner of the room. Knocking into people, they laughed and swore loudly. Old couples looked
sad and lost. Everyone was dressed in their bargain
basement best. Sam imagined what it must be like for
his dad, living with the husbands, fathers, sons, and boyfriends of these sorry people.

"I hope you don't mind," Amy whispered to him.
"But I've invited everyone here to our place tonight for
Christmas dinner."

Sam laughed. *She's pretty cool,* he thought.

A cop stepped into the room and called out: *"Jorgenson?"*

Sam got to his feet.

"It'll be fine," Amy whispered.

At the door, the policeman examined the contents of
the paper bag Sam held. "Can you make sure he gets
this while I'm in there with him?" Sam asked. "It's
kind of a Christmas present."

Nodding, the policeman took the bag and led him
through a metal detector, then into a long, fluorescent-
lit room. A couple of other cops were pacing back and
forth while the visitors sat in cubicles along a glass
wall. As he followed the policeman to a seat in the end
cubicle, Sam glimpsed the faces of the inmates on the
other side of the glass. They looked so sad—even when
they were smiling or laughing. It was as if the vacant,
hollow eyes had become a part of their work shirt and
dark trouser uniform.

Then he saw his father through the glass partition.

His eyes were still the same—clear and kind. But someone had given him a bad haircut, and it made him look
like an overage marine recruit. With a lopsided smile,
he ran a hand over the short, grey-brown bristles of
hair that stood up on his head.

Sam tried to smile back. He sat down in the cubicle.
There was a grilled circular metal disc in the window
that allowed them to speak. But Sam couldn't think of
anything to say.

"How are you, Sammy?" his father asked.

Sam stared at the number on his work shirt. He
shrugged. "Fine, I guess."

"I like your sweater. She give it to you?"

He nodded. "Christmas present."

"She's got good taste, your mom has."

"She gave me your presents, too," Sam said. "Thanks."

"Not much of a surprise, I'm afraid."

"The skateboard was. But she won't let me keep it.
She thinks it's too dangerous."

"She's your mom. You've got to respect her decision."

Sam glanced at the smeared fingerprints near the
base of the glass divider. He couldn't quite look at his
father. His eyes had been avoiding him ever since he
sat down.

"Are you taking your medication?"

"Yes."

His father said nothing for a moment, then his voice
dropped to a whisper. "Do you hate me, Sam?"

He looked up. "No, Dad. I miss you."

He'd been so uncomfortable, so afraid his father
might cry. But now, Sam felt the tears burning his own
eyes. "I'm sorry, Dad," he said, past the tight pain in

his throat. "I didn't think it would turn out this way. It's all my fault—"

"Stop that," his father said. "I put myself in here. You didn't. I don't want you crying for me, Sam. I did a terrible thing twelve years ago, and I deserve everything I've got coming to me. Now, please, stop crying."

"I can't help it," Sam murmured, wiping his eyes. "I miss you, Dad—"

"Quit it!" His father seemed angry. "Stop acting like a baby. There are people around. Want everyone to see you?"

"I don't give a shit," Sam said, his voice quivering. "Why are you acting like such a hard-ass all of a sudden?"

"Just stop," his father whispered. "It kills me to see you cry when I can't hug you, Sammy. Please, save it for later, when I won't see." He touched the glass with his fingertips. "Okay?"

Sam just nodded.

"Thanks, kiddo."

"What's going to happen to you?"

His father idly traced a circle with his finger along the bottom of the window. "Well, I took you across the state line, and that's a federal offense. So I'll spend some time in a federal—place. Most likely down in California. But since there was no 'criminal intent' —I mean, like holding you for ransom or abusing you— my lawyer says it'll probably be only a year or two before I'm out again. And I hear the federal prisons are pretty nice compared to here—better conditions, better food . . ." He worked up a smile. "A better class of criminals."

Sam grimaced. "Has anyone tried to—y'know, beat you up or anything? I mean, you hear all sorts of stories about what goes on in jails."

"Don't worry, Sammy. No one's tried to rape me if that's what you're thinking. I've got a lot of years on most of the guys here. They leave an old fart like me alone."

Sam leaned forward, "But what's it like, Dad?"

His father shrugged. "Oh, it's not half as bad as I thought it would be. Missing you is the worst part. Outside of that, I guess my only complaint is the way the newspapers always refer to me as 'Carl Dean Jorgenson.' Makes me sound like a serial killer from the boonies or something—with the middle name in there. Know what I mean?" He grinned, but only for a moment.

Sam knew it had to be awful for his dad, living with drug dealers, murderers, rapists, and robbers. Hell, his father could hardly tolerate litterbugs. He thought about those two loud, obnoxious teenagers in the visitors' waiting room; and if his dad had seen them, it would have really gotten him mad. He had no patience with rude people. And yet, now he had to eat breakfast every morning with people who were much worse than that.

"Speaking of reporters," his father said, "I guess you and your mom have had your share of them. I'm sorry to put both of you through that. I'm sorry for everything, Sam."

"She says it's a lot easier to handle compared to the last time she had her name in the newspapers."

"She's a good woman, Sammy. You know, this meeting here—you and me—it's totally unorthodox.

But she agreed to it, because you asked. I thought I'd taken you from a bimbo and a dumb-ass greaser. But I was wrong about your mother."

Sam cracked a tiny smile. "On the other hand, you were right about *him,* Dad. I met the guy."

"Give him a chance."

"I'd rather wait for you."

His father was shaking his head. "Sam, if I'm paroled, one of the stipulations would be that I don't try to contact you for a number of years. I'm pretty sure about that."

"But if I talked to her, I'm sure she'd let you come visit me at least. I mean—"

"That wouldn't be fair to your mother—or your real father. Now, don't get teary on me again, please, or I'm going to lose it. You can still write to me . . ."

A cop came up behind him. His father turned. Sam couldn't hear what the policeman said, but he handed the bag to his dad, then walked away. His dad turned again and gave him a puzzled smile. "What's this?" he asked, fingering the thin paper bag.

Sam shrugged. "Kind of a Christmas present."

His father reached inside the bag and pulled out the blue spiral notebook. He smiled, but his eyes watered up, too.

"I didn't read it this time," Sam said.

"I never thought I'd get this back," his father whispered, clutching the journal. "How in the world did you find it?"

"Craig and I went to the apartment yesterday. He says to tell you 'hi,' by the way."

Wiping his eyes, Carl nodded and smiled.

"Anyway, I sent him home," Sam continued. "Then

I started looking through your room. I didn't want the movers or the new tenants to find it. Took me close to an hour. Anyway, I figured you missed it. And writing in it would give you something to do while you're here—someone to talk to, kind of. I stuck a picture of us inside." He shrugged. "Not much of a Christmas present, but then it hasn't been much of a Christmas."

"Oh, you're wrong, Sammy," his father said, smiling at the photo of them together at the Space Needle's observation deck. "This is the best present I ever got. If I'd made a Christmas list, this would have been at the top. Thanks." He slipped the photo back inside the notebook. "Listen, you better go, Sammy. I think I'm about to get a little teary here."

·"I still love you, Dad," Sam whispered. He got to his feet.

Carl smiled. "Be good to your parents. Make me proud."

His head down, Carl remained seated at the cubicle for another minute after Sam had left. He physically ached from the emptiness in his heart. He didn't want anyone to see him crying. If he could ride it out for another minute, concentrate on his breathing, count the seconds, then he might make it back to his cell without sobbing. Once there, he could curl up on his cot, face the wall, and cry. But not now. Not here, in front of the other inmates and guards.

He took several deep breaths, and when he looked up again, Amy Sheehan was sitting in the chair Sam had vacated. His eyes were still watery and red; and somehow, her watching him cry was even worse than having the guards and inmates see him. He just wanted to mutter an apology and shrink away from her icy gaze. He had no license for self-pity in her presence. How she must hate him.

Carl quickly wiped his eyes. "I'm sorry," he whispered.

She just stared at him with such pain and wonder that Carl could say nothing else. He couldn't bring himself to look at her.

"Why me?" she said finally.

Carl was silent. Even if he tried to explain, it wouldn't bring Sam back. It wouldn't make her hate him any less.

"Why my baby? If you wanted a child so badly, why didn't you adopt one? Why did you have to steal my son?"

"I—I don't expect you to understand," he muttered. "Twelve and a half years ago, I thought I was going to be a father. I lived in your neighborhood. I'd see you at the store, the neighborhood pool. You were pregnant at the time, and I used to imagine my wife looking like you in a few months. I wanted to be a father so much. But my wife . . . Well, it didn't happen. I felt gypped. Then I saw you at the pool again one day, and I followed you and your husband around that night—to the movies, then the hospital. I was there when he was born. I didn't want any other child. I wanted him."

"You've got to be sick," she said.

"I guess I was—back then," he said. "It was a crazy, terrible thing I did. I've always regretted that you got hurt. More than just 'hurt,' I know—"

"But you never felt bad enough to give him back, did you?" Amy said. "All I got were postcards—telling me what I was missing. And even those stopped after four years."

"I never knew if you got any of those," Carl said, his eyes avoiding hers. "It was selfish of me to send them. I didn't have anyone else to talk with about Sam. You were the only person who cared as much as I did. They weren't meant to hurt you."

"I was glad to get them," she admitted, shrugging.

"All these years, I've imagined how you must have felt—the hell I put you through. Now, I don't have to imagine it, because I know what it's like to lose him."

"Am I supposed to feel sorry for you?" Amy asked.

"No. I just want you to understand how bad I feel for causing you so much pain."

Amy let out a tiny, pitiful laugh. She shifted in the chair. "A couple of weeks ago, I met a woman. I'd taken something of hers. So I know what it's like to *take* and cling to something. I hadn't meant to hurt her. I told her so, too. I gave her pretty much the same speech you just gave me. And you know what she did? She slapped me across the face. I wanted her to understand me, and wound up with a fat lip. Now, I realize I deserved to get slapped. It's so insulting to hear that: *'I know what I did to you was horrible, but I feel bad about it, so you should have some compassion for me.'* Well, it doesn't wash."

Carl just nodded.

"Don't you see? It doesn't begin to make up for all the Christmases and birthdays I didn't get to spend with my son, my baby. He's a young man now, and he's mine once again." She leaned forward, her eyes wrestling with his. "But I never got to be that *little boy's mommy.*

And nothing you can do or say will ever bring those lost years back."

"I know," he whispered.

"And I'm not the only one you hurt. There's his real father, his grandparents, my mother—all of us are just strangers to him now."

"I know. I'm sorry."

"I hear him crying in his room at night," Amy said. "And I know he isn't crying for himself, or for me. He's crying for you."

Carl felt a pang in his gut. He moved a finger along the base of the glass partition, then slowly shook his head. "I wanted so much for him to be a happy, healthy, normal kid. Guess I've screwed up on that one, huh?"

A tiny smile tugged at the corners of Amy's mouth. "I think he'll pull through this," she said.

"I hope so."

"I wish he hated you," she whispered. "That would make it easier. I wish I hated you too . . . but I don't."

Carl stared at her on the other side of the glass.

Amy shrugged. "Sam went to a friend's house yesterday afternoon. Well, you know—Craig. Anyway, when Sam called for me to pick him up, it was from your apartment. He had a shopping bag. I didn't ask about it. But later, Sam and my mother went to midnight mass. I said I had a headache and stayed home. I found the bag in his room. There were Christmas presents for my mother and me, and something of yours too . . ." She nodded at the notebook in Carl's hands.

"Did you read any of it?" he asked. His face felt hot, and he was blushing. He couldn't look at Amy Sheehan, because now she knew his private thoughts.

"I read the whole thing," she replied steadily. "There's

a lot in there that might help you at the trial—the times you got in trouble at work when he was sick and you stayed home; sticking with that job you didn't like; letting your love life and social life take a backseat to him; his welfare coming before everything else. You could probably sway a jury to give you a lighter sentence if some of it got read at the trial. Maybe that's why Sam gave it to you."

Carl shook his head. "I think Sam gave me this notebook so I could write in it while I'm here—and so I could read and remember how it was when we were together."

She stared down at the base of the glass partition. "If you think it might help you at the trial, you should use it."

"I won't," Carl said. "I don't really care about a lighter sentence—at least, not enough to make this public." He tapped the cover of his journal. "I won't be able to see him for a long, long time. That's the real punishment. He's all I ever had."

"But then, you know you will see him," Amy said. "It might be a long, long time, but you'll see him again. You're sure of that, aren't you?"

"I can't give up hoping," he replied.

"Neither did I—for twelve years." Amy frowned, then stood up. "I better go," she said, but then she hesitated, and the lines around her mouth softened. She glanced down at the notebook. "I read about how you weren't sure you were a good enough father to Sam. That came up again and again . . ."

Carl looked up at her.

She touched the glass divider, near where his hands were resting. "My son is a nice boy, Carl," she said, unsmiling. "He loves you very much—even now. You were a good father to him, Carl, a very good father."

As he watched her walk away, Carl thought about what she said. He was a good father. That thought would get him through the next several years without Sam. Hell, it would get him through anything.

EPILOGUE

Trembling, Sam stood and listened outside the door to his *jather's* apartment. *The baby screamed and screamed. It wasn't the TV; it was real. He had a baby in there. All at once, Sam just hated his father. He thought about finding the nearest phone booth and calling the cops on him.*

"C'mon, sweetheart, settle down," he heard his father say. "Give those pipes a rest."

Sam exploded. He started pounding on the door. "Goddamn bastard!" he yelled. "How could you? How could you?" He didn't care who heard him. He didn't care that the door panel split a little more with every crashing blow from his fist.

The door flung open, and his father looked as if he were about to grab him by the throat. But he hesitated. "Sammy?"

Sam attacked him. He swung at his face and connected, cuffing the corner of his father's mouth. His dad stumbled back for a moment, then lunged forward, grabbing Sam's wrists before he could take another swing. For someone who had looked so old a minute ago, his father still had a powerful grip. Sam struggled to get free. "Son of a bitch!" he cried. "How could you? How—"

His father pinned him against the doorway frame. "Calm down!" he said. "My God, Sam, what's wrong with you?"

"Should I call the police?" a woman yelled.

Sam noticed her for the first time. She stood a few feet behind his father. Gaping back at him, she clutched the baby to her bosom. She was plump, with a round, rather pretty face and honey-colored hair. She looked about thirty-five years old, and wore jeans with a lavender pullover.

"It's okay, Rosie," he heard his father say. "This is Sam." Slowly, his father released him and smiled. "Sammy, this is my wife, Rose. And our daughter, Claire. Are you okay now?"

After a moment, Sam finally caught his breath. "I thought you'd done it again." He started to laugh and cry at the same time. "I thought . . ."

"It's okay," his dad said, embracing him. After four years, Sam felt his father's arms around him again. Sam's lips brushed against his scratchy cheek, and it was moist with tears.

His dad pulled away first, holding him at arm's length and looking him up and down. "I almost didn't recognize you."

Sam grinned. "You just passed me in the lobby a minute ago."

His father's smile ran away, and his eyes, narrowed. "Does your mother know where you are?"

"She thinks I'm home," Sam mumbled.

"And where is she?"

"On her honeymoon in Hawaii."

Rose went into the bedroom with the baby, while his dad called information for the number of the Royal Mahana Hotel in Hawaii. Ignoring Sam's protests, he dialed the hotel, then handed the phone to him. Unfortunately, when Sam asked for the honeymoon suite, his mother was in. He told her where he was, and who he was with.

"Oh, Sammy, how could you?" she said. Her wounded tone made him feel horrible. *"Why didn't you talk to me first, honey? God, I thought I could trust you. I feel so betrayed . . ."*

What killed Sam was that she didn't yell at him for snooping in her notebook (it was obvious now that he had), or for using her car, or even for ruining her honeymoon. She was upset because he'd gone back to him. At least she didn't start crying. Sam could hear his new stepfather, Dan, trying to calm her down. Dan was a graphic artist his mom had been dating for a year now. Sam liked him. Dan finally got on the line, asked Sam for the phone number there, and said he'd call back in ten minutes.

His mother seemed more forgiving by the time they called back. She thought that Sam's dad had shown good judgment in making him call, and she didn't blame him. *"You and I are going to have a long talk when I get home,"* she said. *"In the meantime, I love you, Sammy. Now, I'm putting Dan on. Get a pencil and paper. We've booked you on a flight out of Eugene tonight."*

His dad would drive him to the airport in an hour

*for the last direct flight to Seattle that evening. A lim-
ousine would be waiting for him at Sea-Tac Airport
upon his arrival. And he was to call the Royal Mahana
the minute he got home. As for the Toyota, he'd screwed
himself out of a car for the duration of his mother's
honeymoon. They'd figure out how to retrieve the car
later. They trusted his dad with the car, but not with
him.*

Rose and his dad took turns checking on Claire,
who wouldn't fall asleep. Rose insisted that Sam eat
something before he left, and she reheated some sloppy
joes. She and his dad seemed really happy, and Sam
didn't quite know how to feel about it. Did he want his
dad to be happy without him?

The apartment was tidy and nicely furnished. He
recognized lamps, chairs, some bookends, an end table
that he'd chipped long ago, now mended; and the old
sofa, reupholstered. The last time he'd seen all these
things, they'd been left behind in a vacated apartment.
Now, they seemed to have a whole new life. Sam saw
pictures of himself with his dad on the living room
wall. There were pictures of Rose and Claire, too; and·
Sam found himself counting to see who had the most
pictures. Rose won.

She was a good cook. At least her sloppy joes were
tasty. "Want some more, Sam?" she asked, before taking away his plate.

"No, thank you, ma'am." He sat at the head of their
kitchen table next to his dad.

She grabbed Sam's plate, then patted his shoulder.

"Oh, just call me Rosie. We're practically family, aren't we?"

"How old is the baby, Rosie?" he asked.

"Ten months. And let me tell you, Sam, she's like a gift from heaven. We'd been trying for over a year."

"What?" Sam glanced at his father.

Rosie hadn't heard. She was at the sink, and couldn't see the look that passed between him and his dad. "I'm leaving you guys alone for a bit," she said, heading toward the baby's room. "You've got about ten minutes before you should get a move on."

His dad was pressing a Baggie full of ice cubes to his lip from where Sam had hit him. "Are you adding up the months, sport?" he whispered.

Indeed he was: "trying" for over a year, nine months pregnant, ten-month-old baby. His dad must have been out of jail for at least three years.

Sam shook his head. "What happened? Did you get an early parole or something? Why didn't you write and tell me when you got out? I would have come—"

"You would have come sooner?" his father cut in.

Sam stared down at the place mat. He didn't answer.

"And you would have come, too," his father continued.

"Is that why you stopped sending me letters? Is that why you didn't write and tell me you were married and had a kid and everything? You didn't want me around?"

"That's exactly why," he answered steadily. "It was part of an agreement."

Sam's eyes wrestled with his. "What do you mean?"

"Sammy, your mother dropped the charges. She didn't

want you on a witness stand, having your entire childhood put under a public microscope. Not that I had any say in it, but I didn't want you to have to go through that either." His father set down the ice pack. "They kept it from the press. While you were in Chicago with your grandmother, the lawyers got together and a deal was made. I only had to serve six months."

"What are you talking about?"

"Six months in jail, and a year of outpatient psychiatric counseling, which I needed. Your mother knew that just from one peek at my childhood memories in my journal. I agreed not to live in Washington state as long as you were there. And I agreed not to contact you except through her lawyer."

"But how could you let me keep on thinking that you were in jail?" Sam murmured. "You tricked me, both of you . . ."

"We had to, Sammy. You said so yourself, if you knew I wasn't in jail, you'd come running to me—like you did tonight. Your mom doesn't deserve that."

Sam frowned at him.

He dug out his wallet from his back pocket, then opened it up on the kitchen table. He flipped past a photo of his baby girl, and there was a picture of Edward "Sam" McMurray from the high school yearbook. It was taken the year before. Sam was in his junior varsity basketball uniform. "That's a pretty normal kid there," his dad said. "Not some freak kidnap victim whose life gets dissected on the 'Geraldo' show. Your mom was making sure you turned out okay, Sam. This arrangement allowed all of us a second chance—you, your mom, and me."

"Where did you get that picture?" Sam asked. The last time he'd sent his dad a snapshot of himself was three years ago.

His father pried the photo out of the wallet and showed him the back. Sam recognized his mother's handwriting. It said:

We're happy. He's a great kid.

5'10", 154 lbs.

"I haven't talked to your mom in a long, long time," his father said. He slipped the photo back inside his wallet. "Then this arrived a few months ago. I hope it's true—that you're happy, Sam."

He nodded. "I guess so. She's a neat mom." He cracked a little smile. "How's your mouth?"

"I'll survive." He put his wallet back in his pants pocket and picked up the ice pack. "You were pretty damn angry at me, weren't you?"

"I didn't know you had a family now. I thought you'd done it again. I heard the baby—"

"It's okay, I know." He patted his hand. "What I did was terrible. If someone ever tried to steal my little Claire away, I'd kill them. And I put you through hell. That punch was long overdue, Sam."

Sam hesitated, then pulled his hand away. "I still get mad at you sometimes, when I think about it. But the worst part was that your letters stopped coming. Now I understand. But for a while there, I thought maybe you'd stopped loving me."

His father smiled. "Oh, I'll never stop loving you, Sammy. You know that."

Sam took hold of his father's hand, then kissed him on the uninjured side of his face. "I've missed you so much, Dad," he whispered. He felt his father's shoul-

ders tremble, and heard him stifle the sobs. Sam managed to say what they were both thinking: "I guess we better not see each other for a while, huh, Dad?"

His father just nodded. They sat there at the breakfast table and hugged each other until Rosie came into the kitchen with Claire in her arms.

"You two better get the show on the road," Rosie announced, over baby's soft cries. "Guess who just won't settle down tonight? Sam, you want to take her for a minute?"

He wiped his eyes. He'd never held a baby before. "What do I do?" he asked.

"Nothing, just hold her in your lap," Rose said. Before Sam could protest, she lowered the whining infant into his arms.

Claire wiggled and still complained, but at least she didn't start shrieking. Sam smiled down at her. And he felt his father touch him on the head.

The baby was ten months old. Was I with you at this age? Sam wanted to ask his father. But he knew. He'd been with him even sooner than ten months. His dad had been there from the beginning, on the day he was born.

THE ONLY WAY . . .

A home provides more than comfort and shelter. It stores memories . . . and hides secrets. Divorcée Caitlin Stoller and her children recently moved into a charming old Tudor-style house in the coastal town of Echo, Washington. The place was a bargain, but as weeks pass, Caitlin starts receiving messages— first friendly, then unsettling, hinting at the property's dark past . . .

YOU'LL STAY ALIVE . . .

Caitlin's teenage daughter, Lindsay, isn't fitting in at school. To make matters worse, there are stories about local high school students who've disappeared without a trace—all star athletes, like Lindsay. Then there are the rumors that their new home is cursed. Caitlin doesn't want to believe the whispers, but something strange is going on. Personal items go missing, and there are too many accidents . . .

IS IF HE NEVER FINDS YOU

The Watcher knows how to get inside the Stollers' home—and inside their heads. The rumors are true . . . but the full horror is even worse. There's no escaping the nightmare that started here long ago, and no place to hide from a killer who knows exactly how this story will end . . .

Please turn the page for an exciting sneak peek of KEVIN O'BRIEN's newest suspense thriller

HIDE YOUR FEAR

Coming soon wherever print and e-books are sold!

CHAPTER ONE

Deception Pass, Washington
Saturday, May 21—1:57 A.M.

"Where are we going?" Sara Goldsmith asked with a tremor in her voice. From the driver's seat, she glanced in the rearview mirror.

The masked person in the backseat of the Goldsmith family SUV didn't utter a word.

The clown mask was a strange pale peach shade that almost looked translucent—except for the wide scarlet grin, a blue-painted nose and white stars that framed each eyehole. Sara had no idea who it was in the backseat, brandishing a gun in one gloved hand. The stranger wore a black, hooded raincoat. All she could see was the clown face, leering back at her in the mirror.

A few drops of rain hit the windshield. The headlights pierced through the mist hovering over the lonely roadway. Tall evergreens bordered both sides of the two-lane thoroughfare.

At this time of night, traffic was light on Highway 20. Sara hadn't spotted many cars, not a single police car. Then again, it wasn't as if she could have flashed her headlights or signaled anyone for help. Her passenger in the backseat seemed to be watching her every move. Still, with more cars around, at least she might have hoped for some kind of intervention. Right now, she felt so lost and alone—and doomed.

She wondered if she'd never see her son again.

Sara's window was open a crack. Her shoulder-length, ash-blond hair fluttered in the cool breeze. People were always surprised to hear she was forty-two—or maybe they were just being nice. In the last few months, stress, too much drinking, and not enough sleep had all taken its toll. She looked sallow, tired, and puffy. Her booze of choice was bourbon, specifically Jim Beam, because it was usually on sale at the Safeway in Echo.

What with everything that had recently happened to her and her family, she'd come to rely on booze—and sometimes Valium—to put her to sleep every night. But she usually didn't start self-medicating until after her thirteen-year-old son, Jarrett, had gone to bed.

Tonight Jarrett was staying over at his friend Jim Munchel's house, leaving her alone at home. Sara realized she'd never actually spent the night alone in the house before. She blamed so many of her troubles—and even their recent tragedy—on the big, isolated, old Tudor at the edge of town. It had seemed so charming when she and Larry outbid another couple for the place seven months ago. That was before they knew the house had a disturbing history. That was before the creepy, anonymous phone calls, texts, and emails. That was before all the trouble began—the infidelity, the accidents, and the death from which she'd probably never recover. The house on Birch Street was cursed. At least that was what *Bobby* said. Bobby was obviously watching them, and sending those cryptic, ominous messages. On the phone, Bobby's raspy, gender-indistinguishable voice reminded her of the demon in *The Exorcist*.

She'd once read that Mercedes McCambridge, the Oscar-winning actress who had dubbed for the devil-possessed Linda Blair had drunk weird concoctions and choked herself with a scarf to get that gravelly, sinister voice. The demon's superior, all-knowing tone reeked of evil. Bobby sounded the exact same way, croaking at her over the phone.

The first call, which came two weeks after they'd moved in, was disturbing—mostly because of that voice. "Are you all settled in?" it whispered. Then the line went dead. Sara tried to dismiss it as a wrong number.

The next call came two weeks later: "Sara, I think you should know, you won't have a happy time in that house."

"Who is this?" she demanded to know. Her phone pad screen showed CALLER UNKNOWN.

There was a long pause on the other end. "It's Bobby," the raspy-voiced stranger finally purred, "from down the block."

Sara heard a click on the other end. She tried star-six-nine, but a recording told her that the number dialed was blocked. The closest neighbors, an older couple, were nearly half a block away. She asked them if they knew someone named Bobby. She asked a lot of people in Echo the same question. Everyone seemed to know someone named Bobby or Bob or Robert or Roberta. But nobody knew anyone with a voice like that.

Bobby's calls became more frequent—and then came the emails, texts and notes. Bobby never used any foul language or made threats. For Sara, it was almost as if she had some meddling, omniscient neighbor watching her and her family—an unwelcome anonymous friend who relished sharing bad news about things to come.

Bobby didn't have to sign the notes and emails. Sara always knew who they were from, like the piece of notebook paper folded up and stuck under the windshield wiper of the SUV. It was written in a child's scrawl:

> *YOUR DAUGHTER MICHELLE*
> *IS DOING THINGS SHE SHOULDN'T* ☹

When Sara asked her daughter if there was any basis in fact to the strange note, Michelle turned livid. "How can you even ask me that? Do you actually believe this stalker freak is telling the truth?"

She and Larry went to the police, who increased patrols on Birch Street. But it really didn't do any good. Sara changed her phone number and email server. But Bobby managed to track down her new contact information and got to her nevertheless.

"Jarrett's going to hurt himself on that skateboard someday, I'm sure of it," was all it said in an email. When Sara tried to reply, she got the same notice she always got MAILER-DEMON: UNABLE TO DELIVER.

Within a week, Jarrett wiped out on his skateboard

and got a broken arm and a concussion. He was in the hospital for two days.

It was obvious this person was watching their home. More than that, Bobby seemed to have gotten inside the house at times. He or she seemed to know everything about Sara—her quirks, habits and vulnerabilities. Bobby knew what was going on with Larry and the kids even before Sara did.

One afternoon, coming home from a brief trip to the Safeway, Sara found a Post-it stuck to her bedroom dresser mirror. She immediately recognized the childlike handwriting:

I DON'T THINK LARRY IS HAPPY WITH YOU . . . ☹

Bobby told her about every dose of trouble that was coming her way—the accidents, Larry's philandering, and Michelle's drug problem. Sara couldn't help wondering if this gravelly-voiced phantom was making these things happen—or merely trying to warn her.

After all, how could one person cause all these horrible occurrences? Was it just bad luck? Or was it the house?

"Why don't you just move?" Bobby had asked more than once over the phone. "You should leave this place . . ."

But for months, Larry refused to budge. He didn't think the house was cursed. He didn't believe in curses. Sara had a feeling he didn't even believe Bobby existed. He seemed to think she was making up this stalker person. She had to show him one of Bobby's emails before he started to believe her. But he still didn't take Bobby seriously. He maintained that they were having a bad patch—that was all. He wasn't about to be forced out of his own home. This *Bobby* person was probably part of some sort of elaborate real estate scam. At least, that was what he told the police when Sara insisted they make their fourth or fifth harassment report.

Ironically, Larry ended up forced from his house.

Sara had kicked him out eight days ago. For the time being, he was staying at the Oak Harbor Best Western. He said he didn't want a divorce. He thought they should see a couples' counselor, and if she wanted to unload the house, that was fine with him. In fact, he was all for it.

But Sara refused to have anything to do with Larry. She wouldn't agree to any of his suggestions—except selling the house. They needed to get out of there before something else happened.

With Jarrett spending the night at the Munchels', she'd considered getting a room at the local B&B, the Bayside Inn. She didn't want to be alone in that awful house. But it didn't seem worth the peak-season, weekend rate of one hundred ninety bucks for just one night. Besides, except for a few minor accidents, nothing bad had actually happened *inside* the house.

So Sara had resolved to brave it at home, treat herself to carryout chicken teriyaki from Wok Delight and *The Sound of Music* on demand. She knew it was silly, but she wanted a movie *event*, an epic that would take up most of the night and help her forget her troubles for a while. She'd always loved *The Sound of Music*. Last year, she'd tried to make a movie night with it for the family. Michelle had been on her mobile device during most of the movie; Jarrett kept saying, "This movie is so gay," and Larry fell asleep about a third of the way through it. Sara had ended up shutting off the movie and going to bed early.

Not tonight.

She ate off a TV table and sat in Larry's recliner. No one else in the family ever used it—unless Larry was out of town for something, and even then, rarely. But he had no claim on it tonight—and possibly never again.

The Baroness was just breaking up with Captain Von Trapp when the house phone rang.

It was 10:07 according to the cable box in the TV console. The tiny screen on the cordless showed CALLER UNKNOWN. Bobby hung up after three rings. At least, Sara was almost certain it was Bobby.

He or she usually called on her mobile phone. But then, Bobby probably knew she was alone tonight.

Her heart racing, Sara glanced at the darkened windows of the family room. She couldn't see anything, just her own timid reflection. She had a feeling Bobby was seeing the exact same image—only from outside, somewhere in the dark.

Sara quickly closed the drapes. She double checked the locks on the doors and first floor windows. Minutes passed and the phone didn't ring again.

She told herself that the Unknown Caller could have been anybody.

Still, Sara wasn't able to concentrate on the movie after that. Every little sound inside and outside the house became cause for alarm. At least five times, she put the movie on pause to investigate some strange, new noise.

She decided a little Jim Beam would help her relax. But when she opened the kitchen cabinet, she found

only one bottle there—about a third full. She could
have sworn she'd bought an extra bottle yesterday for
backup. Had she gone through it already? Had she gotten that bad about her alcohol consumption? Or was it
possible Jarrett had stolen the bottle and taken it to his
friend's house? It was just the kind of thing a thirteen-
year-old might do. She could see him and his pals all
trying to be cool, passing around her bottle of Jim
Beam in someone's basement.

It was too late to go out for more booze. She'd have
to stretch out what she had. A carefully measured shot
with some ice and a little water helped calm her nerves.

It was after midnight by the time Maria, the Captain,
and those Von Trapp kids had finally fled the Nazis
and were hiking over the Alps to a chorus of "Climb
Every Mountain."

Sara convinced herself that the call earlier must have
been a wrong number. But she was still feeling too
edgy to sleep—too edgy and too sober. She poured herself another Jim Beam, straight this time. Then she
switched channels to *House Hunters*.

She was beginning to nod off when the phone rang,
startling her.

She glared at the cordless on the TV table and started
to get mad. She'd had enough.

Swiping the cordless off the TV table, she clicked it
on. "What?" she bellowed. "What do you want?"

She didn't have to look at the cable box clock to
know it was nearly one in the morning. She didn't have
to look at the Caller ID screen on the cordless to know
it read CALLER UNKNOWN. She knew it was Bobby.

There was silence on the other end. But she could
still hear someone breathing.

"Goddamn you!" she barked. "What the hell do you want?"

"Jarrett's asking for you, Sara," the Unknown Caller said in that all-too-familiar crawly voice. "He's very badly hurt. He needs his mommy . . ."

Horrified, Sara listened. She didn't remember a time when Bobby had ever lied to her. For a moment, she couldn't talk or breathe. "What—what happened?" she finally asked.

"He's going to die if he doesn't get some help."

Hunched forward in the recliner chair, she clutched the phone tighter. Tears filled her eyes

"Are you listening to me, Sara?"

"What have you done to him, you monster?" she cried.

"Come meet me in front of the teriyaki place where you picked up your dinner earlier. Don't stop to call anyone else. Just grab your keys, get in the car and drive. Do you understand?"

"Where is he?" she asked, getting to her feet. "Is he there with you?"

"If you're not here in ten minutes, I'm going to let Jarrett die."

There was a click on the other end of the line.

With a shaky hand, Sara automatically dialed Jarrett's smart phone. She hoped against hope it was all a lie. But after three rings, Jarrett still hadn't picked up. In the middle of the fourth ring, she heard a click.

"Jarrett?" she asked anxiously. "Honey?"

There was no answer. Had it gone to his voice mail? She couldn't tell.

Then she heard a sigh on the other end—and that raspy voice: "Jarrett can't come to the phone, Sara. I already told you that. Now you only have nine minutes to get here. I'm not even sure Jarrett will live that long. He's lost a lot of blood."

Then the line went dead.

Sara dropped the cordless onto the seat of Larry's recliner and ran to grab her purse off the kitchen counter. Frantically searching for her keys, she headed out the side door that led to the garage. At last she found the keys. She stepped outside and shut the door behind her. It locked automatically.

She shuddered from the night chill outside.

The garage's pedestrian door was just a couple of steps across from there. In her rattled state Sara couldn't get the key in the lock. Tears streamed down her face. All she could think about was her son, stabbed or shot by this maniac. How else had Bobby gotten ahold of Jarrett's phone? Was her boy still alive? Was he really asking for her?

She finally got the key in the lock and opened the door. Stepping into the darkened garage, she blindly reached over and flicked on the light switch.

Nothing happened.

She tried the switch next to it. Still nothing.

The overhead light didn't work—and neither did the switch to open the garage door. But the electricity was working. Their second refrigerator was humming— over by Larry's workbench. She couldn't see it in the blackness, but she could hear it.

Was someone else in the garage with her?

Sara was able to see the outline of the SUV amid the shadows. She pressed the unlock button to the device on her key ring. The vehicle's emergency lights flashed for a second, and the interior light went on.

Making her way around the front of the SUV, Sara opened the driver's door. She reached inside for the remote device on the sun visor and pressed the button for the garage door. There was a click, and the motor overhead started up.

Sara was about to jump inside the car, but hesitated. It suddenly occurred to her that she hadn't checked to see if anyone was hiding inside the SUV.

But she was too late.

A shadowy figure popped up in the backseat.

Sara gasped. A hooded clown-face grinned at her. The masked stranger wore some kind of dark raincoat—and gloves. She could see the gun in one hand. It was pointed at her.

Over churning mechanics of the garage door opening, Sara heard that all-too-familiar gravelly voice behind the clown mask: "Get in and drive, Sara, and maybe we'll reach Jarrett in time to save him."

Her heart racing, she climbed behind the wheel and started up the car. She looked into the rearview mirror and tried to stop shaking. "We're not going anywhere until you tell me what's happened to my son."

"My partner got a little carried away and shot him."

Sara let out a frail, little cry. She covered her mouth with her hand.

"You didn't think I worked alone, did you?" Bobby asked behind the mask. "Jarrett's in a safe place. He seems stable for now—"

"But you just said he might not last even ten minutes," she cut in.

"Ten minutes or ten hours, who knows? As I said, he's lost some blood, and he's asking for you. My partner will text me updates as Jarrett's condition changes.

The sooner we reach them, the sooner you can get your son to a hospital. Now, let's go before the garage door closes on us. We're wasting time sitting here, Sara . . ."

That had been nearly an hour ago.

So many times when Bobby had telephoned in the last few months, Sara had asked, "Who are you? Why are you doing this?"

She'd never gotten an answer.

During their journey tonight, she asked those same questions—over and over again. But her passenger didn't respond. Sara still wondered if Bobby was behind everything that had happened—or just the gleeful harbinger of horrible news.

"Why is this happening to us?" she demanded to know. She glanced at the rearview mirror again. "Why my family?"

"I warned you early on that you should get out of that house," was the answer that finally came from behind the clown mask. There was no further explanation.

As they drove by a sign for Deception Pass, Bobby took a phone out from the pocket of that dark raincoat and checked it. "Jarrett's lost consciousness, but his breathing is steady."

Sara tightened her grip on the steering wheel. They were headed for the bridge. Was Jarrett somewhere on the mainland? Three months ago, her daughter had died from a heroin overdose in an alley behind a bar on Highway 99 in North Seattle. Was Jarrett destined to die in Seattle, too?

After the bridge, it would be at least another ninety miles to Seattle. If Jarrett was really so seriously hurt, she needed to know when they'd reach him. "How much further?" she asked, her voice cracking.

"Not too much. Keep driving, Sara."

She had a feeling that behind the disguise, her passenger had a grin that matched the one on the clown face. Bobby must have felt extremely smug to see her so unhinged and helpless. Sara tried not to cry, but couldn't help it. Jarrett seemed so far away.

She saw the Deception Pass Bridge ahead, partially obscured by a cloud of mist. The old, narrow, two-lane viaduct was actually two bridges, suspended 180 feet over the choppy waters of Skagit Bay and the Strait of Juan de Fuca. One bridge spanned nearly a thousand feet, connecting Whidbey Island with small, uninhabited Pass Island; the second section was just over five-hundred feet—from Pass Island to Fidalgo and the mainland. Lights along the pedestrian walk railing helped navigate the way.

But the mist and mild rain on the windshield obscured Sara's view. She switched on the wipers. The road felt slick beneath the SUV's tires.

Just last week, another person—some poor, pitiful, miserable woman—had leapt to her death from this bridge. It wasn't reported on TV. *The Seattle Times* buried the story in their back pages. That seemed to be the local media's policy: *Don't report it, don't give people ideas*. She'd read on the Internet that close to 450 suicides had occurred on Deception Pass Bridge since its construction in 1935.

Right now, hers was the only vehicle on the old bridge. With her window open a crack, she felt a slight spray on her face. She heard the wind—and the water rushing far below.

"I don't have much gas left," she announced edgily, "less than a quarter of a tank. I don't know where you're taking me, but if we're headed to Seattle—or even Everett—we'll have to stop for gas."

"At the end of the bridge, you'll turn into the parking area for the tourists."

She eyed the clown mask in her rearview mirror. "Is that where you've got Jarrett? Is that where he is?"

"You'll see . . ."

During the day, Deception Pass Park was crammed with people, most of them taking pictures. Sara imagined that at night, the place might have been a lovers' lane or a spot for teens to hang out and smoke or drink. But at this hour—on this cold, drizzly night—the park was probably deserted.

Is this where Bobby's partner had brought Jarrett after shooting him?

Biting her lip, Sara switched on her indicator and turned into the lot for the Deception Pass Park. Beyond the rain-beaded windshield, she didn't see any other cars. Certainly, Bobby's partner had a car. She'd imaged the two of them speeding away in another vehicle while she helped Jarrett into the SUV and then rushed him to the nearest hospital.

Of course, her scenario was based on the foolish assumption that Bobby and Associate were human with some traces of compassion.

How could she be so stupid? What was she thinking?

They hadn't brought her all this way in order to save her son's life. They'd forced her to come here for some other reason. Did they want her to watch Jarrett die?

Sara glanced around the empty lot. There was no

sign of anyone. The lights of the bridge peeked through the tall evergreens bordering the lot. It was too dark to see the water, but she could still hear the rushing current.

"What's going on?" she asked. "Where's Jarrett? Is he even here?"

"Park the car."

Sara pulled into the first parking spot she saw. She swiveled around and glared at the figure in the backseat. "Okay, where is he?" she asked anxiously. "Where have you got my son?"

Bobby nodded toward the front passenger side. "Check the glove compartment, Sara. Go on . . ."

She turned toward the dashboard, and pressed the button on the glove compartment. The panel door fell open. She noticed a bottle of Jim Beam in there. Was this the bottle that had been missing earlier tonight?

"I thought Jarrett had made off with this," she murmured, taking the bourbon out of the glove compartment. "But it was you . . ."

"Why not have a hit?" croaked the passenger in her backseat.

Though she was tempted, Sara quickly shook her head. "Where's Jarrett?"

"He's at his friend Jim Munchel's house—asleep, I assume. Jarrett probably doesn't even realize his phone is missing. But then, he really isn't too bright, is he?"

"What are you saying?" Sara whispered, clutching the bottle to her chest. "You mean my son's all right?"

"Snug as a bug in a rug," Bobby replied from behind the mask. "Aren't I the naughty one to tell such a lie? But I needed you here, Sara, and I needed you to cooperate . . ."

She let out a sigh. Jarrett was safe.

"Now, after a scare like that, I'd say you need a drink. Go ahead . . ."

"I'm fine," she lied. The truth was, she desperately wanted a hit of bourbon—just to calm her nerves. But she needed to keep a clear head right now.

"I know you want it," the gravelly voiced stranger purred. "Don't pretend. I've watched you when you think you're all alone, Sara. You drink yourself into a stupor and stagger up to bed. Go ahead, have a few gulps. You'll feel better. Drink up." Bobby raised the gun a bit. "In fact, I insist."

She glanced down at the bottle in her grasp—and then into the eyeholes of the clown mask. Who was behind there? Why were they doing this to her and her family?

"Go ahead . . ." it said.

She unscrewed the top and realized the seal was broken. It had already been opened. She hesitated. "What are you going to do to me?"

"You don't want to hear the answer to that while you're sober."

Sara didn't move.

"Better you hear it after a few gulps," Bobby whispered. "I crushed up some of your Valium, and put it in there to help things along. You just need to relax, Sara. I'm simply trying to make this easy on you. Now, go ahead, take a hit. Swallow it down like a good girl."

Sara thought about her dead daughter and her ruined marriage. What did she have to live for anyway? She didn't care anymore. A big part of her was already dead.

She brought the bottle to her lips and took a gulp.

The bourbon burned going down, but then almost immediately it warmed her and made her feel better. She wiped her mouth and stared at the figure in the back seat. "What—what are you trying to *make easy* for me? What are you planning to do?"

"Take another healthy swig, and I'll tell you."

The truth was she desperately wanted another blast of the bourbon. She took two more gulps from the bottle. "All right," she gasped. "What are you trying to *make easy* for me?"

"Dying," Bobby answered.

Sara wasn't sure she heard right. "What?"

The bottle slipped out of her hand, and bourbon spilled down the front of her. She could smell it on herself. She felt so stupid. It was humiliating.

She heard a sinister cackle from behind the mask. "The police will know you were drinking, of course. And they'll assume that at some point, on your way to the bridge, you tripped and hit your head . . ."

On her way to the bridge?

Before she could ask what that meant, Sara saw Bobby raise the gun—even higher this time, near the ceiling of the SUV. In an instant, the butt of the weapon came slamming down on her head.

She heard it smack against her skull. The pain was excruciating.

Just before she lost consciousness, in that split second, Sara realized what was happening to her. She'd been set up. Bobby would drag her to the bridge and throw her over the railing.

Everything turned black.

But Sara could still smell the Jim Beam, and she could still hear the rushing current.

The Seattle Times, Monday, May 23:

ANOTHER DECEPTION PASS
SUICIDE

*Echo Woman Hangs Herself
From Bridge's Walkway*

Only eight days after a Monroe woman leapt to her death from Deception Pass Bridge, the Western Washington landmark became the site of another apparent suicide. Early Saturday morning, traffic on the bridge was halted for two hours after motorists reported someone hanging by the neck from a rope tied to the railing of the pedestrian walkway.

Friends of the victim, Sara Rogan Goldsmith, 42, of Echo, WA, said she was still despondent over the drug-related death of her daughter, Michelle, 16, in February . . .

The article mentioned that Sara had called the police on several occasions to report that someone was harassing her, but the authorities were unable to substantiate her claims. Apparently, the notes and emails from Bobby that she shared with the police were neither threatening nor malicious enough for them to be too concerned. There was every indication that Sara was depressed and mentally unbalanced.

The piece concluded that she was survived by her husband, Dr. Lawrence Goldsmith, 44, and a son, Jarrett, 13. No mention was made of Sara and Larry's marital problems.

The article was buried in the back pages of the front section of that Monday morning edition.

On page two of the same newspaper was another article. Unlike the story about Sara, this one featured a photograph. It was a school portrait of a teenage girl with a narrow face and straight, shoulder-length blonde hair. She had a pretty smile.

The article was about Monica Leary, a junior at Capital High School in Olympia. Monica disappeared after a party at a friend's house that Saturday night. The friend lived only two blocks away from the Leary house on Goldcrest Drive. Monica was last seen at 10:30 p.m. She'd left the party early, because she had a swim meet the following afternoon.

She never reached home.

Connect with U s

Visit us online at
KensingtonBooks.com
to read more from your favorite authors, see books
by series, view reading group guides, and more.

Join us on social media

for sneak peeks, chances to win books and prize packs,
and to share your thoughts with other readers.

**facebook.com/kensingtonpublishing
twitter.com/kensingtonbooks**

Tell us what you think!

To share your thoughts, submit a review,
or sign up for our eNewsletters, please visit:
KensingtonBooks.com/TellUs.